Spirit Ponies

by

M.A. Moone

Other books by M.A. Moone

The Lord's Bit
Grits to Granola
An Amazing Aptitude

Original cover art by Francis A. Bâby Jr.

Published in the United States by M.A. Moone

Printed by CreateSpace.Com—an Amazon.com Company

Available from Amazon.com, CreateSpace.com and other retail outlets.

Chapter One

Marshall Duncan let out a mumbled shout and opened his eyes. A slice of sunlight, intruding through the closed drapes, was the only light in the room. He closed his eyes, savoring the quiet, remembering his dream. He seldom remembered his dreams and even more rarely dreamed of real people, places or, in this case, animals. Yet, in this dream, Max, their golden retriever, now buried beneath the maple tree behind the barn, had been leaping to retrieve a high-flying Frisbee. Marshall's shout had been for the good catch. *Good old Max! What a great dog he was!*

It had been almost a year since the old dog had to be put down. He and his wife, Helen, had recently talked about it and decided they were finally ready for a replacement puppy. But, finding the time had been a problem. Even last night he had worked until after 2 AM to put the finishing touches on the designs for restoration of the city of Alexandria's train station. *Time to relax for a bit now. I think the dream was telling me that it's time to start puppy shopping today.*

Marshall stretched and opened his eyes to look at the alarm clock. It was 9:30. There was a note propped in front of the coffee carafe beside it. He grinned and yawned before reaching for his glasses and the note. It read:

> *Good morning, sleepy head. I saw your final rendition. It looks really good, especially the handicapped access. What a good solution! You deserve to sleep in. Here's your coffee and the paper.*
>
> *The horses have been fed and watered. I put Octane in the front pasture to work off some of his energy. He was really full of himself this morning. Please put him back in his stall. I'm off, first to the feed store, then to have my hair done at Monique's. I'll grocery shop on the way home. Yes, I'll remember to get more club soda. I love you.*

1

I love you too, Marshall thought as he sat up and propped pillows behind his back. He looked at the carafe and paper on the bedside table, yawned again and ran a hand through his thick, gray-streaked, auburn hair before reaching for the coffee.

He sat back, mug in hand and poured himself a half-cup. The house was very quiet. He smiled to himself. *It was never this quiet when we had kids at home. God! What a happy, crazy household...and Helen was the ringleader.* He smiled, remembering the general bedlam.

Outside the big windows he could hear baby birds cheeping and realized there must be a nest in one of the ivy-covered, redwood trellises he had designed to soften the north side of the tall brick house. After a minute, he took a long sip, enjoying the quality of light created by the stray beam of sunshine. Although he had designed the house more than 15 years ago, he still got great satisfaction from how well the spaces related to each other and how the windows and skylights made the house cheerful on the gloomiest of days. He threw back the dusky, rose-colored duvet with one hand and swung his long legs over the side of the big four-poster bed. Holding his mug carefully, he hitched up his boxer shorts and went to open the drapes.

With a smile he observed that the Virginia spring was in its glory. The daffodils and tulips were in full bloom. The plum and cherry trees in the orchard beyond the woodpile were already dropping blossoms, but the apple trees were only starting to show green. Marshall nodded in satisfaction, thinking of the fruit to come. A movement caught his eye. In the front pasture, Helen's new horse had evidently run to the far fence that fronted the county road and was now floating back toward the house in a high-action, extended trot. He was energy contained. With his head and tail up, muscles bunching, he moved for movement's sake. Marshall frowned. He had not wanted Helen to buy this colt. He was too hot, bred to run and jump and be a champion. He was not meant to be some middle-aged woman's hack. He took another drink of coffee, watching.

When the gray three-year-old came to the fence, he made a graceful pivot and then broke into a full gallop. Neck stretched and back flat, he lengthened his stride. *Holy shit! What's he doing?* The pasture was perhaps a quarter-mile long, the fence, five feet high. *Is he going to try to jump the goddamned fence?* At the last minute, the colt threw himself into a sliding stop that brought him into hard contact with the wooden fence. Marshall spun, set the mug on the nightstand and rushed for his clothes. *That crazy son-of-a-bitch is testing! He means to jump the fence!*

He raced down the stairs and out the front door, his mind focused on the job to be done. *How in the hell can I get that crazy devil stopped long enough to get a halter on him? Grain won't work. Not in a million years! He's too pumped up with all that energy and no place to go.*

Marshall ran towards the gate shouting, "Octane, here boy!" He grabbed the halter off the gate post, let himself through and whistled using his thumb and middle finger. It was loud and piercing--a command for attention. Octane, trotting back and forth against the end of the pasture, his head over the top rail, eyeing the pastureland on the other side of the road, ignored the sound. Marshall stood helplessly, watching.

He started walking toward the horse, then whistled and called again. This time, Octane turned to look at him, frozen in place. Head raised, ears pricked, he was a thing of beauty. Sweat had turned his gray coat into the color of iron and he looked for one moment like a magnificent statue. "Octane! Here boy!" Marshall whistled a third time and watched as the horse once again flattened himself into a ground-covering run.

3

Almost too late, Marshall realized it was not him, but the open gate that drew the horse. "Christ!" He shouted and sprinted for it, hearing the pound of hooves behind him. He shoved the gate shut, threw the bolt and flung himself to the side in a reflexive action. With his back turned, he felt, rather than saw the horse, unable or unwilling to stop, fold his legs and sail over the gate. As Marshall lifted his head, he saw Octane stumble in the gravel, recover and then race down the driveway towards the county road.

"Son-of-a-bitch!" Marshall rolled under the fence in one smooth move. He paused to watch the colt shy at the ditch on the far side of the road and then turn left. Marshall jumped to his feet and raced back in the house, halter and lead rope in hand, to retrieve the keys for his Jeep. "Thank God!" he said when he found them in the basket on the kitchen counter. He ran for the Jeep.

In seconds, gravel spewing from under his back tires, he drove down the long driveway and turned left onto the county road. The colt was nowhere in sight. He pressed on the accelerator, watching for breaks between the fences where Octane might have left the road. Water filled the ditches on both sides of the road. The colt did not like water; that much he knew. Ahead, the road curved and he could see where the fencing stopped and a hedgerow started. The open ditch disappeared into a culvert. Still, there was no colt. But there was a driveway. Ignoring the sign that said, NO TRESPASSING, he made a sharp left. The hedgerows on either side were tall and dense--no chance for Octane to slip through. The gravel drive ended in a circle. An old, boarded-up barn and toolshed were on the left, a small, well-cared-for, white house with a fenced yard was on the right. Washing hung on a clothesline. The garage door was up, the car gone. There was no sign of Octane. *Shit!*

Marshall doubted the horse would brave the strange territory here, especially with the clothes

4

flapping in the breeze. He roared around the circle and headed back the way he had come.

Not more than another 500 yards down the county road he saw the colt on the left, lying tight against the tall hedge. His first thought was: *The son-of-a-bitch has broken his leg!* Marshall slammed on the brakes, jumped from the Jeep and rushed towards the struggling animal. Then he saw the long strand of barbed-wire, part of an old fallen-down fence, which had wrapped itself cruelly around one slender foreleg.

Marshall threw himself on the horse's head, knowing it was the only way to keep him still. He turned so he could look at the leg. With horror he saw the deep, jagged gashes and the steady pump of blood. "Help!" he yelled. "For Christ's sake, if anyone can hear, help me!"

Under him, the horse jerked briefly. He looked up and down the road, praying for a car. His heart was pounding, his breath heaving. He closed his eyes, made a quick decision, jumped to his feet and raced toward the Jeep.

It felt like it took more time than he had to get the Jeep turned around. *That old toolshed – it's bound to have a pair of fence cutters of some sort. It's got to-- or else that colt is as good as dead.*

The toolshed was not locked, only latched. He threw open the door and stepped inside. A nightmarish jumble was visible in the dim light. His hand fumbled for a light switch on the wall. Feeling nothing, he tried the wall on the other side of the door and found the switch there. Two naked lightbulbs revealed some farmer's lifetime habit of saving everything. *Jesus, what a junk pile!* He picked his way down the narrow path among the stacks of rusted machine parts; broken appliances; damp, decaying boxes holding Mason jars; bicycles in various stages of disrepair and ancient farm equipment. He finally found a pile of rusted tools and sorted through them with shaking hands. He found monkey wrenches, screwdrivers, files, hammers, pliers,

5

but no wire cutters. Marshall grabbed a small pair of pliers and looked at them closely. *Wait! These are for cutting baling wire. Will they work?* Knowing he had no other choice, he sprinted for the Jeep.

Octane lifted his head at the sound of screeching tires sliding to a stop on the pavement. "Hang on fellow. Hang on boy. I'm going to help you. Just lay real still buddy. That's a good boy," Marshall crooned as he looked at how the colt's struggles had caused the old fence to partially right itself. A rotted post was being held nearly upright by the tension. He could not force himself to really look at the nearly severed leg. Kneeling, he put a hand on the bow-string taut wire, ignoring the blood that was everywhere. He grasped the wire with the small cutters and using both hands and all his strength, he squeezed on the short handles.

Feeling the wire move, Octane struggled one last time to escape the torturous pain. His final thrashing caused the old wire to separate with a sharp pop. It caught Marshall just under the chin, severing his jugular vein as it sliced through the air like a writhing, barbed snake.

No! Jesus, God, please... No! He staggered to his feet but his world turned and he swayed then stumbled, reaching for support that wasn't there. A black cloud slid over his eyes and he fell onto the soft spring grass. He struggled to raise his hands to the ragged wound at his neck, but could not. His mind whirled on the brink of consciousness. Images of his childhood... His mother's perfume... His father's laugh... He and his best friend, Will, riding like wild Indians on Will's horses... Helen and the children... Peter's first pony... Putting up the basketball hoop for Willie... Carrie as a toddler, crawling into their bed... Helen as his bride in a white gown that flowed on and on in his mind until that was all there was--a welcoming tunnel of white. A soft, golden glow suffused the tunnel's end. A whisper as gentle and melodious as the good memories bid him to come. He felt himself begin to float and thought he heard a dog bark.

Chapter Two

Helen Duncan looked at herself in the brightly-lit salon mirror. The black nylon cape did nothing to camouflage the fact that her chin line showed the definite beginnings of jowls; did nothing to soften the laugh lines around her eyes; or the fact that her eyelids were beginning to droop.

"Kellie, if I didn't like you so much, I swear I would not sit myself in front of this disgusting mirror. I would hack my hair off with my sewing scissors and tell everyone it was the new look."

Kellie laughed. She had been sifting through Helen's heavy, chin-length hair, assessing the amount of gray. "It's time to do something about this gray, Helen. You're starting to look like a mouse. Think about letting me add some highlights."

Helen had heard Kellie's opinion of her hair before. She looked at her image in the mirror, remembering when her chin was angular and the summer sun had created its own brand of highlights in her once shiny brown hair.

"Marshall has been dropping hints along those same lines, Kellie." Helen wrinkled her nose. "I told him I'd think about it, but, not today. Today a cut will do. Marshall is actually taking the day off. I'm going to try to talk him into taking the horses for a long ride at Bull Run."

Kellie dropped her hands to Helen's shoulders and they smiled at each other, with the comfort of long association. "Okay then, let's head for the washing station."

Abruptly, Kellie stopped talking and frowned. In the mirror, she saw Monique, the owner of the salon, striding down the aisle towards them. Kellie said softly, "Uh oh! Something's seriously wrong here."

"My goodness, Monique, what's wrong?" Helen asked as Monique stopped behind them, her face unreadable; her gaze barely touching either woman.

Monique ignored the question and said, "Helen, there is a phone call for you in my office."

The words sounded odd, too controlled. "I have a phone call? Here? Is it Marshall?"

Monique's tight-lipped, silent headshake sent a shiver of goose bumps over her body. "Not Marshall? Then who..."

Frightened by her boss's strangeness, Kellie rotated the chair and pulled Helen from it. "It must be important, Helen. Get moving."

Helen looked blankly at her, as if surprised to find herself on her feet. Then she turned and hurried after Monique.

"Who is it, Monique?" She asked, her voice rising. "Is everything all right?"

Walking in front of Helen, Monique silently shook her head again. The words that needed to be said would come from the man on the telephone. She sat Helen at her desk and put the receiver in her hand. "I'll be right outside, honey." She touched Helen's shoulder softly with long, pearl-white nails, before closing the door behind her and allowing her face to crumple.

Fear wrapped itself around Helen more closely than the nylon cape. She pressed the receiver to her ear and took a deep breath. "Hello, this is Helen Duncan."

"Mrs. Duncan, this is Sergeant Paul Moore, Prince William County Sheriff's Department. Ma'am, there's been an accident. Please wait where you are. An officer should be there almost immediately to get you."

"An accident? What do you mean? Is someone hurt?" Her senses suddenly seemed sharper. She could smell the various odors of the salon's products; hear the murmur of voices outside the closed door. "Oh, my dear God! Is it Marshall? Has he hurt himself?"

There was a short silence on the other end of the line. "Ma'am... Mrs. Duncan, this isn't information to give over the telephone, but I'm afraid it is about your husband. Ma'am, he was trying to save a horse that evidently got caught in barbed-wire and somehow he got caught in it too. The wire cut his neck bad enough..." He paused. "Well, he didn't make it."

A horse caught in barbed wire? In Prince William County? What wire? I've never seen any wire! No one uses barbed-wire for fences anymore. This is some sort of a gruesome mistake. Only Marshall knows I'm at Monique's. It's not Marshall that's dead. He can't be dead. If the officer is calling me, Marshall had to give him the telephone number. I've somehow misunderstood. It must be a horse that is dead, not Marshall. She pulled the white receiver from her ear and balanced it in her palms as she tried, with a ricocheting mind, to make sense of what she heard.

"Ma'am? Ma'am? Mrs. Duncan, can you hear me? If you can hear me, Mrs. Duncan, please don't leave the premises until the officer comes to escort you."

Helen straightened both arms, holding the receiver straight out in front of her, as if she were presenting a gift...giving the words away. Still, they came from the receiver. "Ma'am? I'm sure sorry about your husband. You wait there now, ma'am. You hear? Deputy Allen will be there any second."

A shudder of irritation crawled over her. She didn't want to hear any more words that didn't make sense. It was far too upsetting. She concentrated on her hands as she gently replaced the receiver in its cradle and noted how badly spring gardening had damaged her nails. *I should have scheduled myself for a manicure today as well.*

The roller chair pushed back easily. She rose, feeling weightless, disconnected, and walked to the office door. Both her heartbeat and her breathing were shallow...fluttery. It took great effort and strength of will to turn the doorknob and pull open the office door. With wonder, she saw that both Monique and Kellie were

10

waiting for her, tears sliding down their faces. Kellie was holding her old, tan, canvas barn coat and her leather shoulder bag. She looked at the women as though they were oddly behaving strangers. The only sounds besides their quiet sobbing were the breathy roar of hairdryers and women's quiet conversations. "Goodness," she heard her voice say as from a distance, "An officer is coming to get me, so I'm afraid I must go. Marshall has apparently hurt himself. I'm so sorry."

Kellie hurried forward with her coat and purse. "Wait, Helen. You'll need your coat." Tears continued to make black mascara tracks down her cheeks as she removed the cape from around Helen's neck and helped her into the coat.

A uniformed deputy walked through the door. He immediately recognized Helen from the pictures he had seen in her house. In a gentle voice, he said, "Mrs. Duncan? I'm Deputy Sam Allen. Did Sergeant Moore talk to you?" He held out his hand.

"Yes," she heard her voice say. Ignoring the hand, she put her purse strap over her shoulder, grabbed his sleeve and tugged him towards the shop door. "We must go quickly. I'm afraid my husband has hurt himself."

Her voice sounded only worried, not distraught. She did not see the shocked expressions on the faces of the two women, did not see their eyes riveted on the face of the young officer, asking an unspoken question.

Sam Allen's face registered disbelief, then dismay, as he allowed himself to be pulled through the salon's front door. When Helen released his arm, he rushed to open the back door of the squad car. After helping her in, he leaned forward to secure her seatbelt, as if he were dealing with a small child.

Monique hurried forward, waiting until Sam had firmly shut the door before whispering, "I thought Sergeant Moore said her husband died."

"Yes, ma'am."

"That's not what she just said."

"I know, ma'am." Worry clouded his black eyes. "I heard her."

"What's the truth, then?"

"He's dead. The sergeant and I were the first ones on the scene." He turned on his heel and strode around the car, mumbling to himself, "But if the sergeant told her that, it's pretty clear that she doesn't want to believe it." Sam quickly fastened his own seatbelt and started the patrol car, expertly moving into the traffic and heading east.

Helen's odd, weightless feeling had not gone away. She believed only the seatbelt kept her anchored to the hard leather seat. She knew if she spoke, the words would simply float from her mouth and hang about her head. Her thoughts seemed to hover and bump into each other, dark nebula shadows in her mind. *What did the man on the telephone say? Something about Marshall and a horse caught in barbed wire? What nonsense! Marshall is probably still propped up, drinking coffee and reading the paper. Whose horse could the officer have been talking about? Not one of ours! Everyone except High Octane is in his stall. And it isn't Octane. I fastened that gate myself.* A second shudder ran through her, leaving in its wake, a cold emptiness she'd never felt before. She pulled her barn coat more tightly around herself and huddled into it. *What else had the man on the phone said? It was something important. Right at the end... there had been words...* She closed her eyes, letting whirling dark shadows block her ability to think and, instead, began to silently pray. *Please, dear God, I can't take another second of this. Wake me up now if I'm in a nightmare. Fix it if it's some huge misunderstanding. But do it now, please!*

She only opened her eyes as the car veered onto the steep off-ramp that would take them to State Route 28. A fresh wave of fear crashed through her like shattering crystal. *He acts as though he knows exactly*

12

where he's going--as though he knows exactly where we live!

"Do you know where I live?" Her voice sounded suspicious.

"Yes, ma'am," Sam said. "I'm the one who found the note." His worried eyes flicked from the road ahead to his rearview mirror where he could see how she was hunching her shoulders and rubbing one side of her chin against the corduroy collar of her coat. He looked ahead, judging the amount of time until they hit the narrow, paved county road that led to the beautiful place where she lived. With some of the fruit trees in bloom and the white board fencing, it looked like some movie set from the old black and white movie, "National Velvet." Even the name of the place seemed too classy to be real: Henley Brook Farms. "But, we're not going there, ma'am, we're heading right on past to the scene of the accident." He did not add, "You'll need to identify the body." *I'll let the sergeant handle that whole deal, he thought. He must not have told her right.*

"What note?" Helen's puzzled voice broke his reverie. It was low and hesitant, as if she really didn't want to know.

He waited as long as he dared before answering. "The note that said you were getting your hair done at Monique's."

"You… You were in my house?"

"Yes, ma'am. The door was wide open. I was looking for you or anybody. We traced the location from the Jeep's registration."

The silence in the car lengthened. Helen shivered inside her coat. She had again lost the will to ask questions. A moan of fear and anguish began in a rhythm deep inside her, but she held it there, owning it, feeling it drag her from her weightless state. She started to shiver harder.

Sam was relieved that the questions had stopped. He was even more relieved when he saw Marshall's green Jeep, the patrol car, and the

13

ambulance ahead--parked to shield the gristly scene on the grass behind them from passersby.

Helen felt the car stop and heard Sam get out; heard his soft voice asking and answering questions; heard the crunch of footsteps on the gravel as someone approached her side of the car; heard the car door open. She huddled more deeply inside her coat, her chin on her chest.

"Mrs. Duncan," a deep, southern, male voice said. "I'm Sergeant Moore, the one who called you at the beauty parlor. I'd like you to step out of the car and come and tell us if you know the victim and perhaps the horse."

Helen looked up, confused relief written on her face. "Oh... Yes. Thank you for calling. So, Marshall isn't here, then?"

Sergeant Moore frowned. *Sam was correct. Either she didn't understand what I said on the phone or is in total denial.* He bent down so his eyes were level with hers. "Ma'am, I have to ask you to do a real hard thing. From the pictures in your house, we believe the deceased man to be your husband. We just need you to verify the body for us; the horse too, if you can. We'd like to call a truck and have it removed from the roadside."

"The horse? Are you talking about High Octane?"

"Is he a gray horse, ma'am?"

"Yes. He's a gray thoroughbred."

"Then I'm afraid he's deceased too. Like I said on the phone, he got tangled up in some barbed-wire from an old fence. Of course, I'm not certain it's your horse, but the horse lying by the victim is a gray one."

Watching Helen's face closely, Paul Moore reached out and touched her arm. His drawl was soft and gentle. "I'm sorry I had to be so abrupt, Mrs. Duncan. It's an awful thing to have to say to someone, but I had to make sure you understood. After we do this, we'll take you home. Do y'all have family you can call?"

She raised her head and said, as if from far away, "Yes, our children." Then she turned her legs and stepped from the squad car, focusing tearless brown eyes on the sergeant's. "Please, take me to see what I must see."

Sergeant Moore nodded to his deputy and they both moved in beside her and directed her steps around the back of the ambulance and past the waiting EMTs standing there. He'd said to Sam, in their earlier whispered conversation, "I expect she's in some sort of shock. When she sees the victim and the horse, don't be surprised if she blows. She is liable to throw herself right on the ground. I just don't know. If she does, we won't get in her way or try to stop her. We just don't want her to hurt herself."

As they walked, the sergeant thought, *Thank God the press has left.* Even now, his stomach turned when he remembered how reporters had turned up, taking pictures, asking questions. *Goddamned police scanners! Who wants to see a picture of this kind of tragedy?*

Reflexively, both men reached out to firmly grasp Helen's elbows just as the scene came into view. She stopped, stared and then whirled, jerking her elbows free as she spun. She walked back to the squad car and then she stood perfectly still, eyes cast down, drawing in deep breaths, arms straight and rigid at her sides. After a few seconds she said, flatly. "Yes, that's my husband and my horse...and there is no doubt that they are both dead. Call your truck, Sergeant Moore. Get that horse out of here."

Her matter-of-fact voice so contrasted with her behavior that Sam felt the hair on the back of his neck lift. He nodded and reached to re-open the door and help her in. "The EMTs will handle your husband, Mrs. Duncan, and the sergeant will bring your husband's Jeep. Let's go call your children," he said simply.

15

"Yes," Helen said. "Yes, of course, I must tell them about Marshall. Where did you say those men were taking him?"

Sam felt like he had just run into a brick wall at full speed. He leaned down to where she sat looking up at him, a placid, waiting expression on her face. "Ma'am, he's going to the only place he could be going--the Prince William County Morgue. You'll need to go and sign papers there and tell them what you want done with the remains."

Chapter Three

Deputy Sam Allen sat deep in the Adirondack chair on the Duncans' side porch, shaded from the slanting sun by the overhang. A cold cup of coffee sat on the slatted, wooden table in front of him. He appeared relaxed, boots on the lower porch rail, elbows resting comfortably on the generous arms of the chair. It was an illusion. Despite his best efforts, the day's events were still on constant rerun. He wasn't overly disturbed by the horrific accident. He'd seen far worse in Vietnam.

As he sat waiting, it came to him that mostly he was thinking about the woman in the house. It was the way she was acting that had gotten to him. *What's her deal? Why doesn't she cry? Didn't she care for the victim?* The possibility that Helen was as unperturbed as she appeared made him scowl. *If I died like that, Denise better be crying her butt off!* He thought of his wife and his face moved. He knew, to the bottom of his soul, that his wife of 26 years, upon news of his death, would be inconsolable. *She wouldn't be like this white woman, all in control and sensible. No way she would call her kids on the phone and say, 'Darling, your father has had a terrible accident. I need you to come home as soon as you can.'*

Sam recalled Helen's phone conversation in its smooth, everything's under-control tone. The words she said played again and again in his mind, like a skip in a cracked record. *If the sergeant hadn't taken over the phone, those three kids would have come home thinking their daddy was still alive and that sure wouldn't be right.* He shook his head, so agitated that he had to stand. He hooked an arm around the verandah post and stood staring down the drive, hoping to see a car with a Pennsylvania license plate, the older son's car, to arrive. He looked at his watch. "Three hours," Mrs. Duncan had said when he had knocked on the screen door to ask. She was chopping onions for a pot of beans. "That's what it usually takes them to get here. They live in Philadelphia."

With a sigh, he walked back to the chair and slumped into it. *Only another 40 minutes to wait.* He turned his ear to listen as Helen's footsteps sounded on the plank floor. He thought about the way she'd made her beans. *Never seen beans made up out of cans like that. Sure makes it easy.* Sam decided he'd tell Denise and their kids about it around the dinner table that night. He wondered what they would think.

He put his palms to his forehead and lowered his elbows to his knees. *If I hadn't opened my big, fat, black mouth, I wouldn't be here.* But he HAD opened his mouth. He had volunteered. It seemed like he couldn't help himself when he saw how the thought of leaving her alone troubled his sergeant. That's when he'd said, "Sir, maybe one of us should stay...in case she breaks down. I could just sit tight here on the porch until her son gets here. That way, if she needed something, there'd be somebody here."

The sergeant looked relieved. "That's a good idea, Sam. Thank you. I'll go tell her you'll be on the side porch."

When Sergeant Moore returned, Sam walked with him toward his squad car. Before getting in, the sergeant turned to face him and said, "I asked Mrs. Duncan to leave the kitchen door open so you could hear her through the screen door if she calls out." He shook his head, the troubled look still on his face. "Do you know what she said to me? She said, 'Thank you, sir. If I can think of anything for him to do, I'll give a call.' I got the feeling she'd forgotten why we are all here. She sounded real vague." A deep crease of worry etched his forehead. "But then, right after that, she said she planned to spend the afternoon on the telephone notifying friends--in this real crisp, businesslike voice."

Sam looked at him. "You mean like her voice was when she talked to her kids?"

"Exactly!"

Sam opened the patrol car door and his boss lowered himself in and absently reached for his seatbelt, lost in thought. Then he looked up and said softly, "So, it's not like she doesn't know, right? Maybe she's holding it in, waiting for her son to get here. Or, like you said, she needs privacy to cry. Don't go in unless she asks you to or you hear something you think needs handling. Otherwise, just report out and go on home when you're done."

Sam nodded and gave a two-fingered salute as the sergeant put his car in reverse.

In the kitchen, Helen sat at the old pine table and stared at the telephone on the wall. Her fingertips mindlessly read the braille of a lifetime in the dents and scratches inflicted on the table's satiny surface, each a memory. She had always been glad that Marshall had decided to move it with them from the house in town. She touched the crescent-shaped indentations where Willie banged his pewter cup and the fork tine holes where Peter had barely missed Carrie's arm as she tried to steal a piece of bacon from his plate. Not funny then, but somehow more precious than tears to her now. Almost as a revelation, she thought, *Tears are precious, but I don't have time to cry. I have to call Marshall's friends, dust the children's rooms, call the…place where they put him…and tell them to take him to…* She shoved away from the table, suddenly losing track of thought. Slowly, she rose to her feet, looking at the telephone. The short walk to it seemed impossibly long. *I must at least call the Rawlings. Will and Torrey must be told,* she thought. But instead, she turned and headed for the stairs.

Thinking of Marshall's boyhood friend and his wife caused such pain that, as she climbed, she unknowingly put one clenched fist over her heart. Memories of the family vacations spent at the Rawlings' ranch on the high desert of Eastern Oregon

19

brought with them the scent of sage and the laughter of children. *Torrey, what should I do? How can I live through this? How can I live with myself?* She paused on a stair and bowed her head as if expecting an answer. When none came, she lowered her fist and gave a small sigh. *I wonder if I added enough chili powder and cayenne pepper to the beans for Peter. Funny, how he is the only child to have inherited his father's hot tongue.*

When she reached the landing, she paused, trying to remember what had brought her upstairs. She stood, disoriented, looking around. *Oh yes, I must make sure that the children's rooms are ready when they come. We'll have so much to talk and think about, I don't want to have to worry about cleaning then. There are so many, many details. I must make certain things go well. It is really up to me to set the tone. My children will be counting on me.* Then she remembered. *The dust cloth, I forgot the dust cloth.* She tried to feel irritated and failed. Her eyes wandered down the hallway and her gaze stalled before reaching the open double doors of the master bedroom. She lowered her head, but the picture was clear in her mind--the four-poster bed with its still rumpled duvet-- signs of the last night she would ever spend with her husband. She turned in retreat. *The dust cloth... But first I must make the calls to those... those...two places.*

Back in the kitchen, Helen purposefully lifted the telephone book from the drawer and thumbed through it. Under the word "Mortuaries" it read: see Funeral Directors. With a steady finger, she retraced her path back towards the front of the thick, but flimsy book. When she found the place, she looked blankly at the type, wondering how one went about selecting a funeral home. On the counter beside the book was the number of the Prince William County Morgue, thoughtfully written there by the sergeant. *What was that he had said to her? I was to call them and tell them*

20

who I am. I am to tell them I will come and identify the body after Peter arrives. She remembered the last thing he'd said, "You'll have to tell the morgue to release the body to whichever funeral home you plan to use. Be sure to take identification."

Helen clenched her teeth. *No! I have to do it now. I won't make Peter be a part of this thing.* She willed her eyes to focus. Each advertisement seemed more crassly commercial than the one before it. She looked for those ads that offered cremation. It was the one detail that she and Marshall had agreed upon--no casket, no funeral, only a brief memorial service and ashes in a box. Her first finger trembled slightly as she went down the list, finally stopping at an ad enclosed within a simple black line. It read: Ashes to Ashes Crematorium. Three lines of type followed the name:

- Next day service
- One call for everything
- Dignity at an affordable price

Her fingernail paused below the words 'next day service.' She wrote the number of the mortuary beneath the number of the morgue and then quickly closed the book. Again, she recited to herself, *this must all be done before Peter arrives. I do not want to try to do this in his presence. I must not subject him to...* Then, as before, her mind seemed to empty and she stood staring blankly at the bright Yellow Pages cover. The letters A to Z were printed in a cheerful red above a landscape photograph taken at the Bull Run Battlefield. Black half-dots around the image gave the impression of a postage stamp.

I could improve that design; almost any graphic designer could. For one thing, it needs to be color balanced. She looked inside the front cover for a design credit, but there was none, only one for the photographer. Photo by Kevin Burns, it read. Her unseeing eyes rested on the print until the sound of boot heels hitting the porch boards made her jump. She pushed the Yellow Pages back in the drawer under the telephone and then hurried over to give the slowly cooking beans a stir.

Sam stood and walked down the steps when he saw the old Volvo come barreling up the driveway. He waited as the doors flew open and a disheveled young man in a rumpled suit and wild brown hair erupted from the driver's side. The man strode towards him saying, "Hello, officer, I'm Peter Duncan. Is my mother inside?" His calm voice belied his appearance and his red-rimmed, blue eyes.

A slim, freckle-faced woman had slipped quietly from the other side of the car and had come to put her arm around her husband's waist. "And I'm Patti Duncan," she said softly. She too had been weeping.

Sam held out his square, blunt-fingered hand to her and then to Peter. "Hello," he said, his voice kind, "my name is Sam Allen. I have been waiting for you to come. Yes, sir. Your mother is inside."

Peter looked at the rock of a man before him and grasped his hand like a life preserver. "How is she taking it?"

Sam looked gravely at the two standing in front of him, searching for words. "I don't know for sure," he finally said. "She may not realize…"

"It's so hard to believe. How in God's name did it happen?" Peter broke in, his anguish causing his wife's renewal of tears. She pressed her face into her husband's arm, her shoulders shaking.

"It appeared like your daddy was trying to save a horse that got caught in barbed-wire and in the process the wire got your daddy too." Sam was suddenly glad that he had waited for this boy's arrival. He finally realized where he'd seen Helen Duncan's vague and changeable behavior before. "Mister Duncan," Sam said, in a voice so soft that it made Peter lift his head to listen, "I'm real sorry about your daddy, but it's your mama that I'm worrying about now. She's acting unnatural...like she doesn't seem to care about what happened. But I've seen the pictures all over your walls..." Sam stopped, choosing his next words carefully. "I've seen people act this way before-- when I was in Nam. I've seen soldiers who quit remembering the terrible things that happened so they wouldn't go crazy."

Peter's blue eyes darkened as he looked down at his weeping wife and back up at Sam. Shaking his head, he asked, "What do you think we should do?"

"I don't know for sure. I'd guess I'd recommend asking her doctor."

Peter nodded. "That sounds right," he said. "Thank you."

Sam saw how, even with her weeping, the slender woman still held one arm protectively around her husband and said, including them both, "I sure wish it hadn't happened, but she's got you two to lean on now. You've got to take charge."

Peter stretched out a hand again. "I'll try," he said simply.

Sam enclosed it with both of his own. "You might want to tell the doctor that she hasn't shed a single tear that I know of," he said, releasing the firm grip and stepping back. "Tell the doctor she's acting like she's in shock. She keeps her coat on all the time."

Peter looked at Sam in disbelief. For his mother not to have cried over his dad's death was hard to believe. He shook his head, "My mom cries over Lassie reruns. You must be right about her being in shock. I'll call the doctor first thing."

"Well, then, I'll be leaving." Sam reached up to touch the brim of his hat in the same two-fingered salute he'd given his boss.

The young couple watched the retreating patrol car until it turned onto the county road. They looked at each other in despair. Patti reached up and laid her

23

palm against Peter's cheek. "This is going to be very hard for you, love."

Peter took her hand and kept it within his own. He nodded and drew in a deep, wavering breath. "Here we go," he said, half to himself, as they mounted the steps. He purposefully let the screen door slam behind them, and imagined he could hear his mother saying in a resigned voice, "Peter, how many times do I have to remind you? Hold onto the screen door until it's closed!" But on this day, there was no voice to break the silence, save his own. "Mother," he called, "Mom, we're home. Hello."

Immediately he heard sounds from upstairs and his mother stood on the top step in her barn coat, dust cloth in hand. "Oh darlings, you're here! I'm so glad! I've just been dusting your room. How was the drive?"

Her voice was as bright and brittle as fracturing glass. She flew down the stairs. Peter held out his arms and she rushed in to give him a quick tight hug before moving on to Patti. After giving her the same quick hug, she stepped back to survey them.

"Gracious," she said, "you two look exhausted! Let me make us a quick cup of tea. We have so much to talk about!" Her brown eyes were bright with something that looked like excitement. She turned and hurried toward the kitchen without waiting for their response.

Peter looked at his wife. "What should I do?" He whispered helplessly.

She shrugged and shook her head sadly. "I don't know. Just act natural and let things unfold, I guess." Then she squirmed and tried to smile. "I know the first thing I have to do is go to the bathroom. Don't you?" Without waiting for his nod, she turned and hurried toward the powder room at the end of the hall.

Helen looked at her hands, surprised to see that they were shaking as she held the tea kettle under the faucet. *How silly! Am I cold?* It was then she realized that she was still wearing her barn coat. She glanced at the clock on the wall above the telephone. *Why, I must be cold. I've got my coat on and it's not yet time to feed the horses.* The thought of feeding the horses caused a stab of pain to slice through her.

The trembling in her hands continued and she used her full concentration, willing them to steady as she carried the brimming kettle to the range and turned on the element. Then she lifted the lid on the beans, giving them a thorough stir. *I refuse to be coming down with a virus. The children are all coming. I don't have time to be ill.* She suddenly stood very still; unable to remember whether or not she had called her other two children. Footsteps sounded on the plank floor and she whirled to see Peter and Patti. "Oh dear," she said. "Peter, do you know if Carrie and Willie are coming?"

She could see Peter looking at her oddly. He shook his head. "I don't know, Mom. Did you call them after you and the sergeant called me?"

Helen put her hands to her temples and lowered her head, trying to recall. "I believe I did. There was a man here..."

"Yes," Peter said impatiently. "A Sergeant Paul Moore. I spoke with him. He's the one who told me of Dad's death. Did he help you call Willie and Carrie too?"

They watched in stricken fascination as Helen reacted to Peter's words. She looked like a turtle withdrawing into its shell. Only her protective shell was an old, canvas barn coat. Her shoulders hunched up under her ears and she wrapped her arms around herself, forearms making a cross over her heart. With her eyes on her loafers, she whispered, "Really, Peter, there is a time and a place for everything and this is neither the time nor the place. We have so much to think about."

A silence so complete descended upon the kitchen that when the telephone broke it, Patti jumped and gave a squeak of surprise. Peter leaped to answer it.

"Peter Duncan here." There was a brief moment when he thought no one was on the other end of the line. But then he heard the quiet sobbing. "Carrie? Carrie is that you? Where are you?"

"Oh, Peter. I'm h-h-e-re at the airport in Dallas, waiting for my flight, again. They had to bring the first plane back. I'm so-o-o frus-tra-ted!"

"Well, thank God you're on your way. I wasn't certain you even knew."

"It was on my answering machine at work, Peter. I was teaching a class. I still can't believe it. What happened? I can't..."

Peter interrupted, "Carrie, do you know if Willie knows?"

"I think so. The officer who helped Mom call here said that you had been called and that Willie would be called too. But, Peter, it's three hours earlier on the West Coast. He's probably either in class or at basketball practice. He might not have the message yet."

Peter grimaced. "Carrie, just get your butt on that plane. I'll call Willie, even if I have to call the University of Oregon Coaching Department to find him. Things are tough here."

Carrie's voice changed. "Tough? What do you mean tough, Peter? Is it Mom?"

"Yes."

"Should I talk with her?"

Good old Carrie, Peter thought, *it's not so bad having a shrink-type for a sister. She'll know how to handle Mom.* "Sure," he said. He turned and held out the receiver. "Here, Mom, it's Carrie. She wants to talk to you."

Helen had been hovering over the stove, mechanically stirring the beans into mush. She turned and looked at the receiver with distaste, but slowly walked to the phone. Somewhere, in the past few minutes, Peter noted she had fastened every button on her coat. While he watched, Helen took a deep breath,

26

straightened her shoulders and pasted a smile on her face. "Carrie, darling, where are you?" The crystalline voice was back. Peter caught his wife's eye. He strode from the kitchen to the den where his parents kept their answering machine, thinking Willie might have called. *My father is dead! We should be crying together about this. Why can't Mom let that happen? What in the hell is happening here? What horse got caught in the wire? One of ours? What wire? There's no wire around here! What in the hell happened?*

The red light blinked angrily in the semi-darkness. He jabbed the button and heard his brother's tearful voice. "Jesus! Somebody answer this goddamn phone...please. My roommate brought me the message. Mom, where are you? The coach's brother has a plane. He's flying me from Eugene to Portland to catch Northwest flight 111 to Dulles. I'll catch a cab. Goddammit! Somebody please answer this phone!"

The message ended when the receiver slammed. *This whole thing is a walking nightmare!* Peter jerked the receiver from the phone. "Don't hang up, Carrie," he shouted!" In his ear there was a click.

"I'm here, Peter." Carrie's voice was calm, almost professional sounding. "I believe the click you heard was Mom disconnecting."

"She hung up? She hung up!" He repeated, disbelief making his voice shake.

"Never mind for right now, Peter. I think she's in a state of shock. I'm serious. Something's not right."

Peter nodded into the phone. "That's what the police officer said, too."

Carrie said, "Okay, here's what you do. Call Doctor Henry. I don't think Mom will go, but at least, ask his advice. I've got to go now. If this plane works, I'll be landing at Dulles at 6:40, flight 342, United...your time. Can one of you come and get me?"

"Yes, of course. And Carrie, Willie knows. There was a message on the phone machine. He didn't

27

give me an arrival time, but I can get it. I've got his airline and his flight number. He's pretty shook."

They were quiet for a moment, thinking of their younger brother. Each wondering if their mother had chosen not to take Willie's call.

"Remember when he was so little we could hold things out of his reach?" Carrie asked in a tight voice.

Peter cleared his throat. "Yeah, I do. Funny, how he never got mad about it. We sure can't do it anymore."

"I love you, Peter. Be gentle with Mom. I'm coming as fast as I can."

As he hung up, Peter realized there was much more in what they hadn't said than in what they had. As much as he wanted to unload all his unanswered questions on Carrie, he was glad he hadn't. He took a deep breath then reached for the telephone book, hoping Dr. Henry could see them immediately.

Chapter Four

Willie mumbled a tight-lipped thanks to the flight attendant as she escorted him to his seat in first class. It was the best he could manage. He slid over next to the window and looked out, grateful to at last be able to hide his face. Grateful too, for how things had worked out so that he could make the plane. *It's one thing about playing college basketball; if you're any good, people come out of the woodwork to do nice things for you. Maybe it isn't fair...* He shook his head remembering how his coach had started making things happen, including making the arrangements for Willie to fly in a hot dog Lancair IVP to Portland to catch his flight east.

The little plane was incredibly fast. Under other circumstances, the 20-minute ride would've been a blast.... *Maybe it isn't fair, but it's sure convenient and in this case essential.* The extra space between the seats in first class allowed him just enough leg room for comfort. He finally pulled his face from the window, leaned back into the seat and tried to relax--tried to think of something other than the reason for the trip, but it proved impossible. *Dad's dead! It's so hard to believe I'll never see him again. None of us will.* He closed his eyes and allowed tears to slip down his cheeks, unchecked.

He kept hearing the sound of his mother's voice on his answering machine. It was only because she had identified herself that he could believe the voice on the phone was hers. He had listened to the message again and again as he threw clothes into a carry-on bag. "Willie, darling, this is your mother. I hope you get this message. You must come home right away. Your father has been in a terrible accident."

Then he'd heard a male voice prompting in the background. But the voice was cut off after the words, "Mrs. Duncan, you've got to tell him..." Then, there had been a long silence until his mother spoke again.

29

"Dear, it's very, very bad news... I've called the others... There are so many details associated with all of this. Please come as quickly as you can."

Again there was silence, only the sound of breathing and then a man's voice, sounding almost disgusted, had said, "Mister Duncan, this is Sergeant Moore of the Prince William County Sheriff's Office. I am afraid your father has been killed in an accident involving a horse. His death was immediate. Your brother and sister have been notified. Your brother, Peter, is on his way from Philadelphia. If you receive this message, please call your mother immediately."

Willie sat up in his seat, suddenly realizing why the sergeant's voice had been cut off during the first part of the conversation. His mother had put her hand over the receiver! She evidently didn't want him to hear what the sergeant was saying. She was trying to protect him. Love for her welled up in him and he stifled a sob. *I'm coming, Mom. Hold on. We'll all be there.* He could feel his own anguish mingle with his mother's and become one deep black wave of despair. *Thank God the sergeant took over the phone. Mom's message was so vague I wouldn't have known for sure... I would've gone crazy with wondering.* He shook his head. *But where was she when I tried to call? Why didn't she answer the phone? I hope someone is there with her.* He looked at his watch. Peter and Patti had surely arrived by now. *But what if they hadn't? What if she was all alone?*

Willie didn't seem to be able to control his colliding worries. Questions kept multiplying in his mind. *The sergeant said Dad died in a horse accident. What did he do, try to ride Octane?* Knowing his father, he realized it was entirely possible. *It would be just like Dad to take control, override Mom's objections and get on that horse; especially if the horse was misbehaving.*

The captain's voice came on and rolled over him nearly unheeded, but he automatically checked his seatbelt and then turned his head toward the window again. *Dad's dead! I know he's dead, but it doesn't feel real. Stuff like this just doesn't happen to the Duncan family. We are the all-American stereotype.*

The flight attendant came by to offer beverages and snacks. He shook his head without taking his face from the window, tears again tracking steadily down his face.

At Dulles International, Willie was the first to deplane. He sprinted through the airport toward where the taxis waited and threw himself in the backseat, his bag on the seat beside him. "Take 95 South to Manassas and then I'll direct you," he said tersely to the cab driver who nodded and flipped on the meter without comment.

Long after bowls of chili had been eaten, the dishes cleared and their mother given a sleeping pill and put to bed, Peter, Willie and Carrie lingered around the scarred kitchen table, anchored there by the need for each other's company. Patti had long since gone off to bed, partly to keep an ear out for their mother, who they hoped was sleeping a dreamless, drug-induced sleep.

In front of Carrie lay a spiral notebook and their mother's address book. But, the time for list making was finished and the time for calling friends had not yet come. Tonight, the need was to be together; to absorb and blend the fact that their father was dead, with the feeling of unreality caused by knowing that their lives were forever changed. Everything seemed a little surreal and only each other's presence provided perspective.

Willie sat back from the table; his basketball player legs stretched out and crossed at the ankle, his size 16 hi-tops jutting up into the air. Peter looked at him and said, "Willie, remember the day we realized you could put one leg over Carrie's old pony, Pooh, and stand up without touching her back?"

31

"I do. Remember when we led her to the front of the house and I straddled her, pretending to sit on her while you went in to get Mom?"

Peter chuckled and looked at Carrie. "Mom was dusting under the beds, but I told her we had something special to show her and that she had to come right out. She came right out all right. Whoo-ee!" He pitched his voice to imitate his furious mother. 'William Bradford Duncan, what's wrong with you? Get off that poor pony immediately.'"

Carrie looked from one to the other in surprise. "Why haven't I heard this one before? Where was I?"

The brothers ignored her, grinning at each other. Peter said, "She was all set to thwack ol' Willie with the dust mop when he straightened his knees and stood up so I could lead Pooh right out from under him."

Carrie's blue eyes sparkled. "Then what?"

Willie said, "We started laughing like crazy. I was hamming it up, fell to the ground, was rolling around and laughing my head off like a goofus. I didn't know that Peter had Pooh and was already high-tailing it back to the barn until Mom started to giggle and bash me with that dust mop, saying what wicked boys we were."

Carrie could see the whole thing: the dear moth-eaten pony calmly munching on the lawn; her beanpole brother, all elbows, knees and Adam's apple, on the ground, laughing, unaware that he had been left to face the music alone. She started to grin, remembering the other times she and her older brother had set poor Willie up as the target of pranks. Then she said, "You know, it seems a little strange to be sitting here pulling up all our happy childhood stories on the day our father died, but for some reason, it feels comforting."

The men nodded, feeling the wrench in their gut at Carrie's words, *on the day our father died.*" The words made it true. It was also true that the memories

32

were all they had and that dredging through their private trove of childhood memories, reliving them together, somehow temporarily eased the finality of their loss.

Willie was the first to break the silence. "Remember the year Pooh had Bear? We couldn't get over how tiny a Shetland colt was."

Peter looked at them. "That may have been Dad's best joke on Uncle Will; when he took Bear to him on the airplane in Max's dog carrier."

The memory brought more tears. "What a great dad we had," Carrie sobbed. "I think that all those happy memories are really making it hard for us to realize he's gone."

They sat in silence, looking at each other with red-rimmed, weary eyes. All had cried, though not in front of their mother. She'd made it abundantly clear that she didn't want tears in her presence.

Finally, Willie said, "We were a pretty crazy family, weren't we?"

Carrie responded immediately, "We still are, Willie." She reached out and grabbed his hand and then reached for Peter's, squeezing hard. "I'm so glad we're all here together. I can't even think what it would be like without you guys."

"Awful!" Peter said, leaving his hand in her grip. "I had Patti at least, but before you got here, it was awful! God! I couldn't get Mom to tell me anything. She was off somewhere in the ozone, acting as phony as Astroturf. If that deputy hadn't told me the details of how Dad died, we probably still wouldn't know."

Tears again gathered in Willie's eyes. "That damned horse! I was here when they had the big fight about getting him. Mom acted really weird, like she was practicing assertiveness or something. Every time dad would say something against buying him, she would just say, in that real calm voice she can have, 'But this is the horse I want, Marshall.' Just those words--in that real calm voice."

He dropped his head into his big hands. "Uncle Will and Aunt Torrey asked me what Octane was like when I went to see them at Thanksgiving. They said Mom had called, all excited. I told them Dad was worried about how hot he was. Uncle Will didn't say it; you know how he is. But, I think he was worrying too. He made one of his smart-assed comments about horses in the East being all dressed up in little pancake saddles with no place to go except over a fence."

"At least we all made it home for Christmas last year," Carrie said; her words low and broken under the pain of remembering what Christmas had always been at Henley Brook Farm. "That is one thing that won't ever be the same again."

They sat, heads lowered, each picturing how the farm had looked; the lane and porches glowing from strings of frosted white lights. It was their father who always took charge of fashioning the two magnificent juniper wreaths with boughs sent from Oregon by their dad's oldest and best friend, the man they'd always called Uncle Will.

"God!" Their dad always said after he hung the wreaths on the big, sliding barn doors and stood back to admire his work, "There's nothing like juniper for wreath-making. Those blue berries make it look self-decorated."

Carrie asked quietly, "Willie, remember when you were about 10 and wired the stereo with outside speakers to surprise us all with Christmas music when we were out decorating?"

Willie finally raised his head and they looked steadily at each other. His face relaxed into softer lines. "I was 12," he said.

Peter asked, "How old were you when you fixed the Rawlings' hay baler?"

"I was 12 then, too. You were 17. It was the year Uncle Will fired the irrigation crew and put us all to work."

"Including Julie and Tina," Carrie reminded them.

"Tina Rawling was more trouble than she was worth. All she wanted was piggyback rides," Peter said with a grin.

"And now she's giving them to her own kids," Will said. They sat, remembering Will and Torrey's pesky, youngest daughter, Tina. "Remember the year she got her mare, Sheba, caught in the irrigation ditch mud and how you had to go sneak the tractor out of the shed to help pull her out, Peter?" Carrie asked.

Peter looked at them. "Unless Julie or Tina told, I don't think the adults ever found out about that one."

Willie yawned and stood up. "I saw Bear at Thanksgiving. In his winter coat, he looks just like Pooh used to look--like a fat, dirty, fuzzy snowball. Dewey and I trimmed his feet." He grinned at them. "Actually, I figured out how to get him up on the flatbed, so he would be high enough that Dewey could do the trimming without hurting his back."

Carrie and Peter nodded, thinking of the wizened ranch hand. "He's getting awfully old," Carrie said.

Willie looked down at his siblings, suddenly feeling older than either of them. "If Mom doesn't want to call Aunt Torrey and Uncle Will tomorrow, I'll do it."

Peter nodded. "Just do it. She keeps talking about calling people, but I don't think she's made a single call, so far."

Willie thought about his brother's words and then shook his head. "Naw, I'd better ask her first. Seems like it's important to her that we all mind...just like we did when we were little."

Without further words, Peter and Carrie scraped back their chairs and followed Willie toward the stairs.

Helen struggled to wake. She felt as though she had a hangover, but couldn't remember drinking. There was a bitter, metallic taste in her mouth. She reached out a leg to touch her husband. The coldness of the sheets on the right side of the bed jerked her awake and back into the horror of yesterday. Her eyes flew open and she sat up, looking about without focus. Finally, her eyes settled on the bedside clock. 9 AM! She threw back the duvet and reached for her robe, thinking of her children with irritation, remembering how they had tried to tell her what to do. *Even Willie, when he finally arrived, tried to boss me around!*

Annoyance caused her pale face to flush. *Well I won't have it and I won't swallow any more of those terrible pills!* She swept into the bathroom, snatched the small brown container from the counter, up-ended it over the toilet and flushed. "There!" She said aloud. "That takes care of that!"

She marched, shoulders squared, down the stairs, working up her anger as she went. In the kitchen, her grown-up children were making breakfast. She paused in the doorway to take in the cozy setting. Peter was at the stove flipping the hotcakes. Patti was setting the table, chatting with Carrie who sat at the table rubbing her fingers back and forth mindlessly over the spiral of a notebook. The normality of the scene seemed almost obscene. Helen closed her eyes to wipe it out.

When she opened them, she saw that all activity had stopped and everyone was staring at her, waiting quietly. Unaware that crimson, telltale spots of anger flushed her cheeks, she said brightly, "Hello, darlings, I'm glad you're all up. We've got a lot to do today."

Peter, watching closely, wondered if he was the only one aware, that once again, some warp-speed transition had taken place within his mother. "Where's Willie?" She asked.

Carrie jumped up and hurried toward her mother. "Good morning, Mom. How did you sleep? Willie's out feeding the horses. He should be right in."

36

Peter watched the interchange, noticed how his mother dipped in and out of Carrie's hug like a moth to a porch light. He reached for a mug and poured his mother's coffee. His lawyer-sharp senses collected the details of contrast. *If I look at her, instead of listen to her, maybe I can read her better.* "Hi, Mom. It looks like we beat you out of bed. When's the last time that happened?"

"Oh," she said, "it was that horrible pill Dr. Henry prescribed. But, you can bet that I won't take another. I flushed them all down the toilet." She lifted the heavy white mug from his hand and moved away to stand in the doorway. Then she changed her mind and instead went to stand with her back to the sink.

Peter's eyes flew to Carrie's face, but Carrie was staring at her mother with an appraising expression. *She can't figure this out either,* he thought.

"Now, children, please listen to me carefully." Helen's voice was falsely cheerful but determinedly businesslike. *She sounds like a damned telemarketer. I wonder what my sister is making of all of this.* Peter watched in silence as Helen took a sip of coffee and then theatrically threw back her head. "I won't be bullied. I would like your help. But, I won't be bullied."

Peter listened to his mother's voice in baffled wonder. *She's really pissed about something. 'I won't be bullied.' What a line!*

Helen walked across the room to the counter by the wall phone, set down her coffee and picked up the piece of paper that held the telephone numbers of both the morgue and the crematorium. "Peter, after breakfast, you must call these people and then go fill out the paperwork. That has to be done before they will release…the…the remains. Take Willie with you so you can pick up my car from Monique's. Carrie, I'd like you to call this second number on the list. It happens to be the Ashes to Ashes Crematorium in Manassas. Their advertisement in the Yellow Pages stresses one-day service. That's what your…your…father would like. I know you would like to carry out his wishes about this, now wouldn't you? And could you please write just a little something to put in the paper as well?"

Carrie stood, trying hard to keep her expression neutral. *What's going on here? This is crazy! This is what Peter was talking about...her saying one thing, feeling...or not allowing herself to feel...something else.* She drew a deep breath, trying to calm herself, trying to pull out of the emotional roller coaster being created. Carrie gave a mental shrug. *Well, at least she finally made a direct reference to Dad. That's something, I guess.*

Willie had walked through the kitchen door, bringing a draft of early spring chill with him. He heard the last of Helen's words and he too recognized it. He thought, *that's her 'madder-than-hell' voice. What's happened? What have they said to her to get her so worked up?* He looked at his siblings' faces. They both looked as if they had been slapped. He strode across the room to Helen, sighed and reached down to wrap her in a bear hug. "Hey, morning, Mom. How'd you sleep?"

Helen raised her hands and pushed hard against his sternum and then retreated out of his reach. "Dammit! Do not use that tone of voice on me, Willie. Her gaze flew around the room. Do not patronize me, any of you. I won't have it! First, you drugged me, and then you insist on treating me like a child!"

From a safe distance, she looked squarely up at Willie's horrified face. "I asked your brother and sister for a little help with these dreadful details, and I'm asking you as well. I need to be on the telephone, calling people, letting them know... I do not think it is asking too much of my children when I ask for a little help in making the arrangements."

Helen watched her youngest struggle to control his face, saw the bafflement in the eyes of all her children, but knew if she was going to manage to get through the next few days, she would need every inch of the distance she was creating.

When she felt her control return, she stepped forward and reached up to pat the side of Willie's face. "It's going to be all right, dear," she said in a normal voice and turned to look around the room, her glittering eyes lightly touching on each of them. "You are wonderful people. It's going to be all right for you, you'll see. We just need to get this over with so you can go on with your lives." She gave a small, grave smile, pivoted on her heel and strode from the kitchen. Four stricken faces watched her go.

"Jesus!" Willie said softly, looking first at Peter and Patti, and then at Carrie, "What was that all about? Did I do something to cause that performance?"

Carrie shook her head. "Nothing, Willie. It isn't you, or any of us. It's Mom. It's the situation. That's why she wants to get it over with so fast."

"What situation? What are you talking about, Carrie?"

Peter clenched and unclenched his fists. "The memorial service, Willie; Mom wants us to arrange to have Dad cremated today, if possible. Carrie is supposed to call the place and write an obituary. You and I are supposed to go and identify the...the...remains and bring home the car."

Willie stared at him, digesting his words, watching as Patti went to Peter and put her arms loosely around him before dropping her head to his chest. He could think of no words worth saying until finally he looked at his sister with stricken eyes. "Just like that, huh? Bake him and pour him in a box. Boom! Done! Over with! Carrie, you're the one studying to be a shrink. What are we supposed to do here? Do we have to let Mom do this so fast?"

Carrie slowly lowered herself into a chair, shaking her head in despair. "I don't know what we should do. She's just not our mom right now. It's like something has snapped inside her." She looked at her brothers. "If she is affecting you like she's affecting me, we're all pretty angry with her...and I keep asking myself if that's what she wants."

Peter nodded and absently kissed the top of his wife's head, his smoldering eyes meeting Carrie's. "Damned right I'm angry. I came real close to grabbing her and giving her a smack when she gave Willie that shove."

Willie looked at the empty doorway, hoping to see his mother reappear, his Adam's apple bobbing as if he were trying to swallow his pain, "Jesus!" he said again, shaking his big head from side to side, "This whole deal is so wrong. I don't care if she pushed me, Peter. I'm not mad. And I don't want us to get mad at her. Jesus! Please don't talk about hitting her. Talk about how we can get our mom, the mom we used to have, back."

Chapter Five

Peter shut Patti's door and walked around the Volvo to get in. He shut his own door and looked at her. "This isn't right," he said, anger simmering in his voice. "This whole thing just sucks! What's wrong with her, anyway?"

Patti put a hand on his thigh. "I guess she wants to be alone. Maybe being around you kids is just too painful for her right now."

He turned the key in frustration and threw the car into reverse. "That's too ridiculous to even contemplate! Maybe in some other family…but not this one. We've literally been kicked out of here."

"Do you want to stay?"

Peter shot his wife a quick glance as he twisted the wheel and shifted into gear. "You've got a point," he said grimly, looking over his shoulder and raising his hand in a farewell wave.

From the porch, Helen watched the Volvo until it disappeared around the first curve of the county road. Even though she needed them to be gone, their leaving seemed to have pulled all the heat and energy from her body. She pulled the old, Irish fisherman's cardigan she was wearing close around her and then glanced across the lawn towards the barn. Her first impulse was to go there to find comfort; to hear the soft nickers welcome her as she opened the door; to feel velvety, questioning muzzles asking for a treat; to lean against solid, warm bodies and absorb the strength she lacked. Instead she frowned, shook her head, and hurried back through the kitchen door. *Thank goodness Peter took care of the horses. I have so much to do. How will I ever get it done?*

She caught the screen door with her heel to keep it from banging and then paused to look around the spotless kitchen with a frown. Every dish, pot and pan was in its place. Pink tulips in an old milk glass vase sat on the table--the only flowers in the room. At

41

her request, all the bouquets and sprays sent to the funeral home or to the house had been taken to the various nursing homes throughout the area. When her children had protested, she'd used her stock phrase: *It's what your father would've wanted.* To that she added: *You are all leaving and I certainly don't need them when we have so many lovely spring flowers of our own.*

It was very quiet, a contrast to the kitchen as it had been that morning. She could almost hear the chatter of her determinedly cheerful children. Certainly, it was good that they'd had a few days to visit, but it really was time for them to be gone; to get on with their own lives. *Why did they refuse to understand that getting back to their own lives was my reason for having the memorial service so soon? Carrie, at least, should have understood, should have supported me. She has a comprehensive examination to write, for heaven's sake.*

Abruptly, Helen strode to the table and picked up the tulips. She carried them to the sink and one by one, pulled them from the vase to stuff them into the garbage disposal. *I'm just wasting time; I really must get to my desk. I'm glad I didn't give in to the children and use the telephone. To write a note is really far more civilized. It is so difficult to hear bad news over the telephone. One never knows quite what to say.* She turned on the water and flipped the disposal switch, standing expressionless, watching the flailing spring-green stems being drawn into the growling darkness. Then, she briskly dried her hands and hurried from the kitchen.

Once at her desk, with her address book, a box of plain cream-colored card stock with matching envelopes and the stacks of Xerox copies of the obituary Carrie had written, Helen made a copy of what she planned to say. She revised it several times, but when she was satisfied, she drew the sheets of card stock to her and wrote, one note after the other; each exactly alike.

Dear_____,

We knew you would want to know of Marshall's sudden, accidental passing. He did not suffer. We are all doing as well as can be expected. The service is one he would have liked.

Love,

Helen, Peter, Carrie and Willie

Helen did not stop until the entire stack of 100 cards had been written. Only then, did she put down her pen and started to stretch her aching fingers, but then she stopped herself. The cramping muscles made her nod her head with satisfaction. She deliberately picked up the pen and began to address the envelopes.

Shadows had gathered in the room as she wrote. Birds outside in the ivy were starting their good-night songs. When she had finished the last envelope, she stood and walked to the dormer window in her office. It had nearly the same view as the master bedroom. A restored hump-backed chest sat under the window. She put a knee on it and leaned forward, craning her neck to the left to look out over the orchard, avoiding the empty pasture where she'd left a gray thoroughbred to work off some springtime energy.

Slowly, she turned from the window and looked at her drafting table and then at her desk. She couldn't remember when she'd last done a display layout. Everything before the accident seemed to have happened in another lifetime. *Get used to it, Helen. It WAS another lifetime.*

She walked firmly back to her desk and sat down, spine straight. With steady fingers, she picked a clipping from her stack and read:

MARSHALL JAMES DUNCAN
Howie, Duncan and Beadle, AIA
1938-1995

A memorial service for Marshall James Duncan, 56, will be held at 11 AM, Thursday, April 18, 1995, at the Ashes to Ashes Crematorium, 7200 Jackson Avenue, Manassas, VA. Mr. Duncan, a long-time resident of Prince William County, died tragically while attempting to rescue a horse. Born June 17, 1938, in Colorado Springs, Colorado, Mr. Duncan served in the U. S. Air Force in Korea, and then in 1964, graduated from Clemson University with a degree in architecture. He was active in the Manassas Rotary and was membership chairperson of the Battlefield Country Club. He served as president of the Prince William County Hunt Club from 1990--1994. Mr. Duncan is survived by his widow, Helen Hunter-Duncan and their three children: Peter James Duncan, Carrie Helen Duncan and William Bradford Duncan.

She put the note and clipping into an envelope. They fit nicely. She reached for another, thinking of the second mention of her husband in a paper; one hidden under a stack of files on her desk. She had not seen it and didn't intend to, although she knew about it from the nice sergeant's apologetic call. "I'm real sorry about the picture in the paper, Mrs. Duncan," he had said. "Those vultures listen to our scanners and follow ambulances."

"Thank you, Sergeant Moore," she had answered with a forced calmness, glad that she was alone in the house. "I certainly appreciate being alerted. I would not want my children to open the paper and see such a thing."

"Ma'am, they wouldn't even have to open it. I'm afraid it's on the front page."

Afterwards, she'd hung up the receiver and looked at the clock in alarm, knowing that everyone would be back from the crematorium at any moment. They would pull the paper from the box as they turned into the driveway, just as they'd always done. She rushed down the stairs to retrieve it.

Now, as she methodically continued to stuff and seal envelopes, she found herself glancing at the stack of files under which she'd buried the newspaper. Even though her children were gone, it seemed important that the article remain completely hidden. When the phone on her desk rang, she jumped and then answered it before she stopped to remember that she had decided not to do so.

"Helen, baby, it's Torrey. Willie just called from Portland International. He's waiting on a flight to Eugene. We didn't know about Marshall's death. He thought you'd called us. Helen, he's VERY upset." Torrey's sentences were jerky and disjointed. "He didn't know if you wanted us to call, but God, Helen... We are so, so sorry." Torrey's voice broke and Helen listened to her weeping, feeling her face grow hot.

"Oh, Torrey, I'm so sorry. It's my fault. When Willie asked me if I planned to call you, I told him that I already had. It was just a little fib to comfort him. I knew at the time that I wouldn't have the strength to let you know until after everyone had left. Peter and Patti left just a bit ago, and now I've been sitting here by the telephone putting it off. Please, I'm so sorry. Please, Torrey, forgive me. It's just that I have been unable to..."

Helen let her voice drift into a whisper and stop, unsure what to say next. It was not hard to do. Her throat felt swollen and she suddenly felt faint. Pinpoints of light swirled and flashed in tiny explosions behind her eyes. Inside her head a nameless prayer formed itself. *Please, dear God, don't let her ask how it happened. Don't make me say it out loud, even to Torrey. I can't live through it again.*

"Helen, my God! My God! Don't apologize. We can't even imagine what you're going through. Willie told us what happened, as best he could. It's almost impossible to believe. We were set to get on the next plane coming east, but he said you might not want us. Just tell us what you do want. We NEED to do something... Anything you want us to do. Will is just beside himself. I have never seen him so torn up."

Helen sucked in a deep breath. Above all, she did not want the Rawlings to come to Manassas. "No, Torrey. Listen to me. Please don't come. What I need most is to be alone right now. But thank you so much. If I would want anyone, it would be you two. But I don't. Not now, anyway. What you can do, if you would, is make yourself available to Willie. I know how hard he is taking this."

"Of course we will. You know how much we love him--love all of you. We'll ask Russell, our pilot friend from Burns, to fly to Eugene and get him. Listen, Helen, we're here. If you need us, please call. And, we'll check back in real soon. We love you!"

"Thank you," said Helen. "I know you do. We're lucky to have such friends. Good bye, dear. Give my love to Will."

Torrey replaced the receiver. There was something in her friend's voice that caused her to squint her eyes and stand staring, unseeing, at the wall phone. What it was, she couldn't quite put her finger on. She stood, thinking of her own Nez Perce language and how much more important the tone was than the words. A single word had many meanings, depending on its inflections. That was what was missing in Helen's voice, believable inflections. She turned and looked across the kitchen to where her husband was leaning on the big commercial chopping block. His head was down so that she could only see the top of the sweat-stained cowboy hat he wore. The way he stood caused her heart to wrench so sharply that it seemed she could actually feel his stoic pain entering her body. "Helen's in shock or something," she said, walking towards him. "Her voice sounded real fakey. It's like she was reading lines for a play, maybe. She doesn't want us there, but she asked if we'd call and see if Willie wants to come here."

Will made a sound in his throat and she reached across the block and lifted his head with gentle hands. They stared at each other's grieving faces. Her tears had dried at Helen's tone; his stood, unshed, in the corners of his eyes. She said, "How about us taking a bottle and finding Dewey. We might feel a little better if we offer Marshall a toast and an Indian blessing to help him on his way to the other side," she said softly.

"Yeah. Yeah. That's just what I want to do. Maybe even come up with a few old stories," Will said in a cracked voice. "Dewey likes to tell those old stories, especially the ones about Dad and him trying to ride herd on Marshall and me when we were kids."

Will pushed himself into a standing position and mopped his face on his forearm. "And it is just what Marshall would want us to do, by God! I remember how Marshall and I would slip a little Jim Beam into what our dads and Dewey thought were cans of coke. We'd get tighter than ticks, sitting on the porch at the old house, listening to them tell their war stories while they sipped on that yellow stuff Uncle Pete made and called 'horse piss?'"

47

Torrey tried to smile. "What I remember is our kids and the Duncan kids listening to your dad and Dewey spinning tales about how wild you and Marshall used to be."

Will looked at her sadly. "You think those times can last forever, so you don't pay close enough attention." He sighed. "What were you saying about Russell on the phone?"

Torrey frowned, "Helen did ask us to do what we could for Willie. I told her we'd ask Russell to fly over and get him. The University of Oregon can do without him for a while."

For the first time since Willie had called with the news, her husband seemed able to mobilize himself. "Call the boy right now," he demanded. "If you get his machine, tell him, weather permitting, we'll come and get him whenever he wants--soon as he can come. The sooner the better, by God! Then call Russell. You'll get his answering machine, but at least you can let him know what's up."

Torrey seemed preoccupied, as if listening to an inner voice. "I have half a notion to call Helen back first and tell her I'm coming to Virginia, whether she likes it or not." Torrey paused and looked at the big, solid man in front of her. "She sure didn't sound right, Will."

He lifted his cowboy hat and scratched his head, thinking. Then he looked at his wife. "Call her and then call the boy. It'll make Willie feel better to know you're going. If he can come, he won't mind hanging out with old Dewey and me." He looked at his wife and said sadly, "You know, besides their mother, we're the closest thing to family those three kids got."

Torrey scanned the numbers written on a wall directory, lifted the receiver and dialed. She listened to the hollow ringing of Helen's unanswered phone for long minutes, a frown on her face. Her worried eyes met her husband's as she hung up the receiver. "Helen's evidently not taking any more calls for a while.

She's not answering and the phone machine didn't pick it up." She looked at him, worry etching her face and then shrugged her shoulders and said, "I guess I'll go ahead and call Willie."

Helen sat at her desk listening to the phone ring, glad that she had at least turned off the answering machine. She frowned and reached once again for an envelope. *I really cannot let that phone keep interrupting what I must get done. Why can't people understand what a stressful time this is? I must be allowed to concentrate.* When the caller finally gave up, the silence seemed a blessing. *Thank goodness!* She stared at her telephone for long minutes and then, with deliberate hands, reached out and unplugged it. *I refuse to allow that dreadful jangle to startle me anymore tonight.* Once again, she reached for an envelope. *Tomorrow, I must remember to have all our bills sent to Bob Bennett's firm. That's what accountants are for. I have far too much to do to have to worry about paying bills on time.*

Chapter Six

Torrey and Will Rawling looked at each other over Willie's lowered head. Even the plane ride in Russell Warner's Cessna, over the snowy peaks of the Cascade Mountains, had failed to lessen the lines of grief on his young face. He sat on their old leather couch in the living room of the new guest lodge with his bony elbows on his knees, staring at the floor, alternating between silence and angry staccato bursts of disjointed details; most of the anger directed towards his mother. His tears had stopped.

With Torrey's gentle probing, he shared more and more of the events surrounding his father's death. The couple sat on each side of him, but neither reached out to touch him, knowing his current composure was a thin veneer.

"I can't stop thinking about how wrong she was to do what she did. She had dad cremated before we could even get used to his being dead. Then, she had his memorial service before any of us could let people know about it. She said, 'You have to get on with your lives.'" Willie suddenly stood up and looked down at the Rawlings, his brown eyes snapping with anger, "But then, she didn't do anything. Not one thing! She made us do it."

"What do you mean, Willie?" Torrey asked softly.

"I mean like go fill out the paperwork. She wanted to send just Peter and me, but Carrie came too, even though Mom said, 'No.' We all went into the morgue together. They offered to let us see Dad's body, but I couldn't look. Peter and Carrie wanted me to, but I couldn't. I was afraid I would cry in front of that morgue guy." He shook his head, remembering. "Now, I wish I had. I think if I'd looked, I could picture him dead. As it is, it still feels like I'm in the middle of some bad trip."

Will looked up at his tall namesake and said slowly, as if thinking aloud, "I wonder why Helen did have the service so damned fast? It seems like she intentionally didn't give us time to get there. Hell! We didn't even know your dad was gone and he was already having words read over his...remains."

Willie shrugged, "Don't ask ME why. None of us could figure it out. Any question we asked her, she would just say, sometimes in this real bitchy voice, 'It's what your father would have wanted.' There was no way we could even argue without her getting mad and leaving the room."

Willie looked down at the man sitting in front of him. "Jesus, Uncle Will, the crematorium she picked was called, 'Ashes to Ashes.' Can you believe it? Is that a sick name or what?" He rushed on, "And do you know why she picked it? She picked it because it promised one-day service and one-stop shopping."

Will shook his grizzled head slowly, feeling suddenly confused and on overload. Things weren't making sense. Torrey stood and looked at them both, suddenly glad that she had not gone east. It was clear she needed to be here for Willie. "Willie, the grandmother who raised me would talk of how your mother's true spirit has gone from her body because the grief has left it no room. She would say that this was not your mother who did these things. She would call her behavior 'peleypeley' and would ask the 'tiwet' for a ceremony for the safe return of Helen's spirit." Torrey bowed her head, looking for the old words. "There is a word we have for when grief is too large for the body to hold, but I can't remember what it is. I wish I'd paid more attention back then. Grandmother was missing the first knuckle of her little finger and I saw the knife scars on her arms. Neither was an accident. When she was quite young, her older brother drowned and her own mother, my great grandmother, helped her cut off both her finger and her long braids. Then, one of her aunts showed grandmother how to draw a

51

sharp boning knife across her forearms to let the too-big pain out."

Willie looked at her blankly. "Jesus! That's barbaric! But, I'm not sure what it has to do with Dad's death and how Mom is acting, Aunt Torrey. You think Mom needs to cut herself up?" He looked at Will for clarification.

"Son, she's just tryin' to say your mother isn't herself. If we've got grief, don't you know she's got it worse? It was her horse that caused Marshall's death." His voice broke at the words.

Anger flashed in Willie's brown eyes. He rubbed a hand over his crew cut. "That damned horse..."

Torrey broke in, drawing his attention back. "Willie, I'm also trying to say that back then, grandmother's people found ways to express their grief. They don't seem like good ways to us now, but they worked back then. We've lost our ceremonies, so each person tries to find some way to relieve those terrible feelings. Sometimes what they do hurts others, but they don't mean to."

There was a soft knock at the sliding glass door. Dewey, as rumpled and bent as always, was on the other side, letting himself in. Willie's face softened. "Dewey!"

"Howdy, youngster. Glad you could make it. We've been pretty sad around here."

Torrey noticed, with some surprise, how old and faded his blue eyes looked with their twinkle gone. But his voice still held the gentle kindness that had charmed people for more than 70 years. She watched as Willie leaned over to fold him into a bear hug and then lift him off his feet.

"Here now! Put me down, you big, tall beanpole. Ain't dignified to treat an ol' man so." Dewey's muffled outrage popped the tension in the room like a pin prick to a balloon. Willie was the first to laugh. He loosened his grip, but held the hero of his childhood by the shoulders.

"It really is good to see you." He looked over Dewey's shoulder toward the slider, a puzzled look that quickly turned to worry on his face. "But where's Queenie?"

"Why, down in the barn, with a litter of the cutest blue healer pups you're likely to see. I'll show you. How long you stayin'?"

"Only for the weekend. But I may be back looking for work. No sense staying in school if I can't concentrate."

There was shocked silence in the room. Torrey shot Will a warning glance to keep his mouth shut. Dewey chewed his wispy mustache with his lower lip, then nodded to Willie. "I expect that is some job right now." He looked at Will. "The horses are saddled," he said.

Will stood up without a word and glanced at Torrey. "You still got time to come, babe?"

Torrey thought for a moment and then shook her head and turned to Willie. "We were going riding, so Will could show you something and ask your opinion." She grinned and confessed, "Anyway, we thought being the first one up on old Chainsaw this spring might get your attention off these sad times." She paused, thinking for a moment and then made up her mind. "I'd like to go, but I think I'm going to stay here and try to call Helen again. I'm also going to call Betty Barnes at Burns Travel and see what kind of airplane connections I can get to Virginia."

Relief lit Willie's face. "You mean it? You'd go even if she didn't answer the phone or gave you a real pissy 'no' if she did answer?"

Torrey tipped her head up and looked at him. "I don't know for sure yet. I'm going to think about it while the three of you ride." A question came to her mind. "Does she take your calls, Willie? Since that first call, I haven't been able to reach her."

Willie shook his head. He was standing with one forearm draped casually across Dewey's shoulders; they looked like a gnome and a giant. "Not always. I know the recording machine is off, and I think she sometimes unplugs the phones. Carrie had a hard time reaching her, that I know. But I haven't tried. What would I say to her? You ask her a question and she either gets mad, changes the subject, or pretends she didn't hear."

"Remember that she's not herself," Torrey said firmly.

"You're sure right about that! Have any of you ever heard her tell a lie?" He watched closely as they shook their heads. "Well, Carrie says she lied on the phone. She said she'd called Dr. Henry for some more sleeping pills, but she hadn't... Carrie checked it out because she knew she'd flushed the first bottle."

Will looked sadly at his wife. "Do your phoning!" He turned to the boy. "Like Torrey said, I need your ex-per-tise. We need to ride over to Duck Creek. I'd like to hear your thinking on how it can be diverted into a new patch of sage we cleared."

Torrey said, "Dewey, go ahead and leave Paleface saddled. If I get this thing handled, I'll go check on the first-calf heifers and then ride out to meet you." She had a sudden need to be on her appaloosa, if only for a little while.

Torrey felt the jerk in her stomach again. She leaned down to close the latches on her old blue Samsonite. Will sat on the bed, hat in hand, waiting to drive her into the Burns Airport. She composed her face before straightening. *He's going to worry himself into a puddle if he knows how scared I am to do this without him. He's bad enough as it is.* She put her hands to her hips and said briskly, "Look okay?"

"Hey, you look great, babe!" Will looked at his wife with admiration. Her face showed what 60 years of sun could do to skin, but her height and carriage made her look regal in the black trench coat and the big, silver, hoop earrings she wore. She had pulled her hair

54

back into a low braided bun and the streaks of gray added to the effect. He stood and kissed her gently on the forehead.

"Let's get going then," she said. Will picked up her bag.

At the airport, their friend, Russell, had his little Cessna 182 out on the apron and was finishing his preflight check. He waved at them, got in, and then leaned across and unlocked the passenger door.

As they walked across the pavement Will put his arm around Torrey's shoulders. "Got your ticket?"

Torrey tapped her black shoulder bag. "You know I do. Quit worrying. Make Russell let you pay him when you see him next. You know he's not going to let me."

Will opened the passenger door and put Torrey's suitcase on the backseat. "Howdy, Russell," he said. "I sure can't thank you enough for fitting us in."

Russell grinned as he put on his headset. "No problem. Howdy, Torrey. Hear you've joined the jet set."

Torrey settled herself and let Will fuss with her seatbelt. He said, "Why don't you call me from Boise--if you have time before the plane leaves."

Torrey smiled and nodded indulgently. "Sure." She dropped her purse behind her seat. Then Will pushed her door shut, waved and walked back towards the pickup. Russell handed her a second headset and then reached across to make certain her door was locked. Torrey pulled her seatbelt tighter and put on the headset in time to hear Russell shout, "Clear!" before starting the engine. *What a great way to travel,* she thought and let her mind run, once again, over what lay ahead of her.

She and Will had been east six or seven times before. The last time had been two years ago to visit their daughter, Julie, who had been living with the Duncans, completing her degree at George Mason

55

University. The flight was no problem. She liked flying. It was the other things that made her nervous. It was deplaning at Dulles International without Will to guide her. It was what she would find when she got to the farm. It was what Helen would say when she came knocking on her door after being told not to come. She shrugged to herself and looked out the window as they reached airspeed and Russell eased back on the yoke.

She could see Will standing by the pickup looking like a toy cowboy, waving her out of sight with his big hat. She waved back though she knew he couldn't see her. *I miss you already, but this is the right thing. It is right for us, for the Duncan kids and hopefully, for Helen too.*

She glanced at Russell's stubble-faced profile. He was talking into his microphone to the other traffic in the area. *You are a good man, Russell Warner,* she thought and was not surprised when he glanced at her and smiled. She smiled back and then closed her eyes against the brightness, thinking how times of trouble always sent her out to the sweat lodge. She had used it to offer prayers both for Marshall's safe journey to the other side and for the healing of his family's spirits. The Nez Perce did not pray for themselves in the sweat lodge, only for others. But she had also taken Willie into town to the Episcopal Church and prayed for everyone, including herself, so she figured the bases were covered. In her suitcase was a plastic bag of sweetgrass, one of red bark willow and one of sage; tucked there in hopes that Helen would agree to building a lodge for a healing sweat while she was there.

Helen was no stranger to the little tarp tent Torrey often erected behind the implement shed. They had thrown many buckets of water on hot stones over the years. Perhaps now, Indian medicine would help cleanse what was bad inside her friend. "She may not let me help. It may be too soon. But it is right to go," she'd said to Will, knowing he would agree.

"Sure it is, honey. Don't you know Marshall would have come out here if something had happened to you?"

She looked at him sharply. "Helen would've come too. Do not let your grief turn to anger against her. Think of her anger at herself. Think of her loss."

He'd lifted his hat and scratched his head. "At least you got through on the phone that one time and she knows you wanted to come. I sure hope it works out that you didn't take no for an answer."

Torrey gave a soft sigh. "I hope so too. But it's the right thing, Will," she said again, "even if she turns me away."

Chapter Seven

As Torrey entered the stream of deplaning passengers at Dulles International Airport, she pictured herself as a buffalo moving smoothly among the herd. It helped control her nerves. *Otherwise, I might start my own stampede,* she thought grimly to herself. *Who thinks of so many people flying in the air when they live in Burns, Oregon? It is good to do this again; to remember how big the world really is; to remember how different people are; how many paths there are to walk.* She found her suitcase without trouble; one blue bag in a caravan of black ones trundling in a loop that went nowhere. She lifted it and headed toward the taxis.

It only took 15 minutes for the cabbie to deposit Torrey at the Duncan's front door. It was 7:30 PM, completely dark, and yet the porch light had not been turned on. Torrey frowned as she got out of the car and handed the driver his fare. *If I'm looking for signs, here's the first one.*

"You want me to wait, lady?" The cabbie asked, looking doubtfully at the dark house as he got her suitcase from the trunk.

She shook her head. "No, thank you." To herself, she thought, *Nope, I'm staying. If she won't let me in, I'll sleep with the horses.*

She first rang the doorbell and knocked at the front door. "Helen," she called, "please let me in." She waited, listening hopefully for any sound to disturb the silence. When there was none, she called, "Helen! It's Torrey. Open the door!"

She frowned again in the continuing silence and tried the latch. It was locked, as she knew it would be. She gave a little grunt of sad determination and walked around the porch to the kitchen door, glad the yard security light had come on. A faint glow came through the kitchen windows. She pulled open the screen and looked through the window in the door. The light over

58

the range had been left on. She tried the knob and then rapped sharply, "Helen! Open the door, please." She had raised her voice to a shout.

She pondered her problem. Bluffing was something she was good at. Unfortunately, Helen knew she was. *So I'll gamble. My people are good at bluffing AND gambling.*

She walked back around to the front of the house and stood under the window of the master bedroom. "I'm not leaving, Helen! Give up and let me in." She waited, counting to sixty slowly, under her breath, as she walked back to the front door. Then she shouted, "Okay, Helen, don't worry me like this. I'm about to dig my mobile phone out of my bag and dial 911." She mentally crossed her fingers both for the phantom mobile phone and for what she was about to say next. "I mean it, Helen! Carrie told me you got some sleeping pills from your doctor. I'm calling 911 right now!"

Like magic the front door lock clicked. It was obvious that Helen had been standing silently on the other side. She opened the door and stood facing Torrey in the dim light. She was wearing her old Irish fisherman's sweater over a sweat suit, her face haggard. "Oh, Torrey! You're here! I told you NOT to come." There was no welcome in her voice, only the faked note of surprise.

Thank God! Torrey did not realize how worried she'd actually been. "Hi, baby," she responded nonchalantly. "I just thought I'd drop by. Turn on a light, would you."

When Helen didn't respond, she picked up her suitcase and stepped inside. "I could sure use a cup of tea to calm my nerves," she said as she reached for the light switch. "This part of the country is way too populated for my taste."

The women looked at each other in the soft hall light until Helen dropped her eyes. Her arms were stiff and rigid at her sides. Her face looked as if she were concentrating, perhaps willing Torrey to be magically gone. *Well, it looks like there's to be no hugging going on here.* Torrey could not help but think of past welcomes; of back slaps, hugs and the shouting of happy children.

"Hey, baby, it's good to see you," Torrey said softly and reached out one hand to touch the side of Helen's face. Then she quickly dropped her hand before Helen could jerk away and turned toward the kitchen, turning up the hall thermostat as she went. It seemed colder inside than outside. "Sorry I didn't call you from the airport. It just seemed easier to grab a cab and come."

The kitchen light illuminated the stark cleanliness of the room. Torrey blinked. "Lordy, Helen!" Torrey said before she could stop herself. The clutter in the Duncans' kitchen was legendary. It was the center of the household. The times she'd been here in the past, there were papers on the counter, fruit in a huge bowl and riding boots in a jumble on the floor. In fact, it used to look like her own kitchen, only there were cowboy boots instead of English riding boots in her own mess. She turned and looked at her friend. "Not doing much cooking these days?"

Helen felt as if her worst fears had come true. Her mind was frozen. She knew, from the brief eye contact in the entry, that unless she concentrated with her whole being, Torrey Rawlings would read her mind. She knew she had to keep herself together, had to convince Torrey that she was fine, just needing to be alone. But she also knew that what had worked with her children, would not work with Torrey. There would be no bullying or deceiving this woman. *She will leave only if she's convinced that I'm okay living alone.* Helen drew a deep breath and forced herself to relax, willed her voice to come out strong and steady as she followed Torrey into the kitchen.

"I'm afraid you're right. I simply haven't recovered my appetite. However, if you're hungry, there is food in the freezer that I can pop into the microwave."

Torrey listened to the brittle, forced cheerful tone. *That's her "everything is just fine" voice Willie was talking about. But, just fine or not, she's going to try to give me a snow job of some sort before this evening is over; I'll bet my bloomers on it.* She said, "Well, that would be nice. I've changed my mind about the tea. I'll make us a little drink while you work on dinner."

Without waiting for Helen's response, she headed toward the bar in the den. When she flipped the light on, the story was the same as in the kitchen. There was not one bit of clutter. Not one bit of dust. Magazines were artfully arranged on the coffee table; hassocks were tucked tight against the old, plaid chairs; books were aligned, spines straight on their shelves. The door to the liquor cabinet was neatly shut. Torrey opened it. "Another first." she muttered. "The woman has become a housekeeping marvel." All the liquor bottles were carefully lined up, side-by-side on the glass shelving. The shelves themselves were Windex spotless. The bar refrigerator had been cleaned and disconnected. With Helen's sense of design, Torrey felt as though she were standing on a movie set that had been created to replicate someone's cozy den.

In the kitchen, Helen stood in front of the open freezer door looking at a tidy stack of casseroles given by friends. She nodded with grim satisfaction, remembering that as of yesterday, all of the thank you notes had been written and sent. Like the death announcements, each carried the same message:

Thank you for your thoughtfulness.
I'm sure the dish will come in very handy.
It was a lovely gesture.
Love,
Helen

The words grated through her head. She reached into the freezer and took out the top container without looking at its label, put it into the microwave and programmed it for defrosting. Then she grabbed a package of frozen green beans. *How am I ever going to get her out of here? Why did she come when I specifically told her that I needed to be alone? What have the children told her? What is wrong with people? What's wrong with wanting my space? It's only been eight days. What in God's name do people expect?*

The microwave beeped and the LCD blinked a reminder to check the contents. She turned the container and jabbed the start button, feeling her anger mount. *Torrey, of all people, should understand what I'm going through. Instead, she's going to try to "fix" me, make me better. Damn her!* She turned as Torrey's footsteps sounded on the plank floor. "Find what you need, Torrey, dear?"

Torrey set one glass of bourbon on the counter by the refrigerator and held the other under the ice dispenser. "Yep." She handed Helen her drink, took off her raincoat and went to hang it in the hall closet. She then stopped at the thermostat and fiddled with the temperature control. "I'd forgotten how well your furnace works," she called.

Helen's heart sank. *God! It's like she thinks she lives here!*

As if reading Helen's mind, Torrey walked back into the kitchen and said, "I hope you don't mind me making myself at home..." There was a question in her voice.

Helen turned and smiled, but avoided eye contact. "Not a bit, silly. Thank you for the drink." She

62

picked up her glass and raised it as if toasting, but did not drink. Instead, she turned abruptly back to the stove and busied herself fixing green beans. Torrey's eyes grew watchful. She pulled out one of the kitchen chairs and sat down. Despite the false cheer and bright words, she could feel her friend's distance and discomfort. A deep sadness swept over her and with it, a sense of despair. *She has decided that she needs to feel pain but what pain is it? Why do I keep feeling anger instead of sadness coming from her?*

Torrey raised her drink and took a sip, watching Helen's rigid back, and felt a strong premonition. *She's not going to let me help. I'll be shuffled out the door just as she shuffled her children out the door...and probably any other friends who've tried to offer comfort.*

Torrey took another sip of bourbon, feeling, as she felt so often, at war within herself. She had grown up with two ways of looking at the same world: her father's way; and the way of her mother's people. Her father would say, "Stay no matter what. This woman needs your strength." Her mother, had she lived, would have counseled differently, as would her grandmother. She thought both would tell her, "Accept things as they are. Do not think you know what is best... especially when dealing with the ancestral spirits who've come to guide Marshall on his journey to the Star World. Honor them. Ask for their guidance. You know nothing!"

Several times, Torrey started to break the silence and then did not, knowing whatever she said would be deflected against a shield of suffering. *Should I try my father's way? Should I at least say, "Do you want to talk about Marshall's death?" Should I walk over and put my arms around her? Tell her how sorry we all are?* Instead, Torrey bowed her head and opened her heart and mind, seeking wisdom, asking for guidance.

Into her mind's eye came vignettes of scenes from the times their lives had come together over the years: the Duncans and the Rawlings. Marshall's form came into clear view. He was opening the door of a pet carrier, laughing up at Will's puzzled expression. The children were all dancing around in excitement. Instead of a dog, a tiny pony poked out its nose and gave a squeaky whinny. In her mind's eye, Marshall then turned and seemed to be looking directly at her. His blue eyes seemed to be brighter than she remembered. *Hello, Marshall. Have you come to tell me what to do?* Her silent thought brought her back to the present. She said softly, "Helen, remember when Marshall brought Bear to Will in that pet carrier?"

Helen froze in the middle of stirring what turned out to be a chicken casserole. *Oh no! I'm not going to start the walk down memory lane. I know that ruse. No way!* "Of course I do. I'm not senile yet, Torrey. Would you please set the table? Whatever this is, it seems to be steaming nicely."

Throughout dinner, Helen directed the conversation. She changed the subject or the direction of conversation with the ease of a skilled interviewer, and seemed most comfortable when probing Torrey for details of the Rawlings family. Always, she listened intently, her brown eyes fixed on Torrey's face, while Torrey obligingly told stories about their oldest daughter, Julie, who, after graduating from George Mason, had moved to Paris. She also, and at greater length, talked about their younger daughter, Tina, who lived in Payette, Idaho. Tina had married a minister and produced two rambunctious boys in rapid procession.

At least stories about my grandsons come as easy as opening my mouth, Torrey thought, as she did her part to keep the conversation going. She watched the tremendous effort it took Helen to stay focused. Her food had not been eaten, only pushed around her plate. *Her whole job is to keep this one-sided conversation on safe ground.* Torrey let herself be manipulated without resistance.

It's your show, baby. You run it as you need to...just like I came because I needed to. She realized that the long day, the sadness, the tension, and the bourbon were taking their toll. She looked at her watch and rose from the kitchen table, carrying her plate to the sink. "It's 10:00 here. That makes it 7:00 at home. I'd better call Will and let him know I got here okay."

She did not see the relief written on Helen's face at her words. "You go right ahead. Use the den phone, but plug it back in first. I'll see to these dishes and then afterwards you can tuck into Carrie's room. You must be tired." As an afterthought, Helen added, "Give Will my love."

Will's solid, deep voice answered on the second ring and erased the miles between them with its warmth. Torrey could hear the note of worry and was determined to keep the conversation as light, but as factual, as she could. *No sense sharing all my fears over a telephone wire.* "Will, I swear I feel like I've just been on the Larry King Live show. I can't remember having such a lopsided conversation in my life. It feels like the score is-- Helen seven--Torrey zero-- in the information exchange department!"

"She's not talking, then?"

Torrey shook her head like he could see her. "No, at least not about anything of substance. Most subjects I bring up are off-limits. I asked her how the horses were doing, which I thought would have been safe to talk about, but it wasn't." Torrey cradled the phone, thinking out loud. "Mostly, she's putting up a front, pretending everything is just fine. She's as brittle as a dried stick, but she told me she was refusing medication. There's a gulf between us that I..." Torrey's throat closed and she finished by saying, "I don't think I can be of use to her while she's like this."

There was a silence on the other end of the line. "Remember what you told Willie and me...she's not herself."

When Torrey came out of the den, the hall light was on. Her suitcase no longer sat in the doorway. Presumably, Helen had hauled it upstairs. *She's gone to bed! That bit about me tucking into Carrie's room was her way of saying good night.* Torrey shrugged and then frowned. While talking to Will, she'd looked to see if the answering machine was on and found that it was not. When she told Will, he'd said gently, "She's cutting herself out of the herd. Maybe you're right about letting her go for now. Come on home, unless you decide crowding her would do some good. I'll tell you, Dewey and I would be real glad to see you come. You were right when you said we'd better bring the first-calf heifers into the barn lot. When I got home from the airport, we had a baby on the ground and one in progress that wasn't doing so well. Dewey and I ended up pulling it. It looks like it's going to have to be bottle-fed."

Torrey climbed the stairs feeling defeated and homesick. *I wonder why the heifer wouldn't mother-up with her baby. I wish I had asked. Well, I'll see what tomorrow here brings. Probably more of the same. I suppose I might as well go on back home and help with calving if I can't do any good here.*

She stood at the door of Carrie's room, remembering when Julie had lived here and the girls had so happily shared the space. Then she looked on down to where the big double doors of the master suite had been pulled shut and shook her head, coming to a decision. *She's either set herself, or has been set on this lonely path for some reason. Who am I to think I know what is best? Will's right. I've seen nothing that makes me think crowding her would do any good. At least, I've seen with my own eyes what her kids were talking about. She really doesn't want anyone here. She does not want to be comforted.*

When Torrey opened her suitcase, the scent of sage filled her nostrils. She found the plastic zip lock bag, held it under her nostrils and took several deep breaths. That it had somehow come unsealed seemed to be a gift to her spirit--a sign of hope.

A sudden thought came to her. She nodded, retrieved the other two plastic bags, grabbed her purse from the bed and carried everything into the guest bathroom. After she shut the door, she opened the three bags and with great concentration, wove the sweet grass and sage into a wisp and placed it in the bottom of the sink. Out of her purse, she took her small Buck knife and a packet of matches. After shaving several long thin strands of sweet willow bark into the wisp, she carefully put a match to the pile. *I wish I had paid more attention to my grandmother's ceremonies; I wish I knew the real words.*

As dry bark caught and a pungent spiral of smoke drifted upwards, she closed her eyes and released the thoughts in her heart. *Please,* she prayed, *let the death of Marshall not destroy the woman he loved. He would not wish that. He would wish her spirit to find its way back to happiness; to be the loving, laughing mother she used to be. Her children need her guidance.* Torrey opened her eyes and thought, *And I...need her friendship. With it I have seen myself as better and wiser than I think I am. We have truth and love between us. Do not take that away forever. Let this offering of the sacred smoke help her find her way back to us. Give me a sign that I should stay...or go.*

She closed her eyes again and rested her palms on the basin, breathing in the ancient, symbolic mingling of the odors and waited, with a still mind, for some sense that her offering had been accepted and her prayers heard. Eventually, after the remaining sage had turned to ash, she stood erect, eyes downcast to avoid the face she would see in the mirror. No vision had come to her, only a feeling that it would be futile for her to stay. The time to help Helen had not yet come. She had no place in this house. All that had happened...and had yet to happen...had a purpose...a purpose that she was not part of. As she slowly turned on the tap and washed the remnants down the drain, it seemed she could feel something dark and sad hover

over her momentarily and then descend down the drain with the ashes. A powerful understanding came to her. *Her spirit is gone. It cannot fight that which Helen has become. It has found courage to rise up with the sacred smoke. Only Helen can call it back.*

Torrey turned off the water, filled with certainty that Helen would not be ready to do such a thing until after her pain had run its course. As she gathered up the bags and stuffed them into her suitcase, she wondered how long it might take. More than anything now, she wished for sleep, but knew she wouldn't rest until after she had booked her flight and called her husband again.

On her way down to the phone, she thought of her father. *He would call me a quitter*, she thought with dismay and such a feeling of weakness enveloped her that she nearly stumbled on the stairs. *He would say I gave up too easily; that I didn't stick it out. Is it true? But, which would be best for Helen? How can I know her path? How could my father know her path? How can anyone know except the ancestors?*

Chapter Eight

Helen sat quietly at the old pine table, watching Peter struggle to make one-sided small talk. She wondered again what had made her son finally disobey her and come home, but couldn't bear to ask. Instead, she sat quietly re-memorizing the lines of his face and the sound of his voice. Then she saw him straighten his shoulders and clear his throat. *Here it comes,* she thought, *he's tired of talking about the weather and Patti's morning sickness. Come on, Peter, out with it; I can't have you here too long.*

Peter looked at her, his blue eyes gray with worry. "Listen, Mom," he said, "I came here to say something and here it is." He paused and then sighed so deeply it sounded as if he were clearing his soul. "We've been talking. It's been almost two years. If you don't do something to help yourself get over Dad's death, like starting to see people or getting away from the farm for a while, we are going to buy you a puppy."

Helen felt shock jolt through her. "What? Buy ME a puppy? You're joking!"

Peter shook his head, his eyes never leaving her face. From the look of them, she knew he was not. "I don't want another dog, Peter. I won't have one! Max was our last dog!" Helen's eyes narrowed in anger. *How dare he come, uninvited, to issue this proclamation! Thank goodness I was dressed!*

She glared at him. "I mean it, Peter."

Her son shrugged. "Sorry, Mom, we've decided to take matters into our own hands. Patti has already been looking at puppies. If you don't take charge of making some changes, we are going to help you."

"Oh, no, you're not, Peter James Duncan!" Helen rose from the kitchen chair, the balance of dread and joy she had felt about this unexpected visit shifting suddenly to hostility. She strode back and forth, confining herself to the exact length of the Bokhara rug

69

beneath her feet, as though its fringe was the wall of a cell. "By the way, who is this ubiquitous 'we' to whom you keep referring?"

"Your children, Mother. Carrie, Willie and me... The children you keep refusing to visit. The children you have banned from visiting you since Dad died. The ones you'll barely talk to on the phone. Remember us?"

"Why, that's not true, honey." She stopped her angry march in mid-stride and softened her voice. "I'd love to see you, you know that. I just don't want you to inconvenience yourselves. I know how busy your lives are. In fact, I can't believe you didn't bring sweet Patti with you. There's not something about her condition you're concealing, is there?"

My God, she's turned into a chameleon! Peter held his hands in front of his chest, palms out. "No changing the subject, Mom. We are all fine. I'm FINE. Willie's FINE. Carrie's FINE. I already told you that Patti's doctor said she was FINE. The pregnancy is normal. We're all FINE!" Each time he emphasized the word 'fine,' he gave it an additional tinge of sarcasm. "This is about you, Mother dear. As your oldest son, whether I like it or not, I have been chosen as spokesperson. You are NOT fine!"

Helen put her hands on her hips, brown eyes flashing, voice again hard, "Now you hold on here, Buster. I don't believe my ears! My own children are talking about me behind my back? I won't have it!"

"We wanted to talk to you about it at Christmas, but you still wouldn't let us come." Her son's voice remained infuriatingly controlled. *God, he sounds just like his father,* she thought and felt an unfamiliar sensation in her chest. It was as though her son was inadvertently worming his way into her center, the place where she kept all the pain she had felt and might yet have need to feel sealed away.

She took a deep, steadying breath against the feeling. *I have to get him out of here. I cannot let him make me re-live what I've worked so hard to overcome.*

70

"Peter, I know you've had a long drive and your concern touches me, but you children surely understood that last Christmas was just too soon. I couldn't have handled it. I wouldn't have been strong enough to even pretend."

Helen thought she might drown in the gulf of hostile silence between them and wondered if Peter was remembering Christmases past. *Is he remembering when we did the house, the barn and all the way down the lane to the county road with frosted white lights? Is he thinking how his father always took charge of fashioning the juniper sent by the Rawlings into magnificent wreaths for the barn doors? Or is he simply sitting there, masking the discomfort he feels in my presence, trying to get done the job he has been sent to do?*

"Mom," Peter finally broke the long silence, "Carrie said you would say that. She said to remind you those were your exact words the Christmas before last."

Helen snapped from her reverie. "Peter, please. I do not want to talk about this. Since when has Carrie become the expert on my behavior? Since when have you children decided to play God and put a limit on my time to grieve the loss of your father?"

The words she said sounded good to her. She suddenly felt righteous indignation straightening her spine. She stood taller, again in control. *I am through pleading!* She felt her son's eyes searching her face, but she was no longer afraid, and glared at him.

"Sorry, Mom," he said again. "It's not working. We decided about the puppy during a conference call. By the way, your daughter said you'd probably say that about limiting bereavement time too. That's the trouble with having a psychologist in the family, I guess." He paused, shrugged and tried to smile, but failed. "We don't want to put a limit on anything," he said.

From somewhere safe and far away, Helen listened to his words. She realized that his voice sounded odd...stilted perhaps. A question formed in her mind as to why, but she couldn't seem to care enough to voice it.

"What we want is for you to start rebuilding your life, Mom. We're talking about visiting friends, going to the city to see a play, traveling, inviting us down-- nothing earth-shattering, just the normal routine of everyday living." She heard determination come into his voice. "If you don't at least start getting out, we mean it. We're going to show up, at least Patti and I will...with a replacement for Max. It's time to start living again, Mother...and we think a puppy could help you do it."

Helen put a hand to her cheek. *God, but he sounds like Marshall, all calm and reasonable sounding, while flattening my objections like a steamroller.*

Again, the silence stretched. She could hear her son's deep, regular breathing. She watched as he calmly reached for the teapot and refilled his cup with steady hands.

"I just can't believe Willie is a part of this plot," she said, as if to herself. Of her three children, she felt he was most like herself. Neither of them were big on ultimatums.

Peter paused again, thinking hard about whether or not to say the next words. Finally, he said slowly, "The dog was his idea. Carrie wanted to get you a horse."

Helen gasped, shaken from her cocoon. "No! Oh, no, Peter. Not a horse! Please, children," she said, as if she too were in on the fateful conference call, "not a horse! How could Carrie even consider such a thing?"

Helen sank back into her kitchen chair, remembering. Marshall's voice came seeping past her carefully constructed walls. *"Octane's too young and too hot, Helen. He's been bred to run or jump in the big leagues. Look at him. He's not meant to be someone's*

72

hack. You're looking at years of training before he's as safe and reliable as Junior, if he ever is."

The voice was so real inside her head that Helen closed her eyes and leaned over, crossing her arms as if protecting vital organs. She could hear her own reply. *"But this is the horse I want, Marshall."* Guilt seared through her and she thought *this is exactly why I still cannot see our children.* Around her children, she knew she couldn't forget, couldn't pretend; couldn't control the pain.

"Peter," she whispered, unable to look at him, "why are you doing this? Did you drive all this way just to be cruel? I do not want a dog and I certainly do not want another horse after what happened. Surely you can understand that." Even as she said the words, Helen recognized the pounding of pain in her temples that always came when she thought of how she went about the selling of their horses. It was as if the four of them were galloping through her head, reminding her how, with one telephone call, a horse trader had come in a large, fancy van to haul them away. It had been quick and dirty. She had sent her own horse, Junior, who had taught all three of her children to ride, along with the rest. At age 20, he deserved better. She had known it then. She knew it now. But at the time, his reliability and gentle spirit had somehow seemed an unforgivable affront. She remembered, too, how in some convoluted way, Marshall's death seemed to be partly Junior's fault, not Octane's, not hers. It was Junior's...simply because he was boring. She was looking for a challenge when she found the beautiful, gray thoroughbred.

She could not lift her head to look at her son and he did not ask her to. Instead, he put his cup down and reached across the table to rest his hand gently on the nape of her neck. She wondered: *Can he feel how cold I am? Does he know how empty and dead I am inside?*

73

"Mom," he said, "you raised us to believe certain things. One thing you've always said is: 'If you are going to give someone an opinion or advice, examine your motivation and if it is correct, go ahead.' Remember that? Well, we've examined our motivation, grilled each other, in fact. We've all agreed you need something to get your life restarted. Carrie said a horse, because she thinks you sold all our horses after dad died to punish yourself. She sees a new horse as a symbol of healing. I was the one pushing for a trip abroad or a cruise somewhere warm and sunny. But Willie and Carrie think you need someone or something to love. You know you'd love a puppy, once you got it. We've always had dogs. It still doesn't seem natural for the farm to be without one."

Helen raised her head and he let his hand drop. "Peter, please! Darling, I know you mean well, but you simply have no idea how this is tearing me up." She felt the pain in her temples intensify and began a methodical circular massage with her fingertips. "I really can't talk about this one more second. If I promise to give your word serious thought, will you hold off on this nonsense about a dog?"

Peter considered her request. "Maybe," he finally said. How do we know you're not just stalling?"

The room was again quiet while Helen continued pressing fingers to her temples. She knew Peter was staring at her and heard him sigh. "Mom, it's been almost two years. Look at yourself. You've turned into a recluse. Can you tell me the last time you've been to town, treated yourself to a shopping spree, or called someone to go to lunch? You still won't talk, really talk, to any of us. Are you talking to anyone? Anyone professionally, I mean?"

Helen shook her head, defeated by his persistence. "Not yet," she whispered. "But I know that I must."

"Yes," he said gravely, "you must."

74

Is that disgust in his voice? The thought made her wince. With effort, she raised her chin from her chest and lowered her hands into her lap.

"Okay," he said matter-of-factly, after she raised her eyes to his, "here's the deal. If you make an appointment with a counselor, we'll re-think the puppy." He pulled a piece of paper from his shirt pocket. "Carrie already did your homework. Here are three names of people who specialize in grief and bereavement counseling. She says they are all good."

When Helen didn't take the proffered slip of paper, he put it on the table. "You get some appointments under your belt; let us come home for a visit later this spring; and we would take that as a sign you don't need a dog. Willie can't make it, of course, but Carrie would love to come home for spring break."

Helen's eyes widened. She pushed back her chair and rose to her feet. *They really have planned this whole thing out. The reason Peter's voice sounds so odd is because his speech has been totally rehearsed. The three of them, four if I include Patti, have been plotting and scheming behind my back.*

"I don't believe this!" She hissed, leaning forward over the table. "You have this whole thing planned. You've even memorized the necessary lines. This isn't about a dog--It's about forcing me into therapy!"

Peter nodded grimly from where he sat. "You'd better believe it. We agreed on the plan and I rehearsed it practically the whole way down. You didn't raise children who would sit by and watch you do this to yourself."

"Get out of here, Peter!"

"Nope. I'm not done. This isn't something the three of us discussed, but if you spend time thinking about this conversation, give a thought to Carrie. With all the pressure of her dissertation and living all by herself in Texas, she's been super. I don't know how much her phone bills to the West Coast have been, but

I do know she's been Willie's major support." His blue eyes, Marshall's blue eyes, drilled into her. "Carrie AND the Rawlings, that is. He spends all his off time at the ranch. Uncle Will and Aunt Torrey are the ones who talked him into staying in school. He'd made up his mind to quit and come home, no matter what Carrie and I said."

Helen found she could no longer return his gaze. The pain in his eyes seemed to reflect her own pain and magnify it. *Willie at the Rawlings? Yes, of course, I was the one who asked them to look after him. Torrey and I even talked about Willie's wanting to quit school when she came. I must've forgotten.*

Peter's voice softened. "I've been lucky. I've had both Patti's and Carrie's support during the tough times. They've made me talk and remember all the good parts." Then his voice trailed away, leaving unsaid, thought Helen, the fact that his mother had been unable to aid or comfort either them or herself. A fine quiver started around her mouth and quickly spread to her entire body. Goosebumps covered her arms. Noticing, Peter rose to his feet and plucked her old, Irish fisherman's cardigan from one of the wall pegs by the door. After he held it for her to slip into, he sighed and gathered her in for a long hug. For a moment she stood, rigid and numb, her mind reeling, then she pushed him away with both hands, knowing she was very close to falling into a thousand un-mendable pieces.

"Fine," she said sarcastically, "it's a deal. Thank you all for your concern." She reached out to shake his hand to seal the bargain, an old Duncan family gesture. But then she changed her mind and put both hands behind her back instead. "But, now go. You have a long drive ahead and you've certainly said your piece."

Behind her back her fingers twisted into each other like denning snakes, seeking warmth where there was none. Peter looked at her long and hard and she stiffened her spine under his scrutiny. She knew what

76

he was seeing, knew how much weight she had lost, how shapeless she looked in her old, too large cords and baggy turtleneck. After the accident she'd never gone to have her hair cut; not even once. Now, her thick hair, shot with gray, was simply skinned back and fastened with the barrette at the nape of her neck.

Peter reached out abruptly and pulled a hand from behind her back. Her nails were long and perfectly clean. "These are very different than the hands of the mom I used to know," he said sadly. "That mom was forever complaining about her 'peasant hands.' But, that was because she refused to wear gloves when she worked outside."

The look in his eyes spoke volumes, but she still couldn't begin to meet his gaze. After a quick glance she looked at her feet. "I've given my word. I'll make the appointment," she said woodenly, "Now go."

He glanced at the kitchen clock and handed her the telephone numbers from the table. "Make it now," he said. "Carrie said it can take a while to get in."

"No! I'll do it later. I promise, Peter."

Peter looked momentarily undecided then shook his head. "Do it now," he said quietly and sat back down at the table.

She looked at him then. *Where is this hardness coming from? Do my children now hate me? Of course they do, but no more than I hate myself. No more than I deserve.* She snatched the paper from the table and went to the phone on the wall, punching in the first number on the list. She looked at her fingers as she dialed. It felt as though they belonged to someone else. Her voice, too, was a stranger's. She could hear it saying the appropriate words, answering simple questions, confirming time and date, but she heard it as from a distance.

Peter watched her closely, his head cocked. It looked as though an inner voice was trying to tell him something, but he couldn't quite understand it.

77

"There! It's done." she said, turning towards him. "The appointment is a week from Tuesday. Now will you go?"

He nodded. "Sure. Thanks, Mom."

She couldn't control her sigh of relief and he looked at her strangely as he put on his mackinaw. "Not very flattering for your own mother to want you off the farm," he said, not even trying to keep his tone light.

She did not follow him to the door but went to the window instead. Once outside she saw him stop to look around. The February wind made him button his coat. Instead of getting in his car, he headed for the barn and opened the door to the tack room. She saw the light go on and knew what he was seeing. She had covered every saddle with canvas casings. Stacked on the concrete floor were huge cardboard boxes: two years of boughs from Will and Torrey. She stood at the window, her temples throbbing. *Surely Peter won't scold me for the wasted boughs. I couldn't have been expected to enjoy them, could I? Not after I robbed myself of a husband, my children of their father and Will Rawlings of his best friend.*

She opened her eyes in time to see Peter slide into the Volvo seat. She watched as he fumbled gloves from a pocket with one hand and fastened his seat belt with the other. But he did not start the engine. His gloved hands rested on the leather-bound steering wheel.

"Start the engine," she whispered. "Start the damned thing!" But he didn't. Instead, he sat there, the door open, the frost created by his breathing forming an exhaust of its own.

He suddenly erupted from the car, slammed the door and stood looking first at the house and then at the barn. Helen, knowing he had seen her, let the front drape fall back into place. After a few minutes, she heard his footsteps thumping toward the front door and she met him there. He carried a cardboard box.

"What on earth are you doing?"

"Building you a fire."

"But I don't want a fire. I want you to go."

"The Rawlings were kind enough to send you these boughs--seems like it's only fitting to at least burn them so you can enjoy the odor of the juniper. The ones they sent last year should burn nicely."

"No, Peter! I mean it! Leave now!"

She looked at him, thinking, *how odd that my own son is deliberately disobeying me,* as he moved past her to walk on into the living room.

"I need to start you a fire. If you don't let me, I won't leave at all," he threatened.

"What? Don't be ridiculous, Peter! Earlier you were telling me how buried you were at work. Of course you'll leave." She had pulled the edges of the heavy cardigan around her thinness, but stood in the draft of the open door, unwilling to close it with her son still on the inside.

Peter strode to the fireplace, opened the damper, quickly laid the fire, and struck a match. Unable to remain in the room as the air exploded with the perfume of the Oregon high desert, Helen turned on her heel and left, walking woodenly to the stairs and then mounting them as if climbing a mountain in thin oxygen.

In the growing dusk, she walked to her bedroom and lay full-length across the huge, carefully-made bed. Memories of their Augusts with the Rawlings came crowding unbidden and unwanted into her mind. How they had all looked forward to and loved that special month! Their routine at the ranch never varied. For the kids, it was always an early morning, all-you-could-eat breakfast with Will, Dewey and any buckaroos or hay hands at the ranch. Then it was down to the corrals to help groom and saddle the horses while Torrey and she made the sack lunches. In later years, after the ranch needed extra income, there were other guests as well. Some of them had kids, but there was never any fighting over who got which horse. Will was in charge of that. He had a way of looking at you, like he was sizing you up, that made even the adults walk taller and behave better than they might have otherwise. *God, but things were simple then!*

Afternoons, the children spent damming up the creek, collecting Mason jars full of pollywogs, snakes and frogs, while the adults sat around the swimming hole, drinking beer or lemonade or wandering off to do whatever suited them.

Pain shot through her as she remembered what often suited Marshall and her. She was unable to prevent remembering the time they rode knee to knee across the meadow back towards where Peter, Carrie, Willie and the Rawling girls were playing in the creek, dumping tadpoles into what they called "the tadpole grotto." She remembered that they sat in their saddles, horses still side by side, holding hands, still feeling mellow from their love-making, while they talked with the children. As they turned to ride away, Peter had noticed that she had dust and a few pine needles clinging to the back of her shirt and had called out, "Did you fall off, Mom? You've got dirt on your back."

Marshall's snicker caused her cheeks to flame. "No, Peter, we found a pretty spot to...eat our lunches," she had said.

Helen stifled a moan. For almost two years she had warded off all memories. Now, her firstborn was causing her to unearth all that she had worked so hard to bury.

Flat and emotionless, Peter's voice came up the stairs. "Goodbye, Mom. I'll call you tomorrow."

Helen forced herself to get up and stand by the top of the stairs. "Yes. Thank you, dear. Drive carefully," she said in an equally dead voice.

For a moment she let a foot reach out to begin descending, but then she pulled it back and stood there, waiting for him to leave.

"Enjoy the..." He said as he turned, raising one hand in goodbye. His sentence was left unfinished.

When she heard the sound of Peter's car diminishing, Helen walked down the stairs and stood like a statue in front of the fire...just beyond the reach of its radiating warmth. She stared for a long time at the wrinkled, dusky-blue juniper berries that had fallen off the boughs and onto the carpet. Then, as if coming to a sudden decision, Helen turned and dragged one of the over-stuffed, corduroy chairs up to within a few feet of the raised hearth. She sank into it with a sigh, resting her head against the lumpy softness, soaking in the warmth.

Her body felt as though it had been used as a battlefield, with not one spot left untrampled. Slowly, she lifted both legs onto the hearth and closed her eyes. "Now," she whispered tiredly, "now you can come." She spoke to the misery pervading her body as she would to a familiar friend and waited quietly for sleep and the accompanying nightmares to commence.

Chapter Nine

Helen pulled her sedan into the parking space as far away from the clinic door as she could get and looked at her watch. *Twenty minutes early. Damn!* She knew she had to get out of the car right then, because the urge to slam the Toyota into reverse and escape was making her shake all over. She snatched the key from the ignition, threw it into her shoulder bag and jumped from the car. *Surely there is a decent waiting room,* she thought, forcing herself to walk towards the door. Inwardly, she cursed her children, especially Peter, for making her give her word.

The sign on the door read, "Village Counseling Services." A plaque on the wall carried three names:

Robin Pagglio, Ph.D., CHMC
Alan Austin, MA, MFT
Nina Soames, MSW

She wondered what all the initials behind the names meant, but decided she really didn't care. Outwardly calm, she pulled open the door and was relieved to find a space similar to her dentist's office, complete with aquarium, chairs, magazines and a smiling receptionist.

"Mrs. Duncan?" The young woman's voice carried the question.

Helen nodded. "Yes. Sorry to be so early, but here I am."

"Well, I'm glad. I tried to call earlier, but you'd already left. We like our first-time clients to arrive early to fill out the paperwork and I forgot to tell you that when you called." She was holding out a clipboard. "May I get you a cup of coffee or tea while you work?"

Helen started to shake her head and then changed her mind. She smiled. "Is it good coffee?"

"It is. We're all coffee snobs in this office. I'll bring you a cup. Cream or sugar?"

Helen shook her head. "Black, please."

The receptionist smiled again. "My name is Deena."

Helen took the clipboard from her, sat down and began filling in the blanks. When Deena brought her coffee, Helen was fumbling in her billfold. Looking up at the cheerful, young face, she said, "Thank you. I suppose you have your Social Security number memorized. My children all do."

Deena nodded. "Yes, I do. I suppose it's a sign of the times."

"Perhaps," Helen said absently as she began to read and fill out the data on her insurance coverage and then to answer the questions relating to her own physical and mental health.

Remarkably, the questionnaire seemed particularly pertinent, as though it had been tailored to her. Changes in: sleep patterns, activity level, eating habits, ability to concentrate, sexual activity? Helen's pen flew through the list, checking the 'yes' box. There were 59 questions, 17 of them read: 'If you mark yes, please explain.' On those, she simply wrote 'change due to husband's death' and then moved on to the next question. Under occupation, she wrote, "graphic designer-- retired." Her coffee got cold as she wrote, stopping to think long and hard about question number 58: *Why are you seeking therapy?* And question number 59: *What outcomes do you hope to obtain from therapy?* She decided to be candid on number 58 and wrote, "Because my children made me promise to do so. Otherwise, they were going to give me a puppy." On number 59 she simply wrote, "I would like to learn how to forgive myself--or at least learn to live with my grief and my guilt."

"Good job." The receptionist said when Helen brought the filled-out form to her.

"Let's hope so." Already, she felt exhausted. She returned to her chair and picked up a magazine.

Then, Robin Pagglio, her therapist, came into the waiting room. Helen looked up from her unopened magazine, registering surprise. She had pictured a woman from the name, Robin, not a man. He was tall and hawk-faced, but under bushy eyebrows, his brown eyes were kind. "Mrs. Duncan," he said softly, as he held out his hand, "please, come in."

She managed a small smile. "You're not what I expected, doctor."

"I know." He said shaking her hand. "People tell me my good Italian last name reminds them of the owner of a shoe company, not a therapist. And I certainly don't look like a bird, do I?"

"Yes," she said, "you do. Though more a hawk or an eagle than a robin, I would say."

She found she was pleased by his chuckle. "Thank you. I like that comparison much more than that of Ichabod Crane, which is one I've frequently heard."

His office, Helen noted with surprise, made a very strong statement and her design sense clicked into analysis mode. She had expected something restful and unobtrusive. Instead, the colors were more cheerful than subdued. Pillows, some in solid colors, some done in prints with great zebra-stripe splashes of coral, golden-yellow and lime, were scattered randomly on the forest green, velour couches. The area rug was done in rust, navy and sandy beige, a replication she recognized as a tapa cloth design, done by the South Sea Islanders. The overstuffed couches and chairs took up most of the room, all close enough for good conversation. A floor-to-ceiling wall of books flanked his cluttered desk at the far end of the long room. More books were jumbled about on the floor. A computer monitor and keyboard sat on the desk. The walls were hung with nicely mounted copies of prints done by Gaugin, Rousseau and Winslow Homer. The combinations of art, color and fabric were audacious, but well done. She looked at him, wondering.

He followed her gaze, shrugged and grinned. "I was raised in Hawaii," he explained as he led the way back toward a small teak table with two chairs. Without her asking, he said, "Most of my space is given up to the sitting area because of the group work I do. Many of my clients are people who have survived great loss and find comfort in the company of others who are also trying to rebuild their lives."

She nodded, but said nothing. The feeling of rescue she felt, when filling out the form, evaporated. They sat and he began looking at what she'd written. She watched him read with growing uneasiness. The man radiated something, some energy that she could almost feel. It frightened her. She started to feel trapped. She had no intention of baring her soul to this man.

Dr. Pagglio finished with the form and then looked at her. She had the strange sense that he was seeing inside her, beyond the dry, brittle exterior shell she had become and into her shriveled soul. The warm regard in his gentle eyes seemed to intensify.

"Mrs. Duncan," he said, "I'm wondering if you got the year of your husband's death right. Has it been nearly two years?"

Helen nodded and forcing a calm she did not feel into her voice, said, "It will be two years the 16th of April."

"And last week you decided to seek counseling and called for an appointment?"

"Actually, as I said on the form, my children issued an ultimatum that I do so."

"Why would they do that?"

Helen could hear the falseness of her modulated tone and wondered if the doctor could as well. "It's been a difficult time... My husband's death was very unexpected and I suppose they felt I was not recovering from the loss as quickly as I might have."

"I see. It sounds as though their intervention was not entirely welcome."

"No, not really. On the one hand, I try to appreciate the fact that they are concerned about my welfare. On the other hand, I loved my husband very much. I loved our life together. I have not felt ready to let go of all those memories." A defensive note had crept into her voice and she realized she was not doing a very convincing job of sounding serene. *What am I doing here with this odd- looking stranger who is making me feel more trapped and uncomfortable by the second?*

"Mrs. Duncan, no one can take your memories away from you. I certainly have no desire or intention to do so. However, I do see it as my role to help you live more comfortably with your memories and perhaps help you come to grips with redefining your life as a single person."

Helen winced when she heard the words "single person," and saw him glance down at where her thin, white fingers clutched the purse on her lap. *Did the man miss nothing?* "I AM redefining my life, doctor. Does it matter so much that it's taking some time? Ours was a very, very good marriage." She shook her head. "I'm sorry, Dr. Pagglio, I'm just not made that way."

He looked at her calmly, seeming to ignore the sharpness in her voice and said gently, "Researchers on grieving have determined that although the stages of grief are fairly predictable, the time spent reaching the different stages and the length of time spent in each stage, varies widely. Tell me, is this the first time your children have attempted to interfere?"

Helen could feel her feathers settling. He had not challenged her; had not told her to get on with life-- which is what she was sure her children had expected him to do. Instead, he seemed to think it was perfectly okay for her to still be missing Marshall so desperately and to resent her children for trying to force her to do their bidding. "Yes," she said. "Although, I would have to say, they probably would have sooner, except I have made a conscious effort to help them keep directed towards going on with their own lives, instead of worrying about what's to become of me."

"How did you accomplish that feat?"

"You mean encouraging them to stay focused on their own lives?"

The doctor nodded and waited quietly as she put her thoughts together.

"First of all, I have wonderful children. Our oldest, Peter, is married, has a new baby on the way and is a lawyer in Philadelphia. Our daughter, Carrie, is finishing her doctorate degree in psychology at the University of Texas; and Willie, our youngest, is on the West Coast, attending the University of Oregon on a basketball scholarship. So they are all very busy."

Helen allowed a touch of pride to enter her voice as she finished describing the lives of her children and then realized, belatedly, as the doctor sat waiting patiently for her to continue, that she had not answered his question. "They're so busy it's easy to keep them from coming home." She still had not answered the question; had not admitted she refused to allow them to come; often did not answer or return their calls.

"Ah! Do they want to come home?"

"I suppose so. Ours was a loving home. I'm sure they have good memories. But really, it would be selfish of me to expect it."

Helen was painting a false picture and she knew it. Her voice sounded just the same as when she was talking with Peter--superbly controlled; she was an actress making the best of an ad-lib. She looked at her watch and knew she'd made a tactical error.

"Is this conversation making you uncomfortable, Mrs. Duncan?"

Helen sighed. "Not at all, though I do have a lot to accomplish today."

"I see. I noticed that before retiring, your occupation was that of a graphic designer. Did you enjoy that work?"

Helen nodded. "Yes." She looked around the room again. "Clearly you have design sense as well."

Dr. Pagglio was not deterred from his line of questioning. "Did you retire prior to or after your husband's death?"

"After. His life insurance was such that I am well taken care of."

"Do you ever consider going back to work, not for the money, but for the sense of accomplishment?"

Helen knew that they were treading very close to a path she did not want to go down. *Please, dear God, do not let him ask what I do with my time,* she begged silently.

"Yes, I think about it. But not right now. I still find concentration difficult. It wouldn't be fair to my clients." She mentally crossed her fingers. "Besides, I am seriously considering a year of travel. It was something suggested by my children as an alternative to getting a puppy."

The doctor had been writing notes in an old-fashioned stenographer's notebook from time to time. He glanced up and said, "Tell me the idea behind getting you a puppy."

She pasted a smile on her face and said brightly, "They think it will give me a kick-start on the road to grief recovery. But I do NOT want a dog and I made that perfectly clear." Much to her dismay, Helen found herself adding, "And, I don't want a horse even more than I don't want a dog."

"A horse? Your children considered getting you a horse? Would there be a particular reason they might want to do that?"

"Not a single good reason, doctor, especially since I am thinking of taking up traveling."

She could tell by the way he looked at her, her glib tone was raising flags of warning in his mind. "A horse," he mused, "how interesting. Are you a horse fan, Mrs. Duncan?"

"Yes. Rather, I was, but am no longer."

When Helen did not elaborate even after the doctor waited patiently, he closed his notebook and asked firmly, "What did you mean on the questionnaire when you said you wanted to learn to live with your grief and your guilt? I understand your grief, but please tell me about your guilt."

Helen looked at him steadily while her mind jumped, looking for a way to evade both his look and his question. Finally, she shook her head. "No, not today. It's too soon."

Dr. Pagglio let out a slow breath before speaking. "Mrs. Duncan, I sense this session has been very uncomfortable for you. It seems you keep dropping hints about therapeutic areas to explore, but then veer away from talking about them. Could it be we are touching on areas too painful for you to share?"

Helen could only nod mutely. His tone, rich in empathy and understanding caused tears to jump to her eyes. "Yes," she whispered, "much too painful."

"I see. Was your husband's death traumatic or unexpected?"

"Both." She managed to choke out.

"Ah." His tone implied a sudden understanding; as if he'd suddenly found puzzle pieces. "Since our time is so nearly up, I believe it would be a mistake to start talking about it under any circumstance. However, I would like to propose that you think about undergoing a light hypnosis in our next session."

Our next session! His words clanged like a gong in Helen's head. *I doubt it!* What she wanted was out of Dr. Pagglio's presence. His eyes were too penetrating; his mind was too perceptive. She smiled. "Just what would you expect hypnosis to do for me, doctor?"

"Under hypnosis you will, of course, be conscious and your free will entirely intact. However, you will have a heightened sense of awareness and clarity otherwise unavailable. It will allow you to experience, in a more relaxed state, those emotions you have been blocking, without them devastating you. Will you think about it?"

Without any intention of undergoing hypnosis, Helen found herself nodding. "Yes, I'll think about it, but I'm not really certain I can continue coming. It will depend upon my travel plans."

The doctor stood. "Mrs. Duncan, I must be very frank with my professional opinion. You have many symptoms of a person struggling with severe emotional stress. If you will allow it, therapy can help relieve those symptoms and bring you some measure of peace. Don't you deserve that opportunity? Would you at least consider giving yourself permission to do the work...instead of running away?"

Helen continued to sit for long seconds. Then she looked up at him. "Yes, yes," I'll consider it," she said brightly and then rose from her chair and offered her hand.

Chapter Ten

Helen had paced the floor of her bedroom through the cold, gray, predawn hours, resolved at last to call and break her appointment with Dr. Pagglio. Instead she had, at the last minute, thrown on a once too-tight wool dress that now hung like a sack, pulled her hair into an old-fashioned French twist, and broken speed limits to arrive on time.

She now sat rigidly across the teak table from him, still surprised at what she had done. She made no pretense of being at ease, but instead allowed the doctor to see her as she really was, a woman too exhausted to do other than hold herself upright--and that, she was determined to do. "Well, I'm here," she said.

"I knew you were having second thoughts. I'm glad you came." Dr. Pagglio sounded sincere.

"Until an hour ago, I was certain I would not be here today."

His bushy eyebrows raised a fraction at her frank admission. "I see. Why was that?"

"I...really, really do not want to do this. It would be far easier for me to consider suicide than to consider dredging through all the pain I have been experiencing these last 23 months."

Her words of anguish caught the doctor's attention. He leaned forward in his chair and asked bluntly, "Have you been considering suicide, Mrs. Duncan?"

She looked directly at him for the first time; looked at him with her soul exposed so he could see how dead she already felt. "If I did not have children, I would have ended my life long before this."

"But, you do have children and so you are here, where you don't want to be, because you gave them your word, is that right?"

Helen nodded. "Absolutely!"

"Mrs. Duncan, do you believe you can recover from being in so much pain? Do you believe it is possible for you to rebuild and enjoy your life?"

Before she could stop herself, she cried, "I DO NOT deserve either of those things."

"Ah! I see." He paused. "At least I think I might." The doctor's brown eyes lost their softness and bored into her. "There are things you have experienced that are too painful to contemplate sharing with a virtual stranger, and yet, in order to gain some peace, you know you must. On the other hand, how can you possibly share your pain in hopes of feeling better, when you don't deserve to? Is that your conflict, Mrs. Duncan?"

Helen nodded mutely. His gaze remained steady. "But that's not all, is it?"

She looked at him in surprise. "What do you mean?"

"It seems that the ultimate fear would be: 'What if I do my therapeutic work and I don't find any relief...what then?'"

There was an intensity about him that made her feel like an insect under a microscope. "Yes," she said, "I suppose you're right."

The doctor sat back in his chair. "There, it's out. The worst fear has been expressed and yet we're both here and the world outside the clinic is going on." He sat quietly for a moment taking in her frozen, rigid posture. "Don't, for a second, think I am not admiring the courage it took for you to come here today. And, it's not only that you came, it's that, unlike last Tuesday, you came today ready to be emotionally honest."

Helen recalled her conversation with Peter, the one moment when she had been emotionally honest with him. "Are you seeing anyone, professionally, I mean?" He had asked.

"No," she had said "but I know I must."

She raised her chin. "Since my husband's death, I've talked to no one. Right after he died, my friend, Torrey, came, using money she could ill afford, all the way from Oregon to help me. But I sent her away."

"That was some time ago," he said.

"Yes," she said, "it was. And now, I don't know how or where to begin. I didn't think I would be strong enough to just sit here and tell you." Her voice shook.

"Not many would be strong enough to do so, Mrs. Duncan. It's the reason many of us therapists use the aid of hypnosis--which is what I proposed for you at our last meeting. Have you considered it?"

Helen nodded. "At this point, I feel I have little choice. The choice was made when I forced myself to come. I realized then, that I have to talk to someone." After so many months of playing pretend with her emotions, Helen realized with a jolt how relieved she was to be able to speak the truth from her heart.

He stood then. "Come," he said, "you will be most comfortable lying on the couch."

For a second, Helen thought of protesting. It was just too Freudian, lying on a couch. She would feel foolish and vulnerable. Then she shrugged in resignation and rose to follow him.

He sat just above her head, as she lay on the green couch. "Now, Mrs. Duncan, I will help you relax. Picture yourself relaxing. Picture yourself filled with warming sunshine. Feel it pouring into you from the top of your head, down through your brain, your neck, your shoulders, and your arms, filling your chest cavity, your stomach, on down your legs, all the way to your toes. It's delightful, isn't it? ...So warm and friendly feeling. It's making you a little drowsy, in fact." His voice would not hurry. It was soft, slightly melodic and soothing. She nodded, or at least she thought she nodded her head.

"Breathe deeply, Mrs. Duncan. Smell the warming earth under a summer sky; feel yourself relaxing even more."

It seemed to Helen that she could smell the rich, earthy odor, feel a soft breeze caress her cheeks.

"Now," his voice said, "you are doing splendidly. Picture yourself at the top of a bluff with a set of rock stairs going down. There are ten of them. Can you see them? They are inviting you to descend. Inside your head, count each step as you go down, staying very relaxed. I will count out loud. When you reach the tenth step you will be fully relaxed and able to answer questions freely..."

Helen felt both heavy and weightless at the same time. She could hear the doctor's even breathing as he quietly counted and was not at all surprised when she heard him ask: "Have you reached the tenth step?"

"Yes."

"Are you feeling relaxed and comfortable?"

"Yes."

"As I said during our last visit, you are still conscious and your free will is entirely intact. However, you will have a heightened sense of awareness and clarity. You will experience, in this more relaxed state, those emotions you have been blocking. Do you understand?"

Helen nodded.

"May I ask you some questions now?"

"Yes."

"What was worrying you when you came to see me today?"

"I knew you would want to talk to me about why I am so sad."

"Yes, I would like us to talk about it. It seems that you have been sad for quite a long time."

"Yes. I have."

"What is it that made you so sad?"

Helen felt tears slipping down the sides of her cheeks below her ears, but couldn't seem to raise her hands to wipe them away.

"I've been very, very sad," she said, "so sad, I wished to die."

"Did you think of taking your own life?"

"Yes. No. I mean, I thought of it and knew I couldn't do it."

"Why not?"

"I have three children. It would be too horrible for them to lose both their mother and their father."

"I see. So, your children have lost their father. That would mean you have lost your husband as well, wouldn't it? Did you want to talk about him too?"

"Y-e-e-s." Helen sobbed. "He died. He died and it's my fault."

Dr. Pagglio's breathing was even and his voice soothing. "This is very hard to talk about, Helen, but you're doing a fine job. Can you tell me about your husband's death?"

"I was getting my hair done. My new thoroughbred evidently jumped the pasture fence. Only Marshall was home and he found the colt on a county road that runs past our farm. It was caught in a barbed wire fence…struggling to free itself, severing tendons and an artery instead."

Helen could feel herself sobbing, but she somehow managed to keep talking. "Somewhere, Marshall, my husband, found some old wire cutters, the sort used to cut the wire on the hay bales years ago. When he cut the barbed-wire, there was so much tension on it from the colt's struggles that it must have snapped horribly. I read in the newspaper, much later, that it sliced his neck."

Her voice stopped. Her eyes darted left and right, imagining each vivid detail. "I didn't know. They came and got me… The ambulance was there… There was so much blood… I had to identify them…lying in all the blood…" She drew a ragged breath. Her voice changed; grew hard with anger. "It should have been me. If someone had to die, I should've been the one.

95

Marshall told me the colt was trouble and begged me not to buy him, but I wouldn't listen."

Helen lay quietly, then whispered, "I am responsible. People came to comfort me, but I sent them away. I don't deserve to be comforted. Our children call. They want to come and visit, but I won't let them. I can't look at them. They know whose fault their father's death is. Inside, I know they blame me, just as I blame myself."

"You feel your children hate you?"

"Yes."

"How do they show this hate?"

"They don't. But I know! I love my children. They are wonderful people. But I can't face them."

"You love them so deeply that you can't spend time together because you're afraid they'll come to share your understanding that you are responsible for your husband's death?"

"Yes."

"So, it feels as though you've lost not only your husband but your children. It must be very lonely in your world right now."

"Yes." Helen sobbed. "No husband. No children. No dog. My son, Peter, came to see me last week and said they were getting me a puppy. I wouldn't let him. I came to see you instead."

"So, Peter came to see you. Did he seem angry?"

"No. He seemed... He reminded me of Marshall... Like he'd made up his mind and we were going to do things his way. He said all three of them, Carrie, Willie and he, were taking charge."

"Did he take charge?"

"No, I sent him away. But he stayed long enough to build me a fire from juniper boughs." Helen's head rocked back and forth. "He said he couldn't leave the house feeling so sad. He said the Rawlings had sent those boughs on purpose after Marshall died ...to remind me of the good times."

"The Rawlings?"

"Will and Torrey Rawling. Will is an old friend from my husband's childhood, Torrey is his wife. They own a cattle ranch in Eastern Oregon... Well now it's partly a dude ranch. We went there on family vacations every year. Willie is named after Will Rawling. They want me to visit."

"But you feel you can't. You don't deserve comfort and you don't deserve pleasure. And most of all, you don't deserve the love of your children or friends, much less a dog. That's why you sent your friend, Torrey, away when she came to help you. That's why you sent Peter away when he came."

"That's right."

The room was quiet other than the whisper of Dr. Pagglio's pen. Finally he put it down, rubbed the bridge of his nose and said softly, "Mrs. Duncan, you have done a very good job of describing your problem. I would agree with you that it is a serious one; one very painful to resolve... But it can be done and together we will do it." The doctor took a deep breath. "In a few minutes, I am going to bring you out of your hypnotic state and you will feel calm, relaxed and more at peace. You will remember clearly what we've discussed and will believe, as I do, that there is hope. But, right now, I want you to take a moment to visualize the tears you have just shed. Visualize them as the body's miracle cleansing agent; a miracle healing agent given only to human animals in such abundance. Picture your tears washing away your grief. Give yourself permission to cry whenever you want and then picture those tears as washing you clean inside. Can you do that?"

Helen nodded. The sound of her quiet sobbing filled the room. Dr. Pagglio waited quietly for her to finish and then said, "All right then, Helen. Here we go. You are standing on the bottom step of your ten stairs once more. Can you see them?"

"Yes, perfectly."

"Good. You are looking up towards a lovely, welcoming light. There is a blue sky and puffy white clouds. You are looking forward to climbing the stairs. Each time you take a step, count backward starting with ten, ending with one. When you say the word 'one,' you will awaken feeling calm, relaxed and more at peace. Take a deep breath and begin when you are ready."

Slowly, Helen began her count. When she reached the number one, she lay quietly, enjoying the tranquil feeling of basking in warm sunlight. She heard Dr. Pagglio's quiet voice say, "How do you feel?"

She moved her head slowly from side to side, feeling the dampness of the tissue pillow cover under her cheeks.

"I'm not sure," she said. "Was I hypnotized?"

"Yes. Can you recall the ground we covered?"

Helen nodded. "Yes. May I sit up now?"

"Certainly. When you're ready."

He reached forward, handing her a box of Kleenex. Then he stood up and walked to the phone. "Deena, bring Mrs. Duncan a big glass of water. Then bring each of us a cup of coffee, please."

Helen wiped her eyes and blew her nose before giving him a genuine smile of thanks, realizing she was parched. "Deena already made me one cup of coffee. But I forgot to drink it."

"I know. I saw. This one will make up for it."

She looked at him, her eyes considering.

"What are you thinking?" He asked.

"About my children." She was pleased that he didn't press her for more information.

Deena came in with the water and a smile saying, "Coffee coming up!"

After Deena had brought the coffee and the door closed, she looked at the doctor and arched an eyebrow. "To think, I wouldn't get to try Deena's coffee, had I been willing to accept a dog from my children."

She could tell he understood her admission and saw humor light his eyes.

He grinned and took a sip of coffee. "I've never had to compete with a dog before. If it was an either or proposition, I'm glad I was the one chosen."

Helen also took a sip of coffee. "Well, my third option was a cruise. So, I guess you could say you were my first choice."

They continued sipping their coffee in companionable silence, until Dr. Pagglio cleared his throat and ran fingers through his thinning, wiry brown hair. ""Next time, I'd like to hear more about your children's reason for getting you a dog. Now, let's talk about your homework."

"Homework?"

"Yes, I would like you to write down how you've been filling your waking hours. Make a log or a journal. I'd like to get a sense of how you have been spending your time now that you have so radically altered your lifestyle."

Chapter Eleven

Where? Helen thought, sitting, head in hands at the kitchen table. *Where do I begin? How do I begin? I have lost the skills for what is being asked of me.*

"Make a list for yourself to accomplish," Dr. Pagglio had suggested as they drank their coffee. "Start it with: Get out of bed. Then, as soon as you rise, make your bed so you won't be tempted to crawl back into it. Make that number two on your list. Then, write down every step of showering and dressing, if you need to. Do it tonight before you go to bed and tomorrow, as you do each thing, run a line through it. Make sure the homework I gave you— writing how you've been spending time— is on the list."

This advice was given after she confessed to lately spending entire days in bed, drifting in and out of sleep, only to spend her nights sleepless.

Outside, it was getting dark. The February wind had picked up and she could hear the rattle it made against the screen door's loose latch. *That's one thing to put on my list, tighten that damned thing!* She thought. With a sigh, she pulled the new spiral notebook towards her.

Writing down the sort of things Dr. Pagglio had talked about was the easy part. That she could do. What she couldn't yet do was think about all the telephone calls she did not return, all the knocks on the door knocker she'd ignored, all the unread, unanswered cards and letters she'd received. *What did one do after nearly two years? Send out a blanket letter on the computer saying, "Guess what? I've decided to start communicating again?"* Squeezing her eyes shut to cut off the tears of defeat stinging her eyelids, she remembered the doctor's advice to "Cry whenever you want." *Well, I've certainly taken that advice! What is this? Cry number three?* She rose from the kitchen chair to get a tissue and pushed the empty notebook away from her.

A vision of the fire Peter had built took her to the living room. There on the floor was the cardboard box still containing several juniper boughs. The knife Peter had used to open the box was still on the hearth. Remembering the crackle and the comfort, she thought, *Why not build one for myself? Dr. Pagglio would approve.* A wisp of a smile crept onto her face. *Funny, all afternoon I've been framing my actions by considering what the doctor would think of them; everything from buying a spiral notebook to really shopping for food in a good grocery store.* She sighed. *At least there's real food in the refrigerator and I do plan to fix myself a meal.* Then, as if defending herself, she said out loud to the empty room, "So what if I'm not ready to see people. I've only had two appointments." And found, to her surprise, that she was already looking forward to Thursday and the next session.

Two sessions a week! At first she had resisted the suggestion, but the doctor had remained firm. "Twice a week is NOT too much. You will be doing yourself a disservice to do otherwise." The doctor had looked keenly at her. "I expect you to keep every single appointment, Mrs. Duncan." After a slight hesitation, she had agreed.

Now, moving quickly, before she could change her mind, she opened the damper on the fireplace, sliced the box into strips, wadded newspaper and made the famous "Duncan teepee" of box, juniper branches and the maple kindling still in the copper boiler on the hearth. She paused as she reached for the match. Before striking it, she pictured first, the faces of her three children and then the kind, weather-beaten features of Torrey and Will Rawling. *Torrey would say this is a significant event,* she thought. *She would say I must do as the Native Americans do and offer thanks before I light the sacred boughs of this ceremonial fire. I must give thanks to Peter for his courage in coming to visit against my wishes; to Carrie for being able to anticipate the roadblocks I would throw up; and to Willie because he wanted to get me a puppy.* "I do NOT want a puppy!" she said aloud as she struck the match and watched with satisfaction as the flaming poof of tinder-dry juniper caught and enveloped the teepee in bright orange flames.

It came to her, as she slipped her barn jacket over her cardigan and went to get more maple from the woodpile, that she was taking an action to give herself comfort. It was the first thing she could remember doing for herself since Marshall's death. Selling the horses? Carrie was right in a way. Selling them was to punish herself, not to comfort herself or make her life easier. At the time, she convinced herself it was because she had too much to do and couldn't manage their care, exercise and feeding. In truth, the association was too raw to bear. She sighed, knowing the guilt would be with her forever.

The chunks of wood felt solid in her arms. It took two trips to fill the copper boiler they'd always used as a wood-bin. On the second trip to the woodpile, she looked up into the nearly dark sky just as a snowflake drifted down and landed on her cheek. She felt the satisfaction of knowing there was food in her refrigerator and a cozy fire in the fireplace. "Go ahead and snow. Tonight, I will sit in front of the fire and make a start at chronicling my non-living life just as the good doctor instructed. I will eat a good dinner. I will sit up in bed and make my list for tomorrow," she said, raising her voice in the wind as she turned; the wood heavy in her arms; her face still upturned to catch the next snowflake; a tiny ember of hope in her heart.

Dear Dr. Pagglio,
 You have asked that I record my daily activities since my husband's tragic death.

Helen took a better grip on her pen and settled deeper into the corduroy chair. She had decided to write the accounting of her time in letter form. It was as close as she could get to feeling as if she were talking to him.

At first, I felt I was super-organized. Now, I realize I was probably in some sort of shock. I couldn't seem to really feel anything. I bossed the children around; made them handle most of the arrangements for the memorial service (the things I couldn't bear to do,); and then sent them back to their own lives. I wrote a card and sent an obituary to everyone in our address book; cleaned Marshall's clothing from the closets; and sold all our horses, saying to the children that I no longer had an interest in riding and good horses needed to be ridden. I believe I was in this mode of false reality for about two months.

After the horses were sold (another guilt I must face), I began, what would be called a quest. Not knowing if you are at all familiar with the rural areas of this part of Virginia, I need to preface what I did next by saying that Marshall's death should not have happened. My colt found what had to have been the last piece of overlooked barbed-wire in Prince William County. The wire he did find was no longer an existing fence, but the remnants of an old one that had long since fallen down and had been covered by roadside grasses and shrubs. I was sure my quest was to find all other possible locations of wire, and to either inform the people owning the property, or to remove it myself. In this behavior too, I confess to ignoring "no trespassing" signs and driving past signs posted as private drives, even when it meant opening gates to do so.

Helen sighed and stretched her fingers to ease the cramping in her right hand. She realized that she was holding the pen too tightly. "And I didn't find any other wire," she said in a sad whisper to the empty room as she wrote the line.

103

The fire had burned down and she got up to throw on another log. It had been a long time since she had worn a watch, but she had the idea that a great deal of time had passed. Still lost in thoughts of the time following Marshall's death, she wandered to the front window and pulled back the drape. The security light over the barn showed a fuzz of snowflakes. She stretched her neck muscles gently and returned to the chair.

> The next part seemed to happen overnight. I remember saying to myself as the van left with the horses, "There, that's done." I had done the same thing after I was convinced that wire would not be a problem for others in our area. The day after I finished looking for wire, I began cleaning the barn. I worked on it every single day, seven days a week. By the time I was done, were you to look into the stalls, you would find no sign that a horse had ever lived there. Now, since I haven't engaged in my cleaning behavior for a while, you might find some cobwebs and dust, but there was a time, after I was done, you could have mistaken each stall for a monk's cell. I also cleaned every piece of tack and the tack room. It took me months to get the barn, tack and tack room just the way I wanted them. Each saddle and its accompanying bridle were encased in a canvas bag that I had designed and sewn.
>
> On his recent visit, my son went to the tack room. I wonder what he thought, seeing the cleanliness and the saddles like that. Even to me, they look like body bags. It must've been very difficult for him.

Helen wrote smoothly and with dry eyes. Her pen seemed perfectly attuned to her thoughts as she vividly recalled the days of frenetic behavior, using energy that should have made for sound sleeping at

104

night. Instead, it made for restless nights, often stalked by night terrors.

I remember clearly when I had the barn and tack room just as I wanted; clean to the point of sterility. Then too, I said to myself, "There, that's done. I'm finished with this. So now, I can start on the house."

I had unplugged the phone machine much earlier, but it was about then that I stopped taking phone calls (except from my children) and putting all of my mail, unopened, into a big box. Already, I had our accountant handling my bills. I cleaned the house from top to bottom, with the exception of the children's rooms. I did not even enter those three rooms. However, the rest of the house was scoured, polished and shined. I removed and boxed many of the items in the rest of the house that belonged to the others; their pictures as well.

On the morning I woke and could not think of a single new thing to clean in the house, I stayed in bed. It felt as though I had run out of energy. I had nothing left to accomplish in this world. I could see nothing in front of me worth living for. It was then that I began to contemplate death. It was then that I got the pictures of my children from the box where I'd put them and brought them into my bedroom. I looked at them every day and I believe they kept me alive.

I told myself, as I returned again and again to bed, that I had been working hard for a very long time and deserved to rest. And so the days went, with me leaving the bed only to get food, drink or to perform bodily functions. I did not totally neglect my personal hygiene, and would, on occasion, get up, dress fully and go to any grocery store where I wasn't known, to stock up on canned and frozen goods.

Until my son came, that final pattern continued. I remember being grateful, on the day he

105

came, that I had planned to go for groceries and had gotten up and dressed that morning. It would have shamed me to be caught, still in my nightgown.

And that, Dr. Pagglio, sums it up. I hope this is the account you wanted.

Helen Duncan
February 21, 1997

Slowly, Helen closed the notebook. She did not check her spelling or punctuation. She did not care. She rose and opened the front closet where she kept her shoulder bag and put the notebook inside it. Then she went to the window to watch wet flakes blur the landscape. After several minutes, she returned to her chair to watch the embers glow. *There are so many details I've left out,* she thought. *It doesn't begin to reflect on how terrible those days were.*

Like a high-speed shutter, images clicked through her mind: The terrible nightmare where she ran, shrieking, through fields covered in blood and body parts; the red, rawness of her hands from scrubbing with strong disinfectants...scrubbing and scrubbing and scrubbing, on hands and knees; rinsing and rinsing and scrubbing again.

She'd worn the tires off the Jeep looking for non-existent wire; burned up the old vacuum using it on the cobwebs, spilled grain, hay chaff and dirt in the barn and tack room. She could remember perfectly, the physical details of her compulsive behavior, but she couldn't recall why she felt compelled to do them or what her feelings were at the time. *Was I simply numb? What am I feeling right this very minute? Do I know?* She sighed and snuggled more deeply into the chair, willing herself to feel....something...anything, anything but numb. "Hungry," she finally said with surprise. "I actually feel hungry." She couldn't remember feeling hungry since the tragedy.

106

I feel like a schoolgirl who thinks she's going to get an A on her paper! Helen thought as she opened the door to the clinic. When Dr. Pagglio opened the door to call her, she jumped from her chair and strode past him.

"Are you looking smug, Mrs. Duncan?"

"Not smug. That's not quite the right feeling. I'm feeling…hopeful," she said as she sat in her chair and looked at him. "Call me Helen, please."

"Hopeful? That's good. That's very good. Tell me why."

They smiled at each other. Helen could tell Dr. Pagglio was truly pleased by her words. She took the notebook from her bag. "Writing down how I filled my time was evidently therapeutic. I even started a fire in the fireplace to comfort myself while I worked."

"Good for you! I'd like to get back to that later, but right now, what else did you do that was hopeful?"

"I actually had an appetite after I finished writing. I can't explain it, but for the first time…since…Marshall died, I started fixing myself dinner, and my mouth was watering. I didn't have to force myself to eat. I had to force myself to stop. It was the same at breakfast. I'd like an explanation, please."

Dr. Pagglio shrugged and smiled. "I haven't the slightest idea why, at least not yet. But, I, too, view it is a hopeful thing. After you had finished eating dinner, what did you do?"

Helen look surprised. "It was 10 o'clock. I banked the fire and took my other notebook up so I could write my "to do" list before going to sleep."

"And did you sleep after you did your list?"

Helen frowned. "A little. I still have trouble with bad dreams."

"Ah, yes. I remember that from your intake questionnaire. One of the changes you noted was a change in sleep patterns. Would bad dreams be part of the reason for the change?"

Helen nodded and whispered, "Very bad dreams."

"The same dreams or different ones?"

"Only variations of one."

"Can you talk about it? Perhaps, together, we can make sense of what your subconscious is doing."

At his question, Helen felt bile rise in her throat and thought for a moment she was going to throw up. She closed her eyes, feeling the room swim. Dr. Pagglio said sharply, "Helen, reach out with both your hands and grab onto mine. Squeeze hard. Do it now! Every time you squeeze, take a breath, a big breath. We'll breathe together."

Helen latched onto his hands and sucked in a breath of air. "Again!" She heard Dr. Pagglio say. He drew in his own deep breath, and she did the same. "Now let it out." And then they were breathing together, in...out...in...out...deep belly breaths.

She opened her eyes and found the doctor still had his closed, concentrating entirely on the deep, even breaths. "I think I'm okay," she said quietly, releasing his hands.

His eyes snapped open. "You nearly fainted," he said.

She nodded. "I had no warning."

He stood up, agitated. "My fault. I'm taking you too fast."

Helen felt a wave of motherly protection engulf her. "No, you're doing fine. I have no idea why my body reacted in such a way. At first, I actually felt as though I wanted to throw up."

"Throw up?"

"Yes. You know that metallic taste that comes just before you do?" The doctor nodded. "Well, that was my first sensation, followed by swirling, black dots before my eyes."

"You turned very pale. How do you feel now?"

"Fine. But it's very odd, don't you think?"

Dr. Pagglio shook his head. "Freud wouldn't think so. He'd think your body was trying to rid itself of the toxin."

"Meaning, my bad dream?"

"Exactly. However, while I never want to underestimate the work Freud did on the unconscious mind, I'm more inclined to think the stress of being here, plus a very good dinner and breakfast, on a stomach unused to eating, might be part of the cause."

"How very 'commonsensical' you are." She smiled weakly. "What now?"

Dr. Pagglio retook his seat. "I don't know. We could either have you continue under light hypnosis, or I could read what's in this notebook of yours. Which do you prefer?"

"Read the notebook!" Helen said without hesitation.

"Do you talk about your bad dream in here?" He tapped the cover with one long, slender finger.

"Not even one sentence. Though after I was done, I do remember thinking about many other things I might have put in my letter to you...the horrible nights being one."

"Horrible nights? The dream comes often then?"

"Yes."

"Does the dream have to do with your husband's death?"

"In a way, I guess. He's not in it--at least not as I knew him." Helen took a deep breath.

"Wait," he said. "Would you rather do this under hypnosis?"

Instead of answering his question, Helen let out her breath, lowered her head, and said in a rush, "It's about body parts; a field of body parts. There's the blood; I'm wading through the blood. It's up to my knees sometimes. I'm crying and blood is coming from my mouth. I don't look down. I never look down. But, I think I know those body parts are there...and I know what they are. They are human heads and arms and horse's legs, protruding from this sticky slew of internal organs and blood. I wade and wade and wade until I am so tired that I stop. But when I stop, I start sinking. And when I start to sink, I wake myself with my moans."

When Helen finished, she raised her head. The doctor was writing madly in his notebook. When he was through he looked up. "That isn't a bad dream, Helen, that's a nightmare or worse. Do you know who you are and where you are when you wake yourself?"

"Generally. Sometimes, it takes me just a bit to reorient myself."

"What do you do afterwards?"

"Nothing."

"Nothing?"

"No. I lie there and try not to think. Years ago I read an article about visualizations and so I picture myself in a glass ball or a snow globe, protected, but still able to see. I do it so the pain I feel won't hurt so much. I've gotten quite good at it."

"Did you ever go to a medical doctor?"

Helen shook her head. "My children got me some sleeping pills from our family doctor, but I threw them away."

"Did you ever get up and make a cup of tea or drink a glass of warm milk? Take a bath? Try to read?"

"No."

"Did you do anything to comfort yourself?"

"I looked at the high school graduation pictures of my three children to remind myself that suicide wasn't an option."

"I don't think I'd class that as comforting, Helen."

She looked at him steadily. "No. No, it wasn't comforting, but it did keep me alive."

The doctor's eyes bored into hers. "I'm going to take a risk here, Helen. I'm going to call you on what I think is an untruth."

His word surprised her. "What do you mean? If what I've said is untrue, I don't know it."

"I think looking at your children's pictures did not keep you alive as much as the need to punish yourself further did."

Helen felt a rush of pure anger. "Good God! What nonsense! Talk about Freudian!"

Dr. Pagglio sat quietly, his eyes never leaving her face. Finally he said, "I've made you very angry with my words."

"Your words are absolute nonsense! Of course I'm angry!"

"Are you angry enough to walk out?"

"Just about!" Even as she said the words, Helen knew they weren't true.

"Are you curious as to what made me say them?"

"Not very," she snapped, knowing just the reverse was true. "But I suppose, in the name of therapy, you plan to tell me anyway."

He allowed one corner of his mouth to turn up. "It's my job. But, I think you need to know first, that I'm already glad I took the risk."

Helen said nothing, even though she was remembering she had had a similar thought when she was working on the notebook. She sat back in her chair and crossed her arms in an attitude of waiting.

Dr. Pagglio flipped back several pages in the spiral-bound notebook and read something he had written. Then he looked at her.

"First of all, I want to say that your husband's death was truly a tragedy in a way that only an accidental death can be. Your feeling of responsibility towards it is quite understandable, as is your guilt about buying a horse over his objections. You chose to deal with that guilt by cutting yourself off from the love and support of family and friends. You felt so guilty that when your children and others continued to care for you, it seemed unfair. You needed them to shun

111

you…punish you. It was what you felt you deserved, so you made it happen."

Dr. Pagglio drew a deep breath, leaned forward and said gently, "Please recognize that you were totally in control. You needed to find a way to make amends and then somehow purge yourself, before you could consider being worthy of redemption. The search for wire was your attempt to make your amends."

He paused and closed his eyes and then shook his head and opened them. "That you couldn't find wire must have been psychically devastating to a highly moral, loving person such as yourself. It seemed you would be unable to make those amends. That failure created the house and barn cleaning phase, which seemed to have two purposes: the purging and the preparing for death. However, it really kept you from committing suicide, because you couldn't do it before completing the task. And the task was really one of cleansing the blood from your dreams."

He stopped and looked closely at Helen. "I know that was long, but am I stating this clearly, whether you agree with it or not?"

"Yes. It seems very far-fetched and based on assumptions, but it is clear!" She said coldly.

"Do you want me to continue?"

"Yes. I'm really interested to see what you came up with in terms of why I went to bed."

"Why do you think you did that?"

Helen glared at him. "No, Dr. Pagglio. You started this story. You finish it!"

He looked at her steadily. "As I said, I believe your strategies did not work. I believe even with all the scrubbing, the blood did not go away. I believe the pain became so great that it wore you out. Lack of sleep and proper food also contributed to make you even more vulnerable. You became so exhausted that you could no longer summon the energy to keep frantically busy, so you stayed in bed hoping to die…perhaps from a broken heart."

After the session, Helen walked out of the office and picked her way through the slushy snow toward the Jeep. The emotional trauma left her feeling like a newborn colt must feel; legs wobbling and not knowing in quite which direction to head. In one hand was a box of Kleenex.

"Take them with you," Dr. Pagglio had said. "Consider them an award for bravery."

"There aren't many left."

"Make it a goal to use them all. Remember to visualize the cleansing. I'd like to suggest your next list be about finding ways to give yourself comfort. Do small things like buying an outfit that fits, getting a manicure, or buying a latte. Do big things, too. Think about joining a health club, taking up hiking, or at least doing something physical. None of those things requires sustained concentration and you can do them without interacting with people unless you want to do so. Remember this: these things are to give comfort. You've got nearly a two-year deficit to make up."

Chapter Twelve

It's a great day to be tucked in, Helen thought. *So, why do I want to be outside?* She took her coffee and went to stand by the window. The skies had been dropping wet, sloppy snow off and on most of the week, and the weatherman said that more of the same, only colder, was predicted for the weekend. *How ironic! If ever there was a day to go back to bed, this is it.*

She walked back over to the table and looked down at her "to do" list. *I want to go outside because I don't want to do what needs to be done on the inside,* she admitted to herself. *There isn't a thing here that I feel capable of doing at this moment.*

She ran a finger down the list. She'd already crossed out the standard six:

1. Get up
2. Make bed
3. Shower
4. Brush teeth
5. Get dressed
6. Make and eat breakfast

Left undone was:

1. Start going through box of unopened mail
2. Write a letter to Torrey and Will
3. Call the children

She looked at the grandfather clock whose pendulum once again swung with metronome precision: 8:00 o'clock. She walked reluctantly to the phone. *Why is this so tough?* she asked herself as she punched the numbers.

"Peter, darling, it's your mother."

"Mom?" The sleepy voice held a note of alarm.

"Yes. Did I wake you?" Helen knew both Peter and Patti loved to sleep in on Saturday mornings. But, she also knew this was the day when they did chores together, and she didn't want to miss them. Besides, it was still too early to call either Texas or Oregon.

"Mom, are you all right?"

"Yes. At least I'm better, I think. I wanted to tell you that I have indeed kept my word. I know you were going to call me, but I thought I'd call you and let you know."

There was a silence. She pictured Peter sitting up in bed, his thick, brown hair sticking up like it always had, his pajamas askew, and smiled.

"Mom," he said then, "it's good to hear your voice." His gladness was so genuine that Helen's throat closed. "Oh, Peter," she whispered, her voice full of gratitude.

"Mom, did you say you'd kept your appointment?"

"Yes." She managed to say, "I have and I am. I called to thank you, Peter. It was a very hard thing you did."

"Are you feeling better?"

Helen paused to consider her words and when she continued, her voice sounded nearly normal. "Yes, better would describe me for right now. But the doctor says, from time to time, I am liable to feel much worse as I come to grips with this whole terrible ordeal." She paused again. "Not only for your father's death, but my behavior afterwards."

"Aw, Mom..."

"S-s-h-h, Peter. Don't say it. Do NOT say, 'It's okay.' It is NOT okay and I'm NOT really okay, but I'm working on it and I want to say I love you all very much. Thank you for not giving up on me."

"Aw, Mom, we'd never do that." Helen could hear Peter's voice grow hoarse and could feel the power of his love melt something tight and hard inside her. Her tears were immediate.

"Goodbye, darling. I have to go," she sobbed. "Don't feel badly about these tears. The doctor has given me orders to cry all I want."

115

"May I call you?"

"Yes. I plan to call the others too. I love you, son. Goodbye." Helen found it difficult to replace the receiver and break the link. She stood clutching it to her chest, allowing her tears to run unchecked, until finally, without lifting the receiver to her ear, she placed it gently in its cradle. *God! Two more telephone calls to go. But not yet. Take it one step at a time, Helen. It's still only 7:00 AM in Houston and 6:00 AM in Eugene. You've got time.*

She walked to the table and with a bold stroke crossed out 3. Call the children. Instead, she wrote, one line below the other: Call Peter. Call Carrie. Call Willie. Then she crossed out the line that said, "Call Peter," threw down the pen and strode to the entry closet for her barn coat and rubber boots. Somehow, giving each of her children his or her own place on the list seemed to give the importance of each call more weight. It seemed fitting. *Before I call anyone else, I must think more carefully what to say so I won't fall apart as I did with Peter.*

With a sense of escape, she slammed the newly fixed screen door and plunged out into the gray, blustering, snowy day. *'Don't slam the screen door!'* rang in her mind.

The slush crunched a little underfoot, a sure sign the weather was indeed turning colder. She pulled the coat more tightly around her bony frame, fastened the buttons and turned up the corduroy collar as she picked her way across the driveway towards the bridle trail behind the barn. As she passed the maple tree where Max was buried, she could barely breathe, her chest felt so tight.

"Breathe deeply, Helen." She could almost hear Robin Pagglio's calm voice. *"In, out, in, out. Concentrate!"* She sucked in the cold air and allowed the wind-driven mix of snow and sleet to scour her face while she breathed to the imaginary cadence of his words.

116

The bridle trail, once a clear-cut swath through the maple, sumac and oak was visible, only because of the trees Marshall had felled. The path itself was overgrown and the going difficult. She slogged along, trampling brush and brambles beneath her tall rubber boots, panting from the effort. In no time at all, she ran out of strength and breath. *This is what comes of staying in bed day after day. What a weakling I have become! The barn is still in sight, for God's sake!* In disgust and frustration she turned to retrace her steps and then stopped; the wind was against her back, the cozy picture of a snow-covered barn and house in front of her. *From this distance, it's easy to imagine life as it was,* she thought forlornly.

Had it been the other lifetime, Max would be bounding in front of her, hoping for a rabbit or squirrel to chase. On the way back from their walk, they would stop to visit the horses in their stalls. Max would be searching for stray bits of dropped sweet feed and Helen would be petting the horses, kissing each nose, checking to make certain the children had cleaned stalls and fed the horses before leaving for school.

Helen shivered. Her feet in the rubber boots were numb with cold. She did not lift her eyes again, but made her way back to the house trying not to think how empty it would seem. She could hear the jangle of the telephone as she opened the screen door.

"Mother! Thank goodness! Where were you?" Carrie's voice sounded frantic with worry.

"Hello, darling. I went for a walk so time would pass until it was time to call you."

"Oh Mom!" Helen listened to her daughter's voice soften. "Mom, I'm so glad you went to get help. Peter called me. I'm so glad you called him. He's been really pissed with me for making him come see you."

"Please, Carrie. You know I cannot tolerate that word!" The age-old response to her children's swearing rolled automatically from her.

"You ARE better," Carrie crowed. "Definitely better, if you're starting to tell me not to say 'pissed!'"

"I did not yet classify myself as better, dear. But, I am working on it, thanks to you and your brothers. Carrie, I need to repeat this to all of you. I don't want a dog and I certainly do not want a horse. I do, however, thank you for your concern and for forcing me to take action."

"Yes, Mother, Carrie said demurely. "And, I didn't mean better in the clinical sense. Only that you sounded more like your old self. Doing something to help yourself is more like the mother we used to know."

"It was time," Helen said simply.

"I'd love to see you."

The wistful note in Carrie's voice caught at Helen's heart. "I know. I want to see you too, but not yet. I need more time. Perhaps by your spring vacation..."

After a little silence, Carrie said, "I'll try my darnedest to get the time free, Mom." And then she asked, "Are you happy with your therapist?"

"Robin Pagglio? Absolutely! He's very kind, but he's tough. I intend to see him twice a week. Thank you for the recommendation."

"Twice a week? Oh, Mom, that's so great! You sound really determined."

"Yes. I am feeling...determined. It comes and goes, unfortunately. But, practically every thought I have is somehow framed around what Dr. Pagglio might think; which is useful in its own way."

"Very useful. Very, very useful. I won't pry further. One's relationship with one's therapist is a very private matter."

Helen smiled at how professional Carrie sounded and pictured her slender auburn-haired daughter, freckles on her too generous nose, Marshall's nose.

"Carrie, are you well?"

"Mom, I can't tell you what a load has lifted by

118

just hearing your voice. I'm slogging along on my defense, but I have so missed you; missed the sound and the smell and the feel of you."

Helen closed her eyes, absorbing the words. *Could it be true then, that her children did not blame her for the death of their father?* She knew she was not yet strong enough to ask. "Oh Carrie, I love you so. Love all of you. I'll work as hard as I can to get back on track. Your..." Abruptly, Helen ended her sentence. On the tip of her tongue was to speak Marshall's name and she knew it would be stretching herself too far. Instead she said, "Darling, let's end this conversation on a positive note. I'll call you in a couple of days and that's a promise."

Carrie did not protest and Helen was grateful.

"Do you need to hang up, Mother?" The professional sound was back in her voice.

"Yes, dear. And you needn't call Willie. It's on my list to do once it gets late enough to call the West Coast. I seem to take great comfort in marking things off my 'to do' list."

Helen heard Carrie's sharp intake of breath.

"Um, Mom, I don't know about Willie. He's still pretty upset. Mostly, he keeps it under control, but Torrey says he goes through phases where he...um, wishes you'd been more... available."

Helen closed her eyes, observing how the pain caused by Carrie's words was centered in her chest. She could think of nothing to say. She'd read between the lines of Carrie's words. Willie was angry with her, maybe he was even bitter. She felt deflated—defeated, because Willie's disgust with her behavior was what she deserved from all three of them.

After a moment, Helen put her thoughts into words. "I can't say I'm surprised. I guess I should be grateful that all three of you don't feel as Willie does."

"We don't...and he loves you, mom, don't think that he doesn't. He's just really, really hurt."

"Yes, I can understand that, perfectly. What I

did to you children was very hurtful. I... I...need to think about this. What do you think I should do?"

"I think maybe you should write him a letter instead of calling. Or, if you do decide to call him, be ready for his reaction. He needs to know you still love him, even if he hangs up on you."

"I do need to call him." Helen said quietly, resolve in her voice.

"Okay then. Do you have a pencil? He has a new address and phone number. He's living in the fancy guest cottage of some guy who's a big fan."

As she hung up the receiver, Helen realized her hands were shaking. *It's partly from emotion,* she decided, *but partly from the fact that I'm standing here in my wet canvas jacket and I'm chilled to the bone.*

She leaned her forehead against the wall by the telephone and with numb fingers began to fumble with the coat's buttons. *God, Willie! What have I done to you? What words can I find to ask for forgiveness when I'm still having such a hard time forgiving myself?*

She pulled the sodden coat from her shoulders and hung it on the wall rack, knowing she had to make the final call, even if she was going to wake her son from a sound sleep--but how she dreaded the outcome!

"I can do this," she said through chattering teeth. "I will do this, and then I will have a hot shower."

Helen found her old sweater on the back of the couch and slipped it on before dialing Willie's new number. She made up her mind to simply say what was in her heart. If he wouldn't listen, then she would write the words in a letter. The need to hear her youngest son's voice was now irresistible.

The phone picked up on the fourth ring.

"Whoever this is, you'd better have a damned good reason for calling this early!" The sleepy voice growled into the phone.

"Willie? Willie, did I wake you?"

There was a silence and Helen tried to

anticipate her long-limbed, gangly son's reaction to hearing her voice. "Willie, it's Mom. I'm calling to say how sorry I am for the way I've been behaving; for the way I treated you; to say I love you and that…someday…I hope you'll be able to forgive me."

There was a long silence. Helen stood, clutching the receiver, forcing out the words, shivering despite the heavy wool sweater.

The fuzz of sleep was gone from Willie's voice when he answered. "Jesus! Just like that, huh? You pick up the phone and wake me up to say 'Sorry I dropped out of your life for two years.' Is that what you're saying, Mother?"

The anger and sarcasm in Willie's voice made Helen feel physically ill. She did not try to disguise the tremor in her voice. "No. Not for dropping out of your life. It's much more than that. I don't know where the mother you used to know went when…your dad died, but she was no longer here for anyone, including herself."

"You're telling me! The person who was there was no mother, no friend, not even a widow who looked out for her husband's memory! You were nothing! No, I take that back. You were a real bitch! Aunt Torrey told me how you practically kicked her out of the house when she came to help you. And, do you know what she said to me afterwards? She said, 'Don't feel badly, Willie, your mom is doing the best she can.' But, you know, Mom, I don't think so! You think you're the only one in pain? Well, think again!" Willie's anger ran over the line like lit gunpowder.

Helen bowed her head, fingers fumbled in the cord, as she absorbed his words and nodded. "Yes, I'm so terribly sorry, son. I have thought about it again and again. I understand that you may never be able to forgive me. But, I must try to forgive myself, if I can."

"Fine! Forgive yourself. Go on with your life. That's what you told us to do. It felt like you were saying, 'Never mind that your dad is dead. Pretend it

121

didn't happen. Get out of here. Get on with your life.' So, that's what I did. So, don't just decide to call me up and expect me to roll over and wave my feet in the air." Willie was panting into the phone as if he'd run a full-court press.

"No. No, I don't expect you to do that, son. I realize how little I know about what you've been doing; how you are. Thank God you have Torrey and Will out there. I'll say goodbye now." Helen's voice was little more than a whisper. "Goodbye, Willie. I love you very much."

Willie groaned as he heard the line go dead. His sense of fair play caused him to instantly regret his outburst. Her calling like that had caught him off-guard. Lately, with Carrie's coaching, he had been able to think in a kinder way towards his mother. He also immediately regretted bringing Torrey Rawling into the conversation. She wasn't at all angry with his mother. Her calm face came to him. Her black eyes were full only of love. *Your mother is not herself, Willie. Her grief is too big. Her spirit has gone... Don't let bitterness spoil your memories.* The words seemed to flow through him, against his will, softening him. But he steeled himself. She had not allowed them to properly grieve the death of their father and even worse, he had been cheated of her love and comfort when he needed it most.

Willie gritted his teeth. His mother had to pay and he was the only cashier! Carrie and Peter didn't feel the same way. They were the ones who had arranged the conference call. They felt something had to be done to help her. At the time of the conference call, he had sarcastically suggested they get her a puppy. Carrie hadn't seemed to pick up on his tone and ran with the idea, suggesting instead that they get her a horse.

He threw himself back onto the bed, the

receiver on his chest, aware that his outburst had not given him the relief he thought it might. If anything, the pain in his chest had intensified.

Helen walked away from the phone, making directly for the stairs. Her eyes felt hot and gritty, her skin felt numb with cold. *Try to be grateful he still feels something for you. He couldn't carry that anger unless he did. What was it that Dr. Pagglio had said? "Anger is often easier to feel than sadness."* She reminded herself to be glad that Peter and Carrie did not seem to feel the same way.

Halfway up the stairs, Helen stopped and returned to the kitchen table. Deliberately, she picked up her pen, bent over her list and crossed out: Call Carrie. Call Willie. And then she crossed out item number three, 'Take a shower,' and wrote instead: Take a long, hot soak in the bathtub. *I'm on my way,* she thought. *In more ways than one, I'm on my way.*

Chapter Thirteen

"You did what?"

Helen handed the doctor her list. "I talked to each of my children and then I filled the bathtub with very hot water and had a comforting bath with vanilla bath oil."

She was gratified to watch the doctor's eyebrows rise as he read her list with its crossed out items. "This is a long list."

"Yes. Calling the children was the hardest. My youngest son is very angry with me, and since we talked, I've had to fight tremendous feelings of remorse. Keeping busy helped."

"Remorse?"

Of course, remorse. I've behaved very badly."

"What do you mean?"

"I cut myself off from the world, more specifically, my children. In essence, my children not only lost their father, they lost their mother!" Helen's head was up and her shoulders were straight. It felt good to say the words. She saw Dr. Pagglio was writing furiously. When he was done, he looked up at her in a considering way.

"What are your thoughts?" She asked.

He smiled and leaned forward, recognizing his own words coming from her mouth. "A lot of things are running through my mind," he answered. "First, did I hear you say you took a bath after you talked with your children?"

Helen nodded. "Yes. I was very cold from the walk and felt even colder after I talked to Willie." She dropped her eyes. "He's very bitter."

"Are you surprised?"

"No, not really. I thought about it and cried in the tub. Then I came to the conclusion that I felt relief. I think I need someone to be angry with me. Neither Peter nor Carrie seem to be."

Dr. Pagglio was silent and after a moment Helen said, "What about all those things that were running through your mind?"

124

"I was remembering a bit of research that I just read. There is evidence that willingness to disclose our deepest feelings to another person has a good effect on the central nervous system, and that, in turn affects the cardiovascular and immune systems. Conversely, when we don't confide our problems, both the body and the brain work overtime to suppress our emotions."

Helen nodded her head. "I don't know that this is improving my heart or my health, but I do know for certain that I was trying to suppress my emotions. As I told you, I tried to build a snow globe around the pain and that seemed possible only with total isolation."

He nodded and continued, "In essence, I believe, subconsciously, you felt it was the only possible course. Your self-imposed exile, seeing no one, was an effort to help your body and brain do just that--shut down. It made it easy for you to go to bed." He looked at her and smiled. "And then you decided to see someone. It turned out to be me. So my last thought was, 'I wonder if the fact that you are now willing to honestly explore those deep feelings is having an effect, not only on your mental health, but on your physical health; if therapy actually can help the entire body recover from a trauma.'"

Helen sat quietly, absorbing the doctor's words, and then said, "I think it is possible. Remember how hungry I got after I did my first homework assignment? That was after I decided not only to see you but to trust you. The return of appetite has to mean something. On the other hand, you should have seen my activity level when I was looking for wire and cleaning everything."

He sighed. "Yes, you were very active," he acknowledged. "Let's just, for the moment, accept my theory of atonement and redemption. Let's build on what you said about 'trust.' I agree with you that it is a critical component. That, and the fact that you finally did something to comfort yourself, even after confronted with your son's anger, is very significant. It shows how determined you are to succeed."

Helen lifted her chin again. "Yes. Yes, I am. Even when Willie was shouting at me over the phone, my determination never wavered. I'm proud of that. The list making has become my life raft. You were right about crossing off each item. But, more than that, I can't tell you how good it feels to have a positive thought or two about myself."

"Good! Think about what you're feeling as you finish each task. Give a name to the feeling if you can." Dr. Pagglio leaned back, lacing long fingers behind his head, "So what else have you been up to? Or is it all on the list?"

"Everything is on the list. If I think of something that needs doing and it's not on the list, I put it on and then I do it. Yesterday, I called the accounting firm to take charge of my bills again, but not until I'd put it on the list. I also started to read a box of un-opened mail." Helen frowned. "That one is going to take some time. Oh, yes, I also put, 'Clean off drafting table' on the new list.

"Clean off your drafting table?"

"Yes. When the nightmare comes, I try to replace it as soon as I can with some sort of design problem."

"Excellent! But why did you put cleaning your drafting table on the list?"

"The next time the nightmare comes, I can get up and go to work instead of lying in bed feeling victimized."

Dr. Pagglio's eyebrows shot up again. "Great idea! Was this your idea, or have you been reading something helpful?"

Helen smiled mysteriously. "I've been doing some reading, but mostly the idea grew out of your assignment to find comfort for myself. I found the thought of doing some design work to be comforting for some reason."

They sat in silence. Helen could see his mind wrapping itself around her words, seeking their essence. He started to say something and then shook his head and remained silent for a long moment before looking up and grinning at her. "You don't know how your progress tempts me to move you forward instead of letting you pick the pace. I felt that I had done that once before, remember? So, I've just had a little talk with myself. Please excuse me."

"Why don't you want me to move forward?"

"I do. I certainly do! But the pace is yours to pick, not mine. My job is to assist you by asking about things you bring up, to notice when you avoid areas, and to suggest techniques, such as list making. Right now, I'd like us to go back to the telephone calls you made this morning. In particular, I'd like to hear about the conversations with your children. And Helen, when we start talking directly about your husband, I want us to use his name."

Helen's back stiffened. Her eyes narrowed and she felt anger welling up inside her. The sense of well-being she had worked so hard to sustain evaporated. "I take it you believe I have been avoiding the use of my husband's name for some reason?"

"Yes," the doctor said blandly, "I have been wondering about the significance of the avoidance."

Helen felt as though she'd been dropped over a cliff and was in free-fall. She jumped from her chair and stood, hands on her hips, glaring down at the calm-faced therapist. "I do not want to talk about my husband with you. Is that clear?"

Dr. Pagglio looked at her, his gaze level, but puzzled. He then said, "Yes, it is clear that my suggestion to use Marshall's name has upset you tremendously. Could you tell me why it has upset you so much?"

Upon hearing Dr. Pagglio use Marshall's name, Helen jerked as though stuck by a pin. She dropped her hands to her sides and lowered her head, squeezing her eyes shut. She could feel her heart pounding in her chest. A small, unbidden voice whispered inside her, *What is this about, Helen? Look at yourself. You are absolutely furious! Why?* The insight came immediately. She opened her eyes and sank back into her chair, looking at Robin Pagglio's concerned face. "It's having to use his name in the past tense," she whispered. "It's about really accepting the fact that... Marshall is dead."

Helen nosed the Jeep into the garage and sat behind the wheel, thinking about the therapy process. She was trembling with fatigue. *Who would ever think talking would be so exhausting? How does he do what he does? How does he know when to insert himself into the process? God! Is he as tired as I am? How does he do it all day?* She thought of her daughter and wondered if Carrie really knew what she was in for. *Of course, she's not going into private practice... Or is she? I know very little about the plans of my children during these past two years. If Peter hadn't shared the little bits and pieces about them when he came, I'd know even less.*

Helen stepped out of the Grand Cherokee, feeling deeply sad and 100 years old. With a sigh, she closed the door and turned towards the house. Then, she stopped and really looked at what she had allowed Henley Brook Farms to become. Without the horses to keep it cropped, the spring grass waved tall in the pastures. Weeds choked her flowerbeds so that the daffodils and tulips had to fight for space. She grimaced, wondering what had become of her peonies.

Slowly, she walked to the far side of the house, noticing the buds on the rhododendrons. The weeds poking up through the mulch began to offend her. She reached down and grasped a dandelion by the roots and carefully extracted it, root and all. She pulled another and then another. She realized that the fact that the weed came up so easily was a tribute to the past care she'd given the soil. *I am so glad!*

Suddenly, her fatigue dropped away and she sank to her knees. Before her, the beginnings of their dark-red foliage, clearly visible amid the bark chips and weeds, was the first growth of her peonies. These were the first flowers planted after they built the house. "Well," she said, dusting off her hands and straightening her back, "I know what goes on the list for the rest of my life...weeds."

The day was unseasonably mild. She noticed that it was actually quite warm on the south side of the house. She made a peanut butter and jelly sandwich and decided to eat it out on the screened kitchen porch. *It seems a very long time since I brought the black officer his cup of coffee on this porch while we waited for Peter and Patti's arrival... On the day that... Marshall died.* She finished the thought deliberately, and waited for the knife stab of pain. She absorbed it, and in her mind, pictured her strong, vibrant husband. After a bit, she nodded to herself. *Maybe it's going to be all right. Maybe Dr. Pagglio was right to have pushed the issue.* She made a face remembering. *Yes, he pushed the big button. He pushed it right after he said he was going to let me set the pace.*

Helen sat on the steps so she could feel the sun's warmth. She munched the sandwich and sipped a cup of tea. Her thoughts turned to her youngest. *What did Willie say about Torrey? It was something about how I turned her away... No, kicked her out. Those were his words.* She leaned forward and grabbed her knees, remembering Torrey's visit. She thought of the shoebox full of unopened letters and cards, some of which were from Torrey. The Rawling girls too, had written. *Sympathy cards, unanswered letters and two years of unopened Christmas cards and who knows what else is in those boxes that I barely looked at yesterday.* Helen shook her head in dismay. *It's first on the list. I'd better get started. I'll put weeding on as the second item.*

When she'd finished her sandwich, she looked at her wristwatch calculating the time. *I wonder what's going on at 4 o'clock in the afternoon at the Flat Creek Ranch.* She stood up and went into the house, struggling with herself. As she put her empty plate and cup in the sink she thought, *Chances are that Torrey will be in the house. Unless calving season has started, there isn't much that needs her attention outside. If I call and she's there, what could I possibly say to her? What words could possibly explain my rudeness? Torrey and Will don't have the money to throw away on a round trip plane ticket, and yet, she came. What could I possibly say about that? It would be far easier to write so I can think about what I really want to say.*

Even as Helen thought, she headed for the phone. *To hell with a letter, I need to know how they think Willie is doing, and I need to know it now!*

Torrey was in her sewing room in the midst of hemming a pair of Wranglers for Dewey when she heard the phone ring. With careful fingers, she pulled pins from her mouth. "Darn!" She pushed herself away from the old Singer sewing machine and headed for the kitchen. Just before she lifted the receiver, an odd feeling of relief swept over her and she was not surprised to hear Helen's shaky voice.

"Torrey, this is Helen. I wanted you and Will to know that I'm finally behaving rationally again. And I want to say how sorry I am for pushing you away when you came all that way to help," Helen said in a rush.

"Oh, God! Helen, I'm so glad you called; so glad for all of us. How are you, baby?" Torrey's knees felt weak. She pulled the long cord over to the stool by the sink and sat on it, listening intently.

"I...I...had a pretty tough time accepting Marshall's death. Then, last month, the kids decided to take matters into their own hands." Helen's voice broke and an odd sound that was half laugh, half sob came

130

over the phone. "It was either go to therapy or they were going to get me a puppy."

Torrey said, "I know. I know they did. God bless their hearts. I've been sending you prayers. How's it going?"

Helen could picture the tall woman perfectly; could see the love and wisdom shining in her eyes. "I can't say it's not hard and I can't say it's not painful, but I can say it is much, much better than trying not to feel anything at all."

"Your spirit was ready to return." Torrey said. "I believe it used your children as the messenger to let you know."

Helen was quiet, trying to view the world through Torrey's eyes. Her words were comforting. "I don't know about that, but I do know I needed the therapy more than I needed a puppy. Willie wanted to get me a puppy."

"Yes, I know that too. We keep in close touch with him. Actually, Helen, I don't believe Willie was serious about getting you a puppy."

Helen closed her eyes, allowing her son's angry words to wash through her mind. "Willie is one reason for this call. I--I heard from Peter about how much time he spent with you. I can't thank you enough. There are no words."

Torrey's voice rang strongly in her ear. "Don't thank us. We comforted each other. We were all pretty much in shock, but being older, Will and I understand that life on this side doesn't come with guarantees for old age. Willie, partly because of his youth, is having a hard time. I won't soft-pedal it."

"How IS he, Torrey? I know he's very, very angry with me and I understand and accept it. I called him and he really gave it to me. But, I guess I'm hoping he's been able to do well enough in school to keep his basketball scholarship, despite my horrid behavior. Peter did say he was still in school, thanks to you two, so I knew that."

131

"Yes, to both those questions. Yes, he's in school and doing fine. Yes, he's playing basketball and he's doing better than fine. He is the apple of the coach's eye. Will, Dewey and I even drove over to Eugene when he played his first varsity game. He's something special on a ball court, Helen."

Helen felt a rush of relief and then pride at Torrey's words. "Thank God! Torrey, on top of all the other guilt I've got to work through, I don't think I could stand to feel responsible for what I've done to Willie's life if he hadn't managed to succeed in spite of me."

"He's a good boy, Helen. He's still mixed up, as you probably know from talking to him."

"Yes, it really hurt when he unloaded on me. But oddly enough, it hurt in a good way. Like I told the therapist, I guess I needed him to be angry with me. I needed someone to be, anyway."

"Well," Torrey said, "that's over my head. All I know is that with him it is going to take some patience—time and patience. I know that you have plenty of both."

"Yes, yes, I do. Listen, thank you for coming. I know I was awful to you. But it was important that you came. I could feel you in the house long after you left that next morning."

Torrey closed her eyes remembering the sacred smoke ceremony. Perhaps she HAD left a piece of herself. "You're welcome," she said simply.

Helen was quiet for a moment. "I'm so glad I called. Please tell Will and Dewey hello for me. Are things fine with you?"

"Real fine. Both the girls are doing great. Tina has a new baby boy...boy number three, since we last talked." Torrey laughed. "And we've got some new colts to start this spring that Will is really excited about. He's got a new stallion... But that's another whole story. By the way, one of the colts is out of your old mare, Martha."

"That's great...great on all fronts. It makes me very homesick for you all."

"You can come out anytime you want to, baby. You hear me? We'll be waiting for you with bells on."

Helen smiled into the phone. "I don't know yet, Torrey. We'll see. It's just been since...today that I can actually think about Marshall in the past tense."

"Take your time. He was quite a man..." Torrey's voice petered out and the women fell silent. Helen kneaded the back of her neck and finally said, "Listen, I'll write you a long letter, but I need to hang up now. Thank you for the news. And thank you for being there for Willie when I couldn't be."

"It didn't feel like an obligation. You're family as far as we're concerned. But, I want to say again that you're sure welcome here. So do some thinking about coming out this summer."

"Maybe I will. But not right now. I'm going to take my first shoebox full of unopened mail out onto the porch while I still have sunshine, and get some sense of what's been going on in the lives of friends these past two years."

"Ah," said Torrey, "the Christmas cards."

"Yes, cards and Christmas letters. No matter what people think about them, they're one way to get caught up."

"Helen, will it make you sad?"

"I hope so. I hope they will also make me feel happy. I've gotten very tired of feeling nothing. I don't want to ever go there again."

"Well, welcome back, baby. We've sure missed you!"

Helen closed her eyes. "Thank you so much, Torrey. Please give the men my love. Goodbye for now."

"We love you, baby," was the last thing Helen heard Torrey say as she gently replaced the receiver and went to find a shoebox.

"At least ten. I'll read ten and then I'll go work

133

in my flower beds," Helen promised herself as she picked up the first box. The phone rang.

"Mom?"

"Willie?"

"Mom, listen, I'm really sorry about blasting you like that."

"Oh, Willie. Thank you for calling back. Listen. Don't be sorry. I just talked to Torrey and told her what I told my therapist...I think I NEEDED someone to be angry with me, crazy as that sounds. So, in a way, I should thank you."

"Mom! Don't thank me. God! Listen, I called Carrie and told her the whole conversation. She said, 'What are you going to do about it, Willie?' So, here's what I'm doing about it: I want to be able for us to talk once a week until I can be able to trust that I have my mom, the real Helen, back."

Tears sprang to Helen's eyes. "Willie, I couldn't ask for more. That you are giving me this second chance means the world."

She could hear the relief in his voice. "Great, I'll call you next Saturday. We'll be on the road, but I have a cell phone."

"I love you, son."

There was a long silence before Willie said slowly, "I love you too, Mom, but I sure hated that other bitch."

Helen's hiccup of laughter surprised them both. "I really, really hated her too, Willie."

Chapter Fourteen

It had been a seemingly endless flight. Helen fought a severe bout of nostalgia to a standstill

134

somewhere over Indiana, dozed fitfully over South Dakota, and woke with such a strong sense of Marshall's presence beside her that she turned to speak to him. It felt more comforting than discomforting; as though he were supporting her journey. By the time she landed in Denver and caught her connecting flight to Boise, she was finally certain her decision to visit the Rawlings had been right; just as Dr. Pagglio and the group had promised.

Her thoughts turned to the four men and women to whom she gave great credit for helping her find the courage to rebuild her life. A smile warmed her face. She looked down at herself. She was wearing her "ranch garb," the same clothing she had modeled for the group at the last session.

It couldn't be helped that the catalog-ordered Wranglers, though she had already washed them four times, looked brand-new. Her old Wranglers were still a good two sizes too large and had been left at home. But the stiff indigo of her new ones was off-set by her old, hand-tooled belt, scuffed-up Justin boots, and the old, XXX beaver Stetson Marshall had gotten her in Jackson, Wyoming, where they had gone on their honeymoon 36 years before. Her chambray shirt was also new, but came, at no small expense, looking and feeling well-worn.

As she pirouetted before the group, she knew her face was flaming. "Helen, you look like Barbara Stanwyck, when she played on television in *The Big Valley*," Aretha blurted out. "Girl, forget goin' to that podunk place in Nowheresville, Oregon, and get yo'sef straight to Hollywood. They need you, baby."

She had grinned, happily secure. With the group, trust was sacred. They'd seen her at her worst, sobbing and shaking, racked with pain, remorse and self-pity. They'd handed her tissues, patted her shoulder, and asked exactly the same sort of questions Dr. Pagglio had asked--as though they'd been coached. Which they actually had, in a way--since all of them had come, as she had come to him, for absolution; for relief; to have their lives, their sleep, their emotions returned to them. "I do look pretty good, don't I?"

Aretha nodded, absently rubbing the deep, jagged, straight razor scars running across her left wrist, eyes shining.

A soft voice behind her said, "Helen, your workouts are showing." She turned, smiling. James was the oldest in the group. As a young man, he'd been a nuclear engineer in Nevada during the underground A bomb testing in 1957. As a middle-aged man, he watched his wife die of leukemia, and in his old age, his two daughters, both mothers themselves, were undergoing treatment for metastasized cancer; one for bone, the other for breast.

"Thanks, James, you sly devil. I didn't think you'd noticed."

"A man is never too old to look, Helen."

She laughed and patted his wrinkled cheek before sitting down and looking at the tall man sitting quietly, watching her, palms steepled together, index fingers touching just under the tip of his hawkish nose. She smiled at him. "I'm going to dress like this for the trip west: hat, boots and all."

Dr. Pagglio nodded and the twinkle showed briefly. "Would you like to tell us how you came to that decision, boots and all, Helen?"

"Sure. It's simple. These clothes make me feel good. I think, perhaps, I was a cowboy in another lifetime."

No one smiled at her assertion; several heads nodded. She continued, "I remember the day Marshall had this hat made for me as a honeymoon present. It was the same day I rode my first western saddle. I was 20 years old and had ridden an English saddle all my life, but for the first time, I felt I could relax and look around while on a horse." She looked at the group, none of whom cared a thing about horses, but were smiling and nodding, pleased for her. She realized, as she stopped speaking, that she had used her husband's name without feeling the familiar stab of pain slicing through her, and waited quietly for someone in the group to comment. She was not disappointed.

"Helen! You used your husband's name and didn't put your hand to your heart and rock forward like you used to do. Is it getting easier?"

It was tiny Bianca, once a beautiful, popular teenager, now faced with countless reconstructive surgeries to rebuild her facial bones, and countless therapy sessions to help her face the fact that, with the help of alcohol and a new driver's license, she had caused the death of her best friend.

Helen looked directly into the scarred face. "Yes, so much easier, Bianca." Her words sounded like a promise. "When I put on these clothes, I could almost feel Marshall watching me. I think part of what wearing them is about is the fact that I have no bad memories to associate with them, only good memories; memories that bring me great comfort."

Helen jumped when the Captain's voice came crisply over the loudspeaker, announcing their descent into Boise and reminding them of tray tables, seatbacks and seatbelts. She sighed. One more flight on an air taxi and she'd be landing in the dusty, high desert, ex-logging town of Burns, Oregon, 38 miles south of the ranch.

On the telephone, Torrey said both she and Will were coming to pick her up. Once again, she began visualizing how it would be to spend time with them without Marshall and without the children. She tried to imagine how it would feel to ride through the sage, bitter brush and Indian paintbrush, maybe with strangers. Was she setting herself up to fall apart? This was ground she had covered with the group many times.

"Yes, I suppose I could be setting myself up, but I feel I can manage it." She had looked around at the concerned faces. "I'll probably feel sorry for myself from time to time, but I will rejoice at being able to feel something…which I now know is preferable to feeling nothing."

She wondered if any of the buckaroos, besides Dewey, were still there. *Probably not. Things change. I understand that.*

A lanky man with a Burns Aviation insignia on his ball cap and a snoose can in his snap-button shirt pocket walked up to her as she was waiting for the luggage belt to burp up her suitcase. "Mrs. Duncan?"

She nodded and smiled. "Yes, I am. Are you my pilot?"

He smiled down at her and she could see the skin under his lower lip stretch tight over a wad of tobacco. "Yep. Will told me what you'd look like." He paused and then added, "Sorta."

"Sort of?"

The man blushed pink under sandy-colored stubble. "Aw hell, ol' Will ain't never been good at tellin' weights. I know he guesses size-heavy on his fish and his bucks, guess he does on women too." He stuck out a freckled paw. "Name's Russell."

"Nice to meet you, Russell. Please call me Helen," she said as she shook his hand.

When her bag came, she reached down and grabbed it as it came sliding along the belt. Russell reached out, as if to take it from her, but then drew back. "Aw, now, don't tell me you're one of those liberated, got to carry my own bag, ladies?"

"It has wheels," she said, "but to answer your question, if your help is sincerely intended, it is sincerely accepted."

He took the bag from her, set it on its wheels and pulled the handle, then shot her a keen look, but made no comment other than to say, "Follow me," as he pulled the bag across the terminal, headed across the parking lot and towards the small gate in the chain-link fence. A sign on the building behind it read, Boise Aviation.

Helen shouldered her small carry-on and purse before walking quickly behind him. She smiled, watching the little wheels of her suitcase dangling in mid-air. *Yes, siree, Bob. A cowboy is a cowboy whether he is in a plane or on a horse.*

Russell punched the security code on the gate and led Helen through and across the tarmac towards a blue and white Cessna 182.

She said, "In the old days, we'd have to rent a car and drive to the ranch. This is much better."

Russell unlocked the cargo door and hoisted in her bags. "Next visit, you'll be able to fly direct from here to the ranch. Will's putting in a 4,000-foot paved strip."

Helen felt a shock run through her that tasted like fear, and realized how much she needed things at the ranch to be just the same. "I guess that's a good thing," she said slowly. "It will be better for their dude business."

"Better for the GUEST business," he said, as if correcting her grammar.

At her puzzled look he said, "You've got to say "guests," not "dudes." Torrey gets up a fine head of steam if she hears you call them otherwise."

Helen said, matching his serious tone, "Thanks, I'll remember that."

He lead to the right side of the plane and opened the cockpit door for her to climb in. It was the first time she'd ever ridden right-chair. That had been Marshall's place. Her place was in the back seat. *I can do this,* she thought to herself as she removed her hat, fastened her seatbelt, and settled the second set of earphones over her ears.

In minutes, Russell had them in the air heading due west. He grinned at her, reached to adjust her

139

mouthpiece closer to her lips and said, "Say something."

"I've never ridden up front in a small plane before. It's fun to be able to watch what you do."

Her comment pleased him for some reason, she could tell.

He adjusted the wheel, pushed on a knob and then asked, "How long you been comin' to the ranch?"

"I've been coming since the '60s, but my husband spent many of his boyhood summers here. His father and Will's father, Pete, were Army buddies."

Russell looked at her with new eyes. Long-time friendships, especially military friendships, were still respected in the wilds of Eastern Oregon. "I learned to fly with Uncle Sam," he said.

Helen was glad the subject had changed. She looked down at the black ribbon of highway, with its red cinder shoulders undulating through the sagebrush as far as she could see. "Do you enjoy it?"

"Yep. It's a fair livin' now that I'm doin' a little crop dustin' on the side. Gives me the time to do some huntin' and fishin'."

"How did you meet the Rawlings?"

"Just like this. I transport their guests."

He emphasized the word guests and when Helen laughed, he joined her and then said, "I also helped Will design the airstrip."

Helen sighed deeply. "Things change," she said and turned to look out the window, suddenly overcome with the need for sleep.

Russell watched her struggle to stay awake and then said, "Lots of folks find the drone of an engine and the warmth of the sun better'n a lullaby. You've got a little handle on the right side, back by your butt that will let you tip your seat back. Why don't you take a little siesta?"

Helen nodded, found the lever and fell immediately into a dreamless sleep...until Russell's voice crackled through the headset and into her ears.

"Best sit up now, Helen. We are just turning base and I see ol' Will's truck parked in the lot."

In seconds, the plane was down and Helen felt it shudder a little as Russell applied the brakes. It seemed to mirror her emotional state. *Please, dear God,* she prayed silently, *I know this trip isn't a mistake. I know I'm strong enough. But if I'm not, just don't let me revert to the ice princess, the weeping bowl of Jell-O, or worst of all, the control bitch. Let Dr. Pagglio and the group be right.*

She pictured them, encouraging her to take the trip. They would expect a full report, convinced that a week with the Rawlings was just the experience she needed, to finish letting go of the past and to start looking forward to the future.

As soon as Russell parked the plane and said, "Switch off," she lifted the headset, unbuckled her seatbelt, grabbed her hat and opened the door--only then remembering to look back at Russell for permission. He grinned and nodded and then she was gone, trotting across the hot pavement toward the advancing Rawlings, to be engulfed in the warming circle of their welcoming arms.

"Damned, if you ain't lookin' better than a grain-fed heifer." Will's voice growled in one ear.

"Oh my, but it's long past time. Welcome home, baby," Torrey whispered softly in her other ear.

They stood in a tangle of arms, hats askew simply hugging until Will broke the circle and stepped back. Torrey slipped an arm over Helen's shoulder and pulled her tight.

After a second, Helen found her voice. "What a treat to get you both! Don't you have other guests at the ranch?" Seeing Russell walking towards them with her gear, she emphasized the word "guests" and was rewarded with a quick grin.

Will nodded, dark brown eyes twinkling in his weather-beaten face. "Yep. We got two couples... Bird watchers." Will gestured towards the truck with its tarped load. "Shoot we already been all the way to Bend to buy out Costco today. Torrey did try to leave me back to baby-sit. But I told her 'nothin' doin.' I said, 'Them folks can take care of themselves 'til dinner time.'"

He sneaked a quick sideways glance at Helen. She must have created quite a stir at Dulles international Airport, he thought with pride. He had to admit her body looked good without the extra pounds she carried after the kids were born. Her face, though, told the real story and it broke his heart. There were lines where there hadn't been before and a clouded caution in her gold-brown eyes that told him to walk as softly around her as he would around a green-broke filly.

Half Scot, half Nez Perce, Torrey had gleaned the best from both cultures. She was practical, resourceful and carried an inner peace with her even under the most trying of circumstances. The things she felt most deeply about were seldom seen on her face. Now, Will watched how Helen clung and how tightly Torrey held her, walking hip to hip. He knew there was a transfer of strength happening that he couldn't begin to understand. His wife's black eyes caught his above Helen's head and held. Under her hat, salt-and-pepper hair was braided into a single long strand and even in brim-shadow, her face showed the etching of years of work in wind and weather. Will thought her especially beautiful at that moment.

Helen said, "Russell told me you are putting in an airstrip, so I know that's a change, but just tell me that the ranch hasn't really changed." She was amazed by her own fervor. "I can't believe how Boise has changed; all that good ranching and farmland turned into shopping malls and housing developments."

Will snorted. "Why sure the ranch has changed." He raised his hat and smoothed what was left of his gray hair. "We've got more of everything. More holes in the barn roof, more fences needin' mendin', more ditches needin' dug out. Ain't nothing changed other than a little buildin'..." His eyes softened. "Except, I do have some new colts for you to look at. You recall, I was dickering for a buckskin, that Triple Buck stud with the bad leg, last time you folks were here? Well, I got him. I can't ride him, of course, but he's managing to throw colts worth lookin' at."

Helen glanced at Torrey, who was possibly even a better judge of horse flesh than her husband. Torrey nodded and smiled. "Like I said on the phone, one of the three-year-olds is from your Martha mare. Martha hasn't been ridden much because of that colt and another, but Will had one of the boys tack on some shoes and get the witches' knots out of her mane and tail."

"I always knew Martha would throw good colts!" Helen declared with pride, thinking of the sweet-natured, long-legged sorrel mare Will had paired her with all those years ago. "Remember, Will, you heard it from me first."

They were standing in the shade of the airport office when she suddenly recognized that Marshall's name had not yet been mentioned; the children either, for that matter. It seemed time. "By the way, the children send their love. Patti and Peter are totally involved in being new parents, but you know that both Carrie and Willie would give their eye teeth to be here." She took another deep breath and played the words in her mind before saying them aloud. "Of course, they're worried how this will be for me, the first time back here without Marshall."

Will hunched his neck, as if groping for the right words, but finally, he simply reached out, took her elbow and steered her towards the truck saying, "So are we, kid. He was a damned fine man, just like his daddy before him...and a good friend to boot. We figure it might be real hard for you, at first."

Helen smiled, feeling the well of tears, but no numbing knife thrust of pain. "You two are pretty fine friends yourself. Thank you for sending the juniper boughs. It let me know you were thinking of me. Sorry I didn't get your holly sent. I will this Christmas, I promise."

She turned and waved over her shoulder to the hangar where Russell was removing the cowl from a small, battered looking, tail dragger. "Goodbye, Russell," she hollered. "Thanks for the flight and the company. See you on the return trip."

She saw him look up, wave. His voice drifted over the distance. "Have a good week, then."

Chapter Fifteen

Torrey driving, they piled into the dirt-brown club cab pickup with "Flat Creek Ranch" written on the side, and rode in silence. Helen was rendered speechless by the overwhelming comfort of being

144

shoulder to shoulder with her old friends. She was grateful to the point of tears to discover that she, indeed, was still to be included in their inner circle. As they drove north from the sleepy town of Burns through vast hay fields, Helen felt herself relaxing. Both redwing and yellow-headed blackbirds sang their songs from fence posts. A golden eagle drifted lazily in wind currents, looking for lunch on the freshly mown hay fields. The elevation was rising gradually and the fields gave way to sage and rabbit brush.

"How was your snowfall this year?" she asked Will.

"Real good. The top of Woolf Peak showed white 'til damn near the end of May. It should be a fine hay crop—if those boys keep from bustin' up the machinery." He looked at her and said, only half joking, "Where's that Willie of yours when I need him?"

"God, he loved running that swather, didn't he?"

Will nodded. "That, and damming up ditches…never saw such a boy for tryin' to improve my irrigation."

They rode quietly for a while and then Will rolled down his window and turned his head to spit a stream of snoose with the direction of the wind. Then, he said, "Helen, I don't know if you knew Willie came over and spent some time with us after Marshall died."

"Yes." She said, "Yes, I knew. Not at the time. Peter told me much, much later. But, I did know. And I want to…" Helen couldn't seem to stop talking until Will covered her hand with his and she felt the rough hardness of it asking her to get a grip.

"Easy, girl," he said gently. "Then, he came from Eugene by bus on his Christmas break. Torrey and I picked him up at the Burns Greyhound Depot. He did it with his coaches' blessin', by the way."

Torrey said, "We figured we'd better tell you right away that he'd told us some details. We didn't want it to feel like there were secrets between us."

Helen bowed her head and said bitterly, "Did he tell you I wouldn't let him come home that Christmas? That I wouldn't let any of them come home? Did he tell you I sold off all the horses without their permission?" Her voice caught and broke.

"Yes," Torrey said simply, "yes he did. It was a terrible, terrible time for all of you, Helen."

Suddenly, Helen realized that Will had a painful grip on her right hand. She glanced at him and saw he had no idea of the strength he was using. His jaw was rigid and he was staring, unseeing, out the front windshield. The physical pain centered her, allowing the emotional pain to recede. She reached over with her left hand and tapped her nails on his knuckles. "It's okay, Will," she said softly, as he released her hand with a jerk of awareness. "Torrey called it straight. It WAS a terrible time. I'm glad Willie had you on the West Coast to come to, and I thank you from the bottom of my heart. I went to hell for a couple of years, but now, thanks partly to the kids and partly to a good therapist, I'm back. I suppose I'm sadder and still a little lonely, but much, much wiser and stronger, I think."

Silence again filled the cab of the truck, softened only by the whir of the air conditioner; each lost in a jumble of feelings, memories and thoughts until Will reached an arm over the back of the seat and popped the top of the cooler sitting on the floor. He pulled out three icy beers, held by their plastic rings, purposely dripping ice water down Helen's neck as he did so, just like he had done when Helen first came to the ranch as a young wife. "Thirsty, anybody?"

He laughed as Helen jabbed him in the ribs with an elbow before saying, "God, yes, I'm parched. The in-flight service from Boise to Burns was nonexistent."

Will popped the tops and before he'd raised his, said, "Here's to Marshall. I hope he's lookin' down at us right now and givin' us his blessin'."

It took a moment for Helen to raise her beer, but when she did, she searched the rearview mirror to catch Torrey's eye. "And here's to dear friends."

"Ain't that right?" Will said before tipping his head back and drinking half his can with noisy swallows.

Torrey and Helen raised their cans. "To Marshall and to friends," Torrey said and she and Helen clicked their cans before drinking.

Will let out a huge sigh. "Damn me, but I got to say I'm glad we got that little talk done. Now let's get on with the catchin' up. Ask me some questions."

Helen laughed. "How many of your hands will I still know?"

"Well, Dewey is still struttin' around and fluffin' his feathers, tryin' to tell me how to run the place like always. I got the hay mostly contracted out, so you won't know those men. I got four semi-local boys helpin' with the cows that you may have run into some year or another. And we still got both of ol' Bob King's two young bucks, now and again, to help with the guests and do odd jobs, though they tell me this is their last year. I dearly hope it ain't true, as they are sure good with city people..."

Helen saw Torrey glance sideways and make a face at her husband. He laughed and added, "...especially with some of the lady guests, now that they're both shavin' regular and are drinkin' their beer legal." He went on. "You'd be proud to know I hired me a female wrangler and got Torrey a strapper to help her with the heavy work. Ain't I gettin' modern?"

"Interesting." Helen said, not at all deceived. "Why?"

Torrey hooted. "Why? Yes, Will, you tell her why."

Helen took a sip of beer and turned so she could see his face. Will was looking sheepish. "The kid said he was good with colts, but he had the hands of a sod buster and the seat of a circuit ridin' preacher. But

the girl…first time I seen her ride, I knew I was lookin'
at our Tina all over again. That girl made me want to
stomp out a little joy dance, just to see the music she
made, playin' those pretty colts like they was fiddles."

Helen grinned at him. "How is Tina, by the
way?"

Torrey smiled. "Fat! Fat, but happy. Being the
wife of a minister seems to agree with her. She's
pregnant again and praying for a girl. She says if she
gets a girl, she'll name her Faith because she kept the
faith that God would finally send her something to put
ruffles on."

Helen smiled. "I finally got around to opening
my Christmas cards in June and Tina had sent a family
picture. What did she promise those boys to get them
to look so angelic?"

Torrey laughed. "Funny, that's the same thing I
wondered. They are cute, though. Every time they
come to the ranch, I end up just squirting them down
with the garden hose after they are done playing. Then
I strip them down to their skins before I'll let them near
the lodge. 'Course, Mister Big Shot over there spoils
them to damn death and Dewey isn't a lick better."

Helen took a long drink of beer. The easy
conversation and scenery flowed through her veins like
spring water. They talked of the Rawlings' older
daughter, Julie, who had lived with the Duncans while
attending George Mason University on a language
scholarship, but now lived in Paris, France. Helen
handed Will her beer and pulled a picture of her
granddaughter from her wallet. "Here's our Ashley Ann.
Look at that mop of hair! She's clearly a Duncan. They
came down for a visit two weeks ago, and I could tell
Peter really wanted to come with me. He wants you to
meet both Patti and Ashley and he sends his love."

The Rawlings passed the picture back and
forth. Then Helen filled them in on Carrie's post-doc
work at the University of Texas. "I flew down for her
graduation this June. It was wonderful."

The Rawlings already knew that Willie still had his basketball scholarship and the fact that he was spending the summer as a commercial fisherman in Alaska. What they didn't know was that the lucrative job had been offered only to selected athletes by a U of O alumni sports fan, so Helen filled them in. She told them, too, of their weekly phone conversations and how it seemed to be healing their bond.

Will told her how they now offered guest packages at the ranch that included driving the cattle into the high country for the summer graze in the spring; and another when they brought them down to winter on the ranch in the fall. "I hear there's some that's makin' a livin' off guests by just drivin' them poor critters up and down the mountainside all season long, play pretendin' their guests are doing real ranch work." He snorted. "I reckon I'd have to turn in my spurs before then."

They continued north on US Highway 395, still climbing gently. The Rawlings' ranch backed onto a corner of the Ochoco National Forest. They owned 85,000 acres outright and also bought Forest Service grazing permits so they could graze cattle on the lush forest meadows during the summer. They sent over 500 head of beef to market every year. Still, Helen knew the only reason they could survive the falling beef prices, the rise in taxes, insurance and government fees, was because the ranch was paid for. Will's father, Pete, had been wise enough to turn it into a corporation before he died, so they had not lost it to inheritance taxes.

When they came up over a ridge and Helen saw the rock outcropping and a stand of ponderosa pine flanking both sides of the road, she knew they were almost to the ranch turn-off. She was amazed at her serenity. Torrey made a practiced wheel-sliding 180-degree turn onto the gravel road, barely slowing down and Helen's head began a slow swivel so as not to miss a thing. The big gates, as usual, were open and

149

welcoming. The hand-carved, "Flat Creek Ranch" sign high over the opened gates looked newly painted. The road bent suddenly to the right around the rock saddle and she could see the upper hay fields in the distance. A jolt of joy went through her. *Oh, Dr. Pagglio, I've come such a long way,* she thought gratefully as she welcomed the feeling and allowed it to spread.

The old-fashioned split rail fence still snaked its way along the road and, in one pasture, range bulls lay under a ponderosa pine tree, concerned only with chewing their cuds. As they drove up the rise toward the lodge, she could see down the slope to the corrals where, as always, the unused horses stood drowsing, waiting patiently to be turned back out onto the rich pasture at day's end. Up the slope, on a bench, she could see a yellow, D-6 Caterpillar parked on some newly turned earth and knew she was looking at the start of Will's airstrip. Somehow it made her sad. She drew in a deep breath and changed her thoughts.

"It was lovely of you both to come and retrieve me, when you're so busy. I can't thank you enough. I feel more than properly welcomed."

Torrey nosed the club-cab into its spot beside the kitchen door. "Glad we could do it. Lucky you came this week. Next week, the place is going to be crawling with Hollywood types. We've been discovered."

Helen looked at her with surprise. "Discovered?" "Hollywood types? What do you mean? Are you saying Hollywood has discovered the ranch?" She looked at Will.

There was a strange look on his face. Even expressionless Torrey looked a little grim. "I dunno," Will said, as he climbed in the back of the truck, unleashed the tarp and started handing out sacks of groceries to Helen and Torrey. "Maybe so. Last year was their first year. There was only four of them...which was plenty. This year there's ten."

"Ten? Does that mean they rented all five cabins?"

Will nodded. "Only we built two new cabins since you were here last. You're welcome to try one of them... Of course, cabin A is yours, should you want it."

Helen knew what he was saying. Cabin A had been their family cabin; one of two with two bedrooms and a loft. If it was her decision whether she wanted it or not, there was no contest. She was healing, but not healed. "One of the new cabins would be fine, if it's not spoken for."

"It's not. All four of the birders are in cabin B, happy as clams at high tide." He looked at her and smiled. "You're going to like it. Both of the new cabins got little decks overlookin' Flat Creek, mosquito screens and their own little indoor pot, sink, refrigerator, and tin shower...pure heaven."

Torrey made a space on the counter for Helen's load of groceries and took them from her arms. "I'll have Jake, that's my new helper since Will stole my girl, finish the groceries. Why don't you check out your cabin and go on down to the corrals with Will. Don't you know he's dying to show you the colts?"

Will came in carrying two cases of Budweiser beer followed by a lanky, slab-tailed boy Helen didn't know. "This here's Jake," Will said. "Jake, meet Helen. You treat her right. She's family." Jake ducked his head and seemed to be trying to hide behind Will's broad back. Torrey was smiling and Helen tried not to laugh at his obvious bashfulness. "Nice to meet you, Jake," she said, stepping around Will and holding out her right hand.

Jake's face flared as though someone had lit a match to it. He mumbled something unintelligible, set down his load and grabbed her hand, giving it a quick pump and dropping it as though it were covered with nettles. He glanced at Torrey and turned to bolt from the kitchen. "Gotta take the bags to the cabin," came mumbling over his shoulder.

Torrey frowned as she walked over and lifted a key from the peg by the door. "Don't think it's just you, Helen. I believe he's the most backward child I've known and it somehow makes him clumsy. If I could hold his nose and make him swallow a dose of whatever makes those King boys so all fired cocky, I'd do it and he'd be better off for it."

Helen tried to keep her face from showing surprise. It was totally out of character for Torrey to make such an observation; she wondered what else was going on. *Perhaps she feels she didn't get the best end of the staff swap.*

"Here, honey," Torrey said, handing her the key, her voice again smooth, "we call your cabin the Rainbow Cabin because it's built right above that deep hole where the trout congregate in September."

Helen took the key and stepped outside the lodge, glad for the moment alone. She looked at her watch and turned the hour hand back three hours as she walked towards the two new log cabins, nestled at a discreet distance from each other. *5:00 o'clock here means 8:00 o'clock at home. No wonder that beer tasted so good.* She stepped up and into the tiny, screened front porch, with its two willow chairs and pot of petunias on the low table. She recognized Torrey's touch. *This is going to be wonderful,* she thought as she unlocked the door. And it was! It smelled of wax and new wood and sunshine. The bed was also made of pine logs, but the dresser and armoire were of old mission oak. A double wedding ring quilt covered the bed and a rag rug covered most of the floor. A blue crockery pitcher filled with paintbrush, buttercups, wild strawberry blossoms and daisies sat nodding on the dresser. It was cool and quiet except for the soft sound of the creek as it dropped past the final rocks and into the big pool off her back deck. *Heaven!* She thought as she picked up her suitcase from the steps where Jake had left it, closed the screen door behind her and stood on the deck. *I have died and gone to heaven!*

152

Two more willow chairs and a small trunk, holding a citronella candle and an ashtray, sat on the mosquito-proofed back deck. Helen noticed with satisfaction that Will had not ruined fly fishing access to the hole with the placement of the new cabins. She closed her eyes and could almost see her husband raise his arm for a back cast in the slanting light. *Marshall, you would adore this cabin. There are screens on the windows, a lovely breeze and a firm bed.* Suddenly, her body ached for his touch. She closed her eyes and wrapped her arms around herself, almost attempted to lay on the bed and play, "let's pretend," a game of self-stimulation only Dr. Pagglio knew about. Instead she opened her eyes and walked inside to look at herself in the armoire mirror. A pair of haunted brown eyes and a perfect oval face looked back at her from under the brim of her hat. A trip to Monique's had changed her mousy, graying hair to a subtly highlighted tawny brown. She had continued to pull her hair back, usually held casually in place by a heavy gold barrette at the nape of her neck, but it did not look peeled back. The color and a soft body perm softened the effect. Being 5' 8", she was not a small woman, but had gone from a lumpy size 14 to an athletically trim-sized 10, thanks to Dr. Pagglio's advice about the effect of diet and exercise on depression. She still had generous hips and more bust than was fashionable. And even with exercise, her stomach bulged slightly below her belt... *But,* she grinned into the mirror, *not bad for 55 and three kids.* She unbuckled her belt and re-tucked her shirt, smoothing her hands over her hips. "Well," she said softly to the person in the mirror, "Enjoy yourself."

Chapter Sixteen

As Helen walked beside Will, past the bunkhouse and towards the corrals, she wondered abstractly about what she had meant by, "Enjoy yourself." It wasn't the words that worried her, it was her hands on the hips, body posture. Was she trying to look seductive? She shook her head and let the thought go, stealing herself instead against any sadness that might catch her unaware on this first visit to see the horses.

When the children were young, they asked to be let out of the truck as they came past the barn. They were always so eager to see Dewey and the horses, the children trying to guess which horse Will had slated for their particular use.

Helen heard a whoop and looked up. Dewey was striding towards her with his blue-heeler, Queenie, at his heels. "I'll be damned if you ain't somethin'? Takin' your sweet time comin' down to the corrals to see old Dewey like you didn't..." The little man stopped midsentence and snatched his battered felt hat from his head, suddenly remembering Helen's circumstances.

Helen smiled and put her hands on his shoulders. At 5'8", she wasn't really tall, but she towered over him. "Hello, old friend," she said. "As Will and I were walking down here, I was just remembering how, each time when we arrived, the children always asked to be let out at the corrals." She pulled him close for a hug, knowing there was nothing that embarrassed him more or gave him more pleasure. "My, but I've missed you," she said softly. "All the children send their love."

Behind them Will snorted. "Ain't that just like him, the puffed-up, little banty rooster! Thinking all these years it's been him you rush down to see, instead of the horses."

Queenie was sniffing her pant leg, looking for

familiar smells and finding   few. Helen knelt down. "Sorry, Queenie, these are straight from the catalog. Try my hand instead."

They watched as the roan-blue dog's tail began a slow, steady wag. The dog remembered most of the regulars, especially those who spent as much time with the horses as Helen and her family had. Suddenly, she whined, lifted her head and then looked about with expectation.

"Yep. That's her signal," Dewey said quickly, pretending not to notice that his dog was looking for the other Duncans. "Even after almost three years, she remembers you. Ain't she Dewey's little ol' elephant? What a memory!" He gave the dog a gentle boost with the side of his boot. "Now move your carcass, the lady wants to see the horses."

Helen rose to her feet, inordinately pleased that the famous Queenie had seemed to remember her, though she hadn't offered a paw.

It was quiet in the corrals. The horses were standing around in social groups, some nose to tail, some in mixed groups, only a few standing completely alone. All were relaxed, half asleep, waiting for the gate to open and a wrangler to drive them back to the big pasture for the night's feed. Helen climbed up the heavy, log corral and sat on the top pole, looking her fill, working to keep her breathing even as memories crowded in on her. She found she had no desire to get closer, to touch them. Will and Dewey leaned on the fence below her, holding their silence. "Recognize anybody?" Will finally asked.

"Of course!" She was able to answer with a light and steady voice. "Martha has a little belly, but she looks good. Sheba is finally starting to show her age though, isn't she?"

Helen heard Dewey give the bark that served as his laugh. "You let Tina's little hellions on your back and see how you look when they're done. That old mare and Bear deserve baby-sitting medals. Their grandpa'd better find them somethin' a little more ornery so they can learn respect."

Helen only half heard the banter. Her eyes drifted over Jasper, with his apron-faced blaze and high stockings. He was Marshall's favorite. Bear, Sheba's buddy and the only pony in the herd, was sleeping with his head and neck under her belly. Remembering how they brought him to the ranch and how their three kids would take him down to the swimming hole and use him for a diving platform, choked her. *I must be more parsimonious at rationing these precious memories,* she thought as her senses flooded and her eyes filled. She was glad the men couldn't see, as she raised her eyes from the sturdy pony, now grown old to the point of moth-eaten, and focused on the horizon, overcome with surges of emotion she refused to deny. In a moment, her focus narrowed. "There is a rider coming," she was able to say.

"Probably At. She said she was going to wet the saddle blankets of those colts today," Dewey said, climbing up to join her. They watched the pair come through the horse pasture. The colt was tired, intent on rejoining the herd. The rider was insisting they stop and do large, lazy figure eights, both at a lope and a trot with plenty of stops and quiet standing in between. Once or twice, the rider pulled the colt from the trail, crossed Flat Creek and went angling up a side hill and then back down; the colt being asked to take a straight line and clear the obstacles in his way.

Will's right, Helen decided, *the girl reminds me of Tina, too. She's inside that horse's brain, anticipating his every move.*

About a quarter-mile from the corrals, the girl dismounted and loosened the colt's cinch. She stood quietly by the horse's neck. Helen noticed that Will, too, had climbed up and was watching. He nodded when the girl finally stroked the colt's neck and began to lead him in. He turned to Helen. "Ain't she somethin'? She's givin' that youngster one helluva education and not doin' him one bit of harm."

Helen nodded, her eyes filled with appreciation of both the girl and the red, chisel-headed colt with the deep chest and well-muscled rump. By the length of the slender neck and the way it flexed where it joined the throat-latch, Helen knew she was looking at Martha's baby. "He sure has his mother's headset," she said.

Will was unsurprised by her keen observation. Helen had always known her horses, though she had ridden pancake saddles all her life. It was Marshall who taught her Western riding and she'd taken right to it from the first. "Yep, goin' to have Martha's good withers once he gets growed. He's got his daddy's butt though." He gave Helen a nudge. "Come on; let's go see the old rascal. Then we'll have a gander at Sheba's babies and some of the others, so you can see what I mean about being pleased."

Helen followed Will across the ranch yard towards a stout Powder River corral attached to the north side of the barn. There the stallion stood, drowsing in the fading warmth of the sun. Even asleep, the horse radiated maleness and power.

Will gave a sharp whistle just to take pleasure from watching the horse snap to instant alertness. For a moment, he stood poised, ears pricked, neck arched, locating Will. Then he nickered and moved forward, the stiffness of his gait instantly marring the image of perfection.

Helen watched, silently trying to separate the grotesquely swollen, stiff fetlock joint from the rest of the horse and failing. She found it difficult to watch...in fact, almost impossible. *He reminds me of a person with an ill-fitting artificial leg.* It was all she could do not to turn away. She forced herself to say, "He's not in any pain, is he?"

Will shook his head as the stallion gimped towards them. "Not much, anyway. Sometimes he can get feelin' frisky and start buckin' and runnin'. Then he really limps around for a couple of days. Sometimes I pop some butazolidin into him and that helps."

Will's voice drifted to a stop. A puzzled expression crossed his face. *What's wrong with Helen? Her voice don't sound right. And how come she didn't offer the back of her hand to Packer when he come to say hello? She didn't say one damned word about his confirmation, his attitude or his soft eye, like she generally would.*

Will found his feelings were hurt, partly on the stud's behalf, partly on his own behalf. He slid back the gate bar and walked into the corral, shutting it behind him, leaving her on the outside. The stallion flipped his nose in the air and blew a great blast of air. Will laughed and walked straight up to him, grasping the masculine jowls in calloused hands. *God I love this horse! He's everything a stallion should be...except sound. He'll never be sound. Never be rideable. It don't matter. He's imprinted his great potential on his sons and daughters like he was meant to do.*

The two stood like statues, the big man and the big horse. *God damn! I never could've afforded this horse if he'd had four good legs. If it hadn't been for me, he'd be dog food. Don't she understand that?* He absently began stroking the strong, dusky-gold neck. *I reckon you can take a gal out of the city, but you can't take the city out of the gal,* he decided sourly.

Some of the joy had gone out of his day. He jerked his thumb over his shoulder. "That black three-year old is Sheba's. The buckskin, six-month-old filly is from a grade mare I bought just after your last visit." His voice petered out and he made no move to take her into the colt pasture to meet the rest of the youngsters. Helen didn't seem to notice, just shaded her eyes and looked where he pointed in the next pasture without comment. She didn't even seem to notice Martha and Sheba's other babies that were grazing further out in the pasture where the rest of the youngsters grazed.

The stud suddenly jerked his head up, giving some unseen thing quiet attention. The girl, At, appeared around the corner of the barn, leading the unsaddled colt. She saw Helen and Will and stopped. The colt halted respectfully behind her. Will heard her soft, "Good boy!" and then saw the flick of a listening ear and felt better. He watched her walk up to Helen. "Howdy, I'm At," he heard her say before he could get the words out to introduce them.

"Hello, At, I'm Helen. I watched you riding this guy in and admired your talent."

"Thank you, ma'am. Colts this quality make me look good."

They stood smiling at each other. It was only on horseback that the girl looked like Tina, Helen decided. Up close, she was very different. Where Tina, at this age, had been tall and willowy with fine bones and small delicate features, this girl was raw-boned with generous features and a rosy, freckled complexion. "How did you come by the name At?" She asked.

At laughed. "My real name is Marilee, but Will saying, 'Atta girl' to me so often when I started workin' with his colts, got Dewey calling me that....And somewhere along the line, it got shortened from Atta Girl, to At."

Helen laughed a good, clear laugh and stepped forward. "It's how nicknames get started, I suppose." She reached out her hand to let the colt have a sniff. "I know this is Martha's baby. May I give him a scratch?"

"Sure," At said, "but don't let him rub on you. He's had a hard time learnin' not to do that and he's awful tired and itchy right now."

From inside the corral, Will and the stallion watched as Helen first scratched him and then studied the colt. Will supposed it was the first time she'd been even close to a horse since Marshall's death. "What's his name?" he heard her ask.

"Mac. Like a cross between Martha and Packer."

Helen wrinkled her forehead. "Packer?"

At looked over to where Will and the stallion stood. "His daddy's name is Packer," she explained. "So, we call Sheba's baby Shaq and Martha's baby Mac." She smiled at Helen as if she had just shared something very important and then said, "Excuse me while I put this guy away. I worked his little tail off and he deserves a good roll."

Helen watched her back and was struck by the girl's confidence and natural manners. *That's a fine young woman,* Helen thought. *Someone's certainly raised her right.*

Will let himself out of the stallion's corral and stood by Helen as they watched the colt fold his knees in a sandy spot inside the wire gate and plop on his side, rubbing his jaw along the sand before rolling his whole body on one side and then rolling to the other to repeat the process.

"Those youngsters are all keepers, Will," she said softly. He wondered if she realized she had not included Packer in her comment, had made no comment about him at all. He took her elbow and said, "Torrey'll be wondering where we are. Let's go see if we can find us a drink before the hay crew and the birders turn up starvin' for dinner."

Will looked down at the top of her cowboy hat as they walked, glad he could no longer see her face. *There's something eatin' away at her,* he thought. When they left the stud's corral, her face had a pinched, closed look and now her shoulders were hunched like she was cold. He felt like kicking something. Being around her made him miss Marshall something fierce. *God damn those high-strung thoroughbreds and the son-of-a-bitches that breed them up to be basket cases anyway! To what purpose? So they can run around the track a little faster? Jump a little higher over some stupid man-made obstacle*

160

course? How's a man supposed to make sense of that?

All Will knew was that his best and oldest friend was dead and his widow had nearly broken the hearts of three fine kids in her grief. His mind flipped back to how Willie had cried in Torrey's arms...how they'd all cried...and then Will did the only thing he could think of, put him on tall, gentle Chainsaw and took him out to look at the irrigation system. Afterwards, he sat Willie down in front of the big stone fireplace and poured him drinks of Black Velvet and ginger ale until it almost ran out of his ears. When the boy got a little drunk and Will was feeling mellow, they had talked about Marshall.

Will told him some stories he'd never meant to tell. Coming-of-age stories, stories about when they were roommates at Blue Mountain Community College. Stories about his signing up for the Air Force and Marshall signing up for the University of Oregon; high school stories about girls and getting drunk out in the sagebrush under a summer moon; and stealing beer from the Seneca grocery store; and fighting town kids. He went clear back to the beginning and told all the often-heard war stories that had made his own father and Willie's grandfather more like brothers than friends. "You got to give your mom time, son. Best thing you can do is stay in school and try to concentrate, just like she asked. You keep busy and work hard. Make your dad proud," he'd said, just before the boy went to sleep in the big chair.

He thought it was good advice and Torrey had agreed with him. He wished they could have gone east for the memorial service though. He faulted Helen for not letting them know in time--tried not to hold it against her, but he did. He sighed and looked down at her again, wondering what all she had been through these past three years to be able to pick herself up and get back on track. "You still drink Black Velvet?" he asked.

She looked up at him as though she too had let her thoughts drift somewhere far away and then with

161

effort, smiled and nodded. The hay crew was swimming in the pond. The birders were sitting on the front porch of the lodge drinking something tequila-laced and bright orange-pink. Before Will even reached the steps they started raving about their day. Binoculars still around their necks, feet up, drink in hand, they told of ibis, egrets, eagles and songbirds too numerous for any but dedicated birders to remark on. Will listened politely, introduced Helen to them and went on into the lodge, leaving Helen to listen and look at their lists.

"Have you been down to the Malheur Wildlife Refuge?" She asked.

They all look like academics of some sort, she decided. From their odor, they were covered with mosquito repellent. All were wearing good sturdy hiking shoes and shorts with multiple pockets; they looked competent. College professors and L. L. Bean, Eddie Bauer or Land's End shoppers, she decided.

One of the men answered, "We meant to go yesterday, and then for certain we were going to go today. But, we're having so darned much fun and seeing so many new species right on the ranch, we can't seem to get organized enough to go."

Will had introduced the man speaking as Hank. He looked to be in his early 60s and fit. *A runner perhaps?* In fact, as she looked at them, she decided they all looked physically fit. They also looked very comfortable and satisfied with each other's company. She leaned back against the porch rail and smiled at them. "Old friends?" she asked.

They looked at each other. "Better than that," said Hank, pointing to the woman named Meg. "That's my wife and that's my brother."

His brother laughed and said, "and Meg and my wife, Lee, are sisters."

"Gracious!" Helen said, "I hear a good story coming, but first I need to go find Torrey and start earning some keep. I'm working for my room and board here."

Well, that wasn't exactly true, she thought to herself, glad neither of the Rawlings heard her say it. But she felt fragile somehow and not in the mood to make chit-chat with strangers, not even very nice strangers as these four seemed to be.

When she walked into the kitchen, Torrey gave her a big grin from where she stood slicing a head of cabbage into sliver-thin pieces. "How's it going?"

Helen glanced at Jake who slid a glance towards her, turned red and went back to peeling potatoes and carrots in silence. She decided not to add to his embarrassment by greeting him. "Fine, Torrey. Wonderful! Queenie remembered me and the colts are stunning. But, now I'm ready to help and don't tell me, No."

Torrey paused for a moment and looked closely at Helen. "Okay then," she said with barely a pause, "Go stir the beans and then set the table for 14. You remember where everything is?"

Helen nodded, suddenly feeling a world better at having a task to do. She walked past the stainless steel sink where Jake stood, and snatched a carrot slice from his pile. "Thanks!" She said and went right on walking so he would know she wasn't asking for conversation from him, only the carrot. She grabbed a big quilted mitt and pulled the bean pot forward. When she lifted the lid, the smell reminded her how long it had been since she'd eaten. "God, this smells good!"

She said it with such reverence that Torrey laughed. "We do know how to make beans around here." They were made from scratch, thick, dark and laced with hunks of bacon, onion and peppers.

"How long until dinner?" Helen asked.

"About 20 minutes after I whistle the hay crew out of the pond. Will went to make our drinks, but then the phone rang, so we're sort of waiting on him."

Helen grabbed a wet towel and drifted into the dining room to wipe down the red and white checkered oilcloth on the long table before going to the sideboard for the paper napkins, plates and silverware. As she set the table, she counted heads. 14 people meant the King brothers were elsewhere. Will came in and handed both his wife and her a healthy drink of Black Velvet and 7-Up. "Thank you," she said. "By the way, where are the King boys?"

Will smiled. "The're packin' supplies to the buckaroos at the line camp up in the Ochocos, and doing a little fishin' along the way. Once the Hollywood crowd gets here, they aren't goin' to have time to do much more than wipe butts and fix drinks. It's goin' to be, 'Oh, Buck, will you check my cinch, honey?' And, 'Billy, be a darlin' and run get me a real cold beer.'"

Helen looked up at him. "Whew!" was all she said.

Will smiled. "And that was with only four of them. I don't really want to imagine what it will be like with ten." He paused, "But don't get me wrong. To be fair, it was really only the one woman who seemed to think she was God's gift to the country set. She's married to an older, gay man, so maybe that's why she behaved like she did, jumpin' buck-naked into the pond, runnin' her pretty pink nails up them poor pantin' boys' arms and such."

Helen threw back her head and laughed. It felt as though something hard and tight popped right out of her throat when she did it. Will looked a little startled and then snorted. "You go ahead and laugh, but if I can keep Torrey from killin' one of them, it's goin' to give me the chunk of change I need to finish my airfield up on the bench."

He did not add, "I'm sure not going to make it with my calf crop." But, from years past, Helen knew he was thinking the words and it sobered her, though only somewhat. She took a healthy swallow of her drink, feeling feather-light. "Thank goodness it's only for a week then. Surely everyone can behave themselves for that long."

Will leaned against the sideboard and looked at her. "We'll have to let you know," he said.

Chapter Seventeen

At 4:00 A.M., Pacific Standard Time, Helen's eyes opened and she lay quietly, vestiges of a vivid dream still floating on the edges of her consciousness; clouds turning into horses, horses dissolving into wind. She was there, on the scene, but only as an unseen observer, looking up at the movement, enjoying the weightless energy and freedom of the sky horses. What did it mean? She believed dreams could be interpreted, especially those that came again and again. But this was a brand-new dream and carried none of the nightmarish overtones of those she'd lived with for over two years. This one was lovely, almost spiritual. She resolved to remember the details to share with Torrey.

She propped up on an elbow and looked out her window. "Too early," she mumbled to herself. "I'm still on East Coast time." The sky held only a tinge of light, but already birds were rioting in the willows by the creek. She wondered, as she punched her pillow and snuggled back down under the quilt, if the birders were already up, spying on the early morning absolutions of the songsters and smiled. *What nice people! They are so easy-going, liberated, tolerant in their views and genuinely funny. How lucky to have gotten them as fellow guests instead of the Hollywood crowd.*

She sighed. Early or not, like it or not, she was rested and wide-awake. She moved her hands down over her stomach remembering the gigantic meal she'd eaten the night before: pork roast, mashed potatoes, coleslaw with carrots and apples, biscuits, and Torrey's wonderful beans. *Did I really add peach cobbler on top of that? Not the way to keep this new figure,* she scolded herself. *No more of that!*

Her hands stayed on her belly, slowly massaging, hiking her soft, white cotton nightgown up in the process. Almost without thinking, her hand sought bare skin and continued to knead, moving ever so slowly down, down, until her fingers rested lightly on

166

her pubic hair. When her fingers slipped slowly in to touch herself, she whispered, "Oh, Marshall!"

Then, suddenly she opened her eyes and jerked her hand away. *NO! NO! No more playing 'Let's pretend!'*

Lifting her bottom, she roughly jerked the nightgown back down around her legs, flipped over onto her side and curled into a ball. *Keep your hands away from there. He's gone. He's not coming back, and it does you no good to indulge in pretending otherwise.*

The words rolled through her head like a mantra. She and Dr. Pagglio had covered this ground, after a few false starts. "Are you asking for my permission to masturbate, Helen?" he'd asked.

She remembered her shame; remembered burying her head in her hands and shaking it. "No."

The silence had lengthened. He was a master at waiting out a struggling client. *Why did I say, "No?" What did I mean when I asked him what he thought about self-stimulation? Why is it so hard to just tell him it was how I keep Marshall's memory alive? Why can't I just admit that the secret, sexual part of our lives, even after three kids, was our life's elixir?*

In their long married life, they had developed secret looks, secret touches and a code language that personified their desire and their trust in each other. *God, how I miss that physical part of our closeness!*

Helen remembered how hard it was to tell Dr. Pagglio that she missed the closeness of their lovemaking more than she missed their conversations, which sometimes seemed to turn into battles for dominance. In the bedroom there was none of that. Their non-verbal communication was perfect, exciting and fulfilling.

Finally, more tears and then the words had come stumbling out. "I've let him go, except for that one area. When I touch myself, I pretend my hands are his hands. I hold conversations with him in my head. I

167

remember his moans and even try to imitate them. The fingers on my nipples are his. I even put his aftershave on so I can pretend to smell him. I keep thinking of other things to do to make it even more real…"

Dr. Pagglio said softly, "I see what you mean. Something is going on for you that's a lot more than self-stimulation, and it worries you."

"Yes. It feels… Unhealthy. It feels like an addiction."

"How so?"

"I let it dominate my thoughts. I promised myself I won't do it, but then I do."

"Often?"

"On the bad days, two or three times; sometimes, only once."

"Has the frequency been going up or down?"

"Up. Not the frequency, actually, but the time spent thinking about it; actually preparing my bath, choosing the music, lighting the candles…that's going up."

A clenching fear dried Helen's tears. *Oh, my God! He may think I'm crazy; may think I need to be committed!* She raised her eyes and looked at the doctor. His gentle brown eyes calmly looked back. "This is hard stuff to talk about, Helen. I'm proud of you. Let's keep on a little longer and see if we can't find some light in this tunnel. Here's the next question: How do you feel when you're done creating and participating in this fantasy?"

Helen had lowered her eyes, thinking. *How DID she feel?* Again the silence lengthened as she sorted through the tangle in her mind. *How do I feel afterwards? God! There has to be some word in the English language that would work!* But she couldn't find it and finally looked up and shrugged. "A feeling doesn't come to mind right now. I guess I just feel…suspended."

He didn't seem upset by her admission. "Here's the thing: Behaviors that continue are somehow

168

reinforced. Because the attention to the behavior is increasing, there is something in the sequence of events you are setting up, that gives you pleasure…or rewards you in some way."

"And you don't think it's the orgasm, do you Doctor?"

He shook his head. "I don't know. If it is, it seems like you might have said, when I asked you how it made you feel, 'relaxed, fulfilled, happy'…or some other post-orgasmic word…so it should make us wonder."

Helen always noticed when Dr. Pagglio used the word "us." It always made her feel supported and so much less alone.

"You don't think I'm crazy?" she'd asked.

He'd raised his eyebrows, a characteristic gesture, and looked at her without smiling. "Nope." He said simply.

"'Why am I doing this?' is the question you need to ask yourself. Or perhaps, 'When I'm engaging in this elaborate form of masturbation, what am I avoiding'?"

Helen threw back the quilt and got out of bed. She walked to her suitcase and pulled a well-used journal out of a zippered pocket, then pattered to the window to look out at the creek. She was surprised to see a ghostly form just out of clear vision range in the pre-dawn light and convective creek fog. What she could see, though, was poetry in motion; a fluidity of casting skill that marked a master fly-fisherman. *Probably one of the birders,* she thought and then scurried back for the warmth of her bed.

She opened the simple spiral-bound, book and noted: *Monday, August 21, 1998.* Then she began to write.

Yesterday was eventful. Seeing the Rawlings, feeling their love, knowing, without their words, that they do not seem to blame me for Marshall's death, was such a relief. I have not yet told them of my decision to bring his

169

ashes with me. The children know and are delighted. The four of us agreed on the spot. This is a journey I must undertake myself, though. My final letting go of all except memories. Dr. Pagglio says they are mine to keep in trust for our children and grandchildren.

He would be pleased to know I am writing in my journal, instead of masturbating, facing life as it is, instead of playing, "let's pretend..." Though it was tempting.

Lest I forget, the thing of huge significance yesterday, was the fact that I touched a horse; put my hand on his neck and gave him a good scratch. I also laughed out loud. It was a belly laugh and afterwards, I felt different, like it was easier to breathe or something. Perhaps it is due to this high desert air and the company of old friends.

I do not like Will's new stallion, although I can't quite put my finger on the reason for my dislike, other than looking at his horribly injured leg gives me the creeps. I will admit he sires lovely colts. Perhaps, I don't like the stud, whose name is Packer, because Will gives the stallion all the credit and none to the mares. Well, maybe not. Will is quite delighted with him, however, and so is Torrey.

Today, I will ride Martha. At (short for "Atta Girl"), the Rawlings' summer help and horse trainer, has invited me to ride with her when she exercises Sheba's black colt. I could see in Jake's eyes that he, too, would have liked to be invited. Jake is Torrey's kitchen help and he is so shy that it is almost embarrassing to be around him.

All in all, thanks to the preparation that Dr. Pagglio and the group helped me do, returning to the ranch has been definitely more touching than traumatic. The Rawlings are two of God's finest human creations. Oh yes, I must not forget my lovely dream, where clouds became horses and then became wind. There were wonderful impressionistic streaks of sky color on all the horses—not just

6lue, but peach and lilac and coral with streaks of gold. I
wish I could keep the feeling I had when I awoke.

Helen closed the book and shut her eyes; the dream freshened in her mind. Like the belly-laugh of the day before, the dream seemed to mark a change. Dr. Pagglio's words came to her. "If you have decided that including Marshall in your sexual fantasies allowed you to block memories of him from all other, less perfect aspects of your life together, you are right. It's not healthy. To find healthy ways to honor your husband's memory is important. Don't deify him, Helen. There is no saint/sinner combination here."

"Right!" she said aloud to the silent room and then once again got up to visit the bathroom and then to take a quick peek to see what had happened to the person fly fishing. What she saw surprised her. The poetry in motion person was none other than klutzy Jake. *How can this be?* She felt as though she had been given a delightful puzzle to solve, and watched contentedly as the eastern sky took on the colors of her dream.

Jake presented his fly just below the last ripple in the deep hole below her back porch. When a nice trout could not resist and rose in a smooth swirl to take Jake's offering, joy shot through her. She watched as the rod tip came smoothly up and the pool exploded with the waltzing fish.

When the dance was done, she was not surprised to see the boy bend and release the tired fish back into the safety of the deep water. "Barbless hook," she whispered, nodding to herself with satisfaction.

Once Jake had released the fish, he looked quickly at the sky and then towards the lodge. Helen looked at her watch, 5:15, about time for him to head for the "scullery," she guessed. *Oh, Jake, you're deeper than you seem. What forces have molded you into what you are?"* she wondered silently.

171

She smiled as she watched him break down his rod and head towards the lodge, then added aloud to his retreating back, "I am so glad to have been witness to your glory; to see the face behind the mask. What other secrets do you have, Jake?" She wondered if he found time to fish every morning, determined to watch if he did.

Later, on her way to the lodge, Helen stopped to once again admire how the big building sat its site. After it became clear that the falling cattle market was not going to recover any time soon, Torrey wrote matter-of-factly in a Christmas card that they had decided to take on paying guests, starting the summer of 1989. Both Helen and Marshall knew what that decision cost them. Marshall had picked up the phone immediately. "How's the old man taking your news about adding dudes to the ranch roster?" was his first question.

"Well," said Will, "it's about like you'd expect. Yellin' and fartin' all over the place, 'specially when I told him we were takin' out a bank loan to make the necessary improvements. But, Dewey settled him down some. Said, 'Pete, you got two choices: You can sell some land and hope cattle prices come back up, or you can take out a bank loan, build a lodge and start chargin' money so city folks can have a gen-u-ine Western experience.'"

"Well, bless Dewey's heart," Marshall had said.

"Yep. In this case, anyway. The bottom line is that Dad's seen Torrey's books, and he knows cattle prices better than I do. He listens to the farm report ever' day during lunch, so he knows... He just don't like it."

"Well, I still say, God bless Dewey! I forgot about him having to come around too. It sounds like they're both adjusting then?"

Will laughed. "It took Dad a little time. It took us all a little while, to tell you the truth. But you know

Dewey and Dad always take opposite sides, so he really didn't have much choice."

"It's certainly big news," said Marshall. "Luckily, you've got an architect in the family who would give his eye-teeth to have a go at designing a lodge for you. And he's got a wife who's a crackerjack graphic design artist that thinks she can provide you with an irresistible brochure."

Helen's eyes scanned the massive structure in the growing light. It was weathering well. The logs were ponderosa pine they'd logged from a big stand of mature trees on the west boundary of their property. Will had wanted to top them with a shake roof but Marshall had dissuaded him. "Use a metal roof. It's cheaper and impervious to bugs and chimney fires. Use the money to increase the R-factor in the ceilings."

Marshall had also talked them out of trying to incorporate the old ranch house into the new lodge. "Your dad shouldn't have to see the home his daddy built swallowed up by this big, imposing building, Will. Besides, you'll want the lodge farther away from the corrals. Nobody wants to pay 300 bucks a night and go to sleep with the smell of horse and cow shit in their noses. Pick a site with a view."

Helen nodded to herself, lost in thought. Will and Torrey had taken his advice. The site was perfect. It overlooked the ranch operations, but was up on a slight knoll, so it caught a breeze that kept the mosquitoes bearable. There was a view from every window. The porch wrapped around the entire 5,000 feet. It had been Dewey's idea to put in the pond. *Only now it costs 400 per night,* she thought. *Too bad Grandpa Pete didn't live to see his son's success.* She pulled herself back into the present and continued toward the lodge.

Helen found Dewey reading yesterday's paper and waiting for her by the coffee pot in the dining room.

It was his self-appointed duty to make the morning's coffee, pour everyone their first cup, and entertain until Torrey got the breakfast organized. Torrey loved not having people underfoot in the kitchen and the guests loved the stove-up, old buckaroo--especially the children, many of whom wrote to him after they left. His bedroom in the old ranch house had a wall full of postcards and letters tacked to it that said things like: *"Please kiss Star on the nose every night before you turn him out."* Or, *"Moon likes red apples better than green apples. Please make sure people know that."* Dewey's favorite was the one that said, *"My mom says I can come and live with you if I eat all my vegetables and keep my room totally clean. May I?"*

Helen grinned at him and said, "A very good morning to the world's favorite wrangler. Do you have a cup of coffee for a lady suffering from jet lag and an overdose of pretty country?"

Dewey had already risen and was pouring coffee into a thick blue crockery mug before she had the door shut. "Been waiting on you," he said, grinning happily. Then he frowned. "Ain't them the same duds you was wearing yesterday?"

Helen nodded. "Yes. Probably the same duds you'll see me in tomorrow and maybe the next day after that. I've got to get them broken in with a little desert dust and horse sweat so Queenie will recognize me."

His eyes brightened even more and Helen thought again of how they reminded her of sapphires; such a deep soft, flecked blue you could almost see yourself in them. "Speakin' of Queenie reminds me," he said. "I'd like you and At to take her with you today, if you don't mind. Ol' Dewey ain't ridin' so much these days and since the boys are up in the hills, she's gettin' soft."

"Love to! Thank you, Dewey." Helen knew she had just been offered his most prized possession.

174

Grinning, he said. "She's got a little secret maybe she'll tell you. Has to do with Buck King's Cody dog."

Helen laughed. "Oh, no! Surely not! She isn't... Is she? Again?"

His eyes twinkled. "Damned hussy!"

Helen put her hands on her hips. "I don't believe I know the father. Do you approve?"

Dewey lifted his battered Stetson with one hand and ran gnarled fingers through uncombed wisps of fine, white hair. "Well... That's right, you don't. I guess I'd have to say... He's a might young, but he thinks he's studly...sorta like his owner."

They stood grinning at each other. "Congratulations, Grandpa," she said and took him by the arm. "No one else seems to be about. Let's take our coffee, go sit on the deck and admire your pond until we hear sounds of activity in the kitchen."

It was peaceful on the deck. Already, the temperature was rising. Down below, they saw At mount the horse that had been left in the corral as a wrangle horse and set off through the upper pastures to find the herd. They heard the door behind them open. It was Torrey, just finishing the last of her braid. "God, you two are up early!"

"East Coast time," Helen apologized, getting up to give her a hug. "But, I'm ready to set the table and do anything else you might find helpful... I've already made my bed."

Torrey slapped her on the butt. "Get your coffee and come on," she said. "You can help me torture Jake, just by being present." Then she turned. "When you set the table, set it for 10. I don't think the birders are going to be with us.... And if they are, breakfast won't be on their menu."

Helen looked at Torrey with a question in her eyes.

Torrey smiled. "That's the trouble with your new cabin. You can't hear what's going on up here; which is fine for a honeymoon or a tryst, I suppose. But it's terrible for knowing what the latest gossip is."

Dewey cackled and tipped his chair back, balancing his coffee cup on one knee; a trick all three of the Duncan kids had mastered before their tenth birthday. "Bet they don't make it down to the Malheur today, either."

"Nope," Torrey agreed. "Today they'll spend singing those old, 'Whose Idea was it to Drink Brandy After Dinner Blues.'"

"Oops!" said Helen. "We know about that, don't we, Torrey?"

Torrey smiled. "Yes, indeed. I remember singing, 'Damn that Marshall and his Homemade Raspberry Cordial Blues,' very clearly."

The two women smiled affectionately at each other, remembering...recognizing together that Marshall's name and the memory created the smile. "He's been with me all morning," Helen said simply.

Will came up from the barn just as the hay crew was finishing a third round of pancakes, ham and eggs. Helen got up, poured him a cup of coffee and went to the kitchen to get his breakfast from the warming oven. Jake was already doing dishes, and Torrey was finishing the sack lunches. "Here's one for you and one for At. If Will's here, it means she's about ready to go."

"Okay," Helen said, picking up the sacks and drawing a breath. "This is it. Time to get mounted."

Torrey looked up and said with a straight face, "I wouldn't touch that last line with a ten-foot pole... But have a good time anyway."

They heard a choking sound come from the sink and turned to see Jake shaking with silent laughter. Helen found herself blushing. "Don't I wish," she said, and half meant it.

176

Chapter Eighteen

At was waiting outside the corral gate in the upper horse pasture, holding both Martha and the black colt named, Shaq, by the reins. *Okay,* Helen thought to herself, as she let herself through the gate, *you can do this. Focus on the positive memories. Focus on ranch memories. This is Martha, a sweet, trustworthy, mature, gentle mare. Do not give Octane time in your head! Not here! Not now! You will get on this dear mare and follow At wherever she goes.*

Helen's mouth felt dry, her pulse fast. She hoped her inner turmoil wasn't showing on her face. *Thank God for cowboy hats that give both shade and privacy to the human face.* "Good morning, At. Thank you so much for saddling Martha," she managed to say in a normal tone.

"Howdy!" At's open, friendly expression made up for the fact that her family hadn't seen fit to take her to an orthodontist to correct her protruding teeth. She smiled unselfconsciously through brown freckles at Helen. "Ready to ride?"

"I think so. Here's your lunch." As Helen handed over the brown paper bag, she noticed for the first time that their lunches had been labeled with brick-a-brack lettering. "Whoa! Pretty fancy! Who did this for us?"

"Aw, that Jake! And look...I tell him he doesn't have to write Marilee. At's good enough. Takes a lot less time."

Helen looked. The bags were a work of marking-pen art, the letters beautifully drawn to look like the border trim of a Victorian mansion. *Ah, Jake, shy master of the stream, you surprise me once again.* "Yes," she said, "but time isn't the issue here. It's beauty, don't you think?"

"I guess so. One day he did a big fluffy bush and you had to look real close in the branches to see how he'd worked in the letters." At hurriedly stuffed her lunch into her left saddlebag and fastened the buckles.

177

"Goodness!" Helen said, as she tucked her lunch into her own saddlebag and checked her mare's cinch. "Does he do that for everyone?"

At didn't answer her, saying instead, "I'd like it if you'd get on your horse before I do. We might be moving out pretty sudden."

After At was sure Helen was settled in her saddle, she led Shaq away from Martha to give herself room. She gave her cinch a final check and then gave full attention to the colt. Standing close to the stirrup, she pulled both reins short and grabbed a hunk of mane in her right hand, then reached out and took hold of the bridle cheek-piece with her left hand. Pulling Shaq's head toward her and talking softly, she put one long leg in the stirrup and flowed gently into the saddle, still holding firmly to the cheek-piece.

Helen watched with great interest. She'd never seen the technique used before. The colt stood very still, but there was a crook in his tail and a hump in his back. She held Martha still, sitting quietly, waiting for instruction.

"Helen," At's quiet voice came like a song through the air, "I want you to move Martha right past us at a good walk and then break right into a nice trot. I need to give this guy somethin' to think about other than plantin' me in the dirt when I turn his head loose."

Helen did what she was told. *Smart!* She thought. *Very smart! It's hard for a colt to trot and buck at the same time, and having Martha lead the way gives him a good dose of confidence.* She led the way up the path through the big upper pasture. She didn't know exactly how many acres it was, perhaps 100. As she trotted, she suddenly realized how easily, thanks to the distraction of the colt, her transition back into the saddle had been. There just hadn't been time to think of herself, and now she didn't want to. The sun was gaining strength. Martha's ears were up and she was moving at a ground-covering trot up the trail, already puffing a little from the climb. "It's okay, dear." Helen

178

said, reaching over to put a hand on her neck, "We're both a little out of shape for this sort of ride."

She looked over her shoulder. At had the colt's nose on Martha's tail. "Just keep moving out for a little bit more, maybe till we hit the flat spot," she called. "He's doing fine now."

Helen could see that he was. His nostrils were as big as saucers and his breath was coming hard, but his eyes were on the ground and one ear was tipped back so he could pay attention to the woman on his back. When Queenie appeared out of nowhere and ran past them to take the lead, it didn't faze him. Helen was impressed.

As the trail topped the slope and the ground leveled, Helen touched the reins and Martha dropped to a walk, expecting At to do the same with Shaq. Instead, with a great thumping of boots to the colt's sides, she drove him on past, forcing him, with strong legs, to continue on the trail. When she was finally satisfied, she pulled him, still at a trot, in a big wide circle through the sagebrush and back towards Martha and Helen. Only then, did At allow the colt to stop. They were both puffing. At said, "I gotta get this little guy convinced of two things: Number one is that I'm the boss, and number two is that he can trust me. Thanks for your help."

Helen smiled at her. "My pleasure," she said as they turned their horses on the trail, this time, riding side by side on the flat ground in companionable silence.

After meandering through the hills, they stopped early for lunch at Will's newest reservoir. Helen was sore in places she didn't even know got sore from riding. "I feel like a dude," she said with disgust as she leaned down to hobble Martha.

At laughed. "It's good for you; makes you more tolerant, more humble."

"Yeah! Right! When's the last time you were saddle sore, At?"

"Don't remember. Do remember the last time I got bucked off." She took a bite of her apple and went to sit on the edge of the reservoir dam. Helen followed, wishing for more shade than that offered by the scrawny manzanita bushes. The water looked cool and dark. The earth was sun-warmed, the sky a deep, cloudless blue.

Helen leaned back on one elbow trying not to groan, "When was that?"

At gestured with the hand holding the apple to where the black colt was standing, still unsure what to do about the leather strap tethering his front legs. He was watching Martha hopping, holding both front legs straight, from grass clump to grass clump, grazing on the sparse bunch grass with obvious relish. Helen looked at the colt without sympathy, knowing he would soon figure out the system.

"Why do you think I'm so all-fired careful when I get on that little black devil? I'm still packin' a bruise on my butt." At's face turned pink. "And the little asshole would have to do it right there at the ranch, with everybody watchin'."

Helen laughed. "It's good for you. Keeps you tolerant, keeps you humble," she said, imitating At's breezy tone. Then she said, "Will says Jake can't ride very well. That surprises me. I thought all you kids raised in this country knew how to ride."

"No," At said. "Lots of kids raised in town never been on a horse. Jake was raised in Hines, right next door to Burns. His dad worked in the mill there 'til it closed. But, he can sit a horse okay. He just can't teach them anything, and Will was looking for a trainer."

"Ah, yes," Helen said, wrapping half of her peanut butter and jelly sandwich back in its baggie, ignoring Queenie's soulful look of reproach. She was thinking of the difference between the Rawlings' children. Julie looked really pretty on a horse, but had no desire to train one. Tina, on the other hand, couldn't get on a horse without trying to improve its education. "I know what you mean," she said. She also recognized her own style to be the rider-trainer type, but didn't want to dwell on it. "Do you know the Rawling girls?"

At shook her head. "Not really. I've seen the pictures, though. Tina was here with her husband and their little boys, a couple weeks before they hired me." She grinned, showing the deep creases of her dimples, and pushed her hat up off her forehead. "'Course, at first, I was at the lodge and Jake was workin' at the barn. I was the one peelin' the spuds, strippin' the beds, cleanin' the toilets, hatin' ever' minute of it." She reached out and ran a gentle hand along Queenie's side. "Good dog," she said absently.

Helen lay back and put her hat over her face, supremely content. "Does Jake ever get out to ride with you?"

There was a moment of silence. "Nope. I don't ask him and he's too shy to ask me."

"Why don't you ask him?"

"Well, figure it out. Do I look like the kind of girl who knows how to talk to a boy? And Jake don't know how to talk much at all to anybody, boy or girl. You and I done more talkin' today than Jake and I done all summer." There was another silence. "Besides, Torrey keeps him pretty busy."

Helen, half asleep, wondered if she detected the wistful note in the girl's voice. She said, "I was watching his face this morning and, though I can't be sure, it looked like he wanted to come."

After a bit, At said, "Well, the fool should have said somethin'. Torrey said we could take it a little easy this week 'cause of the crowd comin' in next week. She might have given him the time."

Helen said, "Ah! That explains this leisurely day, right?"

"Yep. It explains why Billy and Buck are loafin' around up in the Ochoco Mountains, too."

181

As she drifted off, Helen wondered how At liked being around the King brothers. The last time she was around them, they had been certified rednecks in their humor. And sometimes their teasing and joking had a sharp edge; the sort of humor that was better left between men. *It really isn't their fault,* she thought. *It's the way they've been raised. They've been full of fun and mischief since they were little more than babies.* She smiled inside her head, remembering the whole gang of them--her three, the Rawling girls and the King boys all playing in the swimming hole. *When had the swimming hole been converted to a civilized pond for swimming? It seems like it was done after the lodge, by a year or two.*

The memories played on as she remembered past summers--how all the kids grew like weeds and showed more independence each year. She remembered the summer Will fired two of his hay crew for drinking, and had hired Buck and Peter, the two oldest in the gang, to help instead. Peter had been so proud when they'd left him behind and returned to Virginia. *Had he been 14?* Now it sounded as though the King brothers had taken over Dewey's role as "guest wranglers." She remembered that Buck had been Carrie's first crush at about age 12. It would be good to see Buck and Billy again, all grown up. Just as her kids were...and the Rawling girls. *Life,* she thought, *moves on, like it or not.*

Helen woke to At pushing on the toe of her boot. "Hey, lady," she said, "your carriage is waiting. Time to go."

Helen pulled her hat off her face and looked up. At had re-saddled and re-bridled both horses. The hobbles were re-hooked in the back cinch rings where they belonged. She could see by their wet front legs that the horses had been watered. Before she even moved, she knew she was sore to the bone. Slowly, she sat up. "Listen," she said, "no more saddling my horse for me. I'm not a paying guest. I need to pull my own weight so I don't feel guilty about having so much fun."

At shrugged. "Okay," she said with a straight face. "Want to ride Shaq home?"

"I do not! You silly child--don't you know it would hurt darling Martha's feelings?"

At's hazel eyes twinkled. "Just tryin' to make you feel needed," she said.

Helen got stiffly to her feet and bent to brush her jeans, realizing with satisfaction that they didn't look so new anymore. She took the reins from At's hand and fed her apple core to Martha. "Ignore me if you hear groaning on the way home. In truth, I haven't ridden for several years... Count that as three..."

At interrupted her, "Aw, once you get movin', you'll be all right. Once a rider, always a rider, my dad says."

Helen put a toe in the stirrup and swung up. She looked down at At. "Was I whining?" She asked.

At gave her a big buck-toothed grin. "I didn't hear a thing. Now let's see how much better ol' Shaq does now that he's had a little time to think. We'll do the same drill we did down at the ranch. Only this time, I'm going to put him out front sooner and I'll be cuttin' off the trail and messin' around. Just ignore me and point Martha's nose towards home."

"Right-oh!" Helen waited until At was mounted and then turned Martha onto the trail and broke into a trot, ignoring, as best she could, her aching bones. At passed her almost at once, then angled the colt toward a rise in the ground to the right. Helen watched them go, more than happy to settle Martha into a walk, to rest her aching knees and to watch Shaq's education progress.

Jake was swimming in the pond and Torrey was sitting on the dock, watching him, with a towel around her head, as Helen and At walked up the hill from the corrals. It was a peaceful scene. "Go get your suits on," Torrey called.

"Yes, ma'am!" Helen said walking up, pulling off her hat and dusting it against her leg. "Can I bring you a beer?"

Torrey smiled. "Of course. Bring a cooler with some sodas as well. You never know who will show up next."

Helen's cabin was cool and peaceful. Stripping out of boots and jeans felt wonderful. Her swimsuit, a basic tank, was remarkable only in its vivid dark purple color. She slipped on thongs and a T-shirt, grabbed a towel, and headed for the lodge to collect the drinks.

At came down the stairs from her attic room in the lodge and found Helen in the kitchen. She held out her pale, freckled arms and laughed. "Working woman's tan." Only her hands and face were tan. Her swimsuit was shocking shades of electric orange with bold, black geometric patterns. Both Helen's sense of design and color were outraged for a split second. Then she smiled to herself. *This girl does not seem to know or care that she has chosen the worst possible color for her skin tone, and in truth, does it really matter? The color of my own swimsuit exactly matches the varicose veins in my legs, should anyone care to check and that doesn't matter either.* She felt a little disgusted with herself. At was a wonderful, natural, talented young woman. Helen looked up at her. "How old are you, At?" she asked.

"Seventeen. Be sure you put in a root beer for Jake," she said. "It's about the only pop he likes."

At the pond, Helen handed Torrey a Bud and popped the top of a Coors Lite for herself. "Where are the birders?"

"Flown the coop like the tough old birds they are. I told them, when they finally showed up this morning, that today was the day to go to the refuge if they were going. The weather report says possible thunderstorms tonight and tomorrow. So off they went with sack lunches and thermoses of coffee. They weren't talking much, but they had their books, binoculars and a determined look."

Torrey had run a comb through her hair, spreading it down her back to dry. It looked like a black and silver waterfall. She wore a faded print suit that went well with her bronze skin. Helen spread her towel at the edge of the dock and sat down, letting her hot feet dangle in the cool water. The thunderstorm warnings explained the sting she was feeling from the sun. She smiled lovingly at her friend. "I'll bet Will is fit to be tied about the weather."

Torrey nodded. "He and Dewey are up in the meadow lashing the backs of the hay crew as we speak, and cussing the fact that he let the King boys have time off."

Helen watched At walk to the water's edge and hold a can of root beer out to Jake; neither appeared to speak.

"What about Jake? Can't he help?"

Torrey shook her head. "I don't believe he's ever been on a swather or a baler. Actually, now that Will contracts out the haying, he doesn't even keep the equipment on the ranch."

Helen nodded in quick understanding. A single swather cost in the neighborhood of a hundred thousand dollars. Will had given her that figure several years ago, so they were probably even more now.

Helen looked over her shoulder. Torrey didn't sound or look upset. It took more than potentially wet, unbaled hay to get her going. It was a trait Helen admired. Torrey credited it to her Nez Percé side of the family.

In silence they watched At swim with strong, sure strokes across the pond. Jake had climbed into the punt tied at the end of the dock, and was watching her, sipping on his root beer.

"Was it a good day?" Torrey asked.

"Fabulous!" said Helen. She slipped over the edge of the dock, lowering herself up to her neck in the cool water. She looked up at her friend, "Absolutely fabulous!" She tipped her head back and began a slow backstroke away from the dock, feeling the heat and soreness leave her body as if on wings. The sky was still a cloudless blue. But soon, she thought, if the sting in the sun was any indication, her cloud horses would come rolling in on the feet of wind. She would remember this day for the rest of her life. Slowly, she turned and swam back to the dock. "Torrey," she said, "I have a serious favor to ask of you and Will tonight, if we can find a quiet moment."

Torrey opened her eyes and sat up to look at Helen. "We can find a moment," she said serenely.

"It's about Marshall's ashes," Helen said.

Chapter Nineteen

Helen stepped into the steaming tin shower and allowed the water to do its magic. She felt grounded and at peace. *I've done it. The journey is complete. Ashes to ashes, dust to dust...may his spirit guard us all.* She tipped her head so that the water blasted her face. It had taken her most of the day, but with only Martha, Queenie, and Marshall's ashes as companions, she had ridden to as near the top of Woolf peak as she could. There, with very little ceremony, but with great feeling, she had released his ashes to the winds.

Now, she smiled against the spray, remembering how Will and Torrey had listened to her plan for Marshall's ashes on Monday night. "All by yourself? Shouldn't your kids be in on this?" Will was on ground he'd never walked before and was obviously uncomfortable.

"Under the best of circumstances, I would have loved to have made it a family thing. But, I can't see that happening, can you?"

"How about us, Helen? Would you like our company?" Torrey's voice came so softly it was hard to hear her, even though she was sitting right beside Helen on the darkened deck.

"I would welcome it, under other circumstances... And I know you'd do it, no matter how busy you were. But, this is between Marshall and me. When I get back, we'll find a minute and raise a toast in his honor. That would be perfect."

They'd sat in silence, lost in their own thoughts until Torrey said, "It will be nice to think of Marshall's spirit looking down on us. I will now think of him each time I greet the mountain."

The tin shower had done its work. Helen turned it off and reached for her towel. *Can this really be Thursday? Where has the week gone?* She frowned. *As if I don't know!*

The lovely slow pace of Monday and Tuesday had picked up on Wednesday, and today she could feel the tension, directed toward the Hollywood crowd, beginning to rise. Luckily, today was the birders' last day. They were to leave at first light. Friday and all of Saturday would be devoted to the final preparations for the new guests' arrival. (They now numbered 12; all saying they were good horsemen and wanted to ride.)

The King boys had been bringing in load after load of freshly baled hay and stacking it in the ranch yard. They were also shoeing horses. Dewey was mending tack, combing out manes and tails and making sure there were 12 suitable saddles, bridles, cinches, and saddle blankets. He had checked and oiled every latigo. At was still working the colts, but she was also helping Buck and Billy run irrigation lines and making sure that at least 14 or 15 head of older, gentle, saddle horses would remember what it was like to have guests on their back. Helen was helping her.

"Why so many extras?" Helen asked as she slid off Jasper's right side.

"Will says we've got to have plenty of spares. He says, sure as hell, some of them aren't goin' to like their horse and will ask for another one because of size, sex, color, name or somethin' else foolish."

They got off and on every horse on the wrong side and slid over their rumps. They dropped their reins, dropped their slickers, poked them in the ribs and did everything they could think of to help bulletproof the horses against inexperienced riders. Those horses that hadn't been ridden for a while, they trotted and loped up the trail to the flat part before turning them around and walking them back.

In the process, we had quite a lot of fun, Helen thought, as she dried her hair and slipped on her nightgown. She turned back the cover on her bed and then put on her Levi jacket and went out to sit on her back porch. The night seemed warmer. The thunderstorm had been more noise than anything else, though great fat drops had settled the dust, temporarily. She could hear the whine of mosquitoes outside the screened porch, the chuckle of the creek and the raspy-throated call of a nighthawk. She closed her eyes, picturing Jake working the creek in the early dawn hours. She had watched him each morning, sitting quietly in her chair--if she could get to the porch before he showed up. Otherwise, she simply stood, as she had on the first day, at her window. Was she spying? Perhaps. But if she told him she was watching, she was certain shyness would keep him from fishing this good part of the creek, and she didn't want to ruin the only part of the day he had to himself.

He's a watcher, that one. She wondered in what other ways he expressed his creativity besides decorating At's lunch sacks. There was something about both of the Rawlings' young summer helpers that appealed to her. At, because, despite her physical imperfections and lack of sophistication, she was steady, open and confident; Jake, because she suspected he needed a champion for his talent. No one at the ranch seemed to appreciate or understand that this was a young man with an old soul. Why he kept everything hidden, she didn't know. Anxiety made him awkward and clumsy, not a lack of coordination. Clumsy fingers had not created those designs. She felt honored that he had done one for her.

Helen sighed. Buck and Billy didn't help. It wasn't that they were unkind on purpose; their world was so black-and-white they just didn't notice. Pickup trucks, fancy women and hard liquor were good. Rap music, long-haired men and people who didn't keep their word or work hard were bad. Bashful boys and semi-homely girls weren't worth noticing...except to tease.

On Friday, Torrey started organizing for a half-day of baking and freezing before heading for town. Helen put her foot down and insisted on being allowed to help. "This is fun, Torrey. I haven't really done any baking for such a long time."

Torrey gave in and together, they planned a week's worth of menus, making a shopping list as they planned. While Torrey made bread, rolls and cinnamon buns, Helen made Torrey's biggest kettle full of a spicy tomato sauce, thick with chunks of ground beef and Italian sausage. From it, she made enough spinach lasagna to feed 25 to 30 people. The rest of the sauce she poured into a plastic container for spaghetti. Everything went into the walk-in freezer. It was Jake who reminded them that two of the crowd were vegetarians. So in a smaller skillet, Helen sautéed vegetables and made a vegetarian sauce. "That boy is starting to earn his keep," Torrey said, nodding at the sauce Helen was stirring, knowing Jake could hear. Helen turned and smiled at him and he smiled back without blushing. She felt inordinately pleased.

The grocery list by the back door was getting longer and longer. Helen looked at the list they had both scribbled. "My gracious but that's a lot of booze!" she said, grabbing the list and putting it in her purse as she went out the door.

Torrey laughed, "Baby, that's not for them, they're stopping in town and buying their own. That's for us! Too bad you're not going to be here."

Torrey stayed back a minute to give Jake last-minute instructions on floor waxing, and then followed Helen out the door. "It's not like we've never had 12 guests at one time; we have," Torrey said as they walked toward the truck. "It's just that these folks are going to require more maintenance than those four thoroughbreds you folks used to pamper."

Helen laughed at the truth of Torrey's words. She could think of their horses, even Junior, without pain, since she and Carrie had gone to visit them in their new homes.

"Speaking of our thoroughbreds, Carrie and I went to visit them when she was home in March."

190

Torrey turned the key in the ignition. "Did you? How did it go?"

"The therapy group I attended encouraged me to call the horse trader and find out where they were. I didn't want to. Then, when I called Carrie and told her, she said to wait until she was home for spring break and we'd go together. Having her there helped a lot."

Torrey looked at her kindly. "I'm sure it did, but I'm equally sure it was still tough."

Helen nodded. Neither Will nor Torrey were the type to pry, and because of that, she found herself sharing more than she intended. "Yes, but the best thing was that Carrie made it our journey, not my journey. It was so special and healing to have her support."

"Are the horses in good hands?"

"Mostly." Helen closed her eyes and leaned back in her seat thinking, *Torrey is right. We did spoil those horses.* Aloud she said, "Except for Excalibur, who is with a professional trainer in a fancy barn, they all have come down a little in station."

"What do you mean?"

Helen managed a smile. "They're treated more like you folks treat yours. No more body clips, stalls in the winter, proper exercise, and all those other things I thought were absolutely essential."

"But, are they in good hands?" Torrey asked again.

Helen knew what she meant. "As far as I can tell; their owners all seem kind. Junior belongs to a little girl who shows him and wins blue ribbons. I get the feeling she's more into winning ribbons than into really loving horses, but he certainly is not being mistreated."

They rode in silence until Torrey said perceptively, "I wondered how it would be for you the first time back around horses."

Helen looked across the leather seat and their eyes met. "I wondered about that too. But At had me so focused on how Shaq was behaving, I didn't have time to think. I just did it... And it was fine."

Torrey reached a hand across and poked at Helen's shoulder. "Speaking of At, don't think I haven't been watching you try to be the matchmaker with my staff," she said grinning. "What's that about?"

Helen tried to look innocent. "Staff? You mean At and Jake? Why? What do you mean?"

"You know what I mean," Torrey said. Then, imitating Helen, she said in a sugary voice, "'Jake, I'll wash those dishes, why don't you and At go check on the outflow to the pond. We want it nice and clear for our new guests.'" Torrey grinned, clearly enjoying herself. "Or how about, "'At, why don't you take this root beer out to Jake. He's been weeding all morning and has to be parched. Here take one for yourself and see if you can't get him to sit in the shade for a minute.'"

Helen reached across the seat and poked her back. "Yes, and who did I just hear give them both the afternoon off?" Then she sighed. "If I had another week, I might have worked it. They're both interested in each other, I can tell."

"Well, you don't have another week," said Torrey, changing the subject back to what was troubling her, "but I sure wish you did. I've gotten real spoiled by your help. It seems like Sunday is rolling around faster than I can believe. You're going to be gone and I'm going to be left handling 12 finicky dudes in alligator boots."

Her words registered with Helen. *She's really nervous about this group. She probably doesn't even realize she just broke her own rule and called them dudes. This unflappable woman is flapped.* She thought for a moment. "Well, I'm here for two more days so feel free to make the best use of me you can. Although, I have to say, Torrey, you really seem to have things under control. I mean, what needs to be done that hasn't been--other than last-minute dusting?"

"Oh, it's not that!" Torrey admitted after a minute. "It's what to say and how to handle these people. They're mostly used to having their asses kissed and I'm not very good at that."

"You'll manage, Tor. You always have and you always will. Just be yourself. I can't think of a situation that could come up that you couldn't handle." Later, Helen was to remember those sage words.

Russell poked his head out of the hanger as Torrey rolled to a stop. He grabbed a rag out of his back pocket to wipe the grease from his hands. "Hey! Look who's here! Come to buy me a beer, ladies?"

"Hello, Russell," Helen said. "It's good to see you again."

Russell nodded to her. "Looks like the Rawlings are taking care of you all right. I been meaning to come on out for dinner one night, just haven't found the time."

Torrey handed him a large cooler. "Howdy, Russell. Here's the cooler we talked about. I'm putting the ice, soft drinks and beer in your refrigerator." She turned to Helen. "Don't you dare let him forget it when he takes you to Boise. I want those people mellow when we pick them up Sunday evening. She turned on her heel and strode back toward the truck.

Russell looked after Torrey, then looked at Helen and smiled. "Mama gettin' a little pushy these days?"

Helen grinned and fell into step beside him as he went to help Torrey with the drinks. "A little," she said, not bothering to lower her voice. "One of the guests requested a beer from some microbrewery in Washington State and she nearly jumped down the clerk's throat at Safeway when he said he didn't have any."

"Requested a beer from Washington? What in the hell is wrong with our Oregon beer?" Russell bristled.

"That's not the point. The point is, she sends out these forms so folks can request special foods...like vegetarians or people with allergies. She says specifically on the form that alcohol for personal consumption will not be provided at the ranch. It's a liquor license thing. So, not only does this one guy request it, he requests something that's a lot of trouble to obtain."

Russell laughed. "Makes you wonder where they think they're comin' to." He stopped beside the truck, looked at Torrey and then looked at the ramshackle buildings and patched up runway.

Torrey followed his eyes and then glared at him. "If we're not good enough for them, they can just leave!"

"Yes, ma'am." Russell said mildly.

Helen asked, "How many trips will it take you to ferry them all here, Russell?"

"Well, since we got the Cessna Caravan rented, it's goin' to be easy. I can fit all twelve of 'em into it, plus their under-the-seat stuff. Then I can bring all their big luggage in the 182 when I take the Caravan back to Boise...and bring it out to the ranch. I'll have it there before bedtime...unless they've ignored the luggage weight like they ignored the thing about alcohol. Then, I might have to make two trips. That sure would throw a monkey wrench into things."

Torrey groaned. "I should've made them hire their own plane."

"Now, girl, don't talk that way. That's my new engine money you're talkin' about givin' to some unknown pilot in a big, fancy plane."

Helen picked up a six pack of Odwalla alfalfa juice. "For her vegetarians," she said in way of explanation to Russell.

"Jeesus!" He shook his head and shouldered the case of Henry's. "What some folks won't do to make a livin'."

194

Chapter Twenty

On the way back to the ranch, Torrey was very quiet. Helen looked at her profile. Hers was such a good face. The long braid, now coiled low at the back of her head, emphasized the strength and generosity of her features. Right now, there was a stillness about her, as though her mind were elsewhere. It was a mood Helen had learned to respect; knowing Torrey was seeking a calmness of spirit. She leaned her head back against the top of the pickup seat and closed her eyes. She was tired, but it was a good sort of tired and silence was welcome.

Only one more day with the Rawlings; then home to my drawing table. She had picked up several good accounts, one being window display backdrops for Banana Republic, a nationwide chain that specialized in well-made, casual clothes out of natural fibers. It was going to be fun. Already, she was working with a fabrication firm who promised to have eight-foot tall tropical trees with branches suitable for hanging clothes on ready upon her return. She sighed deeply. It had been a good visit. Marshall and the children's presence had been with her in so many ways. Bless Will and Torrey for bringing them into the conversation so naturally. Bless them for not blaming her. She gave another deep sigh and let the drowsiness overtake her.

Helen woke when Torrey backed the pickup to the kitchen steps and cut the engine. "Wake up, sleepyhead and start unleashing the tarp. I've got to take a pee." Torrey opened the door, climbed down and hurried up the steps.

Helen smiled and languorously stretched, still feeling soft with sleep. Then she heard Torrey's shriek of surprise and the loud, sickening crash of a body falling. With what felt like a slow-motion bad dream, she leaped from the truck and sprinted up the steps. Torrey lay just inside; one leg twisted horribly under her on the gleaming, newly waxed floor. With a sob of horror Helen dropped to her knees. "Oh, dear God, Torrey, are you all right?"

Torrey was not all right. She was either unconscious or dead. Helen started praying as she reached trembling fingers for a carotid artery. *Please, dear God, do not take another from me. This woman is the way humans are supposed to be. Please do not take her. She has grandchildren.* Tears ran down her face. Her teeth clattered uncontrollably. Then she felt the heavy bead of pulse and felt her prayers had been answered. Slowly, she rocked back on her heels and looked around the kitchen. What had happened seemed no mystery. Jake waxed the floors and had not yet replaced the heavy Navajo rug that covered the spot where Torrey, in her fancy-stitched, leather-soled dress boots, fell. Helen got to her feet and walked carefully to the phone to call 911. Her mind was calm and moving at warp speed as she considered her options.

"911."

"This is an emergency. There's been an accident. We need an ambulance."

"What is the nature of the accident?"

"A serious fall. The victim has a badly broken leg and is unconscious."

"What is your phone number?"

"Area code 541-529-1443."

"Address?"

"The Flat Creek Ranch, Highway 395, Burns, Oregon.

"The victim's name?"

"Torrey Rawling. She fell in the kitchen."

Helen felt focused and calm as she gave the necessary information. "Please," she said, "send an ambulance to the big lodge on the knoll. There's a sign on the highway with the ranch name. Tell the driver to park by the brown pickup truck."

"Yes ma'am. Please, don't try to move the victim."

"No, no, I won't."

"If she regains consciousness, please keep her still until the paramedics arrive."

"Yes, I can do that. Thank you. Please hurry."

Helen replaced the receiver and went to the porch to ring the big dinner triangle. With all her strength she beat out the message of her distress to the silent, seemingly deserted ranch. Tears ran down her face anew as she considered where the others might be. Will and Dewey had been down in the machine shop welding a part on an ancient old hay baler when she and Torrey left for town. They were probably already done and back in the upper field, trying to hurry the crew through the last of the baling. She looked down the hill, praying for movement, but there was none. The King boys had both gone home to get extra saddles from their dad and maybe spend the evening raising a little hell at the Stag Room in Burns. But where were Jake and At? She had no idea.

Her arm finally dropped, holding the striker loosely by her side. What she knew was that she could not leave her friend to go find someone. She walked back inside to kneel beside Torrey's twisted leg. It looked bad; the angle so very wrong that she knew it was seriously broken above the knee. With horror, she watched a dark spot of blood soak through Torrey's Wranglers and begin dripping onto the glossy floor. *It must mean one of her bones is penetrating through the skin.* "Do not attempt to move the victim." The dispatcher's words played in her head. *No, I won't move you, darling. I won't even put a pillow under your head, as much as I'd like to. I don't even want you to wake up until the ambulance comes. I won't be able to stand your pain.*

Helen scooted back to Torrey's head and felt again for her pulse. It was there, as strong and steady as ever. She choked back a sob of relief and stood. *Why in the hell is this floor so slick? What did Jake do to it?* She slid the sole of her own leather-soled boot back and forth. *It actually doesn't seem that slick.*

Helen turned back and looked toward the open door. There, on the floor, was a congealing puddle of liquid floor wax with a definite heel skid mark through it. *Oh my God, Jake, what have you done?* Without really thinking, she grabbed paper towels from the holder and leaned over the spot. Methodically, she rubbed and rubbed the spot, removing all traces of the puddle. Then, she hunkered down and used the towels to wipe the blood from where it dripped steadily onto the new wax. From time to time she put her fingers to Torrey's neck to find the pulse and reassure herself.

Ten minutes passed; then 15, then 20. Still she hunkered. *How long does it take an ambulance to come 38 miles? It only takes us 45 minutes in the truck. Surely, they go faster.* She tried doing the math in her head. *If it took them 10 minutes to get organized and leave, and they drove only 40 miles an hour through town and 70 miles an hour up Highway 395, it would take them about 40--45 minutes.*

Torrey moaned. Despite herself, Helen was relieved. She reached out and took the limp hand in both of her own. She looked at the brown fingers with the rough skin, short nails and blunt tips. *This is a hand to be proud of,* she thought. *This is a hand that can smooth away cares, make bread, gentle a colt, arrange flowers, braid hair, and do any number of things equally well. This is the hand of loving competence.* She moved it to her lips and kissed it.

"Torrey, can you hear me?" She asked softly. There was no response, no movement in the still face. She held the hand against her cheek, kissing it from time to time until, in the distance, she heard the ambulance's siren.

With sudden foresight, she gently put Torrey's hand down and hurried to move the pickup so the ambulance could get good access to the door. As she ran for the truck, she could see dust rising from the trail behind the corrals and knew immediately that At, at least, was on the way. *How many miles can one hear a triangle ringing, or an ambulance screaming, in this high desert air?* she wondered.

The truck coughed to life and she pulled it into its parking spot beside the porch. *Please, God, let them hear the siren in the hay fields and know what it means. Please, Will, can't you feel Torrey needs you? No, no, probably not.* She closed her eyes, remembering. Certainly, she did not feel a thing when Marshall died. Instead, she was talking with Kellie Blair, the woman doing her hair, about whether or not it was time to color it.

And then, with a dying wail, the ambulance was there and two crewcut men, with great efficiency, rushed in, took Torrey's vital signs, and gently, stabilized and strapped her leg before moving her, first onto a board then onto a stretcher. With a handheld computer, one recorded data as the other announced her condition. One of the men whistled as he felt the back of her head. "She really banged her head," he said ominously as he took a small penlight from his pocket. He looked at Helen. "Did you check for a concussion?" Helen shook her head, feeling incredibly guilty. He grunted and deftly peeled back each eyelid to check for dilated pupils.

It was at that moment the kitchen began filling with people. It seemed that Jake, At, Will and Dewey had arrived almost together.

"Torrey! My God! Torrey, what in the hell happened?" The bewilderment in Will's bloodless face as he knelt beside the stretcher, sweat-stained hat crumpled in his hands was nothing compared to the pain and anguish in his voice.

A paramedic put one hand on his arm. "Steady now," he said gently. "She has a bad break of the lower femur and probably a concussion from striking the back of her head. But it could have been worse, much worse. Thank your stars that she wears that heavy braid. It acted as a cushion."

Will turned to look with puzzled eyes at Helen. "What in Christ's name happened, Helen?"

Helen looked at the circle of frozen faces around her. At had her hands over her mouth. Jake's eyes were horrified, his face ashen. His long arms hung loosely at his sides. *He knows! Dear God, he knows that this is his fault.* In a heartbeat, she could see how, in his rush to go riding with At, he had missed seeing the puddle of un-spread wax at the door.

She looked at Dewey as she answered. His gemstone blue eyes drilled into her and she wondered if he knew that she lied. "I'm not certain," she said, slowly. "Torrey rushed in to go to the bathroom and I heard her fall. When I came in she was on the floor. I called 911 and then rang the triangle...only no one could hear...and she moaned once...and I felt her pulse..." Helen couldn't seem to put her thoughts together. Fragments of sentences rushed from her mouth.

Will looked down at the floor and realized the big Navajo rugs were missing. "Shit! Where are the goddamned rugs?"

The paramedics had finished their work and had released the springs on the gurney, allowing it to rise. Quickly they rolled Torrey through the door and into the ambulance. The one who had been doing the talking looked at Will. "Would you like to ride with her, sir?"

"Hell yes, she's my wife!" he bellowed.

In seconds, they were shooting down the driveway in a spray of gravel, the siren shrieking. The people left standing on the porch felt the despair of those left behind. Everyone looked at Helen, perhaps for reassurance. She let out a pent-up sigh of relief. To her it felt as though a great load had been taken from her shoulders. "They'll take care of her," she said. "What we have to do is get the truck unloaded; the

200

frozen stuff in the walk-in, the other stuff in the pantry, the cooler or wherever else it belongs." She looked at At and Jake. "I guess you two have horses to unsaddle. Go do that. I know it's early, but let the horses out and then come back and help me."

The two of them fairly leaped through the door to do as she asked. When they had gone, she and Dewey looked at each other for a long moment. She'd sent the kids off together so she could unburden herself, but she found she could not. When she didn't speak, he looked briefly at the glowing floors. "Best get those rugs back on the floor, I reckon."

She walked up to him and put her arms around him. He smelled of sweat, grease and new mown hay. Almost, almost, but not quite, she unburdened her secret. The voice inside her head held her tongue. *To what purpose, Helen? Certainly, Will would fire Jake and then the ranch would be short two hands. Why does the cause of Torrey's fall need to be identified when the accident cannot be undone?* Instead, she rested her chin gently on top of his cowboy hat and said, "Dewey, old friend, the rugs can wait. First, if the hay crew heard the ambulance, you'd better go let them know what's up and tell them what to do in Will's absence. I know he wants them gone before the Hollywood crowd arrives. When you come back," she pointed a finger in the general direction of the horse corrals, "the four of us had better sit down and draw up a new game plan."

Dewey gave her a quick hug back. As he stepped away to do what she asked, his face was a study of whiskers, tear tracks and tobacco stains. "You ain't leavin' us then?"

Helen shook her head. It was something she had already decided, while holding Torrey's hand. "No, of course not, you silly man. The Rawlings have enough on their hands without having folks sue them because of your cooking."

Dewey dabbed his eyes without embarrassment. "Well, that's fine then. That's real fine. I was worryin' some about how we was goin' to get things done."

"We'll get it done," Helen said with more confidence than she felt. "We've got a whole day to get it re-organized. Now scoot while I get on the telephone and get some details taken care of back East."

Jake found Helen that night as she was sitting on her porch. He did not come to the cabin's front door; instead he walked down the creek bank and came to stand at the bottom of the steps, looking up to where she sat in her nightgown and Levi jacket. It crossed her mind then, that he knew her habits, knew that she watched him each morning as he fished the hole.

The moon was nearly half full and shimmered in a cold, ivory light on the ripples in the pool. He simply stood in silence at the bottom of her stairs, his head lowered, as if asking for absolution. "Come on up, Jake," she said softly. "Let's talk."

Jake had come back from the horses and worked like a dervish unpacking the truck and stowing supplies. He had listened intently while At, Dewey and she had formulated their plan, but he had said very little. When Will's call came saying that Torrey's leg had indeed been badly broken, and that she did have a concussion, Jake first listened to the news and then rushed from the kitchen. At looked after him, concern showing in her eyes, and slowly un-straddled her chair. "Excuse me, folks, I'd best go check on him. He's still pretty shook."

Now, Helen sat in the porch shadow, careful not to move, sensing it took great courage for Jake to come, and that any movement might cause him to bolt. *He's like a big, gangly, shy deer,* she thought. An image of Dr. Pagglio came to her. *This is how he must sometimes feel; knowing one false move and the patient might run.*

202

Slowly, Jake walked up the steps and opened the screen door. Helen waited silently until he had closed it gently behind him and leaned against the door jamb. She did not ask him to take the other willow chair. Instead, she said, "I'm glad you came, Jake. I've just been sitting here thinking about you and how glad I am that we've got each other to lean on these next few days."

In the light of the citronella candle, his dark eyes met hers. "Marilee said I'd b-b-better come." His tone of voice said he did not deserve credit for coming.

Helen was not surprised. "Oh?" She said, "Why did she think so?" Dr. Pagglio seemed to be leaning over her shoulder. "Gently now, Helen," she could hear him say. "Don't pry too much. Let him lead."

Jake's mouth moved but no words came out. His hands came up from his sides and he spread his fingers and looked at them. "I-I know I caused Torrey to fall."

"Oh, Jake!" Helen said, allowing sympathy to come into her voice. "You didn't cause her to fall. The fact that she drank one of those Big Gulps from the Dairy Queen and had a full bladder; the fact that she forgot she'd had you wax the floors; and the fact that she was wearing her dress boots, all contributed."

Jake stood silently, still looking at his fingers. Suddenly, he clenched his fists. "Naw! You got a nice way of lookin' at it, but it ain't true. I left before the wax was dry. I didn't put the rugs down."

"Of course you left before the wax was dry." Helen said reasonably. "Had Torrey been there, she would have told you to leave. She had given you the afternoon off. Listen, Jake, despite what Will implied, the lack of rugs probably wasn't the problem. The paramedics and I walked around on that floor and none of us even slipped a bit. We ALL walked around on those floors before we got the rugs back down." She let the words hang in the air. *This,* she thought, *is probably the most useful lie I have ever told.*

203

Jake's fists unclenched. He made a sound in his throat like a stifled sob. He slid down the doorframe until he hunkered opposite Helen, searching her face in the mix of candle and moonlight. She leaned forward so he could see, certain the tired serenity she was feeling would show and complete the deception.

"Is that how you see it?"

"I do. How does At see it?"

He stood and reached over to pull the vacant chair around to where it faced Helen, and lowered himself into it. "Aw...about what you said. She said to tell Will and Torrey I was sorry it happened and let it go...and work real, real hard."

"She's a smart girl. That was very good advice."

"Yeah," Jake said, with what Helen decided was proprietary satisfaction, "she's good at a lot of things."

She wished for more light, sure that his words had turned his face to flames.

Chapter Twenty-one

Helen sat on the long lodge deck overlooking the pond, a small mountain of green beans to be snapped in the pail beside her on the bench. For the first time in many hours, she was able to sit and think as she mindlessly snapped and pulled the strings from the beans before dropping them into the kettle on her lap. Queenie lay at her feet, assigned there by Dewey, who had gone with the nervous Will to get the first load of guests. "Can't tell how the new guests will take to her. Best leave her here," he'd said. From teasing Jake about his "slick floor," Billy and Buck had come up with the brilliant idea to borrow a friend's Wurlitzer jukebox, so that anyone who wanted to could dance after dinner. She smiled to herself. *It's a very good idea. Actually, those two boys are a good idea. Will's right, they're the only ones truly looking forward to the guests, especially to the women. To them, anyone from Hollywood is a "movie star."*

Helen looked out over the pond and noticed how the sunlight struck the reeds. It was very quiet. The haying crew had been paid and finally left, after lunch and a quick dip in the pond. They were on their way to Jordan Valley and had already complained bitterly about the heat that they were sure to find there.

Mentally, she continued ticking off details in her mind. The cabins were ready, or would be when At and Jake got back with the lupine she had sent them to gather. She remembered how much she had enjoyed having fresh flowers in her room when she had arrived. There was extra toilet paper beneath each sink and extra blankets in each closet.

Jake had the idea to buy an ice bucket for each room, just in case some of the guests wanted to have drinks in their cabins. Will had pounced on the idea. "By God, that's a great idea! I'll pick them up when I go see Torrey."

Will and Helen decided the most they could hope to find the time for was to take turns visiting Torrey while she was hospitalized. They would alternate days and they knew it would be at least several days, if not more, before she came home. Because, although the doctor had set and pinned Torrey's leg, he could not cast it until some of the swelling had gone down.

"It's got to be a cast that runs from ankle to the top of her leg," Will told them. When she gets to come home, she'll have to stay put, with that leg up a lot. Then, they've got her on powerful medicine to shrink the swelling in both her brain and her leg." He grinned. "It ain't goin' to be easy on any of us when she finally does make it home, what with her crackin' the whip from her wheel chair or recliner."

Helen frowned to herself, thinking of her first visit to see Torrey. She'd taken the pickup in to the hospital early that morning. It was the first time they'd seen each other since the fall. Together, they re-covered the details. Torrey's skin looked like burnished wood against the white of the hospital sheets. There were deep circles under her eyes, but she smiled gratefully as Helen slipped into her room. "Baby, you're sure saving our bacon," she said. To Helen, her speech sounded a bit slurred and she wondered if it was the concussion or the medication she was taking.

"I haven't done it yet. Let's talk about this in a week to see what you say." Helen leaned over and planted a gentle kiss on Torrey's forehead.

Torrey had not moved her head from the pillow. When she saw the question in Helen's eyes, she said, "I'm supposed to keep still because of the concussion. If I don't, I get real dizzy and want to throw up."

"Well, then, just lie quietly and talk. I won't stay long."

Torrey was looking fondly at her. "You are going to be a lot better at this than I would've been," she said seriously.

206

Helen waved a hand. "You're making it sound as though you'll miss the whole event. What are the doctors saying?"

Torrey grimaced, still not moving her head. "It's going to be a while." She reached out with one hand and drew back the blanket to show Helen her black and blue, still very swollen leg with its sturdy plastic, immobilizing frame. The flesh around the break was as black as Shaq's coat. It was easy to see where the femur had been pinned. Stitches looked even blacker where the doctor had sewn shut the tortured flesh after extracting broken chips of leg bone and then setting it.

Helen stared, transfixed. She felt suddenly faint. Visions of her old nightmare shuddered through her. Remembering Torrey's dripping blood, imagining the glisten of broken bone, and seeing the ragged line of stitches took her back to her nightmares and filled her with panic.

Torrey grabbed Helen's arm with one hand. "Helen, baby, what's wrong? What are you seeing? Talk to me, Helen! Please. Cover my leg back up. I can't reach to do it."

Instead, Helen let out a moan and slumped on the bed, her knees on the floor.

Torrey's understanding was immediate. "Oh, Helen. I'm so sorry. I didn't think. It's Marshall's accident you're re-living, isn't it? Get up. I can't move and I need to hug you." She tugged ineffectually at Helen's shoulder. "Please, Helen. God, I'm so sorry!"

The remorse and need in her voice got through to Helen. She swam back through the forest of blood and body parts and shakily got to her feet. She was very pale, but her eyes held no tears. She slumped over and let herself fall against Torrey's chest, feeling weak arms wrap around her.

"I'm all right." Helen said shakily. "I had this reaction once before in my therapist's office. It has to do with a flashback to an old nightmare that used to plague me."

"Sh-sh-sh." Torrey stroked her hair and kissed the top of her head. "I don't know what you were seeing, but the Nez Percé would say you have an evil spirit inside your body."

"Ah," whispered Helen, "that's exactly what it felt like. But he comes so much less often. Instead, I am now visited by sky horses."

"Sky horses?"

Helen lifted her head and stood, trying to fill her mind with the vision. Without looking down she felt for the blanket and covered Torrey's leg. "Yes. Since I've been at the ranch, I've been having dreams of lovely horses made of light, clouds, pastel colors and wind. It's a wonderful image and I wake feeling as though I have been given a blessing or benediction of some sort. I meant to tell you about it."

Torrey looked at her, black eyes fathomless. "The spirit ponies bring signs."

"Spirit ponies? Signs? What sort of signs?"

Torrey shrugged. "Mostly change of some sort. You will know. When the time comes, the dream or its memory will come, and you will know--at least that is what my grandmother told me."

With a start, Helen realized her hands were lying idle among the snap beans and quickly reached for another handful from the pail. She looked down at Queenie. "She's not going to be up and about for a long time, Queenie. So, what am I going to do about my Banana Republic project?" Queenie's tail thumped upon hearing her voice, but lying on her side in the slanting afternoon sun was too comfortable for more response. It wasn't until she heard the King boys' pickup that she sat up to announce their arrival with a halfhearted bark. Helen put her pan aside and went to greet them.

"Whoo-ee! Come and see, Helen. This is going to make you want to put on your dancin' boots." Buck's eyes were shining. Billy was unlashing straps on a large quilt-covered object, as Helen walked around the porch to the kitchen door.

Buck maneuvered a hand truck into place and in no time, the two of them had the jukebox up the handicapped ramp and into the dining room. With great care, they untied the cords that secured the wrapping. "Close your eyes, Helen. You've got to see her all at once," Buck said happily.

Helen put her hands over her eyes. "Ready." She said. She heard some grunting as they pushed the jukebox against the wall and plugged it in. Then, in the silence, there was a tinkle and a whirring sound.

"Okay. Now look."

She lowered her hands. "It's perfect!" she said, meaning every word. The Wurlitzer gleamed of neon and polished wood. *South of the border, down Mexico way...that's where I fell in love as stars came out to play...* The mellow tune came from the speaker and Helen laughed out loud. "Frankie Laine! You two are something," she said fondly. "This is the perfect Hollywood touch."

The boys let out a whoop at her compliment and begin arguing about the quilts. "Get this stuff picked up," Buck said sternly.

"No, you pick it up. I got to go get on my 'goin' to town' perfume." Billy grinned and dabbed at an ear.

"And I got to go comb my beautiful curls." Buck pretended to slick back his hair. "You pick it up."

"Well I guess I will then." Billy said. "Takes you longer to get pretty than it does me, anyway."

Helen laughed as they tussled themselves out of the room, quilts and straps dangling. "You'd better do what you need to do and get on the road. Our guests are somewhere in the air from Boise as we speak."

She hurried back to the deck to finish the beans, listening to Frankie Laine's velvet voice croon about lost love through the open French doors and wondering where At and Jake were. "Now, how long can it take to pick an armload of lupine?", she asked Queenie, and then smiled, wondering if perhaps a little hand-holding and sweet conversation were going on as well. It sounded as though they were at least talking to each other...if At was giving him advice as Jake had said when he'd come to visit her at the cabin.

She looked at her watch. In less than an hour the first wave would arrive. She grabbed a handful of beans and quickly began snapping, butterflies started to flutter in her stomach. When she finished and went in through the dining room to the kitchen, she was surprised to find both youngsters there. "Hey, I didn't hear you come back."

At grinned. "Must be that old music." She looked at Jake. "That and the fact that, unlike some, we're pretty quiet."

Jake was on a stool handing vases down from the top shelf to her. "Yep, we're pretty quiet." He repeated At's words with a grin.

Helen walked to the range and picked up a long-handled wooden spoon and gave the simmering spaghetti sauce a stir. She looked at the sink. It was full of purple lupines. "Well, stuff those flowers into their vases and hustle them to the cabins. When you come back, I'd like you to set the table."

At nodded and said, "I got extra time to help. Will said not to turn the horses out of the corral until the guests had a chance to see them...sort of like settin' the stage."

Helen smiled. "He's a pro." She bent down to haul the large pasta kettle from the deep cupboard by the range. As she turned to set it on the counter, she saw Jake take one of the lupines and brush At's cheek. Quickly, she turned her back, knowing she wasn't meant to see. *I knew it! I knew it! I can't wait to tell Torrey!* She had no idea why she was quite so tickled, but she was.

Helen was talking to Torrey on the phone when Will came dusting up the drive. She had just finished sharing her news about At and Jake. "Okay, Torrey, they're here. Any last-minute instructions?"

"No. It will go fine. Tell Lucas and Jude and the Lightmanns hello for me. Remember, the four guests from last year we talked about? They're the ones who set this whole group up to want to come. You'll like Beanie because she's so good to Leo. Jude is a different story, but I guess that's because I've never been married to a gay man. I can't understand what life is like for her."

"What? Oh. Will mentioned something about that and I meant to ask you for the juicy details. Now there's no time."

Torrey chuckled. "You'll find out for yourself. Welcome to Hollywood and the beautiful people, dahling!" She said as she hung up the phone.

Helen hurried to the front door and flung it open; her stomach was jumping. Dewey was already working to loosen the tarped bundle in the bed of the truck. Will was handing a tall, long-legged, gorgeous redhead in tight, white pants and high, gold heels out of the cab as Helen walked down the steps. "Howdy, Helen," he said. "This here is, Cleah. She's a dancer."

"Welcome, Cleah!" Helen said warmly, extending her hand. Cleah turned and extended her beautifully manicured fingertips. "Thank you, Helen." Her voice sounded totally sincere.

Will slid the front seat forward and reached his hand into the backseat. "And this is Juana... Pronounce that Wah-na. She's working in commercials on M-TV." To Helen, it was clear he hadn't the foggiest idea of what M-TV was.

Juana was also dressed in white jeans, only her foot gear was crimson, French, stiletto-heeled cowboy boots. Her hair was a cap of glistening black curls. Hers was also a dancer's body. "Hello, Juana," she said.

Behind Juana, two men came rolling out, cowboy hats in hand. "And this is George..." Helen smiled at the short, balding man and shook his hand.

"And this is Lucas, who was with us last year."

This one actually looks like a ranch hand, or at least Hollywood's version of one, she thought as she shook his hand. He was lanky and obviously weathered brown by California sun. Well-worn Levi's hung from slim hips. With a little shock of recognition, Helen realized she was shaking the hand of the gay husband of the, as yet unknown, Jude.

"Hello. I'm sure Will told you of Torrey's accident. She just called from the hospital to ask that I remember her to you."

Lucas smiled briefly and nodded, showing even, white teeth. "We'll miss her," he said in a beautifully modulated voice. She felt her heart give a little flip. *God, this man could sell telephone sex,* she thought.

"George is a director and Lucas is a choreographer," Will said, obviously pleased with himself for remembering all the details. He helped Dewey off-load the remainder of the guests' under-the-seat-luggage and their liquor. Then he hopped back into the truck, leaving behind Dewey, who looked both a little relieved and a little worried.

Will's last words were, "The boys'll be here about 5:00 with the second group, depending upon how long it takes them at the liquor store." He saluted the guests and put the truck in gear for his last trip to the airport.

Lucas immediately separated himself from the group and went to stand where he could look down toward the corrals. Then he turned to look at the hills, at Woolf Peak, the pond and finally at the lodge. His hands were in his back pockets. He was balancing on the balls of his feet. Helen wondered what he was thinking. He didn't look unhappy.

At and Jake came hurrying up, Helen took over the introductions and assigned the two to help if the guests wanted their bags carried. She walked over to Lucas. "Have you given any thought as to where you'd like everyone to be?"

He shook his head. "If you're talking about cabin assignments, better wait for my wife to get here. I'm sure she has ideas... Better yet, just put people where you want them." He shrugged and smiled. "You have the paperwork on us, don't you?"

Helen nodded. "Do you have a preference?"

He shook his head. "No. I'm here. Wherever you put us is just fine."

Thinking of the two women's high heels, Helen decided to offer them the nearest cabin. With a pang of remembering old memories that she hoped didn't show on her face, she walked back to the rest of the group. As briskly as she could muster, she said, "Jake, please take Cleah and Juana to cabin A. At, please show George to cabin B." she smiled at them. "After you've freshened up a bit, perhaps you'd like to wander around the lodge or go down to the corrals. We won't ring the dinner bell until after the last guests have had a chance to get settled."

Lucas set off for the corrals with Dewey and Queenie. Helen hurried to find Torrey's file on the group. Clearly, Cleah and Juana seemed happy to be rooming together, but she'd forgotten who were couples and who weren't. Did George have a partner coming? If not, she shouldn't have given him cabin B. She threw up the cover of the old roll top desk. *I'm not doing very well, Torrey! Why didn't I think to memorize this guest list? Why didn't we talk more about this?* Already, she was feeling behind the curve. *How does one treat women wearing white stretch pants and stiletto heels; women as exotic as tropical birds? Gads, if I'm flustered, I wonder how Jake and At are feeling.*

She found the file, began to study it and realized why Torrey and Will had dropped the veiled comments and left sentences full of doubt and worry unfinished. Beanie and Leo had filled out one reservation form and they shared the last name of Lightmann. But, Jude's last name was LeDeau. She had filled out her own form, as had Lucas, whose last name was Clements. To confuse things further, two men, whose names were Glenn Jerome and Bradlee Petestone, had only filled out one form. Were they a gay couple, or had there been a shortage of forms? Nonetheless, she learned that Glenn was the one who was going to be disappointed at the dearth of Hale's Ale in Harney County, and Bradlee was a vegetarian. One form only listed two first names, Dean and Dee Dee. All the other information had been left blank, although the waiver of liability and assumption of risk had been signed with two illegible signatures.

She scanned the list. The other vegetarian was a woman named Amber Burns. *Beanie, Amber, Jude, Juana, Cleah... Lord! Don't women in Hollywood have real names?* The flipness of her own thought shamed her. *Get a grip girl! These are real people. They've had their hurts and bumps just like anyone else.* She took one deep breath and then another, studying the forms as she drew a yellow pad of paper towards her and began summarizing the data. *Okay, my first decision... Anyone can sleep anywhere, unless Jude has some master plan in mind.* Her next thought was of Buck and Billy. *Please, dear Lord, give them an instant tolerance if we have two gay guys; no crude jokes or rude behavior.*

The thought of everything that could go wrong made her dizzy. The other thing that made her knees grow weak was the fact that every single person, except Dean and Dee Dee, who had marked nothing, had listed their riding ability as excellent.

Remembering the fallen-off places on the trail up to the base of Woolf Peak made her shudder. *While I have your ear, God, please, if you're still listening... For Will's sake, make that data be true. Make these people good enough to ride any horse they get, anywhere they want to go.*

Her hand continued to scroll across the page, trying to get a sense of her guests, her forehead wrinkled in such concentration that she failed to hear the King brothers' return until Billy laid his hand on the horn and blasted her out of her chair.

She rushed outside just as the pickup coasted to a stop. The truck's doors simultaneously popped open, ejecting the two laughing boys, beer cans in hand. "Howdy, Helen, we brought all the pretty ones, left the old and ugly for ol' Will."

Indeed, the King brothers' Dodge Ram club cab held only women. Buck reached in with a flourish and drew forth a small, slightly plump, grandmotherly woman. "This here's Beanie," he said.

Beanie was laughing unselfconsciously and shaking her head. She held a can of tonic in one hand and a tiny empty bottle of vodka in the other. Wagging them in Helen's direction, she said, "Plane food." Her words caused the group to break into gentle laughter. It was infectious. After a moment, Helen found her own face creasing into a grin.

Billy pulled the seat forward and reached in a hand. "This is Dee Dee of the team of Dean and Dee Dee. They do stunt work."

Dee Dee wore a one-piece, sleeveless, black jumpsuit that fit like a body glove. Her black hair was very short and her dark eyes were intense. "Welcome, Beanie. Welcome, Dee Dee," Helen said, deciding simple words were best.

Behind Dee Dee, bronzed legs appeared and a lithe figure followed. The woman, at first glance, seemed barely more than a girl, with raggedy blue jean shorts and a crop top of an icy blue that matched her eyes. She studied Helen briefly and then decided to smile. Charismatically, it changed her whole face and made her beautiful; an angel with platinum hair that dropped like rippling sunlight down her back. "Hello,

215

Helen. The boys told us you were taking over for Torrey. That's very nice of you." Her tone breathed of youth, innocence and sexuality. Unconsciously, she slid a finger under the hair at her temple and gave it a flip, causing her hair to float and then settle once more down her back.

Both Buck and Billy, starting to unload bags, seemed struck motionless by its beauty and stopped their work to watch and listen. "Hello," Helen said, "I'm sorry, I didn't catch your name."

"Oh, sorry! I'm Jude."

JUDE? Jude? This lovely child is married to the handsome, older, gay man? Helen's mind tried to take in the image while her voice went through the ritual of welcome. "Of course, you're Jude. You and Beanie are the veterans here. I'm very glad you liked it enough to bring your friends."

Jude smiled again, creating the effect of giving a rare gift of approval and said, "And, I'm hoping that this year..." Her glance flicked to the attentive faces of Billy and Buck, one delicate eyebrow arched, "...might be even better than last."

"Move your butt, Jude, honey." Jude's words were catalogued in Helen's mind for later chewing as she turned her attention to the last woman to emerge.

When Amber slipped from the truck and stepped forward, she looked so normal it was almost a shock. Her hair was brown and cut in a casual, carefree style; no frosting; no mousse. She was wearing a tailored white blouse with Levi's and soft riding boots. Her makeup was flawless and the diamonds at her neck and ears, if real, were worth many thousands. But, despite the diamonds, she looked like the girl next door. "Hello, Helen, I'm Amber," she said, offering her hand.

"Amber," said Helen, "it's very nice to meet you. It is good to finally be able to put faces with names." *Yes, this is my other vegetarian.*

216

Beanie took a sip of her drink. "Jude and I have been telling everyone all about the ranch since last year. What a treat to be able to come back..." She broke off and turned to look down toward the corrals. "Where is my darling Queenie?"

Helen laughed. "She went down to the corrals with Dewey and Lucas." She looked at Beanie's wrinkled bermudas and jeweled sandals and inwardly shrugged. "Feel free to join them. But..." she said, remembering her decision, "...I'm hoping you'll work out your own cabin arrangements. Cleah and Juana are in cabin A at this point and George is in cabin B." She looked at Jude. "Lucas said to let you decide where you'd like to be. The only cabin not available is one of the new ones, the Rainbow Cabin."

Jude looked at her. "So, it's first-come, first-served, in other words?"

Helen couldn't read her face or tone. "It is, unless you already have a master plan worked out. If so, I'd sure appreciate a copy."

A small frown wrinkled Jude's flawless face. "It seems to me that would have been your job," she said shortly and then turned quickly to Buck. "Come on, Bucky, those little leather bags here are ours. Help me schlep them to that other new cabin you were talking about."

The women stood watching as Buck picked up the bags. Helen's face felt frozen. *If I have ever treated hired help in such an arrogant manner, may God strike me dead on the spot!* She heard a chuckle and felt herself jerked to attention like a wary animal. Her eyes roved the group. Clearly, she was the focus of their attention. *Like a bug under a magnifying glass.*

It had been Beanie's chuckle. She murmured, "You caught that little jibe, did you, dear? Well, never mind. She doesn't speak for the rest of the group." With that, she turned to Amber. "Honey, do you want to room with the other girls or with Daddy and me?"

"Mother, get serious! Please! The way you two snore?" I'm happy to bunk with Cleah and Juana."

Helen took a deep breath, feeling she would be forever grateful to Beanie for the smooth handling of the moment. *So, Amber is their daughter. Different last name... Oh well...divorce, independent woman, stage name... No matter.* Aloud she said, "Ah, here come two people who will be happy to help you with your bags."

The women turned to watch At and Jake walk up the trail from the cabins. Dee Dee reached down and with a smooth, fluid lift, shouldered a small, red duffel bag. Muscles rippled in her shoulders. "I don't want help, thanks. Is there an empty cabin on down this path?"

Helen nodded, noticing, but not placing her slight accent. "Yes. Try cabin C or D."

She moves like a cat--a black panther. She tried to read At's face, but could not. "Did you get the folks settled?"

They both nodded. "They seem to like things fine." At said.

"Beanie and Amber, meet At, our wrangler, and Jake, my assistant." She hastened to say.

Beanie had been sipping steadily on her tonic can. "Hello, youngsters. Now, neither of you were here last year, were you?"

"No, ma'am. This is our first year." It was clear to Helen that At had volunteered for the talking duty. Jake was standing, looking rooted, just behind At. *He'd like to bolt, but he won't,* Helen thought with confident satisfaction.

Amber looked longingly at At. "If you're the wrangler, it means you mostly get to work with horses, right?"

At nodded. "Mostly, I do...'less somethin' else needs doin'. I try to help out wherever I can. You like to ride?"

"I love to!"

Beanie smiled fondly. "This child has been crazy about horses since the day she was born...horses and dogs."

At looked back and forth between them. "You related?"

Amber laughed. "Yes, I know I'm too old to be going on vacation with my parents, but the thought of scrubbing off my makeup and riding for a week made it worth my while. Besides, Daddy is footing the bill."

It took At a minute to chew through her words, then she smiled her generous, buck-tooth smile. "If you'd like, I'll help you put your suitcase away and then we can go down to meet the horses."

Helen could feel herself starting to relax. "What a good idea. Now, Jake, let Beanie point out her bag and take it to whatever cabin Dee Dee didn't take. And, Beanie, how would you like me to put your drink in a civilized glass with some ice?"

Chapter Twenty-two

Beanie followed Helen into the dining room where the icemaker sat and accepted the glass full of ice and a new tonic from Helen, smiling her thanks. She then flopped her oversized purse on the long dining room table and rummaged in it until she produced a second, tiny vodka bottle. "Dear, you wouldn't happen to have just a teensy bit of lemon, would you?"

"Of course I would. Just a second."

When Helen returned, Beanie had lifted one side of the overlapping red- checkered oil cloths and was looking at the individual tables beneath it in a considering way. "You know, dear, it is none of my business, but you might want to think about separating these tables--you know, make six individual tables. I see that there are actually six individual cloths here, so it would be very easy to do."

"Oh?" said Helen, stifling her first hit of irritation; knowing with sudden insight that Beanie was trying to tell her something.

"Well, I don't like to think I'm interfering in any way..."

"No, of course you aren't. Please, I'd appreciate your thoughts. We actually usually have them separated, but I thought you might like one long table so you and the staff could all be together."

"Well..." Helen realized that Beanie was very fond of starting sentences with the word 'well.' "...your idea of one table is probably an excellent one for other groups, but you're going to find, as the week progresses, that with us, little groups begin to form, that sometimes...little 'tiffs' pop up." She lowered her voice, "Petty jealousies, if you will." She paused, as if remembering. "Well, it's easier for the lambs to separate themselves from the wolves without making a scene this way."

Helen's head reeled. *What? Lambs? Wolves? Jealousies? What can she be talking about? Is she drunk? Crazy? Am I about to be caught in the middle of a tabloid exposé?* Aloud, she said, "Are you talking about the guests or our staff?"

"Both."

"Both?"

Beanie nodded. "Believe me, dear, everyone is going to have a lot of fun...each in their own way. And they'll get real close, which sometimes causes problems. Don't you worry a bit. It won't affect you. Well...I think it's just going to be easier at dinner and breakfast, if the tables are separated. You'll see."

Helen didn't see, but she was to remember Beanie's prophetic words. "All right, I'll take your word on this. We'll move the tables as soon as Jake comes. Thank you. I'm really very new at this, as you can tell."

"Oh my! That reminds me. I wanted to ask how Torrey is doing. What a horrid thing! Will told us at the airport, but he didn't say enough."

Helen considered before she spoke. "She was very lucky in that she was wearing her braid in a coil at the back of her head, so when she hit her head on the floor, the back of her skull had its own cushion. She does have a concussion, but it could have been much worse. As it is, she was unconscious for nearly an hour and her leg was badly broken just above the knee. It was an unusual break that requires a cast of the entire leg. She'll not be walking for a very long time."

"Bless her heart! What a terrible thing! Lucas was really very upset when he heard. Of course, he's just like Torrey, you can't tell a thing from his face. But I've known him for a very long time. He can't hide a thing from me."

With that pronouncement, Beanie took a healthy swallow of her new drink and sighed. "Well, I'm off to find my cabin and change into a cowgirl. I must trot down to the barn for a visit with Queenie and Dewey."

Helen was glad to have the time alone. Quickly, she pulled the crudités and dips from their refrigerator containers, spread endive on a pewter platter and arranged the vegetables artistically. Jake walked in just as she was getting down the new ice buckets.

"Oh, Jake!" We've got a couple of jobs to do before I ring the triangle for cocktails. We need to move the ta..." She stopped. Jake's face was a study of confusion. "What is it Jake?" Her protective instincts sharpened as he stood, blank faced. "Has someone said something to you?"

Jake looked at her, for the briefest moment meeting her gaze. Then he dropped his head. "Aw, I reckon I got culture shock, plain an' simple!"

After a moment of startled silence, Helen gave a snort of laughter. "Then, I did too, my friend. I did too." Helen reached out and, with the natural movement of a long-time mother, gave him a tight side-arm hug. "Hang in there."

"Gonna be an interestin' week," he said, looking down on her, not moving away, though they were hip to hip.

"Yes, I expect it will be that." She gave him a quick squeeze and released him. "Now, come and help me move the tables back apart. Thank goodness you and At didn't have time to get them set... And don't ask me why, because, though I'm convinced it's the right thing to do, I don't really know why."

"Okay. By the way, the two guys will be in Cabin B, the Lightmann's are in cabin C. Dee Dee took cabin D and George is in E. Most everyone, except George, has gone down to the barn."

Helen smiled at him. "Thank goodness!" Was all she said.

Helen and Jake were working like a well-oiled team, the tables in place and partly set, when Will's truck pulled into the yard, horn honking. "Okay, Jake, time to meet the final guests." She didn't say, "Let's get it over with," but her tone implied it. Jake grinned and followed her out the French doors.

She stood holding the porch rail as the four guests climbed from the truck, holding beer cans. "Hello!" She called. "Welcome!" *Obviously, the cooler was a success.* "You got here just in time. I'm just minutes away from ringing the triangle for cocktails."

"Howdy, Helen! Howdy, Jake!" Will called. He still looked jovial, but she could see his tiredness. She stepped off the porch and went forward, Jake following. "Hello Will." She smiled at the guests. "Please introduce us."

Two of the men were holding pinkie fingers. They had benevolent smiles on their handsome faces and wore similar cowboy shirts with Indian petroglyph symbols on the yolks. "Hello, Helen, Will told us all about you. What a trooper! I'm Bradlee and this is Glenn."

"Nice to meet you, gentlemen... And this is my assistant, Jake."

Without hesitation, Jake reached out a ham-sized hand and gave each man a silent, but hearty handshake. Will beamed at him, relief written on his face. "And this here's, Dean. I expect you already met his partner, Dee Dee. They ain't twins even though they sorta look it. Happens they're both from Israel...retired Mossad."

Helen thought, *Whoa! Retired Israeli intelligence doing stunt work? What next?* "Yes, of course, now I recognize Dee Dee's accent. Welcome Dean," she said with a smile in her voice. The man nodded to her and then held out his hand to Jake.

"You been pumping iron, man?" he said, with the same distinct accent, measuring the strength in Jake's grip and glancing at the breadth of his shoulders. Jake grinned, turned red, shook his head and started unloading the truck.

Helen turned to the final man. "And you're Leo! I've met your wife and daughter. They are down at the corrals with the others; your daughter with the horses, your wife with Queenie."

The only way to describe Leo Lightmann, she thought, would be to say, compact; small, neat and compact. His feet and hands were small. He flowed in a tight triangle; small hips, sturdy shoulders, no neck, a short and tight haircut. His jeans had creases; his boots were buffed to a shine. His eyes sparkled when Helen mentioned his family. "Ah! Good! Good! I knew Amber would fall in love with this place." He turned back to the truck and reached past Jake for a round metal container. With a quick movement, he snapped the catches and opened the lid. With a grin, he reached in and lifted out a soft Stetson as gently as if it were a puppy. He looked at the hat with great satisfaction and then set it carefully on his head. When he shut the hatbox, he turned to the other guests and said, reverently, "Rodeo Drive. 100% beaver. Goddamn thing cost me over a thousand shekels with the taxes."

Glenn clapped his hands. "Oh, Leo, it's just divine. I'm simply green! Why didn't you tell me we were doing authenticity, you bad boy?"

Leo snorted. "Oh, my God, Will, now these boys are going to want to go back into town and buy out the Ranch Supply."

Helen realized suddenly that she was standing, rooted to the spot, her jaw unbecomingly slack. She then noticed, with some satisfaction, that she was not alone. Will had stopped off-loading bags and boxes of liquor. He was standing, both hands gripping the side of the truck, his expression glazed over, his mouth, if not wide open, was certainly relaxed. After a few blinks, he focused his gaze on Leo. "Huh?"

"They're the damnedest shoppers you've ever seen." Leo thrust his chin towards the bed of the truck. "Half the shit you're carrying is theirs and they have more coming with Russell." His tone was more of admiration than of mean teasing. He grinned at the group and tipped his hat back with a gentle poke.

"Well, come on, gents, get yourself a fresh beer and let's mosey on down to the barn. You heard the lady. It's almost time for cocktails. We gotta keep moving."

The guests trooped down the hill in Leo's wake, leaving a profound silence among those remaining. Without a word they turned and climbed the two half logs that made the deck steps. Single file, Helen leading, they walked through the French doors. Will walked directly to the coffee pot and poured a cup. Helen and Jake went back to setting the tables. Will cradled his mug, watching them work with a seemingly vacant mind. Finally, he mumbled. "I'd best call Torrey. I said I would when I got 'em all here."

Helen looked up, knowing how heavily the week was sitting on his shoulders; knowing how his personal philosophy of how the world should work had been stretched and brought into sharp conflict with the need to make money. "Yes," she said. "That's a good idea. Tell her..." She took a deep breath and looked at Jake. "Tell her everything is under control. At and Jake have been magnificent help."

Will looked at her startled. "But..."

She glared at him. "I mean it, Will. That's the message from me. Tell her the idea of drinks in the coolers was a real hit. Tell her everyone is in the mood to have a good time."

He looked at her and after a moment straightened up from where he'd been leaning against the sideboard. He took a long drink of coffee and then sighed, looking into the black brew as if for inspiration. When he looked up, Helen was surprised to see a twinkle in his black eyes. Then his whole face collapsed. He set his mug down, turned and grabbed the sideboard with both hands then leaned forward, shoulders shaking. For a split second, Helen couldn't tell if he was laughing or crying.

"Heh, heh! Haw, haw, haw! HAW, HAW, HAW!" Great bellowing guffaws rolled like thunder from somewhere deep in his gut. Helen heard Jake's hoot of laughter join in and suddenly she, too, was laughing, feeling only a half-step from hysteria.

Will's voice came out in gasps between bouts of laughing. "My G-o-o-d! What an outfit. Haw, haw! Ain't they somethin'? You couldn't write about 'em an' make 'em sound real." He stopped in sudden thought. "My God! Where are Billy and Buck?"

Jake, still laughing, said, "With the ladies, down at the barn."

"Oh, my God, I've let them two fairies walk right on down there, unprotected. Helen, you call Torrey. Tell her just what you said...and that I'll call her soon as I'm able to. I've got to go and threaten them two randy bucks with castration should they want to get mean."

He rushed out, slammed the tailgate of the truck, cranked it up and slammed it into gear. Helen and Jake watched the bags remaining in the back of the truck bounce and slam as Will careened down the hill. They looked at each other. "We'd better hope that you and Will got all their personal liquor unloaded," she said, grinning at Jake.

"Maybe," he said.

"Okay." Helen drew a deep breath. "Let's get focused." She counted on her fingers. "First the dining room tables, then the rest of the hors d'oeuvres, then the ice for their drinks, then beer and white wine moved into the coolers, right?"

Jake looked at her. "Likely to be a long cocktail hour."

She nodded. "That's why we're having spaghetti," she said simply. Without further words they moved to their tasks. For the first time, Helen was glad of Jake's silence. Her mind was swirling. *Ah, Torrey, my friend, even you, with your strong center and great patience, would be tried by this undertaking. It's going to take a miracle and a little more to pull this week off successfully. May the doctors release you to come and direct this circus as soon as it's possible.*

226

It was obvious to her that she had an ally in vodka-sipping Beanie. The woman also wanted the week to go well. *What was she trying to tell me?* Clearly it had to do with Will and Torrey's exchanged looks of worry. And those looks had something to do with the King brothers; she'd stake her intuition on it. *What had Will just called them? Randy bucks?* She wasn't sure of the term. *It's probably Western slang.* "Jake," she's asked, "What's a randy buck?"

Jake's face froze and then flamed, his big hand still clutching three water glasses. "U-u-h...I reckon it means a male deer during mating season."

"What?"

Jake had put down the glasses. He took a deep breath. "Out here, we call animals, male animals, that is, "randy" if they like the girl animals...the does, I mean."

"Randy? You mean like the man's name? How odd!"

Jake looked at her, his face still crimson. "I dunno. I don't reckon it's a man's name. I reckon it means the same thing as...horny."

It was Helen's turn to blush. "Oh. Well, thank you, Jake. I finally understand, and I'm sure glad I asked you instead of someone else."

Helen chewed her lip as she walked through the swinging door to the kitchen. She stopped short and the door hit her in the back. Still, she stood there. *Of course! Of course, that's what it means. That's what Will means. He's worried that those boys aren't going to behave themselves, no matter how he threatens. He knows that they can make or break this week. That's exactly what Torrey and he have been stewing about; whether those two can walk the fine line...or whether they even want to.* Belatedly, she wondered if she were the only one on the crew so naïve. She put her head in her hands, bringing the image of Dr. Pagglio's hawkish face to her mind, bathing herself in the warmth of his gentle wisdom. *What would he think? In this situation, what would he do?* She straightened her back and raised her shoulders, drawing in a long breath, knowing exactly what he would say. It would be: "Helen, do your job. The other is not your problem. Work on the things you need to work on and let the others worry about themselves."

"Right!" she said aloud, feeling not exactly comforted as much as resolved. "My only job is to keep the meals coming."

"I beg your pardon?"

Helen spun around. Standing, holding open the swinging door, was George. He looked slightly puzzled, but was still smiling. Helen laughed. "Hello, George. You caught me talking to myself."

"Yes." He said, "I did, didn't I? Should I apologize? Is it off-limits to come into the kitchen?"

"Heavens no! I'm just helping myself get organized. Now, how can I help you?"

He smiled. "That's what I came to ask. I see the others walking en masse, up from their visit to the horses, and I wondered if I might be of service."

Helen really looked at him for the first time. His gaze was level, his face open. Intelligence and confidence were words that came to her mind. He wore a green and red plaid cotton shirt, khakis and boat shoes. A sweater was draped over one arm. *Both he and Amber looked too normal for this group.* "Thank you, George. I'd love some help." Helen moved to the counter and took plastic wrap from a tray of cheese and crackers. "Three things: First, please go ring the triangle. Then, if you would take these in to the sideboard and put them beside the vegetables, and if I'm not yet there when the guests come, if you would show everyone where the soft drinks, white wine and beer are in the cooler in the dining room, I'd be tickled."

George smiled. "Of course. No problem."

"Oh, and, George, if people have brought their own bottles, they can put them on the sideboard or

228

they can store them under the counter; you'll see where there is room."

"Right. I'll spread the word. Will you be joining us?"

"I will. Just as soon as I make a quick phone call, comb my hair and freshen my makeup."

Chapter Twenty-three

"Okay, Torrey, this is it. Everyone has arrived. Thanks to Jake and At, I'm pretty much prepared. George, one of the guests is about to ring the triangle for cocktails. If you have any last advice, give it now."

Torrey had answered quickly, so Helen imagined she had the phone on the bed near her hand. She vowed to keep the conversation light, but focused. Torrey's first words were not advice and that fact surprised her. "How's Will holding up?"

Helen laughed. "Good question. From my standpoint, I believe the famous Rawlings' sense of humor has come to his rescue. He, Jake and I just had a good laugh a bit ago. Torrey, this is quite an interesting group of people. I'm so sorry you're liable to miss them."

There was a sigh from the other end. When Torrey finally spoke, her voice choked to a whisper. "Actually, I'm afraid I will, Helen. The swelling still hasn't gone down enough to put on the cast. Besides that, between this concussion and my medication, I can barely think. All I want to do is sleep. Baby, I feel like I've thrown you to the wolves. Are they terrible?"

"Not at all," Helen said quickly. "Granted, I'm on a steep learning curve, but I know with everyone pitching in, we'll get it done. Torrey, you just relax and do what the doctors tell you to do." She put every ounce of confidence in her voice that she could muster.

"Sadly, I have no choice," said Torrey, sounding resigned.

"No, you don't, dear heart. I wish it were otherwise, but it isn't. I have to run now. I just heard George ring the triangle. But I'll call tomorrow after I get everyone sent to the corrals."

When Helen gently replaced the receiver, she leaned her forehead against the wall by the phone and prayed for strength, taking in deep, steadying breaths. Then she grabbed a lipstick from her pocket, ducked into the staff bathroom and hastily applied a coral slash. She looked critically at herself. *This is going to have to do...this and my happy face.* She thought of Torrey's misery and sent up a second prayer. *Okay, God. I hope you have my back because I cannot let these dear friends down. Thank you in advance.*

Helen took the time to check the sauce and turn on the warming oven, preparing it for the garlic bread and plates, before going through the dining room and out onto the porch to watch the guests straggling up from the corrals. George was there, holding two glasses of red wine. "Here, Helen," he said, offering her a glass. "I know you have a lot on your plate, especially this first evening, but this is from my own vineyard and just a sip now and then won't hurt you."

Helen found herself speechless; her throat tight at his kindness. Tears sprang to her eyes. She met his steady gaze and took a deep breath, letting him see what the gesture meant to her. "George," she said, wonder in her voice, "are you an angel in disguise or simply the kindest, most intuitive man on the planet?"

He smiled at her. "Neither, I'm afraid. But, over the years I have developed the ability to put myself in other people's shoes and figure out what they might be thinking and feeling. That's what makes me a decent director."

They looked at each other in silence for a long moment and then Helen raised her glass in the age old gesture, and George brought his up and touched her rim with his. Helen said, "For the record, George, you were spot on and I can't even find the words to thank you."

"There's no need," he said simply. "No need at all. Just say something nice about my wine and we're even."

They turned to watch the guests, all of them now in boots, jeans and hats. Helen could hear laughter and chatter as they came, Dee Dee and Dean well in the lead. She noted Leo and Beanie were holding hands and walking slowly with Dewey and Queenie, bringing up the rear. "What does Leo do?" she asked. "If Will and Torrey told me, I've forgotten."

"He used to be a talent scout and then later on an agent. Now, he's mostly retired though he still represents a few clients, like Jude, Glenn and Bradlee."

"I hate to sound ignorant, but, are they movie stars?"

George turned to look at her, a considering look on his face. "Clearly, you aren't a fan of daytime television."

Helen shook her head. "No, I never have been. It's mostly soaps and game shows; those aren't genres that I'm attracted to."

George chuckled. "Well, you're looking at daytime soap opera stars--two romantic leads and one innocent-looking bitch."

Helen quickly took a deep sniff and then a sip of her wine, buying herself time, her mind reeling. *Gay men play romantic leads? Had George called Jude a bitch or is that the role she plays? Have I insulted his friends? His work?* To cover up her scattered thoughts, she swished the wine in her mouth savoring the round fullness before letting it slide down her throat. Then she thought, *In for the penny, in for the pound.* "Okay, George, here's what I think about your wine, though it might taste differently if I hadn't had my foot in my mouth." Helen turned so they were face-to-face and said, "it doesn't taste like cherries, cranberries, black berries, raspberries, chocolate, cassis or any sort of spice, including pepper. It tastes simply of very mature, very good red grapes, perhaps from organically-grown Nebbilo grapes, carefully processed, put down and aged to perfection,"

George gaped at her, his mouth hanging open. *At least he doesn't look angry,* Helen thought as she turned to greet Dee Dee and Dean as they mounted the steps. "Hello," she said. "Through these French

232

doors you'll find what you need. If you don't, please feel free to ask me."

They paused. Dee Dee said, "We like our cabin, Helen, and we really liked looking over the herd. It is going to be so much fun to ride a horse at other than breakneck speed."

It was Helen's turn to gape. "Dee Dee," she said, nodding towards Dean to include him, "If there's ever a moment, should you care to share, I would so enjoy hearing about your work and how you came to be in the industry. But for right now, I'm just glad you like your cabin and the horses." *She already looks less tense,* Helen realized.

In seconds, Helen was shepherding people in through the open French doors and directing them towards the hors de' oeuvres and the bar. She raised her glass along with her voice. "Please, everyone, help yourself. Torrey wanted me to tell you to make yourselves totally at home. Jake and I will be in the kitchen. If you'd like to take something and head down to the pond, feel free. We'll ring the triangle again in about 40 minutes, when it's time for dinner." It was only then that Helen realized some were missing from those assembled and one of them was Jake. She bolted towards the swinging kitchen door, barely finishing her sentence.

Jake looked up from where he was flattening and peeling garlic cloves, Torrey's recipe for Caesar's salad dressing beside him on the counter. Helen put her hand to her chest. "Good Lord, Jake! When you weren't on the deck with the others, I thought you'd bolted, and I almost had a heart attack on the spot."

He looked at her and said with conviction, "I'm not goin' to bolt, Helen. You can cross that off your list of worries."

Helen grinned. "Well, that's good." She took a sip of her wine. "I'm not sure I could do this without you at my back."

233

"We got each other's backs, Helen. Now, you still okay with using Torrey's recipe with the fresh eggs in the dressing?"

Helen nodded. "She was pretty adamant when we talked. She said in that matter-of-fact tone of hers, 'Helen, do you know exactly how many cases of salmonella have been caused by eggs in the West? Exactly zero, that's how many. These eggs are fresh farm eggs from Billy and Buck's mother. The salad dressing is delicious. Just trust me and do it.'"

This time, Jake grinned. "I've already grated the parmesan cheese and have the pasta water goin'," he said.

Helen blinked and looked around. It was on the tip of her tongue to say, "Who are you and what have you done with Jake?" But instead, recognizing something important was happening for him, she said, "so you have, bless your heart." She wondered how he had managed to sneak back to the kitchen but decided not to ask. "You are going to make this whole dinner seem easy."

"Oh, and At and I think you should sit with ever'body after things get started. We'll take care of clearin' the plates and keepin' the water pitchers filled."

Helen took a long look at him. "Really?" She tried hard not to visualize dropped plates.

"Yep, she showed me just how to do it with a feed pan. Said she learned how in Home Ec. Reckon all I got to remember is to take the plates from the left and if someone asks me to refill their water glass, I do it from the right with my right hand."

"And don't stack the plates when you take them away."

He nodded. "Yep. That's what she said. She also said that she aimed to help us. Reckon you'd best finish the dump cake. I got the oven turned to 350°"

Trying not to look flabbergasted, Helen took another sip of wine and put down her glass. "Yes, sir!" she said and saluted. "But first, I need to make a note of who is in which cabin before I forget. Thank you for getting all that sorted, by the way."

"Naw, I don't get the credit. That older guy, George, just sorta saw what we had and then told ever' one where they were stayin'…except for the blonde. She was set on bein' in the Sunrise Cabin."

As Helen went to write down the cabin assignments, she remembered both the Sunrise and Rainbow cabins had a view of Flat Creek and wondered if Jake would continue with his early morning fly fishing. *Probably not. Unless I miss my guess, there will be no rest for the weary. More fishing will have to wait until after this group leaves. But what a change in that boy!* She offered up one more petition to Heaven. *Okay, God, this one's really important. Please let Jake do well in the dining room. You can see how his self-confidence is improving. You can see how he's taking ownership of this whole endeavor. Please give him a chance to prove himself.*

When the triangle had been rung and the guests were all seated, Will stood at the end of the room and cleared his throat. "While Helen and the kids are bringin' out the food, I got a couple of details to run by you." He grinned affably at the group and gestured at the deer and antelope horns mounted on the wall throughout the big room. "These here horns and antlers are for hangin' hats, should you want to, but you don't have to." So saying, he removed his own battered hat and sailed it towards the closest set of antlers. When it landed neatly over the horns, the entire room laughed and applauded.

"The second thing I got to say is that should you want your cabin cleaned, just don't do anything. But, if you don't want it cleaned, put out the "Do Not Disburb" sign that's hangin' on the back of your door when you come up for breakfast in the mornin'."

"An, speakin' of breakfast; we start servin' at 8:00, but ol' Dewey is here with the coffee and the bullshit he spreads ready by 6:00. Before that, you could probably go into the kitchen and rob some off the stove, but stay out of Helen's way. She knows she's got to get you all fed and down to the corrals by 9:30 with your sack lunches in hand. 'Course, should you want it, we also got a few little coffee makers that you could take to your room. So, I believe we got you covered there."

"Last thing is that our insurance says we got to offer you a ridin' helmet. If you decline, all you have to do is sign one last piece of paper absolving Flat Creek Ranch Corporation of responsibility."

Will looked around and belatedly smoothed down his hair. "Now, I see Helen's already got the chow on the sideboard so, I'd advise you to save your questions until afterwards and just enjoy yourselves. We got a jukebox that the King brothers have brought in for dancin' later on, if you've still got the energy after this day."

Helen noticed how heavily Will sat in his chair. *He's totally exhausted. I've got to get him fed and out of here as soon as possible.* She looked over to where Buck and Billy were busy entertaining their separate tables. She had found the time to tell them it was up to them to keep the guests happy during dinner and that not only Jude might enjoy their attention. Surprisingly, they had meekly agreed.

Will, after listening briefly to something Leo was saying to him, looked up and nodded at her. She smiled at the group and said, "Okay, everyone, please help yourselves. At and Jake will be around to take your plates when you're done. Save room for Torrey's famous Dutch Oven Dump Cake with whipped cream for dessert. I'm going to go put it in the oven now."

She was glad to see Jake's place was with Dewey, Dee Dee and Dean. He'd be safe there and Dewey could carry the entire conversation, if need be. She, on the other hand, being the last to serve herself and sit, found an empty chair with Amber, At and Jude.

236

Lucas, she noted, was sitting at Will's table with Leo and Beanie.

Amber beamed up at her as she sat. "Oh, Helen, At was telling us how well you ride and that you learned on an English saddle."

Helen smiled at At. "That's quite a nice thing to hear, At, especially, coming from you."

At just grinned at her and kept eating, knowing she had to be done before the guests in order to help Jake remove the plates. Helen smiled around the table, trying to specifically include Jude, who seemed to be in some sort of pout. She appeared to be only half listening and her glance kept sliding to where the King brothers sat at their respective tables, both in full entertainment mode. What little was on the star's plate had been barely touched. "How's the spaghetti, Jude?" she asked brightly.

Jude didn't even look up, but Amber smiled at her and said, "It's delicious and I hope it was not too much trouble for you to make some of the sauce meatless."

"Not a bit! Now, tell me which horse or horses caught your eye." She decided on the spot not to worry about Jude and instead concentrate on getting to know Amber a bit better.

"Well, like you, I learned to ride English first, so I'm more attracted to a slender build. At says the new buckskin mare has a lot of thoroughbred in her. I believe her name is Kitty. Then there were two bay geldings...oh, I don't know, Helen. I'll be happy with whatever Will puts me on. I can't tell you how happy I am to be here. I was so envious when Dad, Mom and Lucas came home last year and described their experience here."

Helen could hear the earnestness in her voice. She cataloged the fact that Jude's name hadn't been mentioned as one giving Flat Creek Ranch a rave review. She really looked at Amber then, and saw that she had indeed scrubbed her face. "I'm glad to hear it.

You know, we really mean it when we say we want you to totally relax and make yourself at home."

At said, "She needs to relax, that's for sure. She's been puttin' in 12 hour days."

Clearly, At and Amber had talked about more than horses. "What is it that you do, Amber?"

Amber finished chewing, dabbed her mouth with her napkin, made a face and said, "I'm a contract attorney for people in the industry, and I have way too many clients."

"Good heavens! By the industry, I assume you mean the movie industry?"

Amber nodded. "I do. So, you aren't going to hear me talking about it. In fact, I'm going to try not to even think about work the whole time I'm here."

At looked at Jude and stood, picking up her own plate in her right hand and transferring it to her left. "Miss LeDeau, are you done with your dinner?" She asked politely.

Jude looked up from where she was pushing pasta across her plate. "No. Yes. Oh, just take it, I'm not hungry," she snapped, reaching for her empty wine glass and waving it at At. "And when you come back, bring me more wine," she ordered. "It's the bottle of red on Lucas's table."

Helen stiffened, watching At. She saw hot spots flash bright on her freckled cheeks. *However she decides to play this, I'm going to back her up and damn the consequences,* she decided. *If it were me, I'd drop the plate right in Jude's lap.*

"I'd be happy to do so," At said evenly and scooped up the plate, turning on her heel and striding towards the swinging door. It was all Helen could do to remain seated. She really was beginning to dislike Jude LeDeau, famous or not.

Amber leaned forward over the table and hissed, "God, Jude, stop being such a royal bitch. What is wrong with you? You already have those two cowboys wrapped around your finger. Give them a

238

break and realize they are being paid to mingle with us…all of us, not just you!"

Chapter Twenty-four

239

"It's all going well, Torrey," Helen said. "We have three different rides out. Jake is finishing up the dishes; the beans are on; and when I'm done talking to you, we're going to make the barbecue sauce; and then go clean the cabins. Now, how is it going with you?"

"Whoa, Helen," Torrey said, "not so fast. Things are fine with me. The doctor was in a bit ago and thinks he can put the cast on this afternoon or maybe tomorrow. Now, stop and go back to the beginning. Give me as much time as you have. I'm starting to feel better mentally and am dividing my time between dozing, feeling sorry for myself, and worrying over what's going on out there."

Helen thought fast. *Entertain her. Hit the highlights. Distract her with Will if you have to.* She took a deep breath, remembering how tired he seemed to be the few times she'd actually seen him. Without Torrey, he was struggling, relying on pure grit and his legendary tough mindedness. "Sorry for the pause, Torrey, it's just so hard to know where to begin. You already know Leo, Beanie, Lucas and Jude. So, do you want to hear about the stunt doubles from Israel, the two very nice gay, soap opera guys, the Hollywood contract lawyer for the stars, the gorgeous M-TV gal, the equally gorgeous dancer, or the very kind director named George, who rang the triangle?"

It was Torrey's turn to be silent. Helen rushed into the gap. "Or, do you want to know that everyone did indeed rave about the Caesar's salad, or perhaps the fact that even those who probably never, and I mean never, eat dessert, just had to have some of your dump cake. By the way, Beanie asked me to ask you if she could please have the recipe. Actually, never mind. I know you and I'll just copy it out for her. What you really want to know, most of all, is how your husband and Dewey are doing. Am I right?"

Torrey's laughter floated down the line. "Bless you, Helen. I can tell by your babble that you really are

240

rushed. Yes, of course, I want to hear about my guys first, but then I want to hear it all...only I know you don't have time."

"You're right, I don't. The juicy details will have to wait until I get to come see you on Tuesday. But, just let me say that your husband was magnificent last night. He was tired, but you'd never know it. He stood and gave his welcome speech and sailed his hat to land on the prong horns just like he always can. Bradlee and Glenn, the gay, soap opera stars, positively squealed with delight. They both brought these faux straw cowboy hats with them and are already lobbying to come with me to town. It turns out that Leo brought a gorgeous new Stetson, and suddenly, their hats just won't do. 'Helen, we want to look totally authentic in our photos,' I believe were their exact words. Of course when they said that, Dewey had to leave the room."

Helen could hear Torrey's low chuckle and it warmed her heart. "Had a coughing fit, did he?" she asked.

"Yes, indeed."

"Are Billy and Buck behaving themselves?"

Helen didn't even try to pretend she didn't know exactly what Torrey meant. "Actually, so far, they are. I asked them to try to mingle with all the guests and pick different tables at which to eat, and they did so quite cheerfully; Billy at the gorgeous red- head's table and Buck at Juana, the MT-V gal's table.

"H-m-m. Interesting. So, you separated the tables. You had a reason?"

"It was something Beanie suggested that I do; and so I just did it. She said something about cliques forming..."

Torrey broke in. "I think Beanie is on our side. She likes her vodka, but she's a good heart. Where was Jude in all this?"

Helen tried for a light laugh. "She's a piece of work, isn't she? You could have warned me, Torrey," she said with mock severity. "However, I might have a secret weapon. Her name is Amber. She's Leo and Beanie's daughter and a contract lawyer. I would bet they mentioned her last year."

Without waiting for Torrey's reply Helen said, "Now, dear heart, I have to run. Will still plans to come and see you sometime today. We expect the riders back between 2:00 and 3:00 so it will be before then. Unless something unforeseen happens, I'll be in tomorrow. If I can bring you something, just say the word."

"I don't need a thing other than being out of here. God bless you, Helen. I just can't say it enough."

"It's all worked out so far and I think you should consider giving both Jake and At a bonus. If we do pull this thing off, it will be a lot due to them going the extra mile."

When Helen hung up the phone, she looked to where Jake was scrubbing on the big baking dish that had earlier held a fluffy, cheesy, Mexican casserole. "I meant that," she said, as she walked towards him. "You two are the real stars here."

He didn't look up and make eye contact and she could see the red creeping up his neck, but she heard his mumbled, "Thanks," as she went past on her way to the pantry.

"You're welcome," she said sincerely and then hauled out the sack of onions. "Now, which do you want to do--dice onions, or separate the ribs and remove the fat?"

"If I have a choice, I reckon I'd be better at cleavin' those ribs." He turned and made eye contact. "You put a couple of wooden toothpicks in your mouth when you do the onions, they won't make you cry."

Helen laughed. "Really? Or are you pulling my leg?"

"Naw. I don't pull people's legs. 'Course, wooden match sticks will work too. Try it." He smiled shyly at her and she smiled back.

"I will then." She reached up on the shelf and got down a box of toothpicks.

"You got to chew on them a little while you work," Jake said while he scrubbed out the sink and then dried his hands.

"Okay," Helen said, "I'll try it." She pointed the toothpicks at him. "Once we get this barbecue sauce done, we'll head down to the cabins and make them up. You can show me how Torrey likes it done." With that, Helen popped the toothpicks into her mouth, pulled the vegetable knife from the block and cut the first onion, thinking, *that's the first time that young man has volunteered information about anything as far as I can remember.*

By the time the guests came straggling in, hot and dusty, but seemingly happy, Helen had a cooler full of drinks on the front porch and a stack of towels on a table at the dock. The ribs were in the oven, slowly baking. The lemons had been squeezed for the green beans, the coleslaw was made and in the walk-in. Jake had shucked the corn and had already set the table. Tonight's hors d'oeuvres were nearly a repeat of the night before, with the addition of a fruit plate. All she really had left to do was the baking powder biscuits and the brownies. It was time to take a break.

"Jake, would you please get butter out to soften and then, unless you can think of something else we need to do, why don't you go see if you can help At, or one of the men in any way." She sighed and leaned back, stretching her lower back. "As for me, I'm going to go grab a shower after I greet everyone and tell them they are on their own until the triangle calls them for the cocktail hour. That includes you."

Helen saw Jake's eyes light at the mention of At's name. But all he said was, "Maybe I'll take her a pop."

Helen had laid her new, still clean Wranglers on the bed and had taken the old ones with her to the shower and had thrown them in the pan. *'Necessity is the mother of invention,'* she thought; *another of the good, old adages.* She stepped in on top of her Wranglers feeling the heaven of the warm water while she shampooed her hair and stomped on the jeans. The water in the shower pan was several inches deep due to the clogged drain and a little bluish-brown. She grinned. *Well, they'll at least be cleaner, if not clean,* she thought.

Standing under the spray of the little tin shower, Helen thought the water felt better than that of any five-star hotel she had ever been in. She had been up since 4:00. Granted, she had dozed off in a deck chair for a good half hour after she had eaten her sandwich at lunch, only to awaken with a start, remembering that she hadn't taken the vegetarians' dinner out of the freezer. *What I know about vegetarian cooking you could put in a thimble. Thank God, Torrey made the main courses for Amber and Bradlee ahead of time. I wonder if she had one of her premonitions.*

Helen turned and let the water blast the tension from her neck and shoulders, remembering how tempting her bed looked when she had walked into her cabin. It had been all she could do to keep from flopping down on it. Instead, she had looked over her meager wardrobe, selected one of her shirts from the old days; one that had been too tight and was now decidedly too big and sighed. *Maybe Glenn and Bradlee will help me pick out some new shirts when we go to town.*

Before she left the cabin, Helen laid her wet Wranglers over the willow rocker on her front porch. She thought she looked as put together as she could look in an old, faded red, too-big shirt. Her hair was blown dry, curled slightly with a curling iron and clasped loosely at her neck. Her makeup was basic, but artfully applied. She wore no jewelry, other than simple, gold hoops.

When she walked down her front steps, she could see Lucas standing in front of the Sunrise Cabin, staring at the clouds. "Hello, Lucas," she called as she strode up the path towards him. "How was your day?"

He pulled his gaze from looking at the sky and smiled at her as she stopped in front of him. "Terrific! Just terrific!" he said.

Wow! Robert Redford, move over. This guy has star power! His cowboy hat shaded cornflower blue eyes and since his smile had turned into a grin, attractive laugh lines bracketed them. "Did Will give you the same horse you had last year?"

He turned somber. "Helen, Will told us of your loss and I'm sure sorry for all of you. Marshall sounds like he was a fine man."

It took a moment for the words to sink in. Helen waited for the pain to hit and was surprised when it didn't. She couldn't begin to identify the feeling that came instead. "Thank you," she said simply. "Do you know the details?"

He shook his head. "Only that he passed three years ago and that this is the first time you've been back to the ranch. The reason he told me even that, I assume, is because he paired me with Jasper, the horse his best friend rode."

Helen managed a smile. "Good for you. As you know, he's a great horse. And Will wouldn't have put the two of you together if you weren't a good man." She found she meant what she said. She had absolute faith in Will's love for her husband, and his integrity couldn't be questioned. She looked him in the eye. "And that, Mr. Clements, is a great compliment."

"Yes," he said somberly, "and I take it as such. But, please call me Lucas."

They walked up the path in silence, each thinking their own thoughts. It was clear to Helen that Lucas, if he had his way, would be a regular at the ranch. Yesterday, long after the other guests had come up for cocktails, he had lingered at the corrals, watching as At turned out the horses. Twice today, she had seen him standing by himself simply looking over the ranch or up at the clouds, just as he had been doing now. Once, she thought he had been watching her. *So, I wonder, how does such a marriage like theirs work? Does his gayness give Jude the right to flirt with other men so blatantly?*

When they reached the lodge he looked down on her. "You're doing a fine job, Helen. Torrey would be proud."

"Thank you Lucas. It means a great deal to hear you say that. I'm going to see if I can find Will and get an update on his visit with her. She was expecting to get her cast sometime this afternoon or perhaps, tomorrow morning."

They heard a high-pitched, feminine squeal and simultaneously turned towards the pond in time to see, either Buck or Billy, loft Jude into the air from the dock and then dive in after her. Helen heard Lucas sigh. "Looks like everyone is having a good time," he said simply as he moved to join them.

Helen watched for a moment. It did look as though everyone was relaxed and having fun. They had moved the cooler down to the dock, and the younger crowd was either in the pond or lying around it. Beanie, Leo and George were reading in the shade of the willows. Then she looked towards the barn where Will's truck was parked. *He's back then.* She glanced at her watch. Already, it was past 4:00. *No time to find out about Torrey, I've got to get cracking.*

Jake was already in the kitchen. She saw he'd turned the beans back on low. When she looked in the oven, she saw he'd not only basted the ribs with sauce but had covered them with foil. "Jake, you're a wonder," she said and then asked, "How did At's day go?"

"It went real good. She just had to make some saddle adjustments. She said, after she got used to them, she and the boys got along fine. They didn't do much other than to walk because they had Leo and Beanie along too, but everyone liked the horse Will picked for them and they were tickled with the scenery."

It was the longest Helen had ever heard Jake talk and even then he wasn't done.

"She was some surprised that they all could ride like they said they could. It was a big relief to her. She'll be along to help as soon as she turns the herd out and grabs a shower." He had been mindlessly chopping walnuts while he talked.

On a whim, Helen said, "Jake, why don't you go ahead and whip up the brownies and the biscuits while I see to drinks and hors d'oeuvres. Oh, and by the way, thanks for the tip on the toothpicks."

He nodded without comment, having evidently run out of words. Helen felt a motherly rush as she went through the swinging door to the dining room. *I miss my children, but At and Jake will sure do in a pinch,* she thought fondly. She stopped to survey the room. It looked good. The tables were set. The water pitchers were lined up by the ice machine. She stopped. *What on earth is that?* She strode to the counter and looked down to see what was obviously, Jake's handiwork. Somewhere, he found a small chalk board. On it, whimsically lettered and beautifully decorated in Jake's special style, was the night's menu: Slow Baked Ribs, Lemon Green Beans, Baked Beans, Coleslaw, Grilled Corn on the Cob, Brownies and Vanilla Ice Cream.

He had even listed the vegetarian casserole: Mushroom and Wild Rice with Black Beans and Gorgonzola. *How perfect! When did he find the time?* She heard the swinging door creak and turned to find Jake standing there, his face redder than her shirt. "Jake," she said, "you just kill me! This is so over-the-

247

top perfect that I'm practically speechless. You are so talented! When on earth did you find the time to do this?"

She saw him swallow several times and then step on into the room to come and stand beside her. "I ain't fly fishin' these days," he said, as if it explained everything. "Want me to go down and get the cooler for you?"

Will stood at the end of the dining room, his thumbs hooked in the front pockets of his Wranglers and his legs spread in typical rancher fashion. He was still slicked up from his trip to town and seeing Torrey. He looked out over those assembled and grinned. "First off, Mama's got her cast on and the doc says, 'maybe, just maybe,' I'll be able to spring her come Friday." His grin got wider when spontaneous clapping broke out.

Beanie, self-appointed spokesperson, raised her vodka glass and called, "We'll all drink to that news; it makes a great day even better. We're all so happy for you both."

Will lifted his hat, scratched his head and then, instead of setting it back in place, sailed it to the horns. Then he looked at Leo and said quietly, "After 40 odd years, a fella sure gets used to havin' his woman beside him, doesn't he Leo?"

Leo laughed and covered Beanie's hand with his. "Now, that's a fact."

"Next thing I got to say is that you folks are sure makin' me look good. I come home from town expectin' all kinds of little problems had cropped up and instead, seems like you all liked your horses, your saddles, the scenery and your lunches. If you got complaints, I ain't heard 'em and neither has Dewey. So, unless you got saddle sores or other issues, we'll be repeatin' the process tomorrow. Any day you don't want to ride, just let one of the staff know; so we don't saddle your horse."

248

Will nodded to Helen to bring in the food and started to sit, but then stood up again. "Oh yeah, and while I was in town, I got us a bunch of quarters to put in the jukebox and Billy said to tell you to go ahead and use 'em all. He knows how to get 'em back out of the machine."

Helen came through the swinging door from the kitchen, wiping her hands. She had turned At and Jake loose to do whatever they wanted. Breakfast prep had been finished, the kitchen was spotless; the coffee maker and the big coffee pot were filled and ready. She had heard the jukebox going for some time and saw that the tables had been pushed aside and dancing had started. Patsy Cline was singing "I Fall to Pieces." It was a slow, sad song, definitely country. She scanned the dancers. Lucas was dancing with his wife, Billy with Juana, and Buck with Amber. Beanie was dancing with Bradlee, and Cleah was dancing with Glenn. Leo, Will and George were sitting out on the deck. Dee Dee and Dean were nowhere to be seen. She went through the French doors to the deck, needing a word with Will before she went to her cabin. The men were sipping something yellow. *Oh, my!* she thought, *Will's pulled out his dad's finest.*
"Helen," George said, "I was just about to come looking for you to ask you to dance."
"Well, thank you, George, but I was just coming to have a word with Will and then I planned to sneak off to bed."
"Aw," Will said, squinting up at her, and waving her away, "go on and have a dance." He paused. "Tell you what. I'll come up to the kitchen first thing...say 5:00 and we can talk then. I got some things I want to say to you, too."
Even though Helen's whole tired body screamed, *"N-o-o-o!"* she forced a smile. "Well, in that case, George, I'd love to."
"Atta girl." She heard Will say.

George took her elbow and led her back into the dining room just as Kitty Wells started singing about honky tonk angels. As they took the familiar pose, the first thing that struck her was how different it felt to be in the arms of a man nearly her own height. The second thing she realized was that George was a very good dancer and she had better pay attention.

"You're so busy, Helen, this is the perfect way for me to capture you long enough to find out how you could have possibly known that my wine was made from Nebbilo grapes."

Helen smiled at him. "Your very good wine, I might add, George." Then she sighed. "In another lifetime...before I was widowed...my husband and I did what many empty nesters do...took a trip. In our case, we went first to Switzerland; then dropped down into Northern Italy. Actually, it was just a guess. We learned, while visiting vineyards there, that a few growers in California were trying the Nebbiolo grapes." Helen was amazed how matter-of-fact her voice sounded when discussing what turned out to be the last trip she would ever take with her husband.

"What a co-incidence! I am so glad I tucked a bottle in. Did Jake tell you that I asked him to work up some ideas for my label?"

Helen's feet rooted themselves to the floor. She grinned in delight. "That's wonderful, George! What did he say?"

George smiled, looking quite satisfied with himself. "Let's just say, I left him speechless. But he did nod his head."

Helen was still smiling foolishly at George, her mind buzzing when the song finished and she heard Beanie say, "All right everyone find a new partner."

"Thanks for the dance, Helen," George said, giving her a slight bow before moving off to find a new partner. She decided the opportunity to leave had come, but Bradlee was there holding out his arms.

250

"Helen, isn't this terrific? We think these records were put in the jukebox in the 50s. I wasn't even born yet! He pulled her close as Jim Reeves' velvet voice filled the room with *He'll Have to Go.*

She smiled up at him. "Bradlee, you and Glenn were just the people I wanted to see. If you really want to go shopping, tomorrow's your day. I'll be going in right after breakfast. I can drop you both off at Ranch Supply and then go on to the hospital to see Torrey. When I come back to get you, maybe you two can help me select a couple of new snap-button shirts."

Bradlee pulled her in tight for a quick, spontaneous hug. "Oh, Helen, that would be just perfect. I can speak for Glenn and say that we'd love to go."

As Reeves crooned about putting sweet lips closer to the phone, Helen couldn't help but wonder who was selecting the songs. "Bradlee, who's putting in the quarters?"

"Beanie, of course. She has this whole thing organized. Isn't she just amazing? It's a round robin thing. That way we can include everyone, even those who don't have partners here and, hopefully, keep the blonde brat from causing a fight."

"Wha-a-? Bradlee, what are you talking about? What fight? What's going on?" Helen got a sick feeling in her stomach. She knew exactly who "the blonde brat" was.

"In all honesty," he said, "I would have to admit that I can hardly blame Jude. Those tight buns and that curly black hair...well, let me just say...they're definitely eye candy."

"Billy and Buck? The King boys? They are the ones fighting?" Helen looked up at him in disbelief, trying to make sense of things.

"Not, yet," he said, putting her through a series of intricate steps, "but if 'the evil princess' ups her game a notch, they will be."

251

Helen glanced around the room and saw that Dewey had materialized out of nowhere and was now dancing with Jude. *Thank God! Dewey must know about all this. He won't let anything happen.* She felt herself starting to relax. "Thanks for letting me know, Bradlee. And yes, Beanie is amazing. She's amazing and you, my friend, are a very good dancer."

"Oh, honey, we all are," he said dismissively. "We're from Hollywood! It comes with the territory."

Helen smiled at him as the song ended and he dipped her low. She said, "You know, I was on my way to bed when George asked me to dance. It's been a long day, so I'm going to bow out now."

Bradlee released her and stepped back, looking over her shoulder as he did so. Then he leaned forward and whispered in her ear, his blue eyes twinkling, "Too late, sweetie." Then she heard him say, "Hello, Lucas. She's all yours."

Chapter Twenty-five

Helen practically ran down the trail to her cabin, the path lights offering just enough light to keep her from stumbling. *What the hell! What the hell! What in the hell is wrong with you Helen? Have you lost your mind? Are you crazy?* The scene in the lodge played like a warped record in her brain. When she had whirled to find Lucas standing there, all thoughts of needing to leave immediately left her brain. He'd held out his arms, a quirky smile on his face and she'd melted into them. He pulled her close, almost possessively and they'd danced in total silence. "I'll be There," another Ray Price song was playing on the jukebox. Helen was hyperaware of how closely she was being held; close enough that her breasts were touching his chest. Her hand resting on his shoulder could feel his muscles glide as he turned her and once, just briefly, their whole bodies touched. An erotic shock jolted through her and her eyes jumped up to his face, but his eyes had been closed. She closed her own eyes, her mind a freefall of confusion until the dance ended and he pulled her close once more and whispered in her ear, "Thank you, Helen," before releasing her. She hadn't been able to summon even one word, instead turned on her heel and bolted.

Now, she stumbled up her steps and through the screen door, latching it behind her. Absently, she turned her Wranglers over on the chair so the underside could dry, flipped off the porch light and walked on into the cabin, feeling a bit more grounded once in her cozy room with the door shut. She flipped on her overhead light and went to stand in front of her mirror, grasping the top of her dresser. *Good God, Helen! Get a grip! What is wrong with you? That man is both gay and married...totally off limits. What have you turned into, some sex-starved, pathetic old woman?*

She groaned, pulled the button on her vintage alarm clock, kicked off her ropers and flopped down on the bed. Being in the design business, she knew something of the gay community and what she knew

253

was--if there was attraction--it was all one way. *This is absolutely all in my mind.* She let out a tired groan, turned on her back and threw an arm over her eyes, a tiny voice whispering inside her, *'But, then, why did it feel so right, so terribly, terribly right?'*

When the alarm started its brassy ring at 4:00 AM, Helen had to swim up from the deep and dreamless sleep of exhaustion before she could move to shut it off. Her mouth was dry, a sure sign she had been sleeping on her back—probably snoring. Slowly, the events of the evening before brought her fully awake. She blinked against the light she'd left on and looked down at herself. Sometime in the night, she had wrapped herself in the quilt, but she was still fully clothed. She sat up, yawned and rubbed sleep from her eyes. *No matter what, I've got to get moving. I cannot let the Rawlings down.*

As she slid from the bed a thought popped into her head. *Wait a minute! No one knows. Thank God I'm a woman...even Lucas has no idea of the effect he had on me. None! I didn't pull away, but I didn't rub against him like I wanted to, either.* "Hold that thought, Helen," she said aloud in the little room as she walked towards the bathroom, undressing as she went. "Hold that thought and you'll make it through this week."

By 4:45 Helen had the big coffee pot on the range starting to perk and the little, eight-cup coffee maker was just done. She was pouring a cup when Jake silently slipped through the door a few minutes later. They looked at each other. Helen said, "I know I look like shit, but you don't look much better." She said it with a smile in her voice and instead of just ducking his head, he mumbled, "Yep. An' this is only Tuesday."

"So it is! Lucky us!" She sighed. "At least it's an easy day. Spinach quiche and ham for breakfast and hamburgers tonight...well, tofu burgers for Amber and Glenn. But that's all easy. Why don't you go ahead and start on the fruit plate as soon as you get the dining room set up."

They heard At's boot heels on the stairs coming down from the attic apartment. She came into the kitchen with an elastic band in her teeth, both hands busy with her hair, but her eyes on Jake, standing at the swinging door. Helen saw the look that passed between them and felt a little surge of happiness. *Now, why I feel like the fairy Godmother to this deal, I don't know...but do I ever have a lot to tell Torrey!*

"Howdy, Marilee," Jake said in a voice so tender it made Helen want to hug them both and lecture them about the trials and tribulations of first love. Wisely, she did neither. "Coffee's ready, At. Why don't you grab a cup before you head on down to the corrals? Oh, and by the way, Glenn and Bradlee are coming with me to town, so don't saddle their horses."

At nodded and reached for a mug. "Well, that makes my day a little easier. Thanks for the heads up, Helen."

Then Helen said, "And Jake, before you go, George told me he had asked you to work on a label design for him. If I can help in any way, just let me know." She tried to make her voice conversational and off-hand, as if a Hollywood director asked him to create a label for his new wine every day.

Jake shook his head in a disbelieving way. "Aw, I'm not sure he wasn't just bein' nice, Helen. He's got a kindness about him, you know."

Helen said, "Yes, I do know. Remember how he helped me Sunday night? But this isn't kindness. When he talked to me about it, he seemed truly excited." She made a shooing motion with her hands. "Now, go get busy. We've got an easy meal, but not that easy."

Will and Dewey walked through the kitchen door just after 5:00. Helen knew she looked tough, but they both looked tougher. At took one look at them, took a last gulp of coffee and made for the door. Helen

255

grinned. "Well, boys, what time did the party break up last night?"

Will quirked a sheepish smile and hooked a thumb at Dewey. "He's the one. I turned in when Leo and George quit me on the porch, but ol' Dewey here was playin' field marshal with the troops until about eleven."

"Oh my," said Helen, dividing the last of the coffee between their two mugs. "More coffee from the big pot in a minute."

Dewey took a slurp of the coffee and grumbled, "I'm way too old for this shit! I need my beauty sleep." He plopped himself on one of the stools by the butcher block.

Helen leaned over and looked at him, her curiosity killing her. "So, Dewey, were you able to keep things peaceful?"

"Only because Lucas finally come and took his wife by the arm and said they was goin'." He looked around for Jake.

Helen pointed at the swinging door and he nodded, lowering his voice. "I told Will what I believe...and that is--Jude wants Buck and Billy to fight over her--and until Lucas shut things down, she nearly had her way. My God but that little filly is in heat!"

Turning to Will, Helen nodded and said, "Bradlee told me much the same thing."

Will looked older than his years as he looked between Dewey and Helen before lowering himself to the other stool. "It's a fine mess we've gotten you into, Helen."

Helen waved an arm like she was swatting at flies, suddenly angry. "Oh stop it! Get off the pity pot, Will," she said with fire in her voice. "You're already seeing a train wreck when you don't even see the train. First off, I don't know Billy and Buck very well as adults, but from what I've seen, they not only love each other, but they like each other and always have." She looked at Dewey. "My advice is to tell them what you think

256

Jude is up to. Ask them if she's worth it. Give them some credit for being able to control their testosterone and handle the situation."

Both men were staring at her and she realized she was practically shouting. She glared at Will and said. "And you, Will Rawling, aren't giving our guests enough credit. Didn't you compliment them at dinner last night? Aren't you pleased how much they seem to like the place? Weren't you totally surprised that no one asked for a different horse, complained about their saddle, their cabin, the food, the mosquitoes by the Big Pond Trail? Don't you think they have Jude's number…whatever it is…nymphomania or some other personality disorder like narcissism?"

By now, Helen had her hands on her hips. She drew in a big breath and let it out slowly and said mildly, "Okay, I'm done and I know I'm totally out of line. But I know one thing…you can't afford to fire Billy and Buck and you can't afford to fire me." She turned to the range and pulled the big pot from the fire to let it settle.

Both men sat quietly, watching her. She looked at the clock and then at Will. "What I really wanted to talk to you about this morning had to do with a whole list of details, one of which was how we're going to handle Torrey when she comes home. But, it seems I've used the time ranting. Sorry."

"You are sure one surprise after another, Helen," he said. "You give a fella a lot to chew on. An' I come up to do some apologizing,' but there ain't time for that either. Dewey's got to go get at his bullshit station and you got breakfast to get together."

"Apology? You don't owe me an apology, Will."

He looked steadily at her, his tired black eyes somber. "Torrey sure thinks I do and she's generally right about such stuff. But, like I say, this ain't the time or the place. Maybe we can carve out some minutes after you get back from town and seein' her."

Already, he was moving towards the door. "Wait," Helen said, taking down a travel mug and pouring coffee from the big pot. "Take this with you."

He nodded his thanks, and was gone just as Jake walked back in, going directly to pour cream into a white crockery pitcher. Helen wondered how much he'd heard and decided she didn't care. He mumbled. "I turned on the hot plates, Dewey," as he disappeared through the swinging door with the cream and a pot full of hot water for the tea drinkers.

Dewey rose from the stool, one creak at a time. "I'm getting' too damned old for this," he said again, as he reached for the pot. He filled both Helen and Jake's mugs before disappearing through the swinging door with it. "I'll be on the porch with my coffee and Queenie, should you need me," he said as the door swung shut.

Jake came back in and they looked at each other and then simultaneously looked at the clock. "I believe this is where we pick up the tempo from 'Love Without End, Amen' to 'Achy Breaky Heart,'" she said, turning on the oven before getting the package of ham steaks and two boxes filled with quiche from the refrigerator. "God bless Costco," she said.

Jake had assembled the fruit and was peeling oranges. "How come you know all those country western songs, Helen?" he asked, his voice puzzled.

She looked up from where she was reading the directions on one of the quiche boxes. "For one thing, believe it or not, country western is very popular in the East. I mean, for heaven sakes, The Grand Ol' Opry is in Nashville, Tennessee. But the real reason is that my husband, Marshall, was a country boy at heart. Our kids grew up on Alan, Reba, George, Travis and Garth. He grew up on Willie, Waylon and the Boys, The Statler Brothers, Chet Atkins and Hank Williams Jr., but he loved the old classics too." She gestured towards the swinging door with her chin, her hands busy with packaging. "He would have been able to sing almost all of the songs on that jukebox. For that matter, so can Will."

Suddenly, Dr. Pagglio's voice whispered to her, 'One day, Helen, you will be able to recall and talk about memories of your husband and they will bring you a measure of happiness.' *And that day is now...right now, when I really need it. What a blessing!* she thought.

Guests started straggling through the French doors. From the kitchen, Helen and Jake could hear Dewey making them welcome, pouring them coffee or tea, inviting them to take it out on the porch. Helen put bran muffins in the warming oven and checked on the quiche. It was not quite time for the ham steaks to go on the grill.

She took a sip of coffee, watching Jake take an artfully arranged fruit plate into the dining room and suddenly wondered if he'd had time to put the breakfast menu on the chalkboard. She started towards the dining room but stopped at the swinging door when she heard Lucas' mellow voice break into laughter and felt her breath catch. *Shit!* She clenched her eyes shut and whirled. *Get a grip, Helen. You are being ridiculous!*

She took a deep breath and opened her eyes, concentrating on breakfast details to steady herself. *Yogurt! We forgot the yogurt. Now, you are going to put those little cups in the big red bowl and take it directly into the dining room. Then you are going to greet everyone pleasantly...including Lucas.*

As she walked towards the refrigerator the phone rang. " Good morning! Flat Creek Ranch, Helen speaking. How may I help you?"

There was a silence and then Willie's surprised voice came on. "Mom? Mom...what are you doing there?"

Helen's heart clenched. She and her son had buried the hatchet, but things were still fragile between

259

them. His voice had not sounded especially friendly, just surprised.

"Willie, darling, how wonderful to hear your voice. Are you calling from Alaska?" She knew her words did not answer his question, but she was stalling for a bit of time.

"I'm not in Alaska. I'm done up there. I'm in Eugene and I was calling to ask Aunt Torrey and Uncle Will if they wanted company this weekend." He paused. "Weren't you planning to be there last week?"

"I was here, dear. My mission to scatter your father's ashes was completed and I was ready to return home when your Aunt Torrey took a terrible fall and absolutely shattered her femur."

"What?" Willie's voice sounded shocked and Helen rushed on.

"She's still in the hospital, but will possibly get to come home on Friday. However, they had twelve guests coming in the day I was leaving, so I changed my plans and am pitching in to try to get us through the week."

"Jeez, Mom, I can hardly take this in. How's Uncle Will doing?"

"He's hanging in there, as we all are... Oh, Willie please come. I can't talk any longer. I'm in the middle of making everybody breakfast."

"Okay, Mom. I'm coming as soon as I get a couple of things settled here. You tell Uncle Will he can put me to work any way he needs to."

"Darling, you are a Godsend! Listen, do you want me to see if Russell Warner, the Rawlings' pilot friend, can come and pick you up?"

"Hey, that'd be great Mom. Call and let me know, okay?"

"I'll get to work on it as soon as I possibly can find a second. I can see his name right here on Torrey's wall list. Good bye, son."

Jake came in to start on the lunches and looked surprised to see Helen throwing the yogurt containers into the bowl and then practically waltzing into the dining room. He could hear her say in a voice full of joy, "Good morning, everyone. I trust you all slept well. We're about ten minutes from breakfast."

Will was standing, talking to Cleah and Amber; he too heard her tone. "Excuse me," he said, "I'd better go and see what is wrong with our cook. She sounds too damned happy."

He caught her just inside the swinging door. "What's up Helen? You win the lottery or something?"

She turned and gave him a hug. "Yes, in a way I most certainly did! If you will please call Russell and see if he can fly to Eugene tomorrow, we can have Willie here by dinner time. He said for you to put him to work any way you want."

A smile split Will's face and he looked over his shoulder. "Did you tell him what he was getting into?" he whispered.

"Ha! And have him change his mind? I think not! I did tell him we had twelve guests."

"Well, well," Will said, thinking fast as he strode to the phone. "That big, lanky kid just might come in real handy. I'd best get some shoes on ol' Chainsaw."

Her good mood had stayed with her and allowed her to smile and engage in small chit chat as she carried around the coffee pot to the stragglers, thankful that Lucas wasn't one of them. "Eat up, she said. It's a simple dinner tonight and all you get for dessert is strawberry shortcake."

Helen had Bradlee and Glenn hustled into the truck and was dusting for town before the last guest was mounted. She had left Jake in charge of the final breakfast cleanup and that night's simple dinner prep. "It's an easy dinner, Jake. All the prep you have to do now is to slice strawberries and put a cup of sugar on them so they make juice for the shortcake. Thank goodness Torrey bought those big tubs of potato salad at Costco."

He'd simply nodded and pulled an envelope from his hip pocket. "I made her a card," he'd mumbled, looking at his feet.

Helen was touched on Torrey's behalf. "What a dear thing for you to have done. She'll love it." Impulsively, she had reached forward and given him a hug. "You are going to enjoy meeting my son, Willie." She looked at him, judging his height. "In fact, I'd venture to guess you two will see almost eye-to-eye." Laughing at her own joke, Helen had flipped him a wave and had rushed to get her purse and the things she was taking to Torrey.

In the truck, the lightness she felt over Willie's impending visit continued. She glanced sideways at the boys and gauged their excitement about going shopping to be genuine. Glenn was riding shotgun with his elbow out the window. Bradlee had his right hand on Glenn's thigh. Helen wondered if she should caution them about public displays of affection in a red-necked cow town like Burns and decided against it. *They aren't naïve,* she decided. "So," she said, "Lucky you. You get to meet my youngest son. And in case you were wondering, this is a surprise visit and it has made me extremely happy."

"Oh, that's great, Helen. Tell us about him. Is he straight?" Bradlee asked.

Helen laughed. "Yes, he's straight. He plays basketball for the University of Oregon, but has spent most of his summer in Alaska, commercial fishing. But that's all about him. Now that we have some bench time, I want to know more about you. All I know is that you are actors on daytime television and At says you both are competent riders."

Bradlee laughed. "Well, of course we are, Helen. We started riding lessons as soon as Leo and Beanie invited us to come."

"Wow! Smart boys!"

"Guess who gave us our lessons," Glenn said leaning forward so he could see her face.

"I haven't the foggiest. Sam Elliot, Clint Eastwood, that guy in 'Lonesome Dove' that rode so well?"

"No. Not Tommy Lee Jones and not Robert Duvall. It was Amber. She has a lot of very "horsey" friends. They let us use their horses for the lessons. That was when we fell in love with everything western."

"What a nice thing for her to have done. Is that why everyone in the group rides so well...lessons from Amber?"

"No. Dee Dee and Dean sometimes ride as stunt doubles. Cleah and Juana both had horses as kids. Amber and her parents already knew how to ride...so did Lucas and Jude, which is good."

At Helen's cocked eyebrow, Glenn paused and then said, "Oh, all right, I'll tell you." He paused, "Let's just say Jude is one of Amber's clients, but she can only put up with her in small doses." He looked fondly at Bradlee and then said, "We think if it weren't for Lucas, Amber wouldn't put up with her at all."

Uh-oh! Helen decided, *time to move this conversation in another direction.* "You know, I've been so busy that I hadn't really noticed much. Thanks for the heads up."

They drove in silence for a while, each thinking their own thoughts. Helen's turned to her upcoming visit with Torrey. She smiled inwardly. *You're about to get those juicy details, Torrey...but NOT about my stupid hormonal reaction to Lucas,* she thought grimly. *That goes with me to the grave!*

She pulled her thoughts back and said, "Okay, what I really want to know now, is more about you two. I don't know a thing about daytime soap operas, but I'll listen to that or about your life outside of work."

Bradlee laughed. "Oh goodie, Glenn, we get to talk about US!" And for the next twenty minutes, Helen learned they'd both grown up in Southern California but hadn't known each other until they met in acting school. Both had been waiters from time to time and Bradlee had painted houses for an uncle for a year before he got a small part in a commercial that went well. Glenn got lucky when his agent sent him to a casting call for *The Bold and the Beautiful.* Two years later, when *The Young and the Restless* needed a new romantic lead, Bradlee got the part.

When Helen tried to ask more about their work, Glenn said with a sigh, "Sweetie, no matter how we try to dress it up, acting in soaps is mostly about learning bad lines, hours in make-up, standing around and putting up with pissy directors and petty insecurities."

"Which, unfortunately, is what the big egos are all about," Bradlee added. "But, we're lucky. Our ratings are holding and that can't be said very often in the world of daytime soaps. But, let's not talk any more about work. We're on vacation."

Helen nodded. "I hear you and I respect that feeling one hundred and ten percent. All those years my husband and I came to the ranch for the month of August, we made a pact never to talk about work. It was wonderful."

As they reached the town limits, Helen said, "Okay, guys, here's the deal. I'll drop you off at Ranch Supply. Keep yourselves busy until I get back. I won't be more than an hour and I have my mobile phone in my purse."

Bradlee reached in his pocket and pulled out his phone. "Cell phone service! I'm in heaven! What's your number?"

After she gave it to him she said, "I'd like you to please look through the ladies snap button shirts for me. If you see something that you think would suit me in a size medium and if they do, ask the clerk to set them aside until I come to pick you up."

"Oh, Helen, really? You'd trust us to pick out shirts for you? Don't you know the reputation we gay guys have for flamboyance?" Glenn teased.

264

"No," she said seriously, "I don't. What I know is that my friends in graphic design, who happen to be gay, have excellent taste." She shot them a brief, stern glance as she pulled into the parking lot of Ranch Supply. "Okay, here you are. Go shop 'til you drop."

Torrey was wide awake and waiting for her when she walked into the room. Her leg was wrapped in white plaster from ankle to upper thigh. For a moment they just stood and smiled at each other and then Helen rushed forward and folded herself into Torrey's arms. "I'm glad to see you're still alive," Torrey said with a laugh.

"I am," Helen said as she straightened. "Mostly, I think, because you were so super organized and over-prepared for these guests. You don't know how many times I have said, 'God bless Costco' or 'God bless Torrey.'"

"How much time do you have?"

"About 45 minutes. I brought two of the guests, Glenn and Bradlee, in with me and dropped them at Ranch Supply. I'd like to get back to the ranch by early afternoon. I've left Jake with all of the cabin and lodge cleaning plus a few hundred other things."

Torrey's eyes were bright. Helen noticed that the circles under her eyes had faded and she seemed much more her old, centered self. "How's your pain?" she asked.

"Much better. Now that the cast is on, other than not being able to get out of bed without help, I'm good."

"Then, are you ready for the gossip?" she asked.

"Oh, God, yes! Pull up a chair. But first--Will says things are holding together, but barely. He's afraid Jude is going to cause some sort of a rift between Buck and Billy."

Helen placed a chair where she could not only see Torrey, but could hold her hand. "Yes, I know he is.

So is Dewey. I got in my lecture mode and let them have it with both barrels this morning."

"Whoa! That sounds more like the Helen I used to know." Now, Torrey's eyes were twinkling. "They came to the kitchen to whine. Am I right?"

Helen nodded. "I told them to not only give the King boys some credit, but to realize that the guests were pretty good at managing their own problems."

Torrey raised an eyebrow and drawled, "Did you now? How'd they take it?"

"Dewey didn't stick around long enough for me to find out. He had coffee duty. Your husband seemed to take it okay. I had a whole list of things to talk about and he said you told him he had to apologize to me, but we ran out of time because of my ranting. You wouldn't know what the apology was about, would you?"

Torrey looked solemnly at her. "Men can be so thick headed. Mine included. I'll tell you, but when he actually does apologize, you'll have to promise to let him."

"Sure, I can't think what it could be. We've barely seen each other."

"I know. He's miffed at you, so he's been avoiding you."

"What? When you say 'miffed,' you mean pissed. What in the world did I do?"

"You don't like his stud."

"What? Packer? I've only seen him that once..." Helen stopped and looked at Torrey. "He's right. For some reason, I don't."

"Of course you don't. That's what I told Will. I said, 'Of course she can barely stand to look at him, Will. Think about it for a one minute. When's the last time Helen saw a horse with a mangled leg?'"

Helen's face paled. "Oh, my God! High Octane! Even I didn't get the connection, Torrey. I just remember that it just about made me throw up to be

266

around him. I guess there was so much going on that I didn't really think about it."

Torrey squeezed her hand and looked steadily at her. "Going on at so many, many levels," she said.

Helen nodded and took a deep breath. "True. But it's in the past. Let's get to the present. The first thing I want to tell you isn't gossip. It's that Willie is back from Alaska and is coming to the ranch as soon as Russell can go get him. Will is working out the details."

Torrey lit up. "Oh, baby, this is working out just right. You two need some face-to-face-time."

"Yes," Helen said quietly, "we do." Then she grinned at Torrey. "Now, on to the good stuff..." She rummaged in her purse and handed Torrey Jake's get well card. "I'll tell you what I'm pretty sure is happening between At and Jake while you're reading the card."

"Oh, goodie," Torrey said as she opened the envelope and looked at the card. Helen watched how touched her friend was; watched as she ran her finger over the cover and then opened it. After a moment, she handed the card to Helen and said, "Who knew?"

Helen smiled as she saw Jake's trademark curlicues, beautifully woven into the words, GET WELL. Inside, it simply said, "We miss you." It was signed, 'Love, Jake and Marilee.'

Chapter Twenty-six

Helen rolled out of bed, slapping at her alarm button as she did. For once, she felt fairly rested. *Spending time with Glenn and Bradlee was obviously good for me;* she thought and smiled, remembering.

The boys had done some serious shopping, not only for themselves but for her. Hanging in her tiny wardrobe were three new shirts and a denim broomstick skirt.

By the time she had finished catching Torrey up on the news and getting some serious planning done for how things would work on Torrey's arrival home, it was well over her allotted 45 minutes. It was over an hour before she had gotten back to Ranch Supply.

When she rushed through the doors, she immediately knew she needn't have worried that her shoppers were bored. Instead, they had the whole store in an uproar. It seemed that a shopper had recognized them right away and was a huge fan of both programs. In the time it takes a whisper to reach an ear, everyone, from shoppers to clerks to stock boys, knew the stars of "The Bold and the Beautiful" and "The Young and the Restless" were intent on buying a good portion of the clothing inventory...new boots, hats, shirts, belts...all of which caught their eye, went into the dressing rooms.

Opinions had been asked for and given. Autographs had been asked for and given. Clerks were blushing and scurrying. A few cameras were pulled out and pictures snapped. The boys were posing and joking with each other and anyone within sight. Their pile kept getting bigger. The store manager's smile kept getting wider.

"Helen!" Bradlee said, when he spotted her, "The shopping has been amazing! Just look at us! Don't we look authentic?"

She couldn't begin to keep the grin off her face. In truth, with their lean, good looks, they did look as if

268

they'd just stepped off the set of an old western movie. Both boys were wearing new shirts with the Wrangler logo; Bradlee's red and Glenn's teal and white. Gone were their designer jeans. Now, both wore brand new Wranglers whose cuffs drug the floor, leaving only the pointed toes of shiny new boots showing. Their new western belts had silver buckles the size of dinner plates. "You two are the ones who are amazing!" she laughed.

"No, wait. Wait! You haven't seen our hats. Let's show her, Glenn." With a flourish, they whipped the top from hat boxes and carefully, by the brim, retrieved their choices and put them on. Bradlee was wearing a silverbelly Stetson with a low crown and a flat brim. Glenn's choice was a fawn colored, high-crowned hat with a rolled brim.

"Well, hello, Hoss and Little Joe!" she said, laughing with delight. "You two look obscenely handsome in those hats!"

"Exactly! We thought we'd go with the hats millions of people agreed were cool. And in their day, the Cartwright boys were the coolest!" Bradlee crowed.

"And Helen, we didn't forget you for a minute," Glenn said, his voice ringing with satisfaction. "Look. We think these are totally you."

She hadn't even tried the shirts and skirt on. There was no way she would have rejected any of their choices. Instead, she'd said, "Perfect! I love them. Thank you so much. I can see that you've stretched me a little, but I need some stretching. Now, we have to get moving. Torrey just told me we have to stop and pick up a grocery order, and your Hale's Ale should be in it, Glenn." She smiled at them and said, "Let's get checked out so these folks can recover a little, because I have a feeling that when some of your friends see what you came up with, we're going to have more requests to come to town."

As Helen slipped into her new dark yellow shirt patterned with cowboy boots, she glanced at her clock and stepped up her pace. *Thank goodness for Jake. He'll get the coffee started.*

But, when Helen walked into the kitchen, a single light was on, though Jake didn't seem to be there. "Jake?" she called. *Don't tell me he's in At's room!* She shook her head, rejecting the thought. *It's just not likely; not with these kids.* But she went to the foot of the stairs and could see a light was on. She called up, "At, do you know where Jake is?"

Again her voice met silence. Slowly, her mind working, she mounted the stairs and found the door to At's apartment open and her light on. From the thrown back quilt, Helen could tell her bed had been slept in. *What on earth?* She looked around. *Her boots! Where are her boots?* Alarm bells triggered. She rushed down the stairs and out through the kitchen door and down the steps. *Has she already gone to the barn? But, where is Jake?*

From where the road sloped down towards the barn, Helen could see the lights in the old ranch house where Will, Dewey and Jake lived were also on; so were the lights in the bunkhouse where Billy and Buck slept. She started to run. *Oh, my God! Something has happened.* She stumbled and nearly fell, her breath starting to come in gasps. *Slow down, Helen. Use your brain. Someone might need your help.*

She reached the corrals, empty except for the wrangle horse that seemed glued to the fence, looking or listening to something unseen. On she rushed to the barn. The big doors were open, but it was empty. She heard Will's shout with a sob in it. "Do it now, Goddamn it. Don't make him suffer." Then she heard the shot. *Packer! That came from Packer's corral. Oh, dear God, no!* She felt frozen into place.

"Helen!" from out of the grayness, Will appeared. "What are you doing here? Go back to the lodge."

270

Up close, she could see the tear tracks on his face. "My God, Will! What happened? Are you all right?"

He took her shoulders in his big hands. "You can't help here, Helen," he said grimly. "We had a cougar take down a colt. Packer tried to get out of his corral, and got caught in the fence and broke his good leg. I'm on my way to get the D-6 to dig a hole and bury him."

Will looked at her frozen expression and gave her a little shake. "I mean it, Helen! You go on back to the lodge. I'll send Jake up as soon as I can. In the meantime, it's up to you to get the coffee made and the breakfast going. There ain't a damned thing you can do here."

"Oh, Will. I am so sorry." Intuitively, Helen knew, as much as she wanted to do it, a hug would totally undo the struggling man. "Keep Jake as long as you need him."

He nodded and walked on past her to go and get the D-6, saying over his shoulder. "Hell, I don't need him, Helen. But, seems like At sure does."

As Helen turned to retrace her steps she thought, *What is it about legs? Am I a jinx? First Octane, then Torrey and now Packer…and what about the colt? Is it dead?* She thought it likely. A sob rose in her throat.

As she reached the top of the hill, she saw Lucas tucking in his shirt as he hurried towards her in the growing light. He saw her face and without a word, folded her into his arms. "What is it Helen? I heard a shot. What's happened? How can I help?"

But Helen couldn't tell him, at least, not right away. It felt like a dam of pain had burst free in her chest and she sobbed without control. "It-it's b-a-d," she finally managed. "W-ill lo-st his stallion and a colt." Her tears continued to flow.

271

Lucas simply held her to him and let her cry until he asked, gently, "What's the best way I can help you, Helen?"

Looking up at him to answer, her heart nearly stopped at the tender concern in his eyes. She stepped back out of arm's reach and took a shuddering breath. "I'm supposed to make the coffee and get breakfast started. Will wants business as usual at the lodge."

He reached up and stoked the side of her face gently, wiping away a tear. "Then, I'll help you."

She nodded and turned. He fell into step beside her. "I would appreciate it. I think I won't have Jake for a while. Will said he was with At. I would imagine she's in worse shape than I am."

"How's Will?"

Helen gave a little broken-hearted, hiccupping laugh. "It's a good thing God made those Rawling men so tough. Now, he's lost his best friend, his wife is laid up, he had to shoot the stallion of his dreams, a cougar probably killed one of his colts...and he's worrying about me getting breakfast out on time."

As they mounted the steps, Lucas said, "Just tell me what to do."

When Dewey didn't show up, Helen asked Lucas to go wake Glenn and Bradlee. "I need you to take Dewey's place at the coffee pot in the dining room. So, if you would, wake Glenn and Bradlee and ask them if they would help me flip pancakes and fry eggs..." She had been moving at warp speed around the kitchen, but she stopped and looked at Lucas. "Tell the group whatever you want to. I trust your judgement."

He looked at her steadily for a moment, and then put down the cup he was using to measure sugar for the whipping cream, and walked forward to stand in front of her. Without a word, he pulled her close and stood, rocking her gently for a moment before brushing a kiss to her forehead, turning and walking from the

272

kitchen. Helen was left standing, mouth hanging open. The tender gesture left her feeling dazed. She raised a hand to her forehead. *Whatever that meant, he's a MARRIED, gay man, Helen. Remember that. Whatever else you forget; remember THAT,* she thought as she rushed to get the bacon and eggs from the cooler.

By the time Glenn and Bradlee arrived, faces pale, Helen was nearly herself; being so busy had helped.

"Oh, Helen, sweetie, Lucas told us what happened. Of course, we'll help. Tell us what to do."

She stopped cutting melon and turned to look at them, trying for a smile. "Bless you both. I'll find some way to thank you later. Now, here's what I need." She drew a breath and said, "Behind the doorway at this end of the dining room is a two-burner, propane stove on a stand. Take it out and set it up in the dining room. Then, when the time comes, I want one of you to fry eggs to order. The other will be at the range making pancakes on the griddle. The one in the dining room should try to keep the mood light." She pointed to a cupboard. "Under there are the cast iron skillets." She pointed to the refrigerator. "The butter is in there...and the Pam spray is on the second shelf of the pantry."

She could see the two men were listening attentively. "Got it." Glenn said. "Where are the aprons?"

"Aprons?"

"Yes, you know, the kind men wear when they cook."

"You mean like barbecue aprons that say, "Kiss the cook? Bad-assed Barbecuer? Those kinds of aprons?" she asked in amazement.

They nodded expectantly.

"Well, look behind the pantry door on hooks and see what you can find."

Helen went back to slicing melon, shaking her head. *Maybe I've fallen through a rabbit hole and none of this is real,* she thought as she whisked the melon through the swinging door and placed it on the counter in the dining room. On the way back to the kitchen for the pitcher of cream for the coffee, she made a mental list in her head: Put the yogurt containers in a bowl, put out a dish of Craisins for the granola, put butter on each table, pour a pitcher of orange juice, heat the syrup, get the strawberries out of the refrigerator... *Thank goodness Jake sliced those for me yesterday, even though I forgot to ask him to.* The list continued in her head: Finish whipping the cream, make the pancake batter... *Lucas kissed my forehead.* The thought stopped her cold and the list flew out of her head. *Oh boy! Get your act together, Helen.*

In the kitchen, the men, both in Torrey's aprons, were busy as though they had read Helen's mind. Bradlee was cutting the two pounds of thick-cut bacon in half to fit the skillet and Glenn had found a big mixing bowl and was mixing the Krusteaz pancake batter. He looked up and said, "Oh, sweetie, we feel just like Boy Scouts to the rescue."

"Only, we wish the circumstances weren't so sad. Lucas told us what happened," Bradlee added. Then he said, "Is it okay if I put the eggs in that blue bowl. I think they'll look prettier that way. And I'm going to put a garbage pail under our stand so I can throw the eggs shells right into it, if that's okay."

Helen nodded and started to finish making the whipped cream. "You two are saving my life," she said, her throat closing behind her words, tears again threatening. After a moment, she said, "Torrey and Will Rawling are my very dearest friends and if it weren't for you guys, I would be failing them."

Near silence reigned in the kitchen. The outside door opened and Jake stepped through, his hair standing on end, his shirttail out and a purple bruise starting to show on his cheek. He paused when he saw the activity. He looked first at Helen, frozen at the counter, her questioning eyes on him and then at

274

Glenn and Bradlee busy helping. His whole body seemed to sag. "Thank God!" he said.

"Oh, sweetie," Glenn said, "You look awful. We've got this pretty much handled. I'm going to go get you a cup of coffee." He pointed to the stool by the butcher block. "Sit," he said and left the room. Jake did as he was told.

"Really, Jake, take a moment. As you can see, the self-described Boy Scouts have bailed us out," Helen said, stifling the impulse to go and hug him. Instead, she got a baggie and put ice into it. "Here," she said, smiling warmly at him, "make yourself useful by holding this to your cheek." The need to ask questions was nearly killing her, but she had learned much from Dr. Pagglio, including when being silent was the most important thing of all.

Glenn returned, carrying a cup of coffee for Bradlee. Lucas was on his heels with two more, one of which he handed to Helen. She smiled gratefully. "Bless you! How is it going out there?"

"He took a sip of his coffee. I've told everyone the circumstances as they've come up from their cabins, and that breakfast might be a little late. They are all a little subdued, of course, but I've told them the best thing we can do for Will"...he gestured to include the people in the room... "and for all of you, is to hold onto our curiosity and go on with our morning as we normally would."

Helen nodded and looked at Jake. "Do you think the rides will be going out today, Jake?"

He looked up from his coffee, seeming much older somehow. "I reckon. When I left, Will had Marilee on the wrangle horse--headed for the herd."

"Well, handsome," said Bradlee, looking at Glenn. "which of us is doing the pancakes and which is flipping eggs?"

"We're taking turns," Glenn said firmly... "and I'm doing my own. Want me to take the strawberries and whipped cream in, Helen?"

"Yes, please," she said and then looked at Jake. "Drink your coffee first, but do you think you have it in you to make the sack lunches? I don't see any reason you need to work the dining room this morning." He nodded silently. She would remember the look of gratitude he gave her for years to come.

When Helen stepped through the swinging door with a fresh pot of coffee in hand, it seemed that all the guests were there. *Even Jude, looking as lovely as ever,* she thought. "Hello, everyone, I know Lucas has told you of our tragedy. I thank you all for your concern and caring." She took a deep breath and looked around. The group seemed frozen in place, eyes on her, waiting. *Waiting for what?* Inspiration hit her.

"As you may or may not know, a cougar came down out of the Ochoco Mountains and evidently killed one of the colts. I don't know, but I suspect, Will's stallion, Packer, tried to jump out of his corral to attack the cat." She paused, praying for composure. "Tragically, he didn't make it and broke a leg."

She looked around and noted that Lucas had left and was now standing on the edge of the deck, overlooking the ranch. She turned her attention back to the group, swallowed and continued. "Unfortunately, you just got a huge dose of the tough side of ranching. It certainly is not part of the experience we wanted you to have. Believe me when I say that this sort of thing is the exception, not the rule."

Helen had to stop and swallow, believing at that moment that divine guidance was working on her behalf. Her voice came out stronger when she continued. "I know I speak for Will and Torrey when I say, the very nicest thing you could do for them is to tuck this sad thing in with all the happy things and go on with your week. At is getting your horses in, and Jake is making your sandwiches as I stand here. They'll be in a box, along with drinks, waiting for you at the corral, as usual."

276

Beanie, again the spokesperson for the group, said, "Of course we will do as you ask, Helen. One thing I think we've figured out for ourselves is that you don't need a bunch of semi-strangers around the ranch today. Besides, it's a beautiful day for riding." Helen could have kissed her.

Jude turned a tragic face towards her. "But, Helen, if we didn't want to go riding, could you take us to town?"

Luckily, Helen's jaw did not drop. Instead, gratitude washed over her that Lucas was not in the room to hear his wife. Then, a surprising thought popped into her head. *Oh, Willie*, she thought sadly, *what are we getting you into?* Smoothly, she said, "How about you let me know how many are interested, and we'll shoot for taking you in tomorrow?" And then, in a fit of inspiration she added, "Besides, it's going to take Ranch Supply a day or so to restock after Glenn and Bradlee's visit."

She walked out of the room to easy laughter and a spatter of clapping.

Chapter Twenty-seven

Helen and Jake were cleaning tables in the dining room when they heard the guests laughing and chatting while going down the hill. They both stopped what they were doing and listened to the retreating voices through the open French doors. She looked at Jake and said, "Thank God!"

Jake nodded, but said nothing. He had done everything she asked, including taking sack lunches and drinks down to the corrals, but had said very little all morning. She said, "As soon as you've mopped the floor in here, I want you to go and have a nap somewhere."

Jake's eyes jerked to her face. "Marilee ain't havin' a nap."

"Well she might...at lunchtime. She did when the two of us rode to the new reservoir above the horse pasture." Helen kept her voice conversational, but unanswered questions made it difficult. "By the way, thank you for taking At and the King boys down those pancake burritos and the thermos of coffee; they're going to appreciate it when they're on the trail."

They both had finished eating their own pancake burritos—pancakes rolled around bacon, strawberries and whipped cream. She had also put the leftover pancakes and bacon in the warming oven in hopes that Will and Dewey would soon come in for coffee and something to eat. Twenty minutes later, they did...looking grim. Both were uncharacteristically quiet. "Just pick a table and sit. I'll bring your coffee and some breakfast," she said quietly.

Will nodded and looked at Jake, a soft expression on his face. "That was a hard lesson to learn, youngster."

Jake's face flamed. He nodded, but said nothing. Helen said, "Jake, would you go fry up some eggs to go with their breakfasts?" She poured the men cups of coffee and brought it to the table. When Jake came in with the breakfasts, Helen brought both the bowl of strawberries and the bowl of whip cream to the table. As an after-thought, she poured a cup of coffee for herself and sat down at the table.

Jake looked at them and started to leave, but Will's voice called him back. "Sit down, Jake, you'll want to hear this too...an' I sure as hell don't want to have to tell it twice."

Helen and Jake watched silently as the men demolished their breakfasts. Will sighed deeply and leaned back, pushing his plate away. "Damn! I sure wish I still smoked." He looked at Dewey for a long moment. Dewey still hadn't said a word. Sorrow was written into every line of his body. "Buck up a little, old man," Will finally said. "Remember, hadn't been for Queenie, it could have been worse."

Dewey looked up then, and nodded. "Her and Jake. That boy was out the door afore I even had my boots on."

"Yeah, then I run into that barn door and almost knocked myself out." Jake's face was a picture of misery.

"Still," the old man said. "Shoutin' and yellin' like you done probably's what drove that cougar off."

"Not in time."

Will said, "no, not in time. Big cats don't give warnin's. That filly was dyin' by the time it was drug fully down. An' ol' Packer...well, we got to figure he died in the line of duty." He sighed and looked at Helen. "Three years ago, we'd be saddled up and out on that son-of-a-bitches' trail. Dewey may be old, but he can still track the spit of an ant."

"Why can't you do that now? Won't he just go and find another colt or calf to eat if you don't?"

Will took a slurp of coffee and looked at her with somber eyes. "Since Oregon passed a law in 1994, we got to call in the Department of Fish and Wildlife...which I've already done. They'll confirm it's a cat kill and call in a state-licensed hunter. They're the only ones who can hunt with hounds."

"Are you telling me that you are not allowed to shoot an animal that is killing, or trying to kill your horses or cattle?"

"No, I ain't saying that. I'm sayin' if you don't catch 'em in the act, you got to call in the Oregon Department of Fish and Wildlife...and they call in the hunter allowed to use hounds."

Will thought speculatively for a moment, a quirk in one corner of his mouth. He looked at Dewey. "'Course, we maybe got ourselves a plan. I had me an interestin' conversation with Buck."

He looked at Helen and Jake, then around the room as if searching for eavesdroppers. "Seems like Buck, out on the trail, got in a conversation with Dean. Found out he was a sharp shooter when he was with the Mossaud...so was Dee Dee. This mornin' Dean came up and offered their services." Helen looked back and forth between the men. Dewey had straightened his back and was looking interested. "You sayin' what I think you're sayin'?"

Will nodded. "Maybe. I'm still thinkin' on it. We'd have to tell the guests tonight at dinner." He looked at Helen and Jake. "See, if this ol' tom is hungry and not too spooked, he might come back to his kill tonight. Should he do that, Dean says he can take him out."

Dewey looked disbelieving. "Now, just how in the hell does he plan to do that?"

Will looked around the table. "Buck says the three of 'em figured it out. There's a clear line of sight from the hay mow to the colts' pasture and ol' Dean just happened to stick a pair of night vision goggles in his luggage."

Dewey started shaking his head in disbelief. "Now, that's the damnedest thing I ever heard." He looked at Jake. "You know about them things?"

Jake nodded. "It's old infrared technology now. The military started inventin' 'em during WWII. They

280

hook around your head with a strap, so you got two hands free for shootin'. They give things a green cast, but you can see at night."

For the first time since they'd walked in, the twinkle was back in Dewey's eyes. He knocked a knuckle on the table and leaned back. "Ever' time I think I've seen it all, this crowd throws somethin' else at me."

Will stood up. "Don't go gettin' all fired up, Dewey. Like I said, I'm still thinkin' on it. In the meantime, I'm tryin' to figure out how to find the time to go and see my wife. Nothin's goin' to happen without her blessin'…and that's a fact."

Dewey got up with him. "Well, lookin' at the size of the tracks, I'd say that this is some ol' tom who's been pushed out of his territory an' has been forced to make a livin' on poor groceries, and is turnin' to livestock. He needs killin', so I hope your plan works. We don't need to lose any more good colts, that's for double-damned sure."

Helen said, "Will, I'm not even going to ask you what colt was killed. I don't want to know. I do want you to know that I'm terribly, terribly sorry about Packer."

Will looked at her and said, "An' I'm sorry as hell I didn't figure out why his bad leg bothered you so much."

"Me, too. It was actually Torrey who figured it out for both of us." She got up and started clearing the table. "What's next on your plate?"

"There's plenty to do around the ranch. Besides shoein' Chainsaw, we're coolin' our heels waitin' for the government guy from the Oregon Department of Fish and Wildlife to show up. We got the hole dug for Packer an' we'll go get him drug over with the D-6 an' buried proper."

Sadness shadowed his eyes and he sighed and went on. "Then, we got some fence fixin' to do. The cat pushed that baby right into the barbed wire to catch her. If the guy ain't here by then, I reckon I'll leave

Dewey to deal with him an' go see Torrey. It's not news I want to add to her list of worries, but better she get this news from me than from someone else."

Will turned his eyes on Helen. "What about you? You still think you got the lodge under control?"

"Maybe." She managed a wan smile. "Thanks to Lucas, Bradlee and Glenn, breakfast went off without a hitch." She balanced their cups on top of the plates. "When I get you guys out of here, Jake and I are going to finish cleaning up, and then I'm going to start channeling Torrey and making my lists."

Will touched her shoulder briefly. "You're doing fine, Helen. An' before I forget, Russell's bringin' Willie out for us so you'll be needin' to set two extra places."

"Not a problem. Oh, and Will, before I forget, some of the guests want to go to town tomorrow."

He thought for a second then nodded. "That should work out okay. Good thing they didn't want to go today."

Helen raised an eyebrow. "One of them did."

She heard Dewey snort knowingly. "Queenie don't like that gal even a little. That should tell you somethin'."

Helen was sitting at the butcher block, menus and lists spread before her. Jake was mopping the dining room floor. He had been subdued throughout the morning. The only time he had brightened even a little was when Dewey asked him about the infrared night vision goggles. *Maybe running into the barn door hurt more than he's letting on. Or maybe it was seeing the dead colt and Packer being shot. Maybe it's some sort of dust up with At.* "Oh, for heaven's sake!" Helen slapped down her pen and strode into the dining room.

Jake looked up and saw Helen standing in front of him with her hands on her hips, glaring. "Jake, how do you expect me to be able to concentrate when all I can do is worry about you?"

282

He stood, holding the mop above the bucket, and then slowly dropped it into the water, swishing it slowly back and forth. "Ah, Helen. It ain't nothin'. I reckon it was that I shamed myself in front of my girl."

"Shamed yourself?" she said in disbelief. "How? By running into a barn door?"

His shoulders slumped and he looked at her, misery in his eyes. "I'd grabbed the gun, but when Buck and Billy come out of the bunk house, there I was, flat on my back in the dirt. They ain't goin' to let me forget a thing like that."

Helen thought fast. *Ah, that's why Will talked about the filly dying so quickly. He was trying to let him know he couldn't have saved her, no matter what.* Aloud, she said, "Will and Dewey both know you couldn't have changed the outcome, Jake. That's what matters."

He shook his head. "I gotta come up with a way to redeem myself. That's what I'm thinkin' on. You go on with your organizin'. I'm bound to come up with somethin'."

Helen could think of a million words...only none of them would work to comfort this sensitive young man. Instead she said, "Well, then, I'll think about it too." She turned to go and then turned back. "Thanks for telling me, Jake. I really was worried."

Shoving the mop into the wringer, he looked up. "I know," he said, seriously. "If somethin' had happened to you, I'd be worried too."

She smiled at him and then said, "I guess that means we're friends, doesn't it?"

Two hours later, Helen felt organized. The salmon was in the marinade, the ingredients for the saffron rice were on the butcher block. She had brie cheese softening and big purple grapes snipped into clusters and resting in the cooler. Jake had the rooms cleaned and was finishing setting the tables in the dining room. She looked at her watch. *Time for us to take a break, with sandwiches on the porch.*

While Helen slathered mayonnaise on bread, she again thought of Jake's dilemma. It had knocked about in her brain like a fly against glass all morning. As she backed through the swinging door, carrying sandwiches, she thought, *What things melt a girl's heart? Let's see…there are the traditional things like flowers, candy, going dancing… Dancing?* Helen's eyes flew to the Wurlitzer. "Jake, do you know how to dance?" She asked.

He shook his head. "Well, unless you have religious convictions otherwise, you're about to learn."

He put down the glass he was holding and looked at the jukebox. Helen could see immediately that he hadn't rejected her suggestion flat out. His eyes were considering. She grabbed a handful of tableware and started placing it, letting him think.

"I reckon you mean for me to ask At to dance…in front of ever' body."

"I do. First with At and then with me. After that, it's up to you. I am absolutely positive you can learn. Remember, I saw you fly fishing. I know you have rhythm and good coordination."

He put his glass down and reached in his pocket. "Okay, let's give it a try," he said, pulling out a quarter. "But only on slow songs."

"Let's try "Deep Water" by Marty Robins, but not yet. First, let's go eat on the deck and then, I want to walk you through the steps. I'll teach you, just like I taught my own three. But, before I forget to tell you this…if At says she doesn't know how to dance, just sweep her into your arms and whisper in her ear, 'Trust me.'"

Helen heard Russell's truck and was out the kitchen door before it rolled to a stop. She paused at the top step and just feasted on the sight of her son unraveling his long legs and stepping out. "Mom!" he shouted and rushed towards her as she was flying towards him. They met in a mutual bear hug, and Willie pulled her from the ground and whirled her around before setting her down and holding her at arm's length. "You look great, Mom."

Helen reached up a hand and stroked his new beard, tears standing at the corner of her eyes. "Oh Willie, how I've missed you!"

He grinned a big open grin. "Russell says I'm your reward for bailing out Uncle Will and Aunt Torrey."

She laughed and peered around Willie. "Hello, Russell. Thank you so much for bringing him. You are so right. He is my reward. By the way, we've set you a place, so don't think of leaving before dinner."

He grinned. "Howdy, Helen. Thanks for the invite. I reckon I could be forced to stay and see how ever' body's survivin'."

Helen put her arm through Willie's. "We're surviving, but it's been nip and tuck," she said flatly. "Have Will tell you about the cougar attack. I've got to get back to work. The guests are mostly getting ready to come up for cocktails, so you two go and get Willie settled in the bunk house." She turned and looked down at the corrals where Will, Dewey and At were bringing the colt herd into the corrals with the wrangle horse. "There will be some announcements and updates at dinner, but if he has time, Will might want you to have a preview." She shook her head. "It is astonishing how, when things need to go just right, they can sometimes go so wrong…and then right again," she said mysteriously, simultaneously giving Willie another hug and then shooing them back to the truck.

Helen hurried back into the kitchen, her eyes shining. Jake was efficiently chopping cilantro for the green salad. "Sorry I didn't have time to introduce you to Willie. There's just not time. We've got to hustle."

285

Jake's smile reached his eyes. "Reckon I was a bit of a slow learner," he said. "Took too much of our time."

She couldn't help but laugh. Despite all the day's trauma and sadness, her heart felt light. *I was so busy that I didn't even have time to think about Lucas...and now, Willie is here to further distract me.* Aloud, she said, "Au contraire, my friend. You were such a star, I couldn't help but teach you more than you needed to know," she said as she popped a pan of raw pine nuts into the oven to toast. She closed the oven door and turned to face him. "Just promise me that you won't try 'the fall down dip' with At unless she does know how to dance...and seems willing."

Chapter Twenty-eight

Will stood in the "cowboy stance" and the entire room immediately gave him their attention. "Okay, listen up folks, we have a whole lot on our plate that you might not know, and after introductions, I need to bring you up to date on things before the salmon comes off the grill."

His eyes fastened on Willie, seated at the table nearest the kitchen where Helen always sat and nodded. Then he gestured to where Russell sat with Leo, Glenn and Bradlee. "I reckon you all remember Russell from your plane ride, and some of you have met Helen's youngest son, Willie, who happens to be named after yours truly and plays basketball for the Oregon Ducks." He paused. "That's all the introduction I'm givin' 'em, but you can talk to 'em both later because when Russell found out about the dancin', he decided to park his carcass in the bunkhouse and show us how it's done. An' Willie, we get to keep for a few days." The fondness in his voice was unmistakable.

"Now, without wastin' your time, I got to tell you that the reason the dead filly is still lyin' in the colt pasture is because, with the help of your friends Dean and Dee Dee, we're workin' up a surprise for the ol' tom that's likely to return to his kill."

He looked around the room. "I think it's important for you to know that we, meanin' Torrey, Dewey and I, don't think the cougar is our enemy. They got a place in the ecosystem just like the rest of God's creatures. It's only when they are sick, old or injured and start findin' easy meals in some rancher's pasture that they need to be killed."

He looked around the room again and then spoke, his tone serious. "This here is one of them

287

animals, and Dean and Dee Dee have got a plan, with the help of Dean's night vision goggles, to kill him if he comes back to feed tonight. Now, he don't come, tomorrow a government fella, licensed to use hounds for tracking and killin' cougars, is goin' to show up...hopefully, after you are all out on your rides...those of you who are goin' ridin', at least. Word has it that some of you are headin' in to town."

With that, Will seemed to run out of steam. "Let me finish by sayin' how you can help us is just by stayin' in your cabins, should you hear a shot or other commotion." He nodded at Helen who then took platters prepared with a nest of endive and lemons out to the barbecue on the back deck, for the salmon.

When she did, she saw that Jude was just coming up the back steps from the creek, looking, thought Helen, *absolutely adorable!* Her hair was piled high on her head. Chandelier earrings hung from her ears, emphasizing her slender neck and low-cut blouse. Her outfit was finished by the cutoffs she had worn to the ranch and her cowboy boots. "Hello, Jude. You are just in time; the salmon is coming off."

"I hope it's not too done," Jude said coolly, walking past without making eye contact or slowing her steps.

So typical! Why am I surprised? Helen ground her teeth, trying not to compare her own current state: sweat trickling from her hairline, chewed off lipstick and lank ponytail. She concentrated on the fact that the salmon looked perfect; skin side crispy and flesh side perfectly red and flaky as only Copper River salmon can be. Deftly, with two big spatulas, she removed the four huge filets onto the platter, remembering as she did so, that only Willie, who had probably been living on salmon, wouldn't consider this a real treat.

As Helen carried the platter into the dining room, she nearly dropped it when she saw Jude take the chair that had always been reserved for her and turn brilliant blue eyes on Willie, one hand reaching out and stroking his arm. Helen somehow walked forward and set the platter carefully on the counter. Disappointment hit her in a dark wave. She had so been looking forward to sitting down with Willie and catching up on his life; continuing to mend that rift between them. She forced herself to turn and smile at the guests. "Come and get it," she said and then turned and walked, in what seemed to be slow motion, from the room.

Once the door swung shut behind her, the disappointment turned to rage. *That little bitch! She did that on purpose. What has she got against me? I haven't done a thing to her!* A sob caught in her throat. She braced her arms on the butcher block and dropped her head, fighting for control, and then gave up and headed for the bathroom, tears streaming down her face. A little unheeded voice was saying, "Get a grip, Helen, you are way over-reacting." She didn't care. She was hot and sweaty, tired, weighted down with responsibility, and it felt good to let the tears flow where no one could see her. She grabbed toilet paper from the roll and gave in to it.

Some minutes later, when her tears had stopped, she splashed cold water on her face, applied fresh lipstick and tightened her pony tail. She felt immeasurably better. *But, I'm not going back into that damned dining room and I don't care what Will thinks. I'm just not.*

There was a gentle knock on the bathroom door. "Helen? It's me, Amber. Are you alright?"

Helen opened the door and the two women looked at each other; Helen with a touch of defiance and Amber with compassion. "Willie is bringing your dinners and look—I've brought you wine." She gestured to the butcher block where indeed, a bottle of white wine stood with two glasses.

Helen was speechless. Amber continued, "Some of us thought you might like a little down time with your son, since you've been so busy you can't have had time for a proper catch up."

"Oh, Amber!" Without conscious thought, Helen reached out and folded the younger woman into a hug. "You have no idea..." She could feel tears welling and smiled to ward them off. "I told Torrey you might be my secret weapon, and you sure are. This means the world to me."

Amber grinned, looking satisfied. "I don't miss the details, Helen. I'll say that for myself."

Willie backed in through the swinging door carrying two heaping plates. "God, I'm so hungry I could eat a horse...oops, sorry, ladies, bad idiom for right now."

Helen smirked at Amber. "College boy. Forgive him."

Amber nodded and looked back and forth between them. "Enjoy your dinners." As she walked past Willie who was carefully setting the plates on the butcher block, she reached up and tapped him on the shoulder. "And you, buster, owe me the first dance. If Jude asks you, tell her the first dance is mine." With that she winked at Helen and strode back through the door.

Helen smiled at her son, who was sitting on one of the stools, eyeing his plate with relish. "Go ahead and start, hungry boy. I'll pour the wine."

He looked up. "This is great, Mom. We can talk with our mouths full." He turned a 100-watt grin on her.

Helen felt a laugh bubble up from inside. *How can one be so miserable and then so happy in such a short time?* "I don't know exactly why Jude has it in for me, but she certainly seems to," she said.

Willie shoveled in a huge bite and sat chewing, looking at her thoughtfully. After he swallowed, he said, "I think I do, and I've only been here since this afternoon."

She handed him a glass and sat on her stool. "Really?" She said, raising an eyebrow.

He nodded and grinned. "Face it, Mom, you're a fox, and both George and Jude's husband, Lucas, can't keep their eyes off of you."

"Good heavens! Don't be silly!" Helen said dismissively and then hurried on to say, "But that's enough about me. I am dying to know about you."

Long before they had finished talking they heard the jukebox start. Hank Thompson was singing "The Wild Side of Life." Willie jumped up. "Oops, excuse me Mom, I have to go and find Amber. I believe this is our dance."

Helen waved him away, knowing Jake and At would be bringing tubs full of empty dishes through the door as soon as they saw the coast was clear. "Yes," she said smiling, "it certainly is your dance. Have fun. It was a great catch up. I'll be along to collect my dance from you when we're done here."

Jake was elbow deep in soapy water and At was putting left-overs in plastic containers when Marty Robin's version of "Cold Water," the song Helen had chosen as Jake's song to learn from, came drifting through the door. Jake's and Helen's glances met. He looked at At and started drying his arms. When he was done, he walked up behind her and as he held out his arms, Helen heard him say, "At, would you care to dance."

At whirled and saw him standing there, a proud smile on his face and after the briefest of pauses, walked into his arms. "I thought you were mad at me," Helen heard her say softly. As Helen grabbed the wine bottle and her glass and scurried out the kitchen door, her face lit with a goofy grin. *This is way better for them than dancing in front of all those people,* she thought as she found a chair on the deck away from the light of the windows and sank into it, feeling tired and wired at the same time.

She poured herself wine, listened to the music and the laughter and thought, *I've got to get in there and collect that dance with my son, finish breakfast prep, and then go to bed.* Still she sat sipping her Chardonnay and looking over the pond, watching the swallows give way to bats as the evening deepened past twilight.

She allowed her mind to ramble. *One more day and then Torrey will be here. French toast, eggs and sausage for breakfast should be fairly easy. I hope I have time to go see Torrey and pick up some more strawberries...and maybe some peaches.* She heard boot heels coming her way.

"Helen! I went into the kitchen looking for you, and Jake said you might be out here."

"Hello, George." She smiled up at the little man. "I'm just taking five to get my brain organized."

He sank into the chair beside her. "You must be exhausted. By the way, Jake said At and he could do the kitchen and dining room prep and to please tell you that you were through for the evening."

"Oh, he did, did he? Cheeky devil to be telling his boss what to do, don't you think?"

George laughed noncommittally. "They were dancing when I walked in. I think I embarrassed them a little."

Helen took a last sip of wine and stood. "What do you say we do a little dancing ourselves, George?" She took him by the hand and led him through the French doors. *There's not a reason in this entire world you should be wishing it was Lucas you were asking to dance, Helen Duncan,* she silently scolded herself. *So, stop it right now!*

Inside, it was clear that Beanie had lost control of the jukebox to Russell. Helen saw him slip in a quarter and soon Hank Williams was belting out, "Why don't you love me like you used to do? Why do you treat me like a worn out shoe? My hair's still curly and my eyes are still blue. Why don't you love me like you used to do?"

"Whooee! Billy, you curly-haired, blue-eyed devil, listen. Hank's singin' our theme song," Buck hollered, setting down his beer bottle and grabbing Juana's hand, twirling her onto the dance floor. Billy grabbed for Cleah and Russell bowed before Jude, a grin splitting his face. "Care to go for a spin, gorgeous?"

Halted in the doorway, Helen said firmly, "Oh, no, George. I can't do this. It's way too fast."

"Sure you can," George said with equal firmness as he grabbed her hand and put her into a triple two step, with a walk back and a four step turn. Helen surprised herself and followed him perfectly as the music got into her blood. There was no time to look around or think. Concentration was required. Once, they bumped into Willie and Amber, or Willie and Amber bumped into them. It didn't matter. Everyone was laughing and those not dancing were clapping and singing along.

At the end of the song, Willie handed Amber off to George and said, "It's time for our dance, Mom."

Helen was puffing. She turned to George and said, "Thank you, George. That was great," and found she really meant it. She looked up at her son. "It really was fun, but I certainly hope the next one is slower."

"Um," Willie gestured with his chin, "I don't think so."

Over at the jukebox, Russell slipped in another quarter. "Grab your partners, boys and girls. 'Ol Hank Snow is movin' on." He pointed a finger at Beanie and said, "And, I'm a' comin' to get you, girl."

Just before Willie swept her into the crowd, Helen allowed her eyes to rove the room. Even Will was dancing, putting Juana into a smooth underarm turn, and then another and another. Then her eyes touched on Lucas. He was staring over Amber's head straight at her. Butterflies started doing the triple two-step in her stomach and she jerked her eyes away. *Oh my God! Could Willie be right? Is he looking at me?* Her mind flashed back to how he had held her to comfort her. *Still, he's not seeking me out. That look was just a huge coincidence.* She took a deep breath and when Willie did a reverse turn and brought her back in under his arm she said, in a serious tone, "I just want you to know, should I expire, that my life insurance policy is in the filing cabinet by my desk back in Virginia."

He looked down, saw the twinkle in her eye and laughed, putting her into a combination of sweetheart moves, spins, pretzels and cuddles. "Sure, Mom, I'll remember," he said as he pulled her in close to his side and started executing the side to side rock-step movement that precluded Helen's favorite move--the trust fall.

As the song finished, Helen realized that Jake and At were still not in the room. *I wonder if those two are still dancing in the kitchen?* She smiled at the thought and struggling for breath, said to Willie, "Hand me off to your Uncle. He and I need to talk, and we haven't had time all day. Maybe I can get him out on the deck."

Will was only too glad to leave the room. He was mopping his forehead with a big white cotton handkerchief as they walked out together. "That damned Russell is sure a fool for dancin'...and for gettin' things stirred up," he said.

"It seems like a good thing...keeping it fun and light on such a serious night," Helen said, sitting in the chair she had vacated earlier.

"Yep." Will said, sitting heavily in his chair and gazing a Helen. "You makin' it okay, Helen?"

"I think I am," she said, surprising herself. "I won't say it's been easy, and there's no way you would ever convince me that I've only been doing this for four days. No way in hell."

Will nodded. "Dewey said the same thing. You notice he ain't here tonight?"

Helen blinked in surprise. "Oh, my God! I didn't even realize it. Is he okay?"

294

"He's just had enough for one day. Told me he'd fix himself dinner. Then he and Queenie would go to bed early and hope to wake up to a gun goin' off."

Helen was quiet, thinking. "You know," she finally said, "For all the things that have gone wrong, there are a lot of things that have gone right."

She heard Will snort. "Now, how'd you come to that conclusion? Seems from where I sit, it's been one damned disaster after another; startin' with Torrey's fall."

"Yes, but I was here to pick up the slack. Losing the horses was a terrible, terrible thing…but what were the odds that a guest would have night vision goggles and be a trained marksman…just when you really needed one? And think about this: I don't think we need to worry about Billy and Buck fighting over Jude anymore. That girl is setting her sights higher…much higher. In fact, I'd say she has them set at 6'5"."

"What? Are you talking about Willie? What makes you think that?"

"Evidently, you didn't see what went on in the dining room earlier, so you'll just have to take my word for it."

Will sighed. "Now, I got somethin' new to worry about. That kid's been on an all-male fishin' boat all summer."

"I think we've raised him better. Besides, being a college basketball star has probably given him plenty of exposure to the fairer sex," Helen said nonchalantly. "Now, let's talk about tomorrow. After that, we need to talk about what we need to do for Torrey once she's home."

"I'm all ears," said Will. "You go first."

Before Helen could begin, Dean and Dee Dee materialized out of the darkness and walked up the stairs. Neither had heard them coming. Will looked at Helen in the faint light and then back at the couple. "Dang! I believe you two could sneak up on a jack rabbit!" Will said. "Grab a chair."

"No thanks," said Dee Dee. "We thought we'd go on down to the barn now, while the cat is still keeping its distance because of the noise."

Will tipped back in his chair and looked at Dean. "How'd the rifle shoot for you?"

"We've got it sighted in to suit us," Dean said. He looked at his partner and she nodded in agreement.

"It'll do fine. Good night, now," she said as they turned and walked into the darkness. "Wish us luck."

"Oh, we do. We surely do," Will called after them. He turned to Helen. "I had Dewey take them on up Highway 395 to the gravel pit to sight in my 30.06 this afternoon. He said it seemed to him that they were the real deal."

"You know," mused Helen, "I think that's only the second time I've heard Dean actually talk."

Will chuckled. "Yep. He's the Gary Cooper of this crowd, that's for sure." He was silent for a minute. "It's a nice thing they're doin', takin' turns sleepin' in a sleepin' bag, keepin' watch...waitin'...for an animal that might be miles from here by now. I'm goin' to give them some money back."

Helen said nothing. *Of course he will try to do that. A guest shouldn't have to pay for spending the night waiting to kill a predator when they have a nice cozy cabin waiting for them.* Aloud she said, "Now about tomorrow...Jude was supposed to give me a list of those going to town, but she didn't. So, you'll have to find out at breakfast and get word to At as to which horses to saddle."

Will nodded. "Will you be able to find the time to go see Torrey?"

She nodded. "Absolutely...and I have a few more groceries to get. How was she?"

"Bored just about spitless. Ready to come home. The news about Packer and Kitty's baby hit her hard, but she agreed it would work out a whole lot better if we did the killin'. She said, 'The way our luck is goin', as sure as God made little green apples, that government hunter with his bayin' hounds would show up just when you got the guests mounted.'"

Helen could hear Torrey saying the words and it made her smile, but she was not deterred from getting questions answered. "Did you get the trapeze bar for over the bed rented?"

"I did. And I've rented crutches, and one of those pot things that goes by the bed. I ordered everything the nurse told me to. Tomorrow, Dewey is going to clean up the ATV so we can get her back and forth to the lodge, should she want to do that."

Helen laughed. "I can't really see Torrey staying down at the ranch house. That leather recliner in the great room of the lodge should work for her. We can pull it around to where she can watch the dancing if she wants to. We just have to remember to check on her. She won't be able to get up out of it without some help."

"It sure will be good to have her home," Will said simply.

Helen stood. "Since Jake and At have volunteered to do the breakfast prep, I'm going to turn in. I don't know about you, but I'm bushed."

Will got to his feet and sighed. "I'm tired, but I have a feelin' that I'm goin' to spend my night lyin' in my bed waitin' to hear that rifle go off."

Chapter Twenty-nine

Instead of going down the steps, Helen turned and walked around to the kitchen door, intending to check on her crew before turning in. From the door she looked through the window and saw them sitting on the stools, heads bent over the chalk board; At evidently reading the breakfast menu to Jake as he wrote. Behind them, she could see her kitchen was spotless. *Talk about blessings,* she thought to herself as she silently backed away and went down the steps.

Tiredness hit her then. She trudged down the path, listening to Ray Price on the jukebox singing, "Crazy Arms," as she went. Nearing her cabin, she heard the nighthawk make its raspy-throated sound. She thought, *I wonder if it is the same bird I heard before.* She listened to Flat Creek gurgling over the rocks as it always did. *It's silly for me to be in the cabin farthest from the lodge under these circumstances, but I'm glad it worked out this way.*

"Helen." Lucas's voice came from the darkness, and she felt the familiar jolt hit somewhere around her solar plexus. Despite her best intentions, her feet stopped and she turned, waiting like a fly in a web.

"I was on my porch, waiting for you," he said as he walked down his steps.

"Hello, Lucas. What can I do for you?"

"May we sit on your front porch…or mine, I guess, and have a relaxed, adult conversation about my wife's behavior…and mine, for that matter."

He stopped in front of her and continued. "I'd say, go sit on the chairs by the pond, which is more neutral, but since this is the night Dean and Dee Dee hope to kill the cougar, I think it best we stay here."

His voice sounds sad…no, it's more like…resigned, she thought. She glanced back up at the brightly lit lodge, knowing the party wouldn't be breaking up anytime soon. *Remember, Helen, he doesn't know about your stupid butterflies,* the little

298

voice inside her head reminded her. She managed a smile. "Let's sit on your porch, then."

Lucas nodded. "I won't keep you long. I know how tired you must be, and what time you have to get up in the morning."

There was a bottle of Black Velvet, two glasses and an ice bucket sitting on the little wicker porch table. As Helen sat, Lucas gestured at his glass. "I was having a nightcap. Would you like one?"

She nodded. "The ice buckets for the rooms were a good idea, weren't they?" she asked, realizing how banal she sounded.

He didn't seem to notice. "Everything this ranch does is a good idea, as far as I'm concerned," he said with warmth as he handed her a glass, the ice cubes tinkling. "And I'd rather be talking about it, than what I'm feeling obligated to talk about."

"Obligated?"

In the soft porch light, Helen could see he was studying her face, his eyes soft. "Yes. I have decided I need you to hear my story. Until now, besides Jude, Glenn and Bradlee are the only ones who know it. I would ask you to keep it that way."

A feeling of dread surged through Helen. "Lucas...you...aren't...ill, are you?"

A short bark of laughter exploded from his throat. "I'm ill, but not in the way you mean."

"Then what is it?" Helen's voice was nearly pleading.

"I want to tell you the story of my marriage to Jude," he said in a tone she couldn't identify. "Bear with me and you'll understand why I think it's important to tell you."

Lucas picked up his glass and saluted her, then sighed and settled back into his willow chair before starting without preamble, "Jude and I married 18 years ago. She was 17 when we met. I was 36."

299

Helen felt like she'd been hit over the head with a hammer. *Good God! That child is no child...she's 35 years old!*

Lucas waited for her to make a comment and, when she didn't, he continued. "I was a dancing instructor at the time, just starting to pick up work as a choreographer. She was taking lessons: acting, dancing, singing...you name it."

He took a long swallow from his glass, looked up and shrugged. "She was a dedicated student; beautiful and absolutely driven to succeed. After about a year, she decided she needed a man to be seen with about town, and she picked me."

"Why?" Helen asked softly, intrigued in every fiber of her being. "As gorgeous as she is; why would she choose her dancing instructor instead of someone more famous?"

"Because...because being safe is a big thing with her, and she thought she would be safe with me. The rumor in the industry was that I was gay and for my own reasons, I let everyone believe it. So, she thought it to be true."

Helen couldn't have said a word if her life was hanging in the balance. *But you are gay, her mind was silently screaming.* She took a gulp of her bourbon, feeling the fiery burn, and nearly forgetting to breathe.

Lucas was rolling his glass back and forth between his palms, choosing his words carefully. "When she asked me to marry her, she said that I could have whatever relationships I wanted on the side...and so would she." He looked up at Helen. "That is when I had to confess to her that I wasn't gay. That I had a congenital condition that made it difficult for me to ah...satisfy a woman. She thought about it and then said she was pretty sure we could find ways to make things work...and we did for about two years of our marriage. Then, one day she told me that she had lied...that I didn't satisfy her and never had. She still

300

loved me, but she needed to seek her pleasure elsewhere."

Helen gasped. "What?"

He looked at her then, the pain in his eyes nearly breaking her heart. "You heard me correctly, Helen. We'd never corrected everyone's impression that I was gay. It suited us both. You see, high school was such a miserable time for me that pretending to be gay was how I got through it, through the service, through college and basically...through life. So, as you would imagine, I'm a very accomplished pretender."

Helen was shaking her head, cutting to the chase. "Let me see if I understand this. She knows you're straight--married you as a straight man--but has affairs and puts the blame on you? Why? Why would she do that? Why not just divorce you?"

"Like I said," Lucas said calmly, "safety is a big deal for her; safety and variety. I'm her safety net and she finds variety in a number of places. When I talk of divorce, she threatens suicide and has, in fact, had to have her stomach pumped. Our situation works well for her...and frankly, until very recently, it worked well enough for me."

His voice had changed. Helen's eyes jumped to his face. He was looking at her intently. "What...what changed?" she whispered, setting down her glass and clasping her hands between her knees to hide their trembling. But she knew. Oh, yes, she knew what he was going to say!

"The minute I stepped out of the truck and looked at you, I felt a terrific attraction. It was like I had been punched in the gut and had a sudden revelation. At that moment, I   understood just how badly I had allowed myself to be manipulated. It felt like the life I have been living...its falseness and its lies...was flashing before my eyes. I had to leave the group. You probably don't remember...

"Yes, yes, I do," she said softly. "You stood apart from the group looking out over the ranch for the longest time."

He nodded. "Yes. And in the four days we've been here, I find myself thinking about you almost continually." He tried for a smile. "For the first time, I think I can identify with stalkers because, if I let myself, I'd be following you around like a puppy."

Helen started shaking her head. "No. Don't tell me this."

"But it is imperative that I do. You have to know so you can tell me I'm crazy...you can reject me straight out. Then, at least, maybe I can come back to reality. As it is, I'm building these fantasies. I keep visualizing us together. I see us down on the dock, kicked back, happy just being together. I see you standing in front of the mirror combing your hair. I'm watching you and you turn and smile at me. Then, there's the one when I get in the shower with you... and another when we're just spooning in our sleep, my arms are around you..."

"Stop!" Helen groaned, "Dear God, you are killing me! Why are you doing this?"

Lucas sighed. "Because, for the first time in my life, I have fallen head-over-heels in love. I'm pretty certain that it's as simple as that. Head-over-heels...and I don't know what to do with the feelings," he whispered hoarsely, looking into his drink.

Helen jumped to her feet, intending to leave, but instead found herself kneeling by his chair. "Lucas," she said, "Look at me, please." When he looked at her, she lost her breath. It seemed she could see into his soul and she wondered if he could see into hers. Finally, she drew a deep breath. "I won't lie to you," she whispered. "I'd like to, but I won't...that punch to the gut you felt? I felt it too...for what I thought was a gay, married man. When you kissed me on the forehead, I felt tingles all the way to my toes and have been beating myself up about it since."

302

She took his hand and lifted it, pulling him up. "Now, it all makes perfect sense."

They were standing very close. "God, I love you, Helen," he said, but made no move to take her into his arms. "That you could even return a fraction of what I'm feeling staggers me. If I touch you...stroke your cheek...even put my arms around you and kiss you like I want to, I wouldn't stop until we were both naked and in my bed."

Helen choked out a sound half laugh, half sob. "Oh, my God! I know this isn't funny, Lucas. It's a big fat mess. In all honesty, I don't know if I'm really in love with you, but I can damned sure tell you that I'm attracted."

He laughed and reached for her. "I've changed my mind," he growled. But Helen stepped back. "No! I can't. We can't. You're a married man, Lucas...granted, in name only...but I have to think. I have to think clearly. There's so much at stake here...so many others to think about...not just what we want at this moment."

Lucas dropped his arms and stood looking at her, sadly. He sighed. "I guess I should be satisfied that the attraction wasn't all one way. But you'd better go. Promise me you'll think about what you called 'our big fat mess,' because I can tell you that I'm not going to change my mind. I'm a goner."

Helen opened the screen door of the porch and looked over her shoulder at him. "Good night, Lucas. Just so you know--if circumstances were different, I wouldn't be a widow going off to her lonely bed tonight." She went down the steps and almost ran the short distance to her own cabin, her mind reeling, knowing whatever it meant; her life had just been irrevocably altered. But two thoughts dominated. *He's not gay and he thinks he's in love with me!* It filled her with equal measures of joy and dread.

Inside her room, Helen leaned against the door and put her hand to her chest. She could feel her heart galloping under her hand. *Did that just happen? Did Lucas just confess that he was not gay, or am I in the middle of some sort of unconscious fantasy fulfillment?* She turned and flipped on her light and walked to her mirror. The woman looking back at her seemed old— old and very tired. *Nope, if this were fantasy fulfillment, I sure as heck wouldn't look like this!* She scrubbed her face as if erasing wrinkles and decided every *one* of her 55 years was showing. The best that she could say about herself was that she looked...grubby. *And yet, he didn't seem to care. And why is it that I don't seem to care? Now there's a question!*

She turned from the mirror and started to undress; methodically sitting on the bed to pull off her boots and socks before walking towards the shower, leaving her clothing like a trail of bread crumbs behind her. She turned on the taps, pulled the elastic from her hair and stepped in before the water had warmed. She didn't even flinch under the cold spray. She was trying with all her being to think of a plan that would see her through the next several days. It did not seem possible. Finally, she sighed and decided, *Okay. This much I can do: shower, dry my hair, set the alarm and get into bed. After a good night's sleep, hopefully things will be clearer.* As the water warmed, she lathered shampoo into her hair and thought, *for right now, all you have to do is get the soap out of your hair.*

She couldn't seem to help herself. The next morning she punched in the alarm button and didn't even stretch before getting out of bed. *What am I going to wear?* had been her first thought upon waking, and she wanted every moment available to do her hair and her makeup before going up to the lodge. That she would be seeing Lucas shortly, sent her scurrying.

This is ridiculous, she scolded herself as she pulled the chambray shirt she had worn on the plane from its hanger and the Wranglers she had washed with her feet from the drawer. *Jesus, Helen, get a grip.*

304

Take a breath. But she didn't. She turned on her curling iron, brushed her teeth, darkened her eyebrows, added eye liner, looked at herself critically and pawed for her mascara. *Look at you, Helen! What are you going to do, walk up and throw yourself into his arms?*

That thought sobered her. Slowly, she applied her mascara, added blush to her cheeks and put on her lipstick, thinking hard. *This is the cold light of day, Helen. You are supposed to be thinking clearly. Remember, above all else, that you have a job to do. People are counting on you. Your son is here. Torrey comes home tomorrow.*

Her shoulders sagged, the weight of her responsibilities dragging her back to the reality of the moment. She picked up her curling iron and looked in the mirror. *Still, for 4:00 o'clock in the morning, you don't look too bad. Keep that thought and don't forget your earrings.*

It was only when Helen was walking down her steps that she remembered the cougar. She stopped and looked around. All seemed quiet. The proximity security light was on down by the barn, but that was normal. A barn cat could trip that. Had there been a shot? Would she have heard it? She didn't know. Then she looked up at the lodge and saw lights were already on. *But, that doesn't mean anything either. It could be At or Jake or even Dewey.*

She started striding up the path when an unearthly scream shattered the silence. For seconds she froze, and then turned and sprinted up the path towards the Sunrise Cabin. Without pausing to think, she wrenched open the screen door, ran across the porch and burst into the room, her own scream caught in her throat.

Lucas had just turned on the bedside light. "Helen! My God! Are you all right?" He leaped from the bed, was across the room, and had pulled her to him before she could even nod her head.

"C-Cougar," she managed against his shoulder.

"Yes, I heard him scream. He's not that far away..." Lucas's voice trailed away as he felt her against him. She was trembling. With one hand he lifted her chin and looked into her eyes. "He's some alarm clock," he said, one corner of his mouth quirked up.

Helen blinked as if coming out of a trance. Suddenly, she realized she was pressed, full length against a man dressed only in silk boxer shorts. She gasped and jumped back to look around him at the bed. "W-where's Jude?"

Lucas also looked around at the bed. It was clear only his half had been slept in. "I don't know," he said. "I guess she didn't come in last night."

"Didn't come in?"

He nodded. "Sometimes, she doesn't," he said matter-of-factly and reached for her again.

"But...the cougar...something has happened. It's supposed to be dead. How can it scare the living shit out of me, screaming, practically in my ear, if it's dead? There are lights on at the lodge. I need to get up there, but how can I?"

He stopped her words with the gentle finger to her lips. "Sh-h-h. It's okay. I'll get dressed and then we'll go together. But first, I'm going to kiss you." He slanted his head and found her lips, holding her to him gently.

With a sigh of acceptance of the inevitable, Helen leaned into the embrace, gave in to the sensations, and returned the kiss. She felt suspended in a cocoon of light and time. All too soon, Lucas pulled back and looked down at her. "No matter what happens next, or in the future, you've given me this, Helen. Thank you."

She put a hand up to his cheek. "Wow!" At that moment, she had no other thought in her head.

He smiled and then turned to dress saying, "We're going to be safe enough. That cat is more afraid

306

of us than we are of him, I promise." Haphazardly, he pulled on his socks, Wranglers, his boots and was putting on his shirt as he hustled her out the door.

As they hurried up the path, they noted lights were on in all the cabins, except Cabin D--Dean and Dee Dee's cabin. Suddenly, they heard Queenie's bark from somewhere across Flat Creek turn fierce and desperate. It was unlike any sound Helen had ever heard her make. Then, just as they reached the French doors, came a single shot.

Inside the dining room was a frozen tableau. In the process of moving tables back into place, Jake and Willie had stopped. Their eyes caught. They turned to look at Helen and Lucas bursting into the room. "I guess they got him, then," Jake said quietly to Willie.

"Yes, I guess they did," Willie replied somberly. He turned and looked at Helen, his glance taking in Lucas. "All hell has been breaking loose around here, Mom. It's been quite a night."

Dewey came though the swinging door carrying the big coffee pot. "An' it's goin' to be quite a mornin'. You two best pour yourselves a cup. My guess is folks is about to start showin' up--some full of questions and others full of the answers."

Helen gaped at him. "I h-heard Queenie. Is she okay?"

Dewey nodded. "I reckon she is. I didn't hear no yelpin' and Dean had her leashed up." Dewey set the pot on the hotplate and turned to Lucas. "In case you were wonderin' where your wife was--she's sleepin' off her bender down at the bunkhouse."

The two men stood looking at each other across the big room. Finally, Lucas nodded. "I was wondering, Dewey. Thank you for letting me know that she's safe."

"She's safe, but I have to tell you, Lucas, she created a hell of a ruckus before she passed out."

Lucas shook his head, "Jesus!" he said in disgust, looking at the boys. "Were you two involved?"

307

Surprisingly, Jake answered. "Eventually, one way or another, we were all involved...not the guests, but the rest of us, 'cept At."

Dewey looked at Helen. "No time for this now. Best you get on through to the kitchen. You'll be gettin' the full story from the boss, come breakfast time. I ain't sure the cougar is dead, but were I a bettin' man, I'd make a wager that he was."

Helen looked at her watch shocked to find it was nearly 5:30. "Thank you, guys, for pitching in like this. As long as everyone is safe, Queenie included, I can wait for the details."

Dewey nodded, looking at her fondly. "That's my gal." He turned to Lucas. "I want to go see about my dog. You mind mannin' the coffee pot like you done before 'til I come back?"

"Glad to."

The old man smiled. "Well, we got coffee on, these boys is gettin' the joint back in place, Helen's headin' for the kitchen...I'd say things are lookin' sorta normal."

Willie followed Helen through the swinging door and across the kitchen to where she was opening the refrigerator door. "Mom," he said grimly, "I don't know what's going on here, but something is and I deserve a few details."

Helen spun and looked at him. "Actually William Bradford Duncan, that is what I was going to ask you when time allowed.""

"What do you mean, ask me? Ask me what?"

"Well, among other things...What is a drunk, female guest doing passed out in the bunkhouse?"

Willie looked at her, his jaw rigid. "I really don't know, Mom. Maybe it was because her husband was already occupied with someone else."

Helen gasped. "What are you talking about? Are you suggesting Lucas was occupied with me? How dare you!"

Willie walked up and shut the refrigerator door and leaned down over her. "If you are going to deny it, Mom, then you'd better go in and wipe your lipstick off his mouth."

Chapter Thirty

Helen, with Jake's help, moved like an automaton through the breakfast routine, her movements jerky, but precise. He kept glancing at her, a troubled look on his face, but kept his silence and tried to anticipate what would be most helpful. Helen stood at the stove, dipping bread in an egg batter laced with orange juice, and cinnamon, methodically making a small mountain of French toast, her eyes vacant, an occasional tear slipping down her face. Already, she had fried the bacon and put it in the warming oven.

Jake arranged the fresh fruit on platters and carried them into the buzzing dining room. When he got back to the kitchen, Helen was in the bathroom. He flipped the last of the French toast from the grill and added it to that in the warming oven, praying that At would soon appear and tell him what to do. Somebody had to make the eggs. He could hear Will asking people to take their place at the tables, so he took the heated syrup jugs from their warm water bath and carried them into the dining room.

To Jake, it looked like everyone was present except for Jude, Lucas and Willie. Even Dean and Dee were there, looking as cool and relaxed as they always did. Russell was there too, sitting in a corner, holding his coffee mug in both hands, bent over it as if praying for absolution. Jake noted the green tinge to his complexion and nodded to himself. *Crazy bastard, it's what you deserve,* he thought with secret satisfaction. The man had certainly not helped the situation with Jude at all. *Or did he?* A sudden doubt entered Jake's brain.

"Okay, ever' body. We had an active night, so listen up." Will stood, holding a mug of coffee, looking satisfied. "I reckon you know Dean and Dee Dee killed the cougar about 5:00 this morning, not long after you heard it scream." He paused and let his gaze rest on individual faces, his eyes kind but intense. "That's a

310

sound, just like hearin' the buzz of a rattler...well, it ain't somethin' that you forget." He watched while several people nodded in affirmation and then continued.

"I'm hearin' some of you thought it sounded like it was right on the other side of Flat Creek from the cabins. It wasn't, but that wild sound is one that sure carries. He was really in a big ponderosa pine..." Will gestured over his shoulder with a thumb, not turning around. "...in that stand of timber beyond where Flat Creek turns and heads south between here and the corrals."

"Now, I'm gonna make a long story short. Let me just say that somethin' spooked that ol' tom away from his kill. Dee Dee was on watch, and she saw him start to approach and then decide somethin' wasn't right. Then, he disappeared for about two hours and they thought he was probably gone...until the youngsters we put in the corral started gettin' restless, movin' around, kickin' at each other, the fresh weaned ones callin' for their mamas... That's when they knew the ol' boy had circled around. They snuck out of the barn and Dean could see, using the night goggles, that he was just sittin' beyond the corrals, watchin' from up on the hill."

Will had every eye in the room on him, including Jake's. *Man, he's sure leavin' out a bunch,* Jake thought as he left to get the pitchers of orange juice, and found Helen back at the range calmly scrambling eggs, listening intently as Will's voice carried through the doorway. Jake felt relief. *She's back in control. Thank you, Lord.*

In the dining room, he could hear Will's voice. "An' here's where things evidently got interestin'. The cat musta sensed them and took off, not runnin', just hurryin' a little, towards the trees...and that's when Dee Dee, in the near dark, took off after the cat...right through the creek...no night goggles...Dean was still wearin' those. No rifle...Dean's got that. But she

311

accomplished her mission with just the moonlight. She surprised that cat so much that he did what a cat does and headed for a tall tree."

For the first time, Will grinned and shook his head, looking at Dee Dee. "I'd give my eye teeth to have seen that little scenario."

He took a drink from his mug. "So, now the cougar is in the tree, but it's gettin' lighter and he don't want to stay. Dean's come across the creek with the rifle, but that ol' tom is smart. He's real good at keepin' the trunk between himself and Dean's rifle, and the tree he's picked to climb has a lot of branches gettin' in the way of the line of sight. So Dean hands the rifle to Dee Dee and hotfoots it to the ranch house where Queenie already had Dewey and me up, since she's growlin' and tryin' to chew the handle off the door. Dean tells us he needs Queenie on a leash--needs to make the cat nervous so it will stay in the tree 'til they can get a shot."

Will grinned. "Dee Dee told me just a little while ago the only reason she tackled that creek the way she did was she knew the cat was having trouble decidin' whether to climb a tree or make a run for it. Then Dean and Queenie show up, and for a Queensland Blue Heeler not noted for barkin', she put on a pretty good show and made that cat climb high enough that the branches got thin. Then things got easier. With the tom's attention on the dog, Dee Dee was able to sneak around and get a decent shot...an' we got him hangin' from a singletree down in the barn for those wantin' to see...an' I left a phone message to that effect at the Oregon Department of Fish and Wildlife."

The guests sat silently, mesmerized, thinking their own thoughts. Will felt a surge of relief that they seemed satisfied. Without a hitch he moved the conversation in a different direction. "Now, if I recall, some of you was wantin' to go to town today and others of you was wantin' to ride. I got a note pad at my table and I'd like to ask you to sign up for your preference now, or right after breakfast. We got plenty of transportation either way." He grinned, looking like his old self. "I mean both horse power and truck power. I can free up Buck, or Buck and Billy, to take you if more want to go in. At an' Willie can take the riders." He paused, lifted his hat and scratched his head, looking for the absent Helen. "Reckon, soon as the cook gets here with the grub, we can eat."

Jake and At came through the door carrying platters as he finished speaking. He raised an eyebrow, and Jake shook his head. A feeling of dread pooled in his gut. *What's happened to Helen?* He walked to his table and sat, keeping his face neutral, handing his note pad to Beanie, not at all surprised when she put both Leo and herself on the list to go to town.

Then he sat and watched as some of the guests gathered around Dee Dee and Dean to ask questions and give compliments. He saw Dewey start going from table to table refilling coffee cups, listening to praise for Queenie, bragging happily about his dog, promising everyone that the day would be as dull as they wanted it to be. "This here's your vacation. We've provided all the entertainment we're goin' to…other than the ridin'. Rest is up to you. Want to sleep by the pond? Be my guest." he said as he poured.

Will thought to himself, *That ol' man sure does earn his keep and then some.*

Helen walked through the swinging door carrying a platter full of scrambled eggs. She set them on the counter and turned toward the guests. "Hi, everyone," she said brightly. "I know some of you are off for town and may choose to eat lunch there, so I need to know how many sack lunches to make. Please raise your hand."

Well, she looks like a million bucks, but somethin' sure ain't right with my cook. Looks to me like she's barely holdin' on to her stirrups. He watched as she took a quick count, nodded her thanks, gave a

313

quick survey to the counter, smiled and said. "It's all here. Help yourselves, everyone," and hurried from the room. *Reckon we're gonna have to have a little talk when folks clear out...find out what's wrong and fill her in on last night.* Yet again, the thought flashed through his mind: *Damn it Torrey, why'd you have to go and break a leg?*

In the kitchen, At and Jake were whispering together, but jumped apart when they heard the door swing, their eyes on Helen. "What?" She said, stopping just inside and putting her hands on her hips.

At looked at her with gentle eyes. "Jake was tellin' me what happened in the dinin' room this mornin'. I hope you don't mind," she said in her straight-forward way.

Helen strode past them, walking to where Jake had started setting out the makings for lunch. She stood silently, her back to them and then whirled. "I'm making the lunches today. You two go in and eat. And At, I told Will to get the numbers straight on who is riding and who is going to town. You can check to see if he's done that."

At looked at her feeling helpless. "Oh, Helen..." she said, her voice choking.

Helen threw up her hands like a shield. "Don't, At!" she said fiercely. "Not one sympathetic word. I mean it! I know you kids are worried, but this stuff with Willie will sort itself out. Lucas is already sorted out. For right now, I promise you that I'll hold myself together...because...because, I don't have a choice. But, really, right now, you kids need to go sit down and eat."

Will hooked the corral gate and leaned on the fence. *I could go to sleep just standin' here leanin' on the fence,* he thought. Instead he waved a hand to the departing riders. Surprisingly, Dee and Dean were following At and Amber up the hill and Willie was guiding Glenn and Bradlee through the colt pasture,

314

Chainsaw making the two other horses look like ponies. *Reckon I should be countin' my blessin's. One bad apple is all we got. Other than her, these folks are good people to know.* With the thought of Jude, his face turned dark and he went to find Russell. *I sure owe him a heap of gratitude, sacrificin' hisself that way;* he thought to himself and headed for the bunkhouse.

Russell was sitting on the front porch, holding a beer in his hand when Will walked up. He looked up and smiled wanly. "Shit!" he said. "That woman is one crazy broad."

"Who come up with the plan?"

"Buck and Billy said it was an old trick they'd played on their friends in their younger days."

Will was shaking his head. "Well, you boys got her to quiet down all right."

"We had to. What else can you do when a woman comes bangin' on your door usin' a half gallon of vodka an' hollerin' loud enough to chase that cougar into the next county?" Russell was very careful not to move or raise his voice. He tipped up the beer can.

"How come you didn't put your tongue over the mouth of the bottle like the rest of the fellas?"

"Hell! I could see she was gettin' suspicious that the jug wasn't goin' down as it was makin' the rounds. So I said somethin' like, 'Watch me, pretty lady an' I'll show you how a pilot does it.' Then I wiggled my eyebrows at her like I can do and chugged about a half inch. Then she clapped her hands and giggled, leaned over, grabbed the jug... showin' me some mighty pretty territory with that low-cut blouse, by the way. Well, she upended the thing just like I did...an' the contest was on."

Will looked down at his friend. "You got aspirin in you?"

"Yep. And a bunch of tomato juice Dewey brought me. Lucas came down an' got Jude up and out...I guess while we were at the lodge. So, I reckon, soon as I finish this 'hair of the dog,' I'm gonna go sack out for a while."

Will smiled. "That's a good plan. I owe you...all you boys. That was way above the call of duty."

Russell squinted up at Will. "I wasn't kiddin' when I said I think that woman has a screw loose," he said flatly.

Helen and Jake had finished cleaning up and were sitting on the kitchen stools. Helen's jaw was slack and she was listening intently while Jake unburdened himself. "She did what?"

"Stole Beanie's new bottle of vodka from the dining room and came down to the bunkhouse after the guys was all in bed."

"She walked down there in the dark?"

"Well, I reckon she mostly staggered...she'd already had plenty to drink."

"But you're saying she came to the bunkhouse door. You were in the ranch house. How did you know that?"

"I was sittin' on the front porch with Will and Dewey. They were havin' some of Will's dad's 'horse piss' and we were talkin' real low about things, when she come past on the road, sorta singin' to herself. It was pretty dark until she passed by the security light and it come on. Then, the next thing we could hear was her bangin' on the bunkhouse door with the vodka bottle and hollerin'."

"Oh, my God! The cat! Will must have gone berserk! He was adamant last evening about people staying put and keeping quiet."

Jake nodded. "He said, 'Jake, get your butt down there and do whatever it takes to keep that...woman... quiet. Tell the fellas to keep her there, no matter what.'"

Helen smiled, knowing that Jake had substituted "woman" for the word Will had really used. Temporarily, she was caught up in the story, her misery held at bay. She was amazed that Jake had somehow turned into a story teller. "So, what did you do?"

"I got myself down there. It was easy with the light still on. The door was open when I got there. Jude was standin' there in the doorway, wavin' the vodka bottle and invitin' the fellas to have a nightcap with her." He grinned and looked at Helen. "Never seen Billy and Buck speechless before, but they was. So was your son and Russell. I quick pushed her in and shut the door, figurin' it would maybe keep in the sound from whatever happened next. They was all standin' around lookin' at her; until Billy winked at Buck an' said, 'Reckon I will.' He tipped the bottle up and it looked like he took him a big swig. Then he passed it off to Buck. Buck did the same thing and then handed it back to Jude, said she could have it back for a kiss."

Helen gasped. "What did she do?"

Jake blushed furiously. "Well, first she laughed her ass off and then she said, 'Well, I'll trade a kiss for a little ol' slug of vodka any day.' An' she kissed him. While Buck was doin' the kissin' and the ticklin', Billy was whisperin' to Willie and Russell."

"Good God!" Helen said, "This is unbelievable! Those guys are all adults, but you're not. I am so sorry you had to witness all that!"

Jake looked down and then looked back up at Helen, a brightness to his brown eyes she hadn't seen before. "It was all happenin' pretty fast. But, before I knew it, they was standin' around in a kinda circle, passin' the bottle and tradin' kisses." He didn't add that he had been invited to partake, but declined, saying he didn't drink and he had a girl...and had taken terrible teasing from Billy and Buck.

"Jesus, what sort of a sick party game was that?"

Jake stood up and stretched his lanky frame, suddenly looking tired. "Actually, Helen, now that I finally got it all figured, it WAS a game...or I guess you could say, a trick. See, those guys were puttin' their tongues over the mouth of the bottle when they upended it...not drinkin', just pretendin'. But Jude didn't know that and she was sluggin' it right on down. Then, for some reason, Russell stopped pretendin' and started matchin' her chug for chug."

Helen could see it all in her mind. "Who passed out first?"

"Jude. She just sat down on Russell's bunk and fell over. Buck just lifted her feet up and covered her with a blanket. He said, 'She ain't goin' anywhere or makin' any more noise tonight.' Then I told him that was exactly what his boss wanted."

Helen thought furiously, putting the pieces together. "So, that's why the cat left without going to its kill."

Jake yawned. "Yep. Helen, do you mind if I have a nap someplace?"

Helen smiled and stood. "I don't mind one bit. I'll bet that's just what Will and Dewey are doing this very minute. Why don't you go curl up on the couch in the living room...or try out the recliner Torrey is going to use...see how comfortable it is. Clean the cabin and stock the ice cooler after you wake up. I'm going to get organized and make a quick run into town. If you need anything, just put it on my list."

Jake grinned. "I'm sure gonna need more chalk."

"Yes you are. I'll write it down for you. By the way, has George said anything more about you doing a wine label?"

Jake, in the middle of another yawn, nodded and headed for the swinging door. Over his shoulder she heard him say, with great nonchalance, "Yep. When he gets home, he's sending me a contract to sign. He said he wants to tie up my talent."

Just before she left, Helen put two sack lunches on the dining room counter; LUCAS scribbled on one;

318

JUDE on the other. She doubted Jude would want food, but she knew Lucas had to be famished. As she walked to her cabin for her purse, a little voice in her head nagged her to go knock on their door to see if they needed anything, but in the end, she could not.

In her mind, the horrible scene replayed. The look on Lucas's face when she'd slammed through the swinging door into the dining room, snatched a napkin from the counter, marched up to him and said angrily, "Wipe your lips...and don't come near me again. I mean it! Never again!" nearly broke her heart. She gritted her teeth. *I guess I should be thanking God that only Jake and Willie were there.*

Helen spent the entire drive into Burns reviewing the utter chaos her life had become. *This was supposed to be a good deed...a week of service to my friends. Instead, I fall for a guy who is even more screwed up than I am. I mean this whole thing sounds like the plot of a soap opera!"*

A sob caught in her throat. *Really, it has all the elements: Handsome lead; sex- starved widow; gorgeous setting; horrible, cheating wife.* Lucas's face came back to her. Not in the lodge, but the time he was looking down at her, his cornflower eyes, with the lids just starting to droop, had seemed to be memorizing her face. *And then he kissed me!* Helen groaned aloud in the truck. "It's over, Helen. It really never was. Deal with it! Think about what you are going to say to Torrey. Decide whether you are even going to tell her." Her words rang hollowly in the truck, but she knew the immediate truth of them.

After a few miles, her thoughts turned to Willie. *Way to re-build the relationship with your son, Helen. You sure screwed that up!* And yet, recalling the story Jake had recounted, her sense of fairness asserted itself. *Wait just a damned minute! My son was kissing Jude in the bunkhouse...that's what Jake said. He said the guys took turns passing the bottle and kissing*

Jude…and there she was, dressed in that skimpy little outfit…

Helen sat up straighter in the truck and looked at herself in the mirror. There was a definite glint in her brown eyes. *Maybe two wrongs don't make a right, but neither do two kisses make an affair…and one of them was to my forehead! My son and I are going to have a serious talk before this day is over!*

Chapter Thirty-one

Will woke up disoriented. He was lying on his back in their queen-sized bed, fully clothed, boots on, his hat beside him. He blinked, scrubbed his face, and then came surging to his feet. *What the hell?* He looked at his watch. *It's almost noon. My little snooze lasted near to three hours!* He grabbed his hat and headed for the front door.

Outside, the August day seemed as if it too were napping. The only sounds he could hear were the faint trickling sound of Flat Creek and the drone of bees working the hollyhocks by the front door. He walked to the road and looked up at the lodge. The truck was gone. Only then, Will remembered his intention to talk to Helen and see if he could take some of the strain off of her. *She's on her way to see Torrey. Maybe they'll talk it out. Torrey's better at this stuff, anyway.*

Will stretched out a few kinks, and decided he would go and place another call to ODFW about the cat. *We sure don't need that thing drawin' flies.* Thinking of flies made him remember the dead colt. He looked back at the house; pretty certain Dewey and Queenie were sacked out upstairs. Dewey didn't think that Torrey and Will knew he let the dog sleep on the bed, but they did. Will smiled to himself, remembering the old man at breakfast. *Well, I ain't goin' to crank up that D-6 until him and Russell are done sleepin'. I owe both those boys big time…Dean and Dee Dee too! Them two are somethin'! I got to remember to tell them that!*

He stood and pondered how he might present the idea that he wanted to give part of their money back to them. *Maybe say, I'm givin' them the staff rate. Maybe they'd take it then.* He doubted that they would. Then the idea hit him—the fall branding. He'd invite them to come and stay for free during branding. *Hell, those two would likely be ropin' more calves than any of us before the day was over.* He knew he was onto something and turned back to the house. He was going to call about the cat...but first he was going to call his wife and get her take on his idea. *I reckon Helen's got it all sorted out as to when they're going to spring her, but hearin' her voice ain't gonna hurt me none.*

Helen had decided, by the time she reached the hospital that she would just let her visit with Torrey unfold; certain that Torrey's main focus was going to be on leaving the hospital as soon as it was humanly possible. She grabbed her purse, slid down out of the truck and locked the door. The pain in her heart was still there and when she even pictured Lucas's face, she felt it shatter all over again. *I can be such a bitch!* she thought grimly to herself as she strode through the front doors and headed like a bee to Torrey's room.

"Baby!" The joy in Torrey's voice was unmistakable. She was sitting in a wheel chair, the cast leg elevated, holding out her arms. Helen flew into them. "Guess what?" Torrey said in her ear. "I get to go home with you! I've been released!"

Helen leaned back and looked at her. Torrey was dressed in her old Wranglers with the leg slit nearly to the waist, smile of anticipation on her face. There was not a single doubt that what Torrey said was true. Happiness positively radiated from her. Her make-up was on, her hair freshly washed and her suitcase sat by her chair. Crutches leaned against the wall. "Oh my God, Torrey," Helen said through her grin. "What if I hadn't come?"

"The thought never crossed my mind. It's your day." Torrey waved a hand. "Quick, go find a nurse. The papers are all signed. Get me out of here. I am so in need of fresh air and open spaces."

Helen jumped to her feet and was gone, her mind whirling. *What about the hospital equipment? Will I be able to get it into the truck? Will Torrey wait in the truck while I get the groceries or will she want to go straight home?* Then, suddenly, none of it mattered…her friend was coming home where she belonged. Her husband was about to get the surprise of his life…and it put a wonderful ending on one of the worst days she had ever spent on the ranch.

In the end, it had been simple. Torrey had been well coached on how to maneuver with the cast. By putting the seat all the way back, with the nurse's help, she used the running board with her good leg, and was able to get in. An orderly came with a box and a wheel chair. He helped Helen stow them, along with the crutches in the back seat. Then, she climbed into the cab, started the truck, and rolled the windows down. "Here's your fresh air," she said. "Now, do you need to go straight home? If you don't, I have a couple of stops to make."

Torrey laughed and drew in a deep breath. "Stop anywhere you like. Oh, my God, Helen, I feel all buzzed up…like I've been drinking champagne."

Helen turned and smiled at her friend as she exited the parking lot and headed for the grocery store. "How about a six pack of beer for the ride home? I've called in an order. So, we'll pick it up, along with the beer, and then I have only one more stop."

"Where would that be?" Torrey asked, not really caring, her eyes feasting on everything she could see.

"I have to go to the green front and buy a half gallon of vodka for Beanie. She might not know it yet, but all of hers got drunk last night and I want to replace it."

Torrey's eyes snapped back to Helen. "Oh, oh! I have a feeling the ride home is going to be interesting. Am I right?"

"Girlfriend, you don't know the half of it," Helen said, pulling into the Safeway loading zone and putting the truck in park. "Relax. I'll be right back."

By the time they were ten miles from Burns, Torrey's mouth was hanging open, the beer beside her

323

in the cup holder forgotten, while Helen told her about the previous night. For some time, the main two phrases out of her mouth had been: "She did what?" and, "Oh, my God!" Both were punctuated by her laughter.

Helen took an occasional sip of beer to keep her throat from getting dry. She was pleased by how well she was recounting the story Jake had told her, making it sound like a funny cowboy prank. After she was done with the bunkhouse story, Helen told how Will had done such a good job in the dining room. "Really, Torrey, he gets up there and assumes his wide stance...you know...the one where he puts his thumbs in his front pockets?"

Torrey nodded. "It's not just Will. All over the West, if you see guys in cowboy hats talking, nine times out of ten, they'll be standing just that way."

"Well, anyway, by the time he was done talking Dean and Dee Dee were heroes, and the rest of the guests were feeling quite proud of their friends and their own behavior...and of course, Beanie had Queenie in the dining room...up on her lap."

Torrey shook her head, still laughing. "Unbelievable! And, I suppose my husband turned a blind eye." She finally took a long drink of beer, thinking.

"I wonder what caused Jude to go off the deep end like that. I mean, last year she was a little sluttish, but nothing like what you just described." She looked over at Helen who was chewing on her bottom lip, looking determinedly straight ahead, her eyes dark with pain.

Oh, oh! We have another chapter in this saga... Torrey sat quietly, watching Helen struggle for control. She would not pry. It was not her nature. If her friend had a secret, it was hers to keep...or share...her choice.

After a minute, Helen said brightly, "The other big thing I wanted to tell you was how Jake has changed. You won't believe it! He's actually the one who told me the whole episode about Jude banging on the bunkhouse door with Beanie's vodka bottle."

"Really? Jake? He's actually talking in sentences?" Torrey let the conversation move forward, tucking unanswered questions and nagging worries away to consider later...after she'd picked Will's brain.

"Absolutely...and embellishing them a bit, I think...but maybe not."

"Well, well. He has a girlfriend and you for his champions. Maybe that's all he needed."

"Actually, he has more than that. Our guest, George, has taken such a liking to Jake's artwork that he has asked him to design a wine label for the wine he's producing."

"Oh my God! That's terrific! What other little hidden tidbits do you have tucked up your sleeve, darlin'?" Torrey blurted out, and then could have bitten her tongue.

Helen turned onto the gravel road to the ranch, the look back in her eyes.

"Well," she said, trying for a light tone, "Willie, is again, really mad at me...but that's a story for another time. For right now, we have to shake our tails and start dinner preparations. It's barbecued chicken tonight."

Torrey smiled. "And I've got a husband to surprise!"

Will heaved a sigh when he saw the ranch truck dusting up the road. *By God, I sorta figured we might have finally run Helen off for good.* He started striding up the road to meet the truck at the lodge. Behind him, At was unsaddling horses. Ahead of him, up at the pond, the guests were taking in the last of the warm rays, lounging around the pond, napping, reading, or in quiet conversation. The ODFW official had come and gone. The dead cougar and Kitty's last baby were buried. Dewey was working on the ATV, determined to have it ready for Torrey's return. The King boys and Willie were napping.

Russell had left during the time Will was taking his snooze. Later, Lucas had come to tell him that when Russell left, Jude was his passenger and would be staying in Burns until it was time to fly back to Boise. Will hadn't been surprised, but he had been relieved. He wasn't surprised at Lucas's tight jaw and clipped sentences, either, but he had been sad. He truly liked the man. *Gay or not, he's a fine man and deserves better than the humiliatin' she dishes out.*

He saw Helen fling open the truck door and stepped up his pace so he could help her unload. He thought, *Now that my cook is back, reckon we can get through another day.* Then he stopped and blinked when he saw Helen rush around to the passenger's side and jerk open the door. The first thing he saw was the white cast. The first thing he heard was the sound of his wife's laughter. He started to run. She was calling his name.

By the time he got to the truck, he was panting. Torrey was balancing on the edge of the seat, laughing, her arms outstretched. "Help me down, darlin', and give me a hug."

Will did just that, gazing at her, feeling his breathing settle, but not his heart rate. Finally he could say, "By God, you pulled one on me this time, Torrey. When I called your room and nobody answered, I figured maybe you and Helen had took off for better country." Her hands were firmly on his shoulders, supporting herself. "Just put your arms around my waist and help me slide down and balance," she directed. And then, she was in his arms and he lost his hat burying his face in her neck, taking in her scent, feeling her softness against him, gratitude filling him. "I've sure as hell missed you," he whispered into her ear.

Torrey looked up, put a hand to each side of his face, and leaned in for what turned out to be a very satisfying kiss. "Well," she finally said, "at least we haven't forgotten how." They heard Helen laugh as she brought the wheel chair. "Enough of that, you two! Now, aren't you glad Marshall did such a good job of handicap access to the lodge?"

In minutes they had Torrey ensconced in the kitchen, able to roll around easily in her wheel chair with its special leg support. She batted her way through the swinging door into the dining room, Will pushing her, and found Jake busily at work, putting down fresh place mats and tableware. "Jake! You are just the person I want to see," Torrey said, warmth in her voice.

Jake froze for a second, glanced at Will's grin and then grinned. "Howdy, Torrey," he said. "Welcome home a day early!" She noticed immediately that he didn't blush.

"Thank you so much for the card. Now, come here and let me give you a hug. Helen says you've more than earned your wages, and thinks both you and At deserve a bonus." She looked up at her husband. "What do you think, Will?"

Without pause, Will said, "I think either we got real lucky or God was lookin' out for us when he sent these kids." He turned her chair and pointed to the menu board. "Look what Jake did with the girls' old chalkboard."

Torrey's hands flew to her mouth. "Oh my!" She rolled herself forward and examined the board. "It's beautiful! Oh, Jake, that was a great idea! Now, I really want to hug you!"

Will held up a hand and said, "Not so fast, youngster." Quickly, he leaned down and planted a kiss on her lips. "I'll go haul in the load and then see you at dinner." He looked at Jake. "Okay, now it's your turn," he said, clapping him on the back as he left.

Torrey lifted her arms. She felt her heart fill to bursting, when without hesitating, Jake put gentle arms around her.

When Will strode into the kitchen, Helen was standing with a look of amazement on her face. "Look at this, Will. Look at all that kid has done in my absence. Here, I've been worrying myself half to death that I wouldn't have dinner out on time and three quarters of it is already done!"

On the butcher block, Jake had laid out all the ingredients for corn bread, including the buttered pan. On the counter was the huge bowl she planned to fill with broccoli flowerets, bacon, chopped apples and red onions. Beside it sat a measuring cup full of Craisins and a jar of sunflower seeds.

Jake walked in, pushing Torrey and said, with quiet pride, nodding at the salad bowl, "I got the salad all chopped an' in the cooler, Helen...an' the bacon's fried."

Helen could feel tears well up. She put a hand over her beleaguered heart and looked at the kind faces looking back at her with love and concern. The sense of being loved and cared for nearly overwhelmed her. She wiped away an escaping tear with the back of her hand, looked at Torrey and simply said, nodding towards Jake, "See what I mean?"

To Jake she managed to say, "I don't have the words...Jake, I just don't have the words right now. But I can tell you that you've already done plenty, and to get on out of here into the lovely afternoon. Go find your girl and do whatever you want to do...Torrey and I can handle the rest."

Will nodded and jerked his thumb at the still open kitchen door. "Go on, Jake. Like Helen said, you done plenty. I can unload the truck. At's down unsaddlin'. You want to help somebody, go help her. And by the way gals, before I forget...Lucas told me that Jude left to stay in town. Russell took her in. So, I guess that makes one less for dinner."

Willie found the women sitting in the great room having tea, Torrey in the recliner, Helen in a chair.

328

"Welcome home, Aunt Torrey. Dewey will be up as soon as he can. He's down at the shop cussing at the ATV." He gave his aunt a gentle hug and she smoothed his hair and kissed him on the forehead. "It's very good to be home, Willie. Thanks for coming to help out."

It was clear to both women that Willie was, after delivering his greeting, very uncomfortable. He was practically crumpling the cowboy hat held in his giant hands. Helen thought, *Oh, please, Willie, don't unload on me again. I won't have the strength to stand it.* Then, she remembered the talk she'd had with herself on the way into town. She stood. "Excuse me, Torrey, I think Willie and I need to have a private conversation."

"No, Mom. I don't care if Aunt Torrey hears me apologize to you. You've probably already told her about it anyway."

"Willie," Helen tried to warn, sitting back down, "I haven't..." Then Willie's words sank in and her words died in her throat. *Apologize? Did he just say apologize?*

It seemed that he did. Her son's words came tumbling out. "I guided Glenn and Bradlee today and they explained a thing or two to me after they pretty much cut me to shreds. I just want to say that I'm sorry I jumped to conclusions this morning." He tried for a smile. "Shoot, if you'd looked close enough, you'd probably have seen Jude's lipstick on me...if she had any left on by the time the bottle got to me."

Helen was speechless. *Talk about stealing my thunder! Now, what do I say? What on earth could Glenn and Bradlee have told Willie? Why would they have scolded him? There are too many pieces missing here.* From a distance she heard Willie's halting voice saying, "I guess you don't have to accept it, Mom..." She snapped out of her trance and back to the present, looked up at her son and said, "That was a huge surprise, hearing you apologize, Willie. I'm trying to digest it."

He looked at her sadly. "That's okay. I had the whole ride to think about it, and I'm still a little confused. But I know one thing you taught us is to try not to judge other people—let them live their own lives--and I think I learned today that means your parents too." He leaned down and gave her a peck on the cheek before turning on his heel and striding from the room.

The sound of his boot heels had faded, still, the women sat quietly, Torrey watching Helen's face run through a gamut of emotions. Most other women would have said, "What in the hell was that all about?" That was not Torrey's nature. Hers was to wait.

Finally, Helen looked at her. "I know, I know. I didn't tell you, other than saying Willie was angry with me again."

"You don't have to tell me anything, baby." Torrey said softly. "Not a thing. But, I will ask you to remember about the spirit ponies that came to visit your dreams."

Helen nodded. "I do remember." She thought about the elegant ponies of shifting light, shapes and colors that brought hope to her dreams. "You said they might signify change of some sort." She looked at her watch and stood. "Well, we've had our break; time for me to get cracking." She looked down at Torrey. "I have so much to tell you, but it's going to have to wait; too many parts are missing and I have no idea how it is going to end." Helen checked the brake on the wheel chair and offered Torrey her bent arm to pull against while she stood. It was a bit of a struggle. "We'll get better at this, Torrey, I promise," Helen said as Torrey turned and sat in her chair.

"You're doing fine, Helen. I know you said you didn't want to hear it again, but you need to know how much gratitude is in my heart."

Helen said nothing, as she pushed Torrey through the dining room, noting that both sack lunches were gone from the counter, and felt the same surge of

330

gladness she'd felt when Will said Jude was gone from the ranch. *But how is Lucas dealing with all of this? And how in the hell can I tell Torrey that I'm probably in love with Jude's husband; the man she thinks is gay…and not be able to tell her that he isn't?*

Chapter Thirty-two

Torrey rolled herself through the French doors to the deck. It was time to ring the triangle for cocktails, and Dewey would be joining her to perform the introductions. She admitted to butterflies. She also admitted that she was tired, but only to herself. She glanced to where the old ATV was waiting at the handicap ramp by the kitchen door. *Wouldn't I just love to have Dewey haul me home to my own bed right now?*

Queenie walked up the steps and flopped down beside her. She heard Dewey chuckle from behind her. "I reckon the whole meet an' greet team is now assembled," he said, setting a glass of Black Velvet and ginger ale on the rail beside her. She took it gratefully. "Dewey, you have no idea how good this is going to taste. Thank you."

"Well, reckon I figured you could use a little whistle wettin' with all the glad handin' you're goin' to be doin'," he said, smiling down at her, his eyes as bright and as blue as ever.

"I've missed you, Mr. Peterson," she said, warmly.

"The place sure ain't been the same without you," he said, gruffly, walking to pick up the old iron rod they used to ring the triangle. "But I got to tell you..." He turned and grinned at her. "I got enough stories to keep you from gettin' bored most of this next winter."

The clang of the triangle echoed over the ranch. Torrey watched as the guests trickled from their cabins. Helen had told her, in detail, about their arrival costumes. But these people looked entirely normal.

"Actually, Torrey," Helen had said earlier, during their break together. "I really can't tell you many details. As much as I really would have enjoyed talking with them, I haven't had time. I can tell you, with the exception of Jude, they deserve to be invited back. Everyone has been more than kind. Remember, I told you how George helped out that first night, and then how Bradlee and Glenn pitched in helping with breakfast...Lucas too."

When Helen had said Lucas's name, her face had changed; her voice had sounded tight. *What's that about?* Torrey had thought to herself. Aloud, she said, "Can you tell me other incidents? Because, if you're set on me being part of tonight's greeting committee, it would be nice to have a compliment or comment for them."

"Well, you'll do fine with Leo and Beanie...and their daughter, Amber, is the one who ran interference with Jude so Willie and I got to have a quiet dinner together." Helen thought for a minute. "Shoot, Dee Dee and Dean will be easy to thank because they killed the cougar, and Cleah and Juana are so in love with your horses, just ask them who they're riding and see what happens."

Torrey looked at her and sighed. "I suppose I can do that. Thank you, Helen. You sure make it look easy," she said again.

Helen laughed. "Torrey, if you only knew how glad I am that you're here. I know you can't help much, but I'm telling you, even with a broken leg, you bring me a confidence and serenity that has been sadly missing in my soul. You keep thanking me, but I can tell you that at least ten times a day, I'm saying either, 'God bless Torrey's organization,' or 'God bless Costco.' Just ask Jake, if you don't believe me."

Helen and Jake were in the kitchen. She had just finished the peach cobbler but it was not yet time for it to go in the oven. Jake was in charge of barbecuing the chicken on the back deck. He'd put it on the grill ten minutes ago and had already looked at his watch twice. She could see he was a little nervous so she smiled at him. "Go sit on the back deck and keep an eye on the barbecue, Jake. Take a root beer.

333

When At comes up, I'll send her out there to watch it with you."

"She ain't comin' up right away," he said as he stood. "She and Lucas are taking Mac and Shaq for a spin."

Helen was suddenly flooded with feelings, but she managed to smile at Jake and say, "Scoot," before turning quickly so he couldn't see her face. *All afternoon I have been worrying that Lucas has been in his cabin feeling...Lord know what! I've had him sad, mad, glad, moping...but I never had him on horseback.* She realized she was nearly weak with relief that her imaginings had been wrong.

Wow! Will and At must really be impressed with his riding ability to put him on a green-broke horse. With that thought, she set the timer, took the corn bread out of the oven, covered it with foil and placed it in the warming oven. Then she put the cobbler in, poured a glass of wine, checked her hair in the bathroom, applied lipstick and went to join the guests, with the picture of Lucas following At up the hill behind the corrals lifting her mood.

The minute Helen stepped through the French doors and onto the deck, she could tell the mood was different. *It feels...mellow.* Beanie had pulled a chair up and was sitting, talking to Torrey. When she saw Helen she jumped up, nearly spilling her ever-present drink. "Oh, you dear girl! Torrey explained how my vodka bottle 'unopened' itself. Thank you. It was a nice thing for you to have done," she said, giving Helen a one-armed hug.

"Beanie, it was my pleasure." Helen smiled at her and raised her wine glass. "Here's to you. She glanced around the deck. "In fact, here's to all of you," she called. "I hope you've had a wonderful day...and that those of you who went to town did some serious shopping."

"Oh, we did," said Beanie, ever the spokesperson. "And to come home and find our dear Torrey here...well, it just about made me cry."

Helen couldn't help but laugh, and many in the group joined in. "Beanie," she said, meaning every word. "You are a love!"

George came to stand at Helen's elbow. He said, "When you've finished that glass, Helen, I have a pinot noir I want you to try." He grinned. I made Billy take me wine shopping."

"Count on it," she said.

"I will." He stepped a little closer and dropped his voice, "And, I'll count on a dance too."

"You've got it," she said lightly and excused herself to go and check on the remaining hors d'oeuvres and Jake. She was feeling a whisper of concern that George might have just been signaling that he was looking at her as more than just a friend. *Please, no, dear God. I have more than enough on my plate and you know it. Let me just make it through the evening.*

At came into the kitchen just as Helen was taking the bubbling cobbler out of the oven, the crust a golden brown. "Hi, At." A jumble of questions filled her mind, all of them about Lucas. But instead of asking any, she smiled and said, "Jake's on the back deck. He's just taking the chicken off the barbecue. Why don't you go and say hello and then get a little trail dust off before I ring the triangle?"

At said, "I've been here for a while, visitin' with the guests." She lowered her voice. "You notice how relaxed ever' body is now that Jude is gone?"

Helen set the heavy pan down and looked at her. "I did notice." Then one of her questions would not be denied. "How is Lucas taking it?"

At shrugged. "I don't know. He didn't talk about it. In fact, he didn't talk much at all." She paused and looked at Helen with a question in her eyes. "I reckon he's hurtin'. He did an awful good job with Mac, though. We sure put those boys through their paces, I can tell you that."

Helen nodded. "Yes, I'm sure both those statements are true. At least, it must have made him happy that you and Will thought enough of him to let him ride Mac."

At looked at Helen, trying to read her face and then shrugged. "That was the boss's call. At first, I was some surprised myself. But it all worked out fine."

At turned to go and Helen found herself trying to think of some way to keep her talking about Lucas. She clamped her jaw shut, holding back words. *I'm going to be lucky if he even speaks to me. I wouldn't speak to me, were I he,* she thought as she started dumping tubs of Costco potato salad into a big bowl and adding long spoons both to it and the bowl of broccoli salad. Then, with an elbow to the swinging door, she put a fixed smile on her face, backed through, set the bowls on the counter, and went to ring the triangle. *Only two more dinners after this,* she thought as she started collecting nearly empty hors d'oeuvres trays from the counter. *And they're both pretty easy.*

As Helen sat and surveyed the dining room, she noticed how people seemed to have paired up. *Well, couples...if I can consider Dewey and Willie a pair.* The two men were sitting with Leo and Beanie. Torrey was seated at Will's table, her wheel chair turned to accommodate her leg. They were talking animatedly with Dean and Dee Dee about something. She noted, without surprise, that Buck and Billy shared a table with Juana and Cleah. Even At and Jake were sitting together with Amber and Lucas; Lucas with his back to her table. She told herself she was glad, but even as she had the thought, she knew it was a lie. *Get over it Helen. At least Amber is a healthy person. Put on your happy face right now!*

George brought her back to the present. "Helen, may I pour you a glass of pinot noir?" He asked, lifting the bottle and a clean glass. "It's made right here in Oregon, in a place called the Tualatin Valley. We can't wait to try it."

"Sorry, George, I was distracted for a moment." She looked around the table and saw that Glenn and Bradlee were already in the process of sniffing the bouquet with serious, considering looks on their faces. She smiled at George. "I think it is not going to match what you make, but I'd love to give it a try." She tried not to notice that Glenn and Bradlee were looking speculatively at her.

"So, guys, how did my son do as trail guide?" she asked lifting the glass to her nose.

Ignoring her question, Bradlee closed his eyes and took a sip of the wine, aerated it with an inhale through his teeth, rolled it around in his mouth, and swallowed. His eyes popped open and he looked at Glenn who was doing the same. "Subtle hints of berries, don't you think?" he asked, raising an eyebrow.

Glenn nodded and looked at George. "Very nice, George. I'm detecting cherries, another berry...blackberry, perhaps and...what else?"

"Plums," George said, delight written on his face.

"Oh, you good boy!" Glenn said, as though George had discovered an important clue to a treasure map.

Helen laughed and took her own taste. She, too, closed her eyes as she sampled. After a moment she opened her eyes, raised the glass and gently swirled the ruddy liquid, watching the tannins make it crawl back down the glass. "I'm thinking Saigon cinnamon for sure and perhaps just the faintest whiff of turmeric. And the berry is raspberry."

George looked first at her and then at the two men who were also looking at her. He laughed so loudly others turned to look. "Good lord, Helen. Talk about one-ups-man-ship! If I weren't married, I'd be after you in a nanosecond!" He put his nose back to his glass and then took another sip.

Helen felt a whisper of relief sigh through her. *Married! This is excellent. Thank you, Lord.* She took another sip and looked at George. "But the best thing is that it is delicious." She felt herself relaxing.

"Yes," said George, "it is. I was worried about pairing it with chicken, but now I'm not."

"It's strong enough to stand up to the barbecue sauce on the chicken, where a chardonnay might not be. I think you're a genius." Glenn said, as he got up to fill his plate.

Only later in the meal did Helen realize that neither man who'd ridden with Willie had answered her question about the ride. *And why are they giving me these odd looks? I wonder if Lucas told them that he told me he wasn't gay. I wonder if he told them of his feelings for me. I wonder if they told Willie...but how would that make Willie apologize? It would do just the opposite.* Helen wanted to grab her hair with both hands and run screaming from the room. Instead, when she saw At, Jake and Willie get up and start taking the empty plates from the guests, she politely excused herself and went to get the cobbler and ice cream.

The dancing didn't start immediately. Instead, guests took their drinks out to the deck, sitting in small groups, laughing and talking. Will excused himself and took his wife home to the ranch house. As he rolled Torrey through the kitchen, Helen could see that both were sagging with exhaustion. She leaned over, intending to give her friend a gentle kiss but Torrey grabbed her and held her fiercely. "I love you, baby," she whispered, her normally calm reserve shattered by her need to tell Helen what was in her heart. "I watched you with the guests and I mean it, Helen, I don't think I can do what you do."

338

Helen straightened and smiled down at her tired friend. "You did great, Torrey...and every day it gets easier. Now, home to bed, both of you...Dewey too. I'll send him along. There's no need for us to babysit this crowd, now that Jude is gone."

Will nodded. "I believe you're right, Helen. And just so you know...she's really gone...back to L.A. Lucas told me Russell had called, wantin' him to know Jude was askin' him to take her to Boise to catch her flight. I guess Dewey took the call and passed it on."

Helen didn't even try to fake disinterest when she asked, "Was Lucas okay with that?"

"Yep. Didn't surprise him none. He said somethin' like, 'She don't get her way, she ain't gonna play.' I decided right then an' there somebody needed to do somethin' nice for him, so I put him aboard Mac. Gave him somethin' to concentrate on besides that screwball of a wife."

Helen reached up and kissed him on the cheek. "I know I've said it before, but you are a fine and decent human being, Will Rawling."

One corner of Will's mouth turned up and Helen could see he was pleased. He pushed his hat back a little with his thumb and said, "An' here's somethin' else you don't know. We've invited Lucas, Dee Dee and Dean to come back as our guests for brandin' this fall; goes without sayin' that you're invited too."

Helen looked at them both. "Well, you two are really something" was all she said; not knowing that the sudden bright interest in her eyes was speaking volumes to the watching Torrey.

Helen walked through the swinging door and watched couples swirling to Hank Williams' classic, "Cold, Cold Heart," and knew she couldn't stay more than long enough to send Dewey down the hill to the ranch house. At and Jake were cheek to cheek; Willie was putting Amber through her paces; Cleah and Buck were dancing more than cheek to cheek, but Billy and

Juana were nowhere to be seen, nor was Lucas. Suddenly she couldn't stand it. It seemed like Hank's words were speaking directly to her and she wanted no part of it. She knew George would want to dance. *I can't. Not tonight. I'll tell him he can have a raincheck for tomorrow.*

She located Dewey and George, sitting with Beanie and Leo on the front porch in quiet conversation. Without even softening the words, she said, "George, I know I promised you a dance, but I am bushed, so I'm off for bed with the promise of a bunch of dances tomorrow night."

Then, without waiting for his answer, she turned to Dewey and said, "And you, old man, had better be getting Queenie to bed as well, don't you think? She's had quite a day. At and Jake and Willie have promised they'll shut the place down."

Beanie said, "It has been quite a day, hasn't it, Leo, dear? I was going to suggest we toddle off as well...but then saw it was only nine-ish."

"I'm ready, my dear. Finish your drink and then we'll go. It's not every day one wakes to the scream of a cougar."

As the silence of the evening closed around her and the gentle night sounds asserted themselves, Helen could feel how incredibly tense she was. She stopped and put her hands on her hips, arching her back and looking up at the night sky, the stars brilliant without the ambiance of electric lights. *Almost close enough to touch,* she thought, straightening and drawing in a deep breath. *That's where the sky horses...or as Torrey calls them...the 'spirit ponies' live.*

Once inside her cabin, she found her notebook and took it to the back porch. Sinking into a chair she opened it and, almost without hesitation, began to write.

August, 1998
I have felt as though I have fallen down a rabbit hole. I am confused and a little frightened of my own feelings in this strange place. I would give the world to have Dr. Pagglio sitting here in the other willow chair with his wise eyes and insightful questions. But he is not. Perhaps, tomorrow, if Torrey and I can find time, I'll try to explain things to her. But first, I must be able to explain things to myself.

Helen stopped writing and closed her eyes, picturing Lucas as he stepped from the truck—his tanned leanness, the well-worn Wranglers, the quiet reserve, the blonde hair with its sun streaks and the blue eyes. Oh those beautiful blue eyes! *If Dewey's eyes are sapphire blue and Jude's are icy, glacial blue, then what are Lucas's?* She had called them cornflower blue, but that didn't seem to do them justice. They seemed so changeable; warm one minute, dark and serious the next, the black circle around the iris intensifying the whiteness surrounding it. Helen blinked her eyes open. *Well, this love-sick puppy mooning isn't going to cut it,* she scolded herself and began to write.

Here's the problem: It seems that I am seriously attracted to a man who is probably more screwed up than I am. I mean, what man pretends to be gay when he's not? What man stays married to a woman whose apparent redeeming feature is that she is breathtakingly beautiful? She is self-centered, arrogant and has the value system of an alley cat and yet he stays because of some undefined "congenital condition" that makes it difficult for him to satisfy a woman. WHAT? I mean, even if he didn't have a penis, surely there are ways, when two people love each other, to find sexual satisfaction.

Helen's thoughts jerked from the page. Marshall's face floated before her. He was smiling, one eyebrow arched. "You know what I'm talking about, don't you, Marshall?" she whispered as she lowered the pen and tipped back her head to rest on the lumpy wood and smiled. *I know that 'come hither' look, Marshall Duncan!* Memories nearly swamped her. Resolutely, she banished the image, but not before a little thought managed to worm its way into her consciousness. *We even found ways to give each other pleasure when I was big as a barn and due to deliver.* With that thought she continued to write.

So, like I say, it's not only possible, but probable that Lucas has serious, deep-seated, long-term issues. For one thing, he must be terribly lonely for a close bond that Jude, apparently, isn't willing to forge. Enter the lonely, sex-starved widow in Wranglers. I was probably emitting pheromones or something. Whatever...he was attracted. Well, admit it, Helen, so were you! Knowing, or assuming you knew, he was a married, gay man, didn't matter to you. The zing was there and you definitely felt it. And you might as well admit that you still feel it. Normally, a woman doesn't think a man's droopy eyelids are sexy.

Helen scribbled wildly; honest words seemed to be flowing like black wine across the page. Then she remembered the conversation and the kiss. *God, how I wish I hadn't let him kiss me. Talk about opening Pandora's Box!*

Okay. So where are you now besides in the middle of a big fat mess? Well, for one thing, Willie doesn't seem angry with me anymore and I don't know why. That mystery, I will tackle tomorrow. For another thing, any way you look at it, I owe Lucas an apology. And I know I have to make the first move. What did I say to him? "Don't come near me again?" With those awful words, I made him the "bad guy..." Like it was all his fault and I was the victim!

Helen paused and lifted her head. She put her pen in the journal and closed it, thinking; *Time to act like a grown up, Helen. Whatever his issues, this is a very nice person, whom you treated horribly.* She put

342

the journal on the table and stood, stretching her back, then walked to the screen door and looked up at the lodge, where the lights were still blazing. Faintly, she could hear music. Slowly she pushed open the screen door, walked down her steps, and with measured strides, went to the Sunrise Cabin and up the steps. She opened the screen door and flipped on the porch light. *"I'll just sit in a chair on his porch and wait for him to come down. Then, I'll say my piece and go to bed with a clear conscience.*

When Lucas walked up the road from the pond where he had been sitting with only the stars for company, back towards his cabin, the first thing he noticed was that the porch light was on. His heart lurched, wondering if Jude, once he'd called her bluff and hadn't gone to town to bring her back, had come back on her own. When he saw it was Helen, sound asleep in one of the willow chairs, he found, despite his best intentions, unstoppable hope rising in his chest. Softly, he opened the screen door, cat-footed it to her chair and simply stood, looking down at her, wishing he could see her face.

Helen was sitting straight up, her hands folded in her lap, her chin on her chest. Her even breathing was accompanied by a light snoring sound. That fact brought a soft smile to his face. The glow from the porch light brought out the tawny highlights in her brown hair. He knew the picture had etched itself in his mind, along with a dozen others. After a long moment, he touched her gently on the shoulder. "Helen?" he said gently.

He heard her snoring stop. Then her head lifted on its graceful neck, and she looked up, blinking. "Hello, Lucas," she said, not a trace of sleep in her voice. "I hope you don't mind that I've invited myself to your porch. I've come to offer you a sincere apology...and my back story, if you'll have it."

343

Chapter Thirty-three

When Helen started talking, she couldn't seem to stop. At some point in her narrative, Lucas had pulled the other chair around to face hers. They sat; his knees touching hers. She had meant to only tell him about the accident that killed Marshall. Instead, she told him about her life, her children, their horses, her work as a graphic designer, Marshall's work as an architect, and most importantly, how much she had loved her husband.

Finally, she looked at him and said, her eyes bright with unshed tears, "Now, we come to the last chapter; the one in which, as a menopausal, empty-nester, I ignore everyone's advice and buy a most unsuitable horse. High Octane was his registered name. Only three, he was already gorgeous and living up to his name. One day, he jumped the fence of our pasture and got caught in wire. In trying to cut the horse free, Marshall...died."

Helen dashed a hand at her tears. Lucas shifted up to one hip, retrieved a red cotton handkerchief from his back pocket and handed it to her without saying a word. Helen nodded her thanks and blew her nose before continuing. "That was an awful time for all of us." She looked at Lucas and said, "To cut to the chase, my remorse was such that I wanted to kill myself...but I couldn't...partly because I couldn't rob my children of both their mother and their father, and partly because I felt I didn't deserve to die--I deserved to live in unspeakable emotional pain."

Lucas stood and pulled Helen up by the hands. "Come on," he said. She rose without protest, stuffing the handkerchief in her pocket. He led her through his cabin, to the back porch and down the back steps to where a little bench had been placed to overlook Flat Creek. They sat and he put his arm around her, pulling her close. She put her head on his shoulder, feeling

344

immeasurably comforted. She wanted to tell him about Dr. Pagglio and the long road back to sanity, but she had no more words. Instead, she let the chuckle of the creek seep through her, as if looking at every little nook and cranny for additional dark places and finding few.

She felt Lucas kiss the top of her head. "Thank you," he whispered. Thank you for coming. Thank you for sharing. I was sitting by the pond tonight and trying to imagine life without you in it. I couldn't. I could imagine going back to L.A., and helping Jude check into the Betty Ford Center where she could get the help she needs. I could imagine finally going through with the divorce, and I could even imagine going to a counselor to straighten out why I've let myself float through life; allowing myself to be manipulated and making compromises with every dream I've ever had. But, I couldn't imagine living the rest of my life without you."

Helen stood and turned to him, standing between his knees and putting her hands on his shoulders. "Maybe, just maybe, Lucas, we can find a way out of our mess. I know for certain that I want to. I know for more than sure…that it is terribly important we not take missteps. But for now, tonight is enough." She reached down and gently kissed the top of his head, just as he had kissed hers. "Good night, Lucas. Besides Dr. Pagglio, the psychologist who helped me recover, you may be the world's best listener."

When she dropped her hands from his shoulders, he took them in his own and gave a gentle kiss to each one. "Sleep tight, Helen. We'll play this your way. I think you have the stronger moral compass right now, and above all else, I want this relationship to start off on the right foot because I want it to last as long as we live."

Helen followed the moonlit path to her own back door and mounted the steps, feeling a lightness of being she knew might be dangerous, but she didn't care. *Time. We need to give ourselves time…time to sort through unfinished business…time to communicate with loved ones…time to get to know each other as friends.*

Robotically she got into her nightgown and brushed her teeth, all the while thinking. *It's a good thing he's going home on Sunday. That's what is going to make the 'staying just friends' thing possible.* She got into bed and pulled the button on her alarm. As her head hit the pillow, she thought of Lucas. *Can a man's eyes even be called cornflower blue,* she wondered as sleep overtook her.

Helen awoke before 4:00 thinking of her children. *I need to tell them what's up with me…with us.* She reached out a hand and captured the clock, bringing it into the bed and pushing the alarm button, then lay in the warmth, remembering the previous evening. *What a remarkable person. Just by listening, he made me feel so…cared for.* She threw back the quilt. *4:00 here means its 6:00 in Texas. I'll call Carrie as soon as breakfast is under control. Then on Saturday, I'll call Peter.*

As she threw on her robe, Helen remembered the spirit ponies. They had come again in the night, their colors more vivid and their shapes more defined. She cinched her tie and remembered. *They came to earth on Woolf Peak. I saw them touch down. I clearly saw them crossing the spot where the trail has crumbled away. Where did they go? I have no memory.* She hurried to the bathroom, shivering a little in the early dawn chill, and wondering how Torrey would interpret the spirit ponies coming to earth.

Striding up the path in one of her new shirts, the lovely coppery orange one, Helen realized she was, for the first time, looking forward to the day, and it wasn't just because of her understanding with Lucas. For one thing, having Torrey home was a relief. Another thing was that today's menus were easy. The breakfast casserole Torrey had invented was called, "Everything but the Kitchen Sink Casserole." *Of course, for my*

346

vegetarians, I'd have to call it "Everything but the Kitchen Sink and the Sausage Casserole," she thought to herself, smiling at her own joke.

Helen flipped on the dining room lights and found everything in ship shape. The blackboard was decorated with the breakfast menu. Each menu item, with its curlicues, was designed to fit as part of the whole. Jake had made good use of his new chalk. A thought flitted through her brain as she continued to survey the room. *That kid needs to go to design school.*

Coffee cups were by the hot plate. The tea bag holder had been restocked. She nodded to herself, wondering if Willie had stayed to help the kids. She'd noticed how he had made himself available and made a mental note to thank him. *What we really need to do is sit down and have a long talk. He, of all the people here, deserves to know what I'm feeling about Lucas...and more than that, what I'm going to do about it.*

Helen went through the swinging door and saw that the coffee maker was ready to go. She lifted the big pot on the range and its weight told her it, too, had been filled. She turned on the burner and went to flip the switch on the coffee maker. *What I need is some music to help me put the casserole together.* She returned to the dining room with quick steps, grabbed the five quarters lying on the top of the jukebox and scanned the offerings. *G-9 should do it.* She put in all five quarters for the same selection.

By the time At came thumping down the stairs, Helen was humming along to "Hey Good Lookin,' What You Got Cookin'," as she peeled, seeded, sliced and diced the potatoes, mushrooms, peppers, and the onions--with two wooden tooth picks gripped in her teeth.

"Well, looks like somebody around here is startin' out in a good mood this mornin'," At said. She grabbed a cup and robbed some coffee from the maker and looked at Helen, grinning from ear to ear, as though she knew a secret.

Helen pulled the toothpicks from her mouth. "Good morning, dear heart. How was the dancing?"

At laughed. "You know, it was pretty tame, with all of us doin' the slow stuff, until Lucas came back in and grabbed Cleah and started showin' us some moves we'd only seen on television. It got real fun. He's an awful good teacher...an' he sure was in a happy mood." The mischief in her eyes was unmistakable, as were the questions asking for answers.

The music stopped and then started again. Helen put down her knife and went to get her own cup of coffee. "Okay. You deserve to know, so let me just say this: Lucas and I have come to an honest understanding. We've admitted to the attraction, but are committed to just being friends until his life gets sorted out. Only then will we decide on the next step."

At set down her cup and threw her arms around Helen. "This is the best news in the world. Is it okay if I tell Jake?"

Helen laughed. "Of course. But, don't tell Willie. He and I need to sit down and have a talk...I need to tell all three of my children...not to ask their permission. I'm not saying that. I just need to assure them that I plan to take this journey in a loving, thoughtful, healthy way."

Helen paused and looked at At, loving the warmth and concern in her hazel eyes. "Frankly, there was a time in the recent past, when my behavior was not any of those things."

To her credit, At did not pry. She simply nodded and said. "I'm real happy for you, Helen...for Lucas, too." Then she grinned. "He sure was a different man on the dance floor than the whipped-lookin' dude I put on Mac yesterday." She took a last slug of coffee and headed out the door to wrangle the horses.

When Dewey and Jake walked in, sausage and vegetables were starting to sizzle in the big cast iron frying pans and Helen was making raspberry scones, trying hard to tamp down her mood. *I don't know why I'm bothering. Dewey has always been able to read all of us like a book.* Both men headed for the coffee maker. Jake poured his and headed for the dining room.

"Smells real good in here," Dewey said. He looked at Helen, and went to give the sausage mix a stir. "Not ever' day a man walks into such good smells and Hank Williams singin' good music at 5:30 in the mornin'."

Helen finally turned to look at him, trying for a neutral expression. "It lifts the spirit, that's for sure. How's Torrey?"

"Well, she's up. Thank God, their bedroom is on the ground floor. She ain't real steady or mobile with that cement leg. You're gonna have your hands full keepin' her corralled today."

Helen knew he was worried that she would fall, and nodded as she moved to take the big coffee pot from the heat. "Luckily, this is our easiest day in the kitchen...which reminds me..." Helen walked to the freezer and removed the two baking dishes of frozen lasagna. "These just need to thaw and they're ready to bake. I have bread frozen that Torrey bought when they went to Costco. That means, we just have a salad to make, corn to grill, and chocolate dream dessert to whip up. What could be easier?"

Dewey looked at her over his coffee cup, his eyes considering, but he said, with a chuckle in his voice, "Well that means you'll maybe have enough energy to twirl around the dance floor with an old man tonight." He looked at the clock, picked up the big pot and headed for the dining room with it. "You been workin' awful hard, girl."

Helen called after him. "Where's Willie? We need to talk."

Dewey stopped in the doorway. "He'll be up directly. He went down to close the gate on the horses after At brings them in. Then, he'll help saddle. I believe ever' one is ridin' today an' Will is otherwise occupied with bein' a mother hen."

They smiled at each other, and then Helen grabbed the pastry blender and started cutting butter into her dry ingredients. "He's right where he should be," she said, looking at him and then quickly dropping her eyes.

Dewey stood looking at her for a second and then dropped a bombshell. "Lucas is already down there helpin. Ain't he sumpthin'?" Then he turned and disappeared through the swinging door with a grin on his face. *My, my, but things are sure interestin' around here. It's gonna be a little borin' when ever' body leaves.*

Helen nearly dropped the pan of scones when she came through the swinging door and saw At, Willie and Lucas walk together through the open French doors and head for her table. She put the scones on the serving counter, and then stood fussing with them while she got her thoughts together. *Well, at least no one looked angry.* Both men had, in fact, been listening to At, who seemed to be demonstrating a reining technique. Helen turned around to nod at Will at his table and smile at the room in general. Out of the corner of her eye, she saw that Willie was standing, holding her chair, waiting for her. She turned her head and really looked. Everyone at her table had a secret smile on their face. Her eyes fastened on Lucas, and she felt her heart hitch.

"Okay, ever' body! Let me get this announcement over with," Will called as he got to his feet. "We got all of you ridin' today. There's only three different groups goin' 'cause I need Willie to do some engineerin' on a head gate so I don't lose my next cuttin' of alfalfa. The drill is the same. Lunches and

350

drinks will be waitin' for you down at the corrals." He started to sit and then stood. "By the way, Torrey said to tell you she'll see you later, but on this fine mornin' she just wanted to be home, on her own front porch with the sunshine and her hollyhocks. Now, the cook gave me the nod, so go ahead and dig in."

Will sat down and looked around the room, noting with quiet satisfaction that the guests seemed comfortable and quite at home. He saw Lucas sitting with At and Willie at Helen's table. *By God, somethin' good must of happened to Lucas. He ain't lookin' near the whipped pup. Maybe puttin' him up on Mac was the right thing to do. 'Course, gettin' Jude outta here is givin' him a little breathin' space, too.*

Helen put her plate on the table and allowed Willie to slide in her chair. "Thank you, son," she said. After he had taken his seat she looked around the table. "Okay, you three. What's up?"

Willie turned his head and gave her a long solemn look. "Lucas was telling us, down at the corral, that he had every intention of getting to know you better after he gets his life straightened out," he said quietly, so only their table could hear.

Helen first felt hot and then cold. She clasped her hands in her lap. Her eyes felt frozen to Willie's face. "What did you say?" she whispered.

"I told him what I told you yesterday...that everyone gets to live their own life, including parents. I also told him to call off his attack dogs," he said grinning and looked at the next table, where Glenn and Bradlee made no pretense of looking anywhere but at them. Willie flipped them a wave and made the "okay" sign with his thumb and forefinger.

Only then, could Helen bear to look at Lucas. He appeared relaxed. His smile was gentle and his eyes never left her face as he said, "I told him I was smitten, and would do as you suggested and get my life straightened out in order to deserve to be friends with a woman like you." He did not lower his voice.

She broke Lucas's gaze and looked at At, openly watching and listening. "You knew all this?"

"Shoot, yes. I'm not deaf. It all got discussed when they were helpin' me saddle."

It was only then that Helen was aware of the silence in the room. Gone was the easy buzz of breakfast chatter. She looked around. Only Will sat, shoveling in forkfuls of casserole, unaware that the rest of the group appeared to be holding its breath, including Dewey. She took a big breath and picked up her knife and fork. *So the whole group has an inkling. I shouldn't be surprised.* She looked at the serenity on Lucas's face, and then she turned back to Willie. "I'm going to call Carrie right after breakfast. Do you want to talk to her, too?"

"Sure. It should be an interesting conversation."

"Not really," said Helen feeling surprised at the laugh bubbling up from inside. "I'm just going to tell her what I was prepared to say to you when we had a minute." She turned a soft gaze on Lucas. "But then, someone beat me to it."

Chapter Thirty-four

Dewey brought Torrey up to the lodge in the ATV after the guests left for the corrals. Lucas had wanted to stay behind, but Helen had persuaded him otherwise. "Really," she said, "the best thing you can do is go and have fun. That way, I can get my work done and be ready to spend some time with you when you get back. Maybe we can even lounge by the pond to see if the experience matches what you've been visualizing."

They were in the kitchen, standing very close. Torrey was on the deck having a late breakfast, and Jake had gone to take the lunches to the corrals. Lucas had Helen's hand folded against his chest. He smiled down at her. "You win, if you promise you'll wear your bathing suit. I have a feeling that's the closest I'm going to get to seeing you naked in these next two days."

At his words, Helen immediately pictured them exactly that way—naked—in bed together. She blushed furiously, and he laughed and put his arms around her. "A kiss for the trail, then," he said as he dropped his head and found her lips. The kiss lingered and deepened until their breathing quickened, and Helen found herself pressing even closer. Then, before it got even harder to do so, she pulled away and dropped her head to his chest. He held her for a long moment, while their breathing settled, and then released her. "Jesus!" He whispered and then turned and headed for the kitchen door.

Helen raised her fingers to her lips. *Jesus, indeed!* She thought. Then she sighed and looked around the cluttered kitchen. *A little break on the deck with Torrey, and then Jake and I will tackle this mess together,* she decided.

Torrey was sitting in her wheel chair, with her plate in her lap, her eyes closed. Helen thought she was asleep until she heard her say, "I am sitting here

353

struggling with guilt, Helen, and yet, I know it as a weakness of my own spirit."

Helen was shocked. She pulled a deck chair around and sat so she could see Torrey's face. "What on earth do you mean?" She asked gently.

Torrey opened her liquid, black eyes. "Acceptance." she said, simply.

"Acceptance?"

"Yes. My guilt comes from all that you are doing for us...which means...I think I know more than the Creator about his plan for you...for us, too. Now, as I sit here, looking out over this beloved landscape, I am trying to accept everything that has happened and know that the Creator has a reason for everything."

Helen was silent, turning her head to look at the landscape, but her eyes went directly to Lucas striding down the hill, and she felt her heart give a now familiar stutter step. *God! Even the way he walks turns me on!*

When she turned back, Torrey's eyes were on her, reading her soul. Helen laughed. "Okay, okay! I'm going to tell you. But first, I want to get back to what you were saying. We've talked about this before, and I will admit that I've struggled to understand your belief system. I think you're saying that whatever happens in life is preordained by God."

Torrey nodded. "I wouldn't put it quite that way. I would say that we journey on the star path forever. We touch down to earth from time to time at the will of the Creator, who has a purpose for us."

"So, you are saying, for example, that Marshall's death was the will of the Creator?"

Torrey nodded serenely. "He sends us to teach and to learn things. Our spirits go home when he calls, but we will be sent again. That is what I believe."

"Boy, this is hard for me, Torrey. Really hard!"

"I know," said Torrey, "but I appreciate that you are willing to think about it and not try to...convert me." She smiled. "Enough! Tell me what I want to know about the man who makes you smile and look so dreamy."

Suddenly, Helen felt shy. She remembered thinking that their love story had the makings of a very bad soap opera. Finally, she said, "Do you want it from the beginning?"

"Of course!"

Helen told her, leaving little out, except for Lucas's admission of a congenital defect that made it hard for him to satisfy a woman. Torrey listened quietly, nodding from time to time but asking no questions. When Helen finished, Torrey asked only one question. "What are the spirit ponies telling you?"

"Funny you should mention them. They came again last night, only this time they weren't vague and ephemeral, they were in vivid colors, and from time to time, seemed almost solid." She paused, thinking. "But, here's the thing...they came to earth. I recognized the spot where they landed."

"Ahhhhh!" Torrey's sound of surprise jolted Helen and she blurted, What? What's that 'Ahhhhh!' about, Torrey?"

Torrey smiled. "This coming to earth--was it a place I know?"

"Absolutely," said Helen. "They came down just above where the trail needs repair up on Woolf Peak, which is very near where I scattered Marshall's ashes."

A smile split Torrey's face. "Get ready for big changes, Helen. There is no way to stop them," she said mysteriously.

Helen gaped at her, knowing she was not going to get another word out of her friend. Then, she threw up her hands, smiling. "I know you're not going to tell me more. I just wish I knew whether I was falling in love, or if I'm just in lust. You'll have to admit he's a handsome devil."

Torrey smiled gently. "Lucky you, to have the spirit ponies as guides."

Helen stood. "I think I'm going to need them. Remember, one more day and Lucas heads back to California...and his wife."

"It seems to me she is not a wife, Helen. She is a child...a very spoiled, mixed-up, too-beautiful child."

"Certainly not my favorite person," Helen admitted.

"I watched all their soap operas...Glenn's, Bradlee's and Jude's, while I was in the hospital. I remember thinking that Jude wasn't playing a character...she was that horrid woman I was watching."

"Interesting. Very interesting," Helen said. "But now, time to put all this on the back burner and get cracking...not you...Jake and me. Wonder where he is."

"He'll be along, and I'm coming in to help where I can. For one thing, I can wheel the dish tubs into the kitchen on my lap."

Helen smiled. "Yes, you can. Just don't try to get out of your wheel chair. Promise me."

"I promise. I know Will and Dewey worry about my falling. Dewey is going to help me practice with my crutches later today."

Helen looked around the kitchen. The dishes were done, the floor mopped and the Chocolate Dream Dessert was in the freezer. Jake was finishing the cabins, and Helen had told him to take time for himself when he was done. Dewey was coming to take Torrey back to the ranch house for a rest. *So...how do I want to spend my time while waiting for Lucas?*

She walked out onto the porch where Torrey was waiting for Dewey. The day was glorious—not too hot and not too cold. She stretched and smiled. "I was just thinking of how to spend my free time, and what I have decided to do is go and visit the horses. I haven't even been down to the corrals this week."

356

"There is no better therapy than spending time with horses," Torrey said, not a shadow of a doubt in her voice. She waved her hand. "Get going. Don't forget your hat. Give Paleface a scratch for me."

"I'll do better than that. I'm going to find a brush and curry comb and give at least Bear and Paleface a good grooming. Martha would get one, but she's Juana's mount this week."

Torrey looked at her serenely. "Perhaps by the time you have finished, the riders will have returned."

"Perhaps," Helen said, knowing she was blushing. "A girl can always hope." She leaned over, planted a kiss on Torrey's cheek and said, "Rest well," before heading down the steps to go get her hat.

At the corrals, all was peaceful. The horses were standing, hip-shot, heads lowered. Some raised their heads for a brief glance her way; others did little more than flick an ear. It was beautifully quiet. Only the drone of flies could be heard. "Hello, Bear. Hello, Paleface," she said as she picked up a brush and comb from the wooden box attached to one of the corral posts and let herself through the gate.

Paleface didn't raise her head, but Bear jerked awake and looked at her, giving his funny tin flute of a whinny. Tears sprang to her eyes; precious memories filled her mind. He trotted on tiny hooves across the corral and Helen dropped to her knees. "Hello, you little, moth-eaten character, you. Now, why didn't I bring you an apple?"

Bear was already sniffing her, asking the same question. Helen held up the brush and curry comb. "Never mind. How would you like me to take off some of that extra hair you're wearing; none of us likes wearing fur in August."

While she groomed him, watching the pile of hair around his hooves grow, Helen let the memory of the time Peter and an already 5' 8" Willie pretended that Willie was sitting on Bear's mother, Poo. "It was only when I was in full scold mode and brandishing a dust mop, that Willie stood up and Peter led your mother away," she whispered to the Shetland, hugging him around the neck. "Oh, Bear! We had so much fun! We really did. Do you remember coming to the ranch in the pet carrier?"

Helen was now working on his rump and she could tell the little pony was in heaven. His neck was stretched and his upper lip was quivering. "This is your favorite spot, isn't it?" she crooned, not caring that her Wranglers were now filthy, and every time she said something, she got more of his coat in her mouth.

Finally, she looked with satisfaction at the pile of hair and stood. "That's it for you, Bear. It's Paleface's turn." She walked to the appaloosa mare's shoulder and ran a gentle brush stroke down it. Paleface lifted her head and looked at Helen but made no move to leave. Helen started with long sweeping strokes to neck, shoulders and rump. She used the curry comb only on Paleface's belly and rump. *This is incredibly therapeutic,* she thought to herself, as past memories again engulfed her.

Helen had finished grooming Paleface and was deciding which of the remaining horses to tackle next when the first group of riders came down the hill, Lucas in the lead. Without conscious thought, Helen slipped through the gate, threw her brush and curry comb at the box, climbed the corral fence and started waving her hat. *Okay, so I'm acting like a school girl with her first crush, and I'm laying it right out there for everyone to see. Who cares?*

Lucas saw her, waved back and kicked Jasper into a trot. As he got closer she could see the wide smile on his face. *God, he looks great in a cowboy hat,* she thought as she went to meet him at the hitching rail. He dismounted before Jasper had fully stopped.

"Howdy, cowboy," Helen drawled.

"Ma'am," he said, sweeping off his hat with one hand and reaching for her with the other. When their lips touched, they heard Billy whoop behind them. "Forty-eight seconds! Amber wins!"

Lucas was grinning down at her. "That was the worst ride of my life," he said. "Not only was I not with you, but I took more teasing than you can even imagine." He whispered in her ear. "The whole damned place knows I'm crazy about you, and I don't care. Please tell me you don't care either."

She looked up at him from under her hat brim, her heart full. "Not in the slightest. The spirit ponies have landed," she said mysteriously as the riders began to swirl around them. She saw Billy jump off to help the guests dismount, taking their horses and tying them to the rail while saying to Helen, "I gotta think of somethin' special to do for Amber. She won the pool fair and square."

Helen turned from Lucas to look at him. "Pool? What pool? What are you talking about, you crazy man?"

He pointed a finger at Lucas. "Better let him explain while I take Jasper off his hands."

Lucas handed over the reins and took Helen's hand. "They started a betting pool during lunch. The thing was to guess how long it would take for me to find you and kiss you once we got back to the ranch. Then there you were...waiting. Amber bet it would be less than a minute."

"So, from the time you saw me, kicked Jasper into a trot, dismounted and we kissed was only forty-eight seconds?"

"That's what the official score keeper said. All I know is that it seemed longer than that."

They stood in the shade of the barn, watching while Leo, Beanie and Amber helped tie the horses to the hitching rail and take their personal belongings from their saddle bags. Beanie reached them first. Her clothes were dusty but her eyes were sparkling. "Leo and I have been hoping something like this would happen for you, Lucas, you dear man. We've watched for too many years…" She stopped and fluttered her hand. "Oh, my! I hope you don't mind that we figured it out, Helen. It has kept us all mightily entertained."

Helen couldn't help but laugh. "Of course I don't." She leaned in and said in a low voice, "We're trying to keep the horse before the cart, if you know what I mean. Lucas has a lot to sort out. Still, it is very nice to be able to be together, openly. I am so glad you don't disapprove. It really is quite unprofessional of me."

"Disapprove? Not this crowd! We're from Hollywood where 'happily ever after' is what sells. Lucas was never going to have that with Jude. Not ever…and like I say, we've all watched it for years."

Helen's eyes snapped to Lucas. He looked as if he'd been pole-axed. She understood immediately. *He thought only Bradlee and Glenn knew he wasn't gay all those years, and that the others had just figured out he was not because of his attraction to me.* She stepped close to his side, putting her arm around him. *And so, the web continues to unravel…in a good way,* she thought. Aloud, she said, "Well, Cinderella and her Prince are going to go swimming. I hope we'll see you there."

Lucas found his voice. "Damn you, Beanie," he growled. "I hate it when you know me better than I know myself."

Beanie let out a tinkling laugh and raised one plump hand up to his cheek. "I know you do, dear. So does Leo. Now, take my advice and get the name of Amber's divorce lawyer and get that show on the road as soon as you get home."

As they walked up the hill hip to hip, Helen asked, "Are you okay?"

"I think I actually am. Only, I'm still in a little bit of shock."

"Because your friends suspected all these years, that despite what you said, or rather, in later

360

years, allowed Jude to say to the contrary, you were a heterosexual male?"

"Damn straight! I couldn't have said it better myself."

Helen grinned up at him. "You sounded just like Will."

"I take that as a compliment," he said gravely.

They had reached the lodge and turned right towards their cabins. Helen looked towards the pond and saw that the cooler was already there, and that Jake appeared to be sound asleep in the boat. She pointed him out to Lucas. "I'll bet there's a cold beer waiting for us in that cooler."

He turned to her then, and looked down with serious eyes. "It's like I'm dreaming, Helen...like this is all too good to be true. That after one more day, I'll leave you...I'll leave the ranch...and I'll wake up in L.A. to find none of it was real."

Helen was, at first, tempted to make a joke, but she did not. "Listen, Lucas. This is real only if we make it real. You have a very big problem to face when you get home; her name is Jude. Always before, she's been able to reel you back in. Don't think I'm not aware of that. Don't think for a second that I'm not aware that when we leave, we'll have the entire continent between us, and that part of our attraction comes from proximity and the setting here. All these things worry me...but still, the second I see you, or even hear your voice, it all fades away and my world feels right..." Helen's voice faded. Lucas was looking down at her, listening intently, a look of remorse on his face.

"What is it, Lucas," she whispered.

"I am so sorry Helen. I'm sitting on information you should have about the situation between Jude and me. I should have told you that the pieces on the chess board, known as Jude, have changed. Always before, I have gone after her when she has made a fool of herself or misbehaved. This time I didn't. So, she upped the ante and went back to L.A., certain that worry about her would draw me back. But after I talked to Russell, I made up my mind. I called the Ponderosa Motel where she was waiting for him to come and get her, and told her I would not be coming home when I got back to L.A. I would be staying with Glenn and Bradlee in Malibu. I told her that when I returned, I would be filing for a legal separation."

"A legal separation?"

He sighed and nodded slowly. "Let me be clear. I fully intend to divorce her, but I didn't want to have that conversation with her over the telephone. There's no telling what she would have done. As it was, she called me every name in the book, including the one she knows hurts me the most."

Helen saw the pain in his face. "And what name would that be?" she asked, quietly.

She saw the line of his jaw tighten as he gritted his teeth. "Pencil Dick!" he spat out before closing his eyes and dropping his head.

"Oh, Lucas!" Before his name was out of her mouth, Helen had her arms wrapped around him. It was like hugging a board. After a moment, Helen said, "I'm glad you told me now. Maybe this is just the perfect time to have told me, both about the separation and the congenital condition you had mentioned before."

He pulled back from her and looked down with a puzzled look on his face. "What do you mean, Helen?"

She smiled wistfully. "If you really want to know, I was seriously considering dragging you to my cabin and seducing you--if only to convince you that no matter what your problem, there was no way I would let you NOT satisfy me."

"Jesus!" he breathed, "I'm all for that." He moved to take her into his arms.

"Not so fast, Lucas," she said, putting her arms up between them. "That's what I meant about telling me at the right time. Right now, I'm convinced that

362

having you be able to testify in court under oath, that you have never cheated on your wife will be a critical move…checkmate, if you will."

Chapter Thirty-five

By the time they got to the pond and had their swim, Helen admitted to Lucas that she had less than an hour to "bask." "Unfortunately, the kitchen will call," she said, rolling over and propping herself up on her elbows to pull her watch out of her boot.   "Anything I can do to help?" he asked. The sun was warm on their backs. His voice sounded very relaxed, almost sleepy.

"Not really. I just have to get the lasagna in the oven, get the bread buttered and make the salad. Hors d'oeuvres are little garlic bread sticks to dip in fondue, with veggies and fruit. Compared to some nights, it will be easy." Before she lay back down, she let her eyes slowly travel his length. *God, he even has beautiful feet to go with his elegant hands. Now, I know I'm a goner.*

She turned on her back, her head next to his and whispered, "Lucky you. You have beautiful feet. Some women say it's the eyes...but for me, it's beautiful toes. I'm crazy about them. " She heard him snort and then laugh. He reached for her hand and laced his fingers through hers. "And I'm crazy about you," he whispered, mindful, as she was, that they could easily be entertainment for the other loungers. "I want every dance."

She propped herself on a hip, giving up the idea of a nap. "Too late," she said softly. "I gave promises to George and Dewey. Then, of course, I want to dance with my son and Jake. How about I promise to save the last dance for you?"

"There's a song about that...by the Drifters. "Save the Last Dance for Me." It's not country; it's Do wop." His voice sounded on the edge of sleep. She smiled to herself and disengaged their hands. *There's so much we don't know about each other. Do wop! Now there's a great genre of music. I'll bet he used it when he taught dancing.* She watched his breathing even as he slipped silently into sleep, thinking of her conversation with her daughter. *Carrie said to go for it, as long as I didn't compromise my value system. Willie's okay with it. Now, I just need to talk to Peter.* She realized suddenly how much she was missing her two other children. She pulled her watch out again, checked the time and put it on. *Peter is home from work. Now's the time to call.*

Carefully, she stood and wrapped her towel around her waist and stepped into her boots. She looked at the others, put a finger to her lips and pointed at Lucas. Then she picked up their empty beer cans and walked to where Willie was sitting in a chair under the willows, a beer can looking small in his big hand. "I'm going in to call Peter. Want to come?"

He looked lazily up at her. "Nope. By now, Carrie has already called and told them your news. All they are going to want to do is talk about baby Ashley's brilliant accomplishments."

Helen laughed. "And I can't wait to hear them!"

Willie hooked a thumb in Lucas's direction. "Does he know you're a grandma yet?"

"No, not yet. Lord, Willie, there's so much we don't know; way more than we do know."

He looked at her, his brown eyes kind. "I think he deserves someone like you, Mom. You've been through it. You know how life can screw you up if you let it. So does he."

Helen leaned down and kissed him on the cheek. "You are a fine human being, William Bradford Duncan. Your father would be proud."

Willie's eyes lit up. "He would have been proud of me today. I had to work my ass off, but I got that head gate opening and closing like it has ball bearings." He laughed. "Uncle Will even gave me a compliment. He said I might be worth my keep after all."

"Dang!" She said, smiling. "High praise. Savor it." She turned and made her way up the path, thinking, *I am not going to let our time left together be sabotaged by thinking about the "what ifs." I just have to keep the faith, and do as Carrie said...be true to my own ethics.* She hurried towards her cabin to shower and dress before she called her son.

Peter answered the phone after several rings, as she hoped he might. Luck seemed to be with her today.

"Hey! Hi, Mom. How are things at the ranch? How's Aunt Torrey?"

"Oh, Peter. You sound wonderful. We're all doing okay. Torrey is back at the ranch but the cast hinders her a lot. She has crutches, but the doctor doesn't want her to use them much. He's afraid of another fall. So, she's practicing on smooth surfaces with Dewey as her helper."

"It's really great that you could help them, Mom. What did you do with your accounts?"

"Well, so far, I've only had to sub the Banana Republic account to Marcie Burnett, and really, that project was nearly done. I had other things in the offing, but hadn't signed contracts. I let everyone know right away and recommended Marcie, so I'm good there. However, I do have some news to share, but it can wait until I've heard about my granddaughter...and you and Patti, of course."

Peter laughed. "We're all great, but, remember how we couldn't wait for Ashley to start walking?"

"She was sure trying when she was at the farm."

"Well, what a difference a month makes! She's turned into a zoomer!"

"Oh, Peter, I hope you are getting videos."

"We are, don't worry. I'll bring them when we come at Christmas. Now, tell me your news."

Helen laughed. "I called Carrie this morning to tell her and get her take on it, but Willie was sure Carrie would have called you by now and spilled the beans."

"Willie isn't right about everything. She didn't. What gives?"

"Well, it seems I've met a man here; he's a choreographer from Los Angeles."

After a slight pause Peter said, "That's a good thing, isn't it Mom? It's been three years. Why doesn't your voice sound happier?"

"It's complicated, Peter. He's married but is filing for a legal separation when he goes home." Helen hurried on. "I know it sounds bad, but ask Willie before you jump down my throat. He's seen the wife in action. She's one of those women who is gorgeous on the outside but really ugly on the inside."

"Mom, married is married."

"I know. I know. And I didn't mean to imply that we're sleeping together. Although I'd be lying if I said I didn't want to."

There was silence on the other end, and Helen knew her attorney son was mulling her words. Finally, he said. "Mom, all that I ask is that you not get hurt. Please don't lay yourself out for more heartache. You've had enough."

"I know I have, Peter. We all have. I give you my promise that I will not violate my value system...which is what Carrie also made me promise. I might get hurt. I know that. But, wait until you meet the man, Peter. He's special. Even your Uncle Will likes him enough to give him Jasper to ride for the week."

Peter's laugh rang over the line. "Then, go for it, Mom."

"That's just what Willie said!" A feeling of relief coursed through her. Then she said, "Listen, I've got to go. It's time for me to start dinner prep, but I wanted to tell you that I had a bit of free time and went to the corrals to groom Bear."

"Bear! How is the old guy? Even thinking about him makes me smile. What a character."

"He's cuter than ever. Evidently, Tina's boys ride him a little."

"Geez, Mom, now I'm really homesick for the ranch. Ashley needs to meet Bear."

"Yes, she does. Oh, Peter, I am so glad we had this talk. I felt strongly that the three of you needed to know of my interest in Lucas."

"Lucas. So that's his name. I'm glad you called, Mom. Tell everybody I know hello, including my brother, okay?"

"I sure will. Love to all three of you."

Helen stood by the phone for a long minute, thinking. *The horse before the cart...if I keep remembering the importance of that, Lucas and I have a chance.* She hurried to the refrigerator to take out the lasagna and set it on the counter to come up to room temperature. Then she looked at her list and organized her mind.

Jake came in while she was slicing apples. "Hey there," she said, smiling at him, "how'd your day go?"

He nodded. "Good. Real good. How about yours?"

"I'm all about solving problems these days, Jake. For one thing, I've informed my other two children of my interest in Lucas."

He walked over to her elbow and helped himself to an apple slice. "You wouldn't of had to tell them if they were here...unless they were blind or somethin'."

Helen laughed, knowing the truth of his observation. "Listen, kid. I have this other problem that needs solving."

Jake looked immediately concerned. "Can I help?"

"Probably, since it's about you."

"About me?"

"Yes. I want to know how hard you are going to fight me if I tell you that I think you should apply to a design school somewhere, and that I want to help you financially."

368

Helen watched Jake lower the apple slice and turn to stare at her, his mouth slack, a stunned look on his face. She said quickly, "You don't have to answer now. I know I came out of left field. But think about it, won't you?"

He nodded solemnly. "I will...maybe talk it over with Marilee. You think I've got enough talent to tackle something like that, just from seeing my doodles?"

She grinned at him. "Let me just say that it's going to shock the hell out of me if you don't." She turned back to the apples, saying mildly, "If you have time after setting up the dining room, would you slice and butter the French bread and then wrap it in foil?"

Without a word, he nodded and turned, walking zombie-like through the swinging door.

When Helen was just finishing the green salad, Torrey rolled through the door. "Anything I can do to help?"

"Absolutely!" Helen handed her a tray of apples, pears, peppers and broccoli flowerets. "Here, take these in to the counter and come back for the rest. You look gorgeous, by the way."

Torrey smiled. "Well, I should. Dewey helped me wash my hair and then I washed everything else. God, do I miss being able to take a shower!"

They looked at each other. Helen shook her head. "I can only imagine. I mean, it's that little tin shower in my cabin that makes life worth living."

Torrey's eyes twinkled. "If old blabbermouth Dewey is telling the truth, there are other things happening around here that might make life more worth living, too."

Helen made a shooing motion. "Go. Let's get the hors d'oeuvres out and then we can talk. I'll make us a drink as soon as I bring in the fondue pot and dress the salad. We're on easy street now."

Helen and Torrey felt like naughty kids skipping school when they took their drinks to the back deck. Helen looked at the barbecue and said to Torrey,

"Steaks and baked potatoes tomorrow night. How hard is that?"

"Not hard at all, with Dewey doing the steaks. I think the only tricky meal left is the eggs Benedict on Sunday. Am I right?" asked Torrey.

"Yes," said Helen. "But I don't want to talk about Sunday. You're going to have one really sad woman on your hands when that last truck pulls out."

"Then we won't. I want to tell you something happy."

Helen looked at Torrey who was sipping her drink. The twinkle was back in her eye. "This sounds interesting," she said, her curiosity piqued.

"Will and I think you and Lucas should go riding...just the two of you...after breakfast tomorrow. Since you are staff, our insurance covers it. So, take Paleface and go. Don't worry about getting back. Jake and I can handle it. Like you said, dinner is easy."

Torrey watched Helen's face and thought, *she is at war with her responsibilities here and the pleasure of going riding with her man.* She sat quietly and waited as Helen's expression finally cleared. It was like watching the sun come from behind the clouds. "Oh, Torrey! I was going to say 'no'...but I can't. I simply would love that so much...more than anything I can think of." She jumped from her chair and leaned down to give Torrey a hug. Then she said, with wonder in her voice, "You're really volunteering Paleface?"

Torrey nodded serenely. "Yes. You two will do well together and she deserves more than to stand in the corral day after day. The doctor tells me that it will be more than six months before the cast comes off."

"Good Lord! I had no idea. How long until you can ride?"

"About eight months, if all goes well. There is a rod in my leg that must not be disturbed until the bone has knit itself. Then, there's physical therapy..."

Helen was shocked. "So long! I had no idea. Oh, Torrey, how will you bear it?"

Her wise eyes fastened on Helen. "I will consider it as part of my journey. I will both accept it and learn from it." Then her tone changed and was tinged with anger. "There's only one thing that really pisses me off."

"What would that be?" Helen asked, taking a sip of her drink.

"No sweat lodge!"

Helen nearly spit out her drink. She tried not to laugh, but it was a losing proposition. She threw back her head and howled with laughter. "Oh, my God, Torrey. You kill me! You can't take a shower, you can't ride your horse, you're stuck mostly in the wheel chair until the doc turns you loose with the crutches, you have more guests scheduled, you can't drive, you can't even turn over in bed...and yet the only thing that makes you mad is that you can't take a sweat bath?"

"Yes, I know. Crazy, aren't I?"

"Maybe. I don't know. Tell me why."

"The sweat lodge is a way to heal my spirit. This next six months without one is going to seem very, very long."

Her words sobered Helen. Again, she realized the depth of her friend's connection to the earth. She'd taken sweats with Torrey many times in years past; sometimes with their girls, sometimes only the two of them. Always, she felt cleansed afterwards. *But there's more to it for Torrey...something I'll probably never understand.* Helen said quietly, "I hadn't thought of it that way. I'm sorry I laughed. Will you forgive me?"

Torrey waved her hand. "This, too, is part of the journey. There is nothing to forgive. I walk with a foot in two cultures, and it makes it a little hard to understand me sometimes. I know that. I also know you love me like a sister. It is enough."

When Helen and Jake walked into the dining room with the lasagna pans, she saw that Lucas was already standing behind her chair, smiling at her. It

371

filled her with butterflies...big flapping, stomping butterflies. *Don't get all goofy and drop this pan,* she warned herself as she smiled back, noticing for the first time that Leo and Beanie were also at her table. She nodded to Will and watched him stand.

"Okay," he said. "I reckon since tomorrow is your last day, and since my genius nephew has solved my irrigation problem, I'd better take you on my personally guided ride up Hidden Creek to the prettiest little lake on the ranch." He nodded to his wife. "Torrey calls it 'The Teardrop.' I'm taking a pack horse, so bring your suits, towels, whatever you want. There's not really a trail to it and we don't want one, so we'll be goin' cross country."

Clapping and cheers broke out around the room. Will grinned, looked at his wife and sailed his hat to the antlers on the wall. "Now, Beanie, bein' our den mother, has asked for your attention."

Will sat down and Beanie stood as Helen slipped into her chair, nodding her thanks to Lucas. "I took this page out of Willie's book," he whispered in her ear as he slid her in.

"Okay, everyone, please pay attention!" Beanie waited while the room quieted and then said, "now, you know that tomorrow is our last night and Helen, or rather, Dewey is fixing us steak. So, he has a notepad in his shirt pocket. Be sure to give him your preference as to how it is cooked and he'll write it down. Also, since it is party night, let's dress up a little. Leo has promised to dig out his camera."

Helen saw Glenn and Bradlee exchange smiles and saw Glenn mouth, "Our hats?" Bradlee nodded, grinning.

She thought, *dress up? How in the world am I going to manage that? Oh, wait! I have the skirt Glenn and Bradley found for me and I can pair it with...* She felt Lucas's knee touch hers under the table and lost her train of thought.

Beanie was saying, "He's also taking it down to the corrals to get a picture of each of you on your horses. Okay, that's all I have to say. Back to you, Will."

"Well, then, since the food's here, I reckon I say, 'Let's eat,'" Will called from where he sat.

Beaming, Beanie sat down, looked at her husband, took a swallow of her drink before raising it to Helen and Lucas. "We know you won't be riding with us, but, please do have your picture taken before you go. It's very important to me."

Helen knew she looked surprised. Her eyes shot to Lucas's. He shrugged and smiled. "News travels fast around here. Will asked me if I was interested in taking the cook off his hands for a while and I said, 'Hell yes!' but, I didn't tell anyone."

Helen laughed and put her hand over his. "The town crier on this ranch is Dewey Peterson...always has been."

She heard Beanie giggle. "And I didn't even have to torture him." Then she sighed. "This has been soooo much fun, despite the sadness of losing two horses. Seeing you two together; seeing our daughter blossom back into her old self; watching our friends totally embrace this whole experience...well, it nearly does me in with gladness." She dashed a hand to her eyes and said, "Oops! Mustn't cry and smear my mascara."

Leo looked at Helen. "Isn't she something?" He captured his wife's hand and held it gently. "She really believes in happily-ever-after and tries to make it true for everyone."

"Yes, she's something," Helen said, meaning every word. "I don't know anyone with a kinder heart." She looked towards the line at the counter and saw At and Jake still at their table with their heads together and suspected she knew what they were discussing. *I'll faint if At isn't on my side,* she thought and looked at

373

those around her table. "Want to know a secret?" she asked.

Later, after the dancing, Lucas and Helen, hand in hand, returned to their bench in the moonlight. Before they sat, he drew her into his arms and lowered his head hungrily. With a little moan, she fell into the kiss. His hands roamed up and down her back and once she felt him start to caress her breasts and then stop himself. *I'm glad one of us has will power right now,* she thought. *It sure isn't me.*

Lucas pulled away and looked down at her. They were both panting a little. "Jesus! You make me feel like a cave man. I don't want to hit you over the head, but I do want to drag you to my cabin."

"But, you won't," she said softly, lifting a hand to the side of his face. "We've too much at stake."

He nodded, dropping his forehead to hers. "I'm hoping it's the rest of our lives."

Chapter Thirty-six

Torrey came rolling into the kitchen while Helen was making the breakfast burritos and Jake was dumping a Costco-sized batch of hash browns into the big cast iron skillet. She was carrying something in her lap, a wide smile on her face. "Look what Will found for me in the girls' room." She held up shirts encased in cleaner bags. "You've lost so much weight, Helen, I think one of these will fit."

Helen knew immediately what Torrey was holding. "Oh, my God! You think I can fit into Tina's rodeo queen outfit?" She washed and dried her hands and went to take the hangers from Torrey's hands, sliding the plastic up to reveal a lovely sky-blue shirt with a vined applique in silver. The other shirt was indigo with a border of rhinestones across the yoke and on the sleeve cuffs. As the coat hanger hook turned on Helen's finger, the shirt turned from blue to violet. "These are gorgeous, Torrey. I've only seen them in photographs that didn't do them justice."

Torrey nodded, clearly delighted. "There are matching pants, but even if you don't wear them, don't the shirts just scream 'party'? I'm going to offer At the one you don't choose."

Helen looked at Jake. His eyes were fixed on the shirts. "Which do you think At would like?" she asked, holding both up to him.

"Which ever one you don't choose, I reckon." he said, turning back to the stove.

Before he turned, Helen thought she saw his eyes linger on the indigo and her decision was made. "I'm thinking the sky blue would suit my sunny mood." She slid the plastic protector back down and went to hang the shirts on a peg by the door. "If they fit, At and I are going to be the belles of the ball. Thank you so much Torrey. You're sure Tina won't mind?"

Helen laughed. "She's never going to fit into them again and she's only been blessed with boys, so

375

no daughter to pass them on to. I called her. She's delighted for you two to have them, and sends her love."

Helen leaned over and brushed a kiss on her cheek. "No way to thank you. But the girlie-girl in me is tickled, I can tell you that."

Torrey's black eyes gleamed. "That's good enough. Now, I'm out of here to get a cup of coffee from Dewey and greet the troops. We're going to practice here in the lodge with my crutches today. There's so much more room." Her voice sounded determined.

Helen glanced at Jake and went back to the burritos. He had not said a word about her offer and the suspense was killing her. She'd made up her mind that it was his to bring up. Now, she was having second thoughts. *I have to remember how shy he was and how far he's come. Maybe he just needs a little prod.* Finally, her resolve gave way to curiosity. "So, Jake, did you and At talk about my offer to send you to design school."

He was silent. Helen watched from a corner of her eye while he carefully removed the lid and flipped the potatoes. "She's all for it," he said. "I'm the one…I'd sure like to try it…it would be like a dream I didn't even know I had, comin' true. But, Helen," he turned serious eyes on her, "it's got to be a loan, not a gift. I don't reckon I can take your offer any other way."

Helen felt her knees go weak with relief. "Sure," she said neutrally as she picked up the first pan of burritos and walked towards the oven, "if that's the way you want it. Do you have to discuss it with your parents?"

He opened the oven door for her and said, "Nope. In my family, you reach 18; you're on your own."

Helen slid the heavy pan in the oven and straightened to look him in the eye. "You may be out of the family nest, Jake…but you are NOT on your own."

She walked to the butcher block for the vegetarian burritos. "In fact, unless I miss my guess, the Rawlings now consider you and At, like they do me, family."

"Go, Helen." Jake said. "There ain't a thing left that I can't handle by myself. You know that."

Helen looked around the messy kitchen, her hands on her hips. "I don't think my conscience would let me." The swinging door banged open and Torrey rolled in, a tub of dirty dishes on her lap. "I heard that," she said. "Listen, you are just about out of here for the East Coast. Then it will be just Jake and me holding this place together. Don't you think we'd better get in some practice time?"

Helen saw them look at each other with knowing eyes. She laughed. "You two are so manipulative! Okay. You've convinced me. I'm off." She grabbed the sky blue shirt from the peg and headed out the door. Jake had taken the indigo shirt up to At's room. She would not see it until she came in from the ride. Helen wished she could be a fly on the wall to watch her discover it lying on her bed. *The sleeves are going to be a little short, maybe, but otherwise, it's going to be stunning!*

As she walked to the cabin, she reflected on how Torrey's attitude towards Jake had changed. *But then, so has Jake.* She looked up at the sky. *Torrey would say that it is all part of the journey...and what a journey mine has become!* She remembered Torrey's interpretation of the spirit ponies. *Change. Thank you, Lord. I think no one needed it more than I.* She hurried her pace. She wanted to try on the shirt. The old collar tag had said a size 10, but sizes varied so she wasn't getting her hopes up.

Lucas was waiting for her at the corrals with both horses saddled. He stood off to one side, in the shade of the barn, holding them while the others took direction from Leo as to where to position their horses

377

so he could keep the sun at his back to take their picture. Will was astride a big black horse with a jug head and high white rear stockings. He was leaning over his saddle horn, the lead rope of the pack horse in one hand, watching the melee. *Now, there's a picture,* Helen thought. *I wish I'd thought to bring a camera.*

She walked up to Lucas, feeling her heart do its happy dance. "Do we have lunches in the saddle bags?" she asked.

He nodded, looking her up and down, mischief in his eyes. "Damn if you don't look good enough to eat," he growled, "and that's after I just had breakfast."

Helen felt herself blush, and turned to check her cinch and take Paleface's reins. "Don't mount," he said quickly, reading her intention. "I want Leo to take a picture of us standing together with the horses as a backdrop."

She looked at him with appreciation. "That's a terrific idea. How did you think of it?" He looked at her, his eyes dark with emotion. He reached out one hand and took a strand of hair that had escaped from her barrette. "I thought of it," he said slowly, letting the hair slide slowly through his fingers before releasing it, "because one day we'll be sending out wedding announcements, and I can't think of a picture we could have taken that would be better."

She looked at him, letting the love she felt show naked in her eyes. Her throat had closed. Only with difficulty could she whisper, "I can't either."

Then, Leo stood before them. "All right, you two love birds, let's get your pictures taken and you out of here before you go into a clinch right here on the spot."

Lucas laughed while Helen blushed yet again. He reached out an arm and drew her close. "How about like this?" he said.

Leo was still taking their picture as they rode through the pasture gate. When they turned to wave at the foot of the hill, he took one last shot and then waved his hat and called. "Have fun."

378

"Thanks, Leo," Lucas called back and then reined Jasper around to fall in beside Helen. "Just being here together on these two good horses guarantees a fine time, don't you think?"

Helen beamed at him, feeling as light as a feather. "With you? Absolutely."

"Do you have a plan for where we're riding?"

She nodded. "We're going up the Woolf Peak trail so I can show you where I scattered Marshall's ashes. Then, we're going on just a little farther, so I can show you where the spirit ponies landed."

"Spirit ponies?"

She nodded. "That's what Torrey calls them. They came to me in a dream. I'll tell you all about it when we stop for lunch." Helen lifted Paleface into a comfortable jog trot to keep up with Jasper's ground-covering walk. *If only there were a way to prolong this day,* she thought, and then chided herself. *Choose acceptance...gratitude...faith.* She allowed the words to flow through her head like a mantra as she rode.

They stopped at the reservoir for lunch, hobbled the horses and looked over the water, sitting hip to hip. "Now, tell me about the spirit ponies," Lucas said.

Helen swallowed a bite of ham sandwich and said, "It goes back to the end of the awful days after Marshall died." She closed her eyes, remembering. "Before they came, my nights were full of bad dreams where I was being sucked down into a swamp of blood and body parts..."

"Jesus!" Lucas whispered, twisting to face her. He saw her eyes were dry and her gaze steady. She shrugged. "It was a terrible time. Then, I started therapy, at the insistence of my children, I might add...but that's another story. Anyway, one night, I had this dream, not of human and horse body parts, but of clouds turning into these most amazing delicate horses--in pastel colors that shifted into and out of shape--driven by the wind. I called them 'the sky horses,' but since Torrey identified them as what her

379

grandmother called, 'spirit ponies,' I call them that as well."

Lucas reached out and touched her cheek. "And that was the start of your healing?" he guessed.

She nodded. "I have had the same dream, or fragments of it, several times. But the last time...after we met, the horses were much different. They were in more vibrant colors and their shapes didn't shift much in the wind. They seemed...more solid. I watched them descend in a graceful herd and come to earth just above where the trail needs repair on Woolf Peak. Have you been there?"

Lucas shook his head. "I know about it. Last year, just in passing, Will said he'd try to get it repaired. My guess is that it hasn't happened."

Helen shook her head. "It hasn't. I was there last week. Poor Will. He always has ten places to put every minute of his day."

They sat quietly, each lost in their own thoughts, eating their sandwiches. Finally, Lucas asked, "Do you think the spirit ponies are significant—an omen, perhaps?"

"Torrey thinks so. She says change is coming, and there's not a thing I can do about it." She turned to look at him again. "If you're part of that change, I say, bring it on."

Lucas said, "There's not a doubt in my mind that I am, Helen. It's liable to get rocky, if I know Jude. I guess the good news is that this whole crowd knows Jude. Get this--Dean, who says very little--came up to me and said he would sign an affidavit as to her unfaithfulness."

"Dean? Good heavens! I can't imagine Dean or Dee Dee, for that matter, spending much time with Jude in L.A. They just don't seem her type."

"They're not. It wasn't in L.A., it was here."

"Here? You mean on the ranch?" Helen's head was reeling.

Lucas nodded. "The night vision goggles," he said simply.

Helen blinked and then put her head in her hands and groaned, as the ramifications of what Lucas was saying hit home. Her mind filled with pictures of Buck and Jude in the pond. "Dear God, I certainly hope it doesn't have to go there."

Lucas stood and pulled Helen up by her hands. "We're not going to even think about this anymore. We're wasting our last day together. Show me where you scattered Marshall's ashes."

"I will," she said as she walked into his arms. "it's right below where the trail sluffed off and the view is gorgeous."

"The view is pretty gorgeous from right here," he said softly, dipping his head and finding her mouth.

When Helen walked into the dining room, carrying the salad, she heard Glenn's happy squeal. "Oh, Bradlee, look at our girl. Now, that's totally authentic rodeo cowgirl!" He came rushing over, waited until she put the bowl down and then grabbed her and twirled her in place. "I am so jealous! That blue would look perfect on me!"

She laughed. "Wait until you see the one At has on. It's divine." She looked at both men with appreciation. "You both already look pretty perfect without my shirt, or At's. In fact, you both look better in those hats than Hoss and Little Joe ever did." She could tell both men were pleased. "Now, stand back and really let me look at you."

"No," she heard a voice behind her say, "You guys stand back and let me look at my girl."

Helen spun around and there was Lucas, looking absolutely devastating in a shirt she had never seen. It matched his eyes perfectly. "A present from Beanie," he said at the question in her eyes. She grinned and turned to the two men. "What color would

381

you call that blue?" she asked them, pointing at Lucas's shirt.

"Periwinkle," they said in unison.

"Rats!" she said. "Not cornflower?"

They shook their heads. "Periwinkle," they both said adamantly.

"Okay. So, I was wrong about the color of his eyes, but, I'm still keeping him," she said grinning up at him as she slipped into his arms for a quick hug, and then headed back for the kitchen.

Jake was putting foil-wrapped baked potatoes in the big red bowl when At walked down the stairs in the complete indigo rodeo outfit, her eyes on Jake. The tailored pants fit perfectly. That the hems were an inch short didn't matter. She was glowing. Helen's eyes shot to Jake. She saw him swallow a couple of times, his eyes shining, but unable to say a word. *But she knows,* Helen thought. *His eyes are telling her that she looks beautiful. She understands him and she understands that.*

Dewey walked in from the back deck with a rose-colored silk bandana tied around his neck, carrying the steaks. "Let's get this show on the road," he said.

"At, you look great!" Helen said as she dumped a skillet full of sautéed mushrooms and caramelized onions into a bowl and trailed Dewey into the dining room, knowing Jake would follow with the potatoes after At and he had their moment. She looked at Will and called, "No speeches tonight, boss, the steaks will get cold."

He laughed and waved a hand at the group. "I guess you'd better go get it before they throw it out," he called. "What I got to say can wait until morning."

Helen looked around the dining room. There was a bottle of red wine open on each table. She walked over to George, smiling, "I suspect you are the wine fairy, since all the bottles have the same label."

382

"You're right. Guilty as charged. Can you even imagine having meat this good without a decent cab or merlot?"

"I cannot. Thank you, George. It has been such a pleasure getting to know you," she added.

He looked at her then. "The pleasure has been mine, Helen. And, I've heard, through the grapevine, what you are attempting to do for our Jake. I have some strings I can pull if he is at all interested in attending ArtCenter."

Helen gaped at him. "ArtCenter? The famous one in Los Angeles? You could help him get in there?"

George nodded. "Yes, I believe so," he said modestly. "Let's talk more when the time comes."

She smiled at him. "We definitely will! Go get your steak, George...and I hope it's perfectly done. No one deserves it more," she said, meaning every word.

A silence fell over the dining room as hungry guests dug into their meal, Helen's table included. The conversation was about small things. Willie and Amber told her about riding cross-country and about swimming in The Teardrop. She caught them exchanging puzzled glances from time to time. *I wonder what that means?* Suddenly, she knew. *Surely not! She's older, I'm sure of it.* A little voice in her head then reminded her that Amber wasn't the only 'older woman' at the table. She slid her knee over and bumped Lucas. His eyes shot to her face and she lifted her glass and said, "I want to make a toast to happiness," she said. "That's all, just to happiness." She raised her glass.

When they had all drunk, Amber said, "Well, I want to raise a toast, too. I can't tell you how much this week has meant to me." She suddenly pushed back her chair and stood. "Everybody," she called, "I'd like to offer a toast."

When all eyes were on her, she said, "This toast is to my parents, who managed to get us all here. I want to personally thank them and drink to their

383

health. They are the best parents in the world!" She raised her glass as the room exploded with cheers, call outs and clapping; then she sat down, her face red.

Helen leaned forward. "That was lovely, Amber. They will never forget this moment. Ever! But, I think you'd better go over and give Beanie a hug. She's in danger of totally smearing her make-up."

"You're right. No time to be shy now." Amber jumped back up to thread her way through the tables.

Willie leaned forward, "Actually, not that it's a contest, but I have a pretty great mother too," he said as he got up to help clear the plates.

Helen looked up at him, tears making her eyes sparkle. "Thank you, son. I...I... won't forget this moment either."

Helen sat for a moment, watching the kids clear the plates, her hand in Lucas's and then she jumped. "Good heavens! Do I think dessert is going to serve itself?"

Lucas smiled at her as she bolted from her chair. "Hurry back," he said.

It seemed, after the tables had been cleared, pushed together and the chairs set against the wall, that the group was happy to pour themselves another cup of coffee, have another glass of wine or, in Beanie's case, another vodka tonic with lemon, and talk instead of dance. They took themselves out onto the deck where the nearly full moon was just rising. A few robins were singing their goodnight songs from the top of various trees. Staff and guests were standing around in small, ever-shifting groups, laughing, talking, and reminiscing.

Even the King brothers seemed mellow and relaxed, happy to drink beers and talk hunting, horses, rodeos and wild country. When someone finally put a quarter in the jukebox and Eddy Arnold started singing, "Make the World Go Away," Dean and Dee Dee slipped out to the deck and started dancing in the moonlight.

At and Jake found Helen standing by Lucas, his arm draped around her shoulder. They were simply standing, staring across the pond when At spoke. "Helen, I reckon things are going to get a little crazy around here tomorrow, and I wanted a little quiet time to say, Thank you for everything.'"

Helen and Lucas turned as one. Helen reached out and hugged her. "Oh, At, don't thank me. You and Jake saved my bacon and you know it."

She grinned in admission. "Well, for sure, we had your back."

She glanced at Jake, and Helen had the premonition that he was working up his courage to speak. She waited quietly, encouraging him with her eyes. He cleared his throat. "It's like you came here just for me, Helen. I wasn't doin' too well, and I sure needed the job. Then seems like things changed for me." He reached in his pocket and pulled something out. "She ain't exactly an angel, but she's been in my pocket since I was little and I want you to have her." He held out his hand, taking Helen's and placing something in it. She looked down and in the porch light, dully gleaming, was an old mercury dime.

She looked up at Lucas; a sob caught in her throat and saw him give a tiny nod. She closed her fingers around the offering and threw her arms around Jake. "You are so special to me, Jake...and...and I don't even know your last name."

The sob broke free, giving vent to the pent up emotions she had been feeling. At and Lucas moved in and joined with Jake in holding her and letting her cry. When she was mostly done, she heard Lucas say over her head, "Don't worry. Those are the happiest tears I've ever seen." He pulled a red handkerchief from his hip pocket and handed it to her and said, "Blow your nose darlin'. I believe this is our song." Don Gibson, singing "I Can't Stop Loving You," had come on the jukebox.

Helen did as she was told. "I'm glad you have more than one handkerchief. I plan to keep the other one to take home with me."

He looked down at her. "A souvenir?"

"No, not that; more like as a piece of you."

Lucas drew her close into the dance position and dropped his head to rest on hers. Words were beyond him. It was enough to simply hold her close, feel her against him, and pray that her love would be strong enough to stand the test of the separation and whatever Jude planned to throw at him.

Chapter Thirty-seven

Helen remembered little of the long flight back to Dulles. Saying goodbye to Lucas had been worse than she could have imagined. It felt, as she watched the truck pull out, that her heart was attached to the bumper and was being pulled out of her chest, the pain was so great.

Willie had pulled her tight against his chest and let her cry, knowing her well. "You've never done a thing in your life half-way, Mom. It's what makes you so special," he'd whispered. "If this is meant to work out, it will. Just don't lose faith in Lucas when what he needs is your support."

Helen remembered Willie's words three days later after she had finally landed and hailed a taxi. What she wanted now, was to get home. As she sank into the back seat of the cab and gave her address, she remembered to turn her mobile phone back on and saw she had a missed call. *Lucas!* She pressed the phone to her ear. "Helen, call me, as soon as you can. I'm like a fucking zombie. Having the whole damned continent between us somehow makes it worse. Thank God, for friends. I worry that you don't have anyone. Please, call me when you land. I need to hear your voice. I love you!"

She let her head sink back and tears roll from the corners of her eyes. *This is real,* she thought. *The pain is real. The love is real. The man is real. I refuse to do what I did before, and shut down every emotion in my body. I could really screw this up by doing that.* She sighed and lifted her head and pulled Lucas's red handkerchief from her jacket pocket to mop at her face. Then she put it on her lap and ran her hands over it, smoothing out the wrinkles. *This handkerchief is a metaphor; wrinkles can get straightened out.* Then the ghost of a smile crept on her face. *Oh my, would Jude ever hate being called a wrinkle!*

She and Torrey had talked about Jude just before she left. "Her spirit is all confused. It stands in the center of the universe looking for the star path, but when it looks north, it does not see the star. If you cannot find the North Star, you have lost your way. She is a person to pity, Helen, not scorn."

"I'll try to keep that in mind, Torrey. I mean it. Right now, I fear the worst from her."

"She cannot hurt you, Helen. She can inconvenience you, but she cannot hurt you. Only you can do that. Remember…acceptance, gratitude and faith. I look at you and see who you are. It is all good."

Helen had sighed, somehow feeling comforted and then she managed a smile. "And don't forget, I have the spirit ponies in my corner."

"Yes," Torrey said simply, as though it were an undisputable fact, "and I have had you in my corner. Now, you are leaving and I will have Jake in my corner. I see now, how impatient I was with him. When the time is right, I will apologize." She gave a small, sad laugh. "I believe that my leg has much to teach me about patience."

"Do you really think the two of you can manage the kitchen?"

Torrey nodded. "Our next big group comes at the end of October, when we bring the cattle down from the mountains. By then, he will be masterful in the kitchen and I will be masterful on my crutches."

Helen frowned. "If you need me, just call."

Torrey shook her head. "November. Come for the branding. Not to cook, but to spend time with Lucas." She looked sideways at Helen. "The saying that 'absence makes the heart grow fonder' is true, you know."

Helen groaned. "I honestly don't know how I can possibly get any fonder of that man, Torrey. I even told him I liked his toes."

Torrey had laughed then, her eyes twinkling. "If you and Lucas can manage to negotiate this next stretch of your journey together, you will find even more things to like—little things—unsaid things." Her eyes got dreamy.

"What do you mean Torrey?"

"Like feeling him check in the night to make sure he has not robbed all the covers; like finding manure sprinkled around my hollyhocks when I know he is too busy for such trivia; like having him pull my braid when he walks by; like looking up in the evening and seeing him looking, not at the television, but at me..." Her voice faded and her eyes were far away. She blinked and looked at Helen. "I wish that for you, my sister of the heart."

Helen grabbed at her pocket for the red handkerchief, tears running down her cheeks, the pain in her heart nearly unbearable. "Oh, Torrey," she sobbed, "I so much want that for us, too."

Torrey leaned forward in her wheel chair and placed a hand on Helen's bowed head. She said not one word, but to Helen it felt like a benediction.

Helen paid the driver after thanking him profusely. Generously, he carried her suitcase to the front door. "I'm not leaving until you're inside," he said as he stepped from the verandah. She turned and looked at him. "You are very kind, and I appreciate it. It makes the world a better place."

He nodded and watched the key slip into the lock before retracing his steps.

Once inside, Helen immediately turned up the thermostat. Then she walked to the wall phone and punched in Lucas's mobile phone number. He answered immediately. "I love you too," she said. "I don't know why I didn't tell you at the ranch, but I do...so much that it felt like my heart was being ripped from my chest when you pulled away in the truck."

She heard Lucas's long exhale. "God, Helen, you have no idea how much I needed to hear you say that! I love you too. Don't doubt that for one minute. Where are you?"

"I'm home. I just walked in the door. I'm sorry I didn't call you as soon as I landed, but I needed to be here, in the privacy of my own kitchen when we talked. How are things there?"

He was silent for a long minute, but from Torrey, she'd learned to wait. "It's been a long day," he finally said. "First thing this morning, Amber put her finger under my nose, shook it and said, 'Above all, Lucas, be straight with Helen. She can handle it. You need to get used to being in a relationship with a strong, healthy, loving woman, not a manipulative bitch.'" The pause came again. "I know she's right, Helen. So, I took two numbers from her—one, her psychiatrist, and the other, her divorce lawyer. I have appointments with both."

"Wow! You move fast!"

He let out a harsh laugh. "Not as fast as Jude. Her lawyer has already filed the paperwork for the divorce. He's advised her to get all the press she can from this...I suspect the tabloids are going to have a ball. I would imagine the headlines will read, 'Star of Young and Restless Abandoned by Husband for Cowgirl.'"

Helen groaned. "But, how in the world can they say that?"

"Because they have a copy of the picture of us standing arm and arm, looking very much in love, that Leo took."

"What?"

"You heard me correctly. Leo and Beanie's home was apparently burglarized when they were out yesterday. It was a real burglary, things of value were missing."

"Someone broke into their home? That's terrible."

"There was no sign of a break-in, Helen. But here's the point...Beanie and Leo both lost most of their jewelry, which is covered by insurance, by the way. But then, Leo noticed that the ranch pictures he'd taken and had developed, weren't on the kitchen counter where he'd left them...they were on the floor."

"And one of them was missing," whispered Helen. "Oh, dear God!"

"Yes," said Lucas grimly. "I'm writing the script here, but all the Lightmanns' friends know they have a key hidden under a flower pot by the pool...including Jude."

"But, she'll get caught."

"She probably knows that. Amber thinks she took the jewelry to throw the police off the track for just long enough for her to be able to play the tragic, spurned wife role; and plans to then take the jewelry back with a tearful apology, blaming anger, booze or drugs...thinking they'll forgive her...as they have...as we all have, in the past."

"But, Lucas, how could she possibly know about the pictures?"

"We're pretty sure it was George's wife."

"What?"

"Yes, we think she put on her 'nice Jude' personality, called Effie, George's very sweet, clueless wife, and asked her how he liked the vacation. And Effie said something like, 'He loved it!' I just looked at George's copies of the pictures Leo took, and it looks like everyone did."

"Lucas, I want to come out there to be with you."

"No!" he barked. "Hell, no! I don't want you anywhere near this mess, Helen." His voice softened. "As much as I want you in my arms--to see your name and face splashed across "Star Magazine" or "The National Enquirer," would just about kill me."

It was Helen's turn for silence. Her mind was whirling, but she felt a clarity in her own thinking that amazed her. "Listen, Lucas. Here's what I think. My role in this is simply to love you and support you in any

391

way that I can. You are probably right that I would become immediate fodder for the tabloids. Right now, when that picture hits the press, I'm just a face and a first name." She thought furiously. "I've got to hang up right now and call Torrey and Willie and you've got to call everyone who came to the ranch with you. Please tell them, 'if someone calls to ask for my last name, to play dumb.'"

"I'll do that. It will sure help, at least for a little while. Besides," he said, "they might not even know it. We were mostly on a first-name basis."

"Right," she said. "But they can find Willie's last name and link it back to me. Still, unless I miss my guess, Jude thought of me as hired help…which means I must live in Burns, right?"

"Hang up and make your calls. We can give it our best shot."

"Okay. Give Glenn and Bradlee my love…and Lucas…with your permission, I'm going to talk to Torrey about what's happening. She helps me see things clearly."

"Sure. That's a good idea."

"If it seems right, I'd better tell her about Buck and Jude, too."

"I trust your judgement, Helen," he said gravely. "You can tell her that Dean is still willing to testify. Will you call me back before you go to bed?"

Helen felt warmth pool like sunshine in her stomach. "Of course…and when I go to sleep, I'll be visualizing your arms around me."

"I might be visualizing more than that," he said.

She laughed, noticing how alive she suddenly felt. "Don't you dare let anything get in the way of the branding in November, Lucas Clements!"

When Torrey got off the phone with Helen, she realized how unclean she felt. *God, do I ever need a sweat!* She glanced at her husband nodding in his chair. He had still not recovered from the week of guests. She hated to wake him, but knew she must. She rolled her wheel chair to the foot of his recliner and pulled on the toe of his boot. "Wake up, Will. We have a problem."

By the time she finished sharing Helen's news, her husband was wide awake and sitting straight up, glaring, not at her, but at the situation. "I reckon I knew those boys wouldn't be able to hold out from all those charms being thrown their way," he said, grumpily. "You think it was only Buck dippin' into the nectar, or was it Billy too?"

"I think it doesn't matter as far as the situation is concerned. What matters is doing all we can to prevent Jude from unfairly and maliciously trying to ruin lives."

Will stood up. "Reckon I'd better call the King Ranch, and tell them boys not to talk to anyone...and to get their butts back over here first thing in the morning." He swung around. "I sure hope to hell them two knew enough to keep their dicks covered, 'specially with the likes of her."

Torrey said, "I think I can wait and talk to At and Jake in the morning. No one will be coming to the ranch tonight."

Will looked at her usually serene face and saw the tension. "You okay, babe?"

"I don't know," she said. "But, I'll tell you for sure that tomorrow I will be burning sage bundles everywhere on the ranch that Jude touched...including the saddle she rode!"

She rolled away shaking her head and he heard her mutter, "Peleypeley...crazy woman."

The next day, Helen wandered around empty rooms in her too-big house and realized, other than very occasional visits from her children, not one thing tied her to Virginia any longer. Then she corrected herself. *Dr. Pagglio. I'm still connected to him and to the group.* She looked at her watch. She had managed to get an afternoon appointment with him. *Only two hours to go. Maybe I'll do my grocery shopping first. I really am tired of this place!*

Her thoughts turned to the West Coast. Lucas was going to call at 5:00 his time; which made it 8:00 her time. She took her mobile phone from its charger and put it in her purse, checked her make-up and hair in the hall mirror and was headed for the door when the wall phone rang. It was Willie. "It's a good thing you called last night, Mom. They're already here."

"What? Who's there, Willie?"

"The paparazzi."

Helen felt herself go numb, as the ramifications of what Willie was saying hit her. "Oh, son! I am so, so sorry. You do know this means you are likely to become infamous, don't you?"

"Give me a break, Mom. What are they going to do? Splash a headline that says, "Basketball Star's Mother is a Tramp?"

"Yes," she wailed, "that's exactly what they'll do. Oh, my God, Willie, what will you do? What can I do to help? I am soooo sorry."

"The first thing you can do is calm down and listen to me."

He sounds just like me, she thought. Peter can sound like Marshall, but Willie sounds like me. She took a deep breath and said, "I can do that."

"Okay. I've already given a heads up to the team's attorney. He said, if they printed one false word about me...or you, as an extension of me, the University of Oregon is prepared to sue their ass off. If you print false things, it's called libel, Mom."

"Oh, Willie you are something. But will you be able to go about your business, or will you have to stay holed up?"

"The attorney is calling the magazine's legal team...and they have a big one, and telling them that I am giving an interview tomorrow...and that they can take all the pictures they want."

394

Helen gasped. "But, Willie...what can you possibly say?"

He laughed. "Don't worry, Mom. Amber is helping me. We're emailing back and forth so I'll have my prepared statement all ready to go."

When Helen hung up the phone, there was no doubt in her mind that her younger son was not only going to be prepared; he was looking forward to the challenge. *Hmmm. Amber's helping? Interesting!* She picked up her purse and walked out the door.

The first thing Helen noticed, as she sat facing Dr. Pagglio, was that there was a smile on his face. "Well, you look wonderful, Helen. How are you feeling? How was the vacation? I notice you canceled last week's appointment. Deena said it was because you had extended your stay."

"Yes, I did. My friend, Torrey, broke her femur. I stayed to help with the incoming guests."

"Isn't Torrey the one who came to see you right after Marshall's death?"

Helen nodded. "She's my best friend; we're like sisters."

"Was it rewarding to be of help to her?"

"Absolutely! I worked like a slave, but I made wonderful new friends...and I fell for a married man." She watched with satisfaction as the doctor's eyebrows shot up.

After a barely discernible pause, he asked, "And how did that work out for you?"

She laughed. "It's a work in progress, but I want to tell you the whole story, from my perspective, of course. Then, when I've finished, I want you to correct my errors in thinking."

When Helen finished her story, she noticed for the first time that not once had Dr. Pagglio picked up his notebook. She sat quietly while he steepled his forefingers under his nose as he did when in deep thought. "I think," he finally said, "that, from the events

395

you have described, this person, Jude, is in dire need of qualified in-patient, psychiatric treatment, but that she won't willingly go. It is only when she is declared a danger to herself, or others, that an involuntary commitment can be made on her behalf."

He looked at her. "That is not in your control. Your behavior is in your control. I believe your commitment to your children and to your own sense of ethical behavior is going to stand you in good stead."

"Yes, I believe so as well. Remember when I told you I would never try to shut down my emotions again?"

The doctor nodded. "Yes, I do."

"I started to, but then I recognized what was happening and made a conscious decision to allow myself to feel the pain and deal with it. So that lesson has been learned."

He looked at his watch and stood. "What you have is a very unconventional love story going, Helen." He held out his hand. "I, for one, wish you luck. I also think you don't really need counseling any longer."

"I think you are right. However, I would like to come and say good-bye to the group."

They smiled at each other. "I think that is an excellent idea," he said.

Helen realized she was checking either her wristwatch or the wall clock every few minutes while waiting for time to crawl by until 5:00 o'clock on the West Coast and decided to go for a walk to help the last hours go by. She threw on her old cardigan and stepped out into the lovely autumn evening. *Already, the leaves have turned and the nights are getting longer,* she thought as she started walking towards the old bridle path through the woods, thinking how overgrown it had become. *Someone else needs to own this wonderful property and give it the tender, loving care we once did.* With that thought, but without really knowing it, Helen's attachment to her family's home, the home Marshall and she had dreamed of and then built; the home where they had raised their children, lessened. The spirit ponies called.

Chapter Thirty-eight

At noon the following day, Helen was fixing herself a salad when the phone rang. Her heart jumped. *It isn't Lucas. It's way too early.* Still, she couldn't help hoping.

"Helen, it's Beanie, do you have a minute?"

"Oh, Beanie, it's so good to hear your voice. Of course I do. Lucas told me about the burglary, and I'm so sorry."

"Well," said Beanie, "that's not how Leo, Amber and I are looking at it."

"You're not?"

"Oh, hell, no. We're looking at it as a gift from Adonai."

Helen pulled the cord on the wall phone over to the table, and plopped down in the chair on rubbery knees. "Did you just say that losing your jewelry, possibly having a friend violate your trust, and the potential of having a picture of Lucas and me sold to the tabloids is a gift from God? Did you really say that, Beanie?"

With Beanie's laugh tinkling in her ear, she thought, *Uh-oh! Here I go down the rabbit hole again.* "Yes, yes, I did," Beanie answered. "Are you sitting down, dear? This is going to take a while."

"As a matter of fact, I am…and I have all the time you need. Lucas isn't calling until 5:00 your time and my last appointment with my therapy group isn't until 3:00 my time."

"Well, first I want to say, Jude is NOT a friend. She doesn't know how to be a friend. She is in our lives only because of dear Lucas. Then, I want to give myself credit and say that I had this tiny, little premonition that I should tell the nice officers, who came to investigate the missing jewelry, about the one missing photo and to ask them to dust the ones we found on the floor for finger prints."

Helen felt her heart rate accelerate. "Did they agree?"

"Well, not until I told them that the stolen photo was likely to either be sold to the tabloids, used in a divorce case, or used for blackmail! Then, they put every one of those photos into an evidence bag and took them away. After that, a team came to dust my jewelry case and the drawer where Leo keeps his good pieces...including his grandfather Lightmann's gold pocket watch."

"Oh, dear! If it's Jude, I hope Lucas is right and that she plans to return everything."

"Helen, dear, that's not the point. Here's the point. The nice sergeant asked me if I wanted to press charges if Jude's prints were found. I said, 'Let me think about it.' Because, you see, my tiny premonition was growing into a plan."

"What sort of a plan, Beanie?" Helen was realizing that for a woman who had just been robbed, there was an odd quality in her voice; one that she couldn't quite place.

"Well, after talking it over with my family and getting the green light, I called Jude." Beanie's tinkling laugh came across the line again. "I was most devious in expressing my sympathy for all that had happened to her and invited her to the Polo Club for lunch. She couldn't resist...as you could imagine...for a number of reasons."

Good heavens, now I know what I've been missing...that's a 'cat who ate the cream' voice, if I've ever heard one. "Right!" Helen said. "I get it. If you're friendly, and inviting her to lunch, you aren't suspicious. Then, too, a sympathetic ear would be like balm to her ego."

"Exactly. I know I'm taking too much of your time, Helen..."

"Good God, Beanie! You have me on the edge of my chair. I am beginning to think you may be holding the key to our happiness. I need to hear every word."

"Well, I won't keep you in suspense." Helen heard the rattle of ice cubes, and imagined Beanie had just taken a sip of her vodka and tonic. "What I said to Jude, after a bit of chit chat and the ordering of cocktails, was this: 'Jude, you little shit, we've got a deal to make. If you give Lucas an uncontested divorce and avoid any publicity about it, Leo and I will not press charges for burglarizing our home. It is totally your choice.'"

Helen put her hand to her chest. She found she could barely breathe as she waited for Beanie to continue. But clearly, by the silence, she knew Beanie expected her to say something. "Beanie! For God's sake! You're killing me here! What did she do?"

"Well, first she played the part of the innocent, tragic victim. I'll tell you, Helen, it almost made me laugh. She said, with an utterly convincing look of shock, 'You've been burglarized? I didn't know! That's just terrible! I can't believe it. But, Beanie, you can't seriously think I had anything to do with it. How could you even think such a thing?' Then she started to cry…right there in the Polo Lounge."

Helen realized she was starting to enjoy the story. It had to have a happy ending, she just knew it; Beanie's voice gave it away. "Waterproof makeup?"

"Oh yes," Beanie confirmed. "And a part of me was sitting back watching the quality of her acting with approval. But the other part of me was leaning forward and saying. 'I can think of it, because some very nice policemen have the photos that were tossed on our kitchen floor and are dusting them for fingerprints as we speak.'"

Then, there was a pause and Helen heard the ice rattle again. She waited, elbows on the table, pressing the phone to her ear with both hands. *Please, dear God, let this be the happy ending I want it to be.*

"Sorry, Helen, dear, I had to wet my whistle, if you know what I mean," Beanie chirped. "Anyway, right before my eyes the tears stopped, and she morphed from sweet, tragic, charming Jude to the blonde bitch we know so well--blood practically coming out of her eyes."

Beanie giggled. "You wouldn't believe the names she hissed at me over her lovely squid, arugula and hearts of palm salad. Then she picked up her glass of water, threw the water in my face and stormed out."

"Wow!" Helen said. "Dramatic exit! Were you okay?"

"Of course I was. I was more than okay. I felt like celebrating, so I ordered another cocktail, asked the waiter to put my very nice, uneaten pastrami sandwich in a take-home box, and proceeded to eat Jude's salad. It seemed silly to waste a twenty-two dollar salad."

"Oh, Beanie, I can see it all. You were magnificent!" Helen laughed. Then she asked quietly, "What do you think she will do now?"

"I don't know. I do know she will go home, lick her wounds, try to think of every scheme that can make what I said work in her favor. She's a survivor, that one."

"Then, the ball is in her court. We'll just have to wait and see."

"Yes, but not too long. Lucas is already advising his lawyer of this latest event. And the last thing I called to her as she stormed out was, 'You've got 24 hours to decide and then I proceed.' I said proceed, because I didn't want to yell 'press charges' across the Polo Lounge, you see."

Helen laughed weakly. "Yes, I see. Oh, Beanie. No matter what happens, you've done your best, and Lucas and I are the winners."

"What do you mean, dear?"

"Like Torrey said, Jude can't really hurt us unless we let her. You know the old saying about sticks and stones. Lucas and I haven't violated our value systems. Instead, what this has reinforced for us is that

401

family and true friends are the most important things there are."

Beanie's voice changed. "Well," she sniffed, "speaking for the Lightmann family, we saw what you did for the Rawlings--how you pitched in and worked yourself half to death. Then we saw Lucas, before our very eyes, fall head-over-heels in love...his words, by the way. Well, like I told you, I believe in 'happily-ever-after.' We've watched Lucas try to 'mother that calf,' as Will would say, for 18 years. So, if the Lightmann family can help get the show on the road to the happy part of his life, we're delighted."

Helen had a sudden, gut-wrenching thought. "Oh, God! Beanie...Willie is set to give a press conference today. The paparazzi are in Eugene."

"Oh, sweetie, don't worry. Amber is all over that little brush fire. You know she's sweet on Willie, don't you?"

"Yes. I saw it spark at the ranch. They were giving each other these seriously puzzled looks...like, 'what in the hell just hit me?'"

"You don't object?"

"Why on earth would I object? Because she's older? Hardly! I'm older than Lucas, you know."

"No, dear. Not that. I wonder because she's divorced and...Jewish."

Helen snorted. "You kill me, Beanie. You really do. Why on earth would I mind that?"

"Some would, you know."

"No one in the Duncan family, I can assure you of that!"

Beanie sighed. "Well, that's good then. Once we get you two settled, perhaps we can sit back and watch the next love story unfold."

"Oh, Beanie, you really are a dear! Who knows what the future holds...we might even end up as mothers-in-law."

Helen's head was reeling when she finally hung up the phone. *Torrey! I have to call Torrey. I shouldn't be glad she has a broken leg, and I'm not, but at least I know she'll be at the lodge or in the ranch house.* But she wasn't. Helen left a message saying she would call back when she could and hung up, looking at her watch. Her final meeting with the group was scheduled in two hours. She forced herself to take deep breaths. When she had counted to ten, she walked to where she had been making a salad for lunch...which seemed like a very long time ago.

The ramifications of Beanie's story started to take root. *Anything is possible. Beanie knows Jude well...so does Lucas. Don't get your hopes up, Helen. The fall back to earth would be too painful.* The rainbow-colored ponies came into her mind. *Well, shit! No wonder the Creator sent an entire herd. Just one might not be enough to hold me up.*

Helen left for the group session with her mobile phone, Lucas's red handkerchief and Jake's dime in her pocket. She still had not been able to get through to Torrey and time had run out. She would not get home from her session until just before 5:00, and then, at 8:00, Lucas would be calling. Just thinking about his voice made her stomach flip.

Thinking back to their morning conversation, she found she could recall almost all of their conversation; not just the important things, but the small things as well. Now, she knew they had both been raised as protestants; she, Episcopalian, he, Methodist. They were both registered as Democrats in college, but had switched party affiliation to the Republicans. Lucas always slept in his silk boxers; Helen in a nightgown. As she drove, she blushed thinking where that conversation had gone.

When Helen walked into Dr. Pagglio's office carrying one of Deena's delicious cups of coffee, the whole group was there, standing around a table with a cake that said,

You've done it!
Congratulations, Helen!
Best of Luck!

"Dr. Pagglio called us," Bianca said, rushing to her and wrapping her in thin arms. "My mom made the cake."

Then, they were around her and she was grabbing them and hugging them as fast as she could. Dr. Pagglio was the last to step forward. "I'd like one of those too, Helen. Then, the group would like to hear your story, if you'd care to share."

Helen grabbed a napkin from the table. "Oh, thank God!" she said, laughing through her tears. "I tried calling Torrey, because I needed to tell someone my news, but she wasn't home and I'm ready to burst with it," she said, stepping into his hug.

When Helen had finished her story, there was complete silence until Althea sighed and said, "Girl, that's what I was talkin' about. Hollywood. You're goin' to end up in Hollywood."

"Helen smiled. "Maybe. Maybe not. But, I WILL end up with Lucas somewhere…sometime. Count on it! And I want to say, thank you, to all of you. You literally helped save my life." She included Dr. Pagglio with her eyes.

As the group was breaking up, Dr. Pagglio came up to her and said, "Thank you for sharing, Helen. You give us all hope."

Helen thought about his words driving home. Hope! She could remember when she had none. Now, it was all she had. Dr. Pagglio, as he was closing the session, had said. "Sometimes it is good to look at life as a series of chapters. If we look at Helen's life, we can see she has closed one chapter and is looking forward to starting the next one."

God bless them all, she thought. *Dr. Pagglio is right. I am really looking forward to this next chapter! Thank God the children forced me into therapy. What a blessing he has been to me.*

She walked into the house with her groceries, set them down and went directly to the den to check the answering machine. The light was blinking. Torrey's voice came on when she pressed the play button. "Sorry I missed you, Helen. I was out on the ATV spreading a healing blanket of sage smoke over this ranch. Call me when you can. Your voice sure sounded like you had good news and this place could use some."

Helen looked at her watch. Lucas would be calling in ten minutes. There was not enough time. *Besides, he might have more news, and I can put even more pieces into place for Torrey.* She went to make herself a cup of tea, already feeling her heart rate accelerate in anticipation of Lucas's call.

Helen was sitting at the table waiting, when the phone rang. She jumped for the phone and had it before the second ring. "I love you!" she said as she put the receiver to her ear and heard his laugh.

"God, Helen. I am sitting on the deck, overlooking the Pacific Ocean; Glenn has just put a glass of wine in my hand in celebration of a very eventful day; and then I call you and hear the exact words I wanted to hear. I think my life would be just about perfect if you were here, too."

"You have no idea how I wish that were true, too, Lucas. We would be sitting as close together as possible, talking about how our day had gone, instead of having three time zones between us."

"Can you believe what Beanie did?"

Helen laughed. "In a word: Yes! But she was very clear that Jude, if she figured out an angle, could still be a huge issue."

"Yes, I don't underestimate her. I understand that her drug and alcohol abuse are now all my fault."

405

"Of course," Helen said matter-of-factly. "Obviously, you are just a monster. She should be glad I'm taking you off her hands." She heard his surprised bark of laughter.

"God, I love you Helen," he said. "You make me realize who I used to be."

"Thank you for saying that, darling. That's a great role for me, don't you think?"

"Yes, I do," he said softly. "Now, let me tell you about the visit with my attorney. It was very productive. We've asked for an uncontested divorce, with an equal splitting of all assets. We each keep our cars and our personal possessions. Neither has a claim on the future income of the other. Our home is to be sold, unless one party wants to buy the other party out."

Helen interrupted. "Do you want to buy her out?" Her heart was in her chest.

"No. Even if I did, it would become a battle over the price and I'm simply not going there."

"Oh, I'm so glad," she whispered.

"What? Why is that?"

"Because, I don't think I could live very happily in Jude's house and sleep in Jude's bed with you, Lucas. I'd do it if I had to. But it seems I don't, and I'm very glad."

"I totally get your point. When you put it that way, it becomes crystal clear that I don't want that for us, either."

"What do you want for us?" Helen asked. "If you could have your dream for us come true, what would it be?"

There was a long silence on the line. Finally, Lucas said, "Jesus, Helen, do you know what just popped into my head?"

"I haven't a clue, but listening to the lightness in your voice, I can't wait to hear."

"You. Horses. A dog. A little ranch with a barn that's not really a barn; it's a school of dance." She could hear the excitement growing in his voice.

406

"That night at the ranch, when I was teaching everyone some of the more advanced moves in Western Swing, I realized that I really miss teaching dance...especially to kids starting out in the industry."

"Oh, Lucas! That sounds wonderful! It also feels real. We can do that. If you want to know the truth, I was looking at the farm yesterday and thinking it needed new owners." Helen stood up and started walking back and forth as far as the phone cord would let her, her excitement rising to match his. "There's not a thing keeping me here except your fears that Jude would exploit us being together."

Lucas sobered. "She would in a heartbeat, Helen. Believe me. But, things are moving forward quickly. It might not be as long as we thought. Her attorney will have my paperwork tomorrow. Jude has a deadline to respond to Beanie's offer tomorrow at noon. When I call you tomorrow night, I might know something solid enough that we can start making real plans...like flying you to L.A. or me to Virginia. This bi-coastal thing isn't working worth a damn for me."

"That sounds wonderful to me. The sooner the better!" Helen laughed. "Willie tells me I never do things half-way...so what would you say if I said I want to talk to a real estate agent about putting this place on the market?"

"Talk to your kids and then do it! Do it...and I'll start looking for a ranch."

Helen looked at her watch. She and Lucas had talked for two hours. It was 10:00 and she wasn't a bit sleepy. She decided to call Torrey.

"God, Helen! It's about time! I have been hovering over the phone. What took you so long?"

Helen laughed. "Busy day. But just now, I was talking to Lucas and then I had to pee."

"Well, fill me in fast, before I explode."

"I will. But first tell me about the sage."

"I did a cleansing ceremony all over the ranch where Jude had been. I even had At go out and bring in the horse she rode, so I could smoke her...and then I had Dewey show me the saddle she used...and the bunkhouse...Lord, I nearly lit that place on fire!"

Helen started laughing, able to picture Torrey, broken leg and all, smoking out any remnants of Jude's bad spirits. "I'm sure Will and Dewey were pleased to help," she said when she could.

"Hmmm," Torrey said. "They are still barely talking to me. They were afraid I would fall. At and Jake were good help though...which reminds me...George called Jake and told him to send some of his work. He planned to visit ArtCenter as soon as he got the samples. If they were encouraging, he was going to send Jake an application."

"That's wonderful, Torrey. Please tell him I carry the 'angel dime' with me everywhere."

"Okay, enough of this, Helen Duncan. Spill!"

Helen started knitting the story together for a silent Torrey, remembering what an excellent listener she had always been. After she had finished--including her decision to put the farm on the market and Lucas's intention to start looking for a small ranch within driving distance of his work, Helen said, "Here's the strange thing, Torrey. Lucas and I have known each other less than two weeks. Yet, in my final session with Dr. Pagglio and in my good-bye meeting with the group, not one person said a thing about the fact that I might be rushing into things."

Torrey was silent and Helen waited. "Perhaps, Helen, it is because it doesn't feel rushed...it feels...right. To me, it feels like you have waited many lifetimes to have this relationship again."

It was Helen's turn for silence. *Yes. Yes. As much as I loved Marshall, this is different. Of course it is...but I know what Torrey is saying. It's like Lucas and I are two halves of one whole...and that the Creator has just given us the opportunity to be put back together.* "Thank you, Torrey," Helen said, gratitude filling her voice. "You put into words--exactly what I've felt from the first time I saw him."

"You need to be together." Torrey made the statement sound like a fact, not a judgement.

"God, don't I know it! But, Lucas doesn't want me in L.A. until the divorce gets settled and Jude has had a chance to do her worst."

"Then, come back to the ranch. God knows I could use your help, especially since At is about to have to go back into Burns for school. Come for the cattle drive...stay for the branding if you like. Invite Lucas. You can have At's apartment in the lodge. I was going to let Jake have it, but I know he wouldn't mind giving it to you."

"Oh, my God, Torrey, that sounds too good to be true. I wonder if there is any possibility that Lucas can get away again so soon."

"There's only one way to find out, that's for sure...call him."

Helen stood by the truck watching Russell's Cessna enter the downwind. Her heart was pounding in her chest. She took off her hat and waved it to the sky. She watched the wheels grease the tarmac and saw Russell apply brakes and turn to reverse direction on the runway, heading straight to where she stood. *You have to wait,* she told herself. *Like Russell said, 'Don't you rush out there and get cut to pieces by my propeller, Helen. That wouldn't do anybody any good, and it would make a big mess to clean up.'*

And so, she waited. She waited until she saw the propeller stop and then she started to run. They met half way. Lucas lifted her off the ground, twirled her around and set her down, his lips already seeking hers.

The world went away. All Helen could feel were sensations from the top of her head to the tips of her toes and salient points in between. They were both breathing hard by the time they had finished exploring each other's mouth. "Just you wait, Lucas Clements. Just you wait until we're really alone," she whispered.

He had not released her. He looked at her, his blue eyes dark with emotion. "I can't wait. I can't wait...but a part of me is terrified."

They looked at each other. Helen saw the vulnerability in his eyes and knew what he was implying. Jude, and perhaps others as well, had made him doubt himself and a vital part of his masculinity. She reached up on her tiptoes and gave him a kiss with all the love she had. "By this time tomorrow, you are going to be too tired to be terrified," she whispered against his lips.

Epilogue

For a man who likes to keep a poker face, Torrey thought, *my husband has given away the pot.* She had seldom seen him quite so excited, though she suspected he came across to Lucas as agitated. Except for Will, they were all sitting in the great room of the lodge, a fire in the massive stone fireplace to ward off November's chill. Will was pacing up and down the room, his head bowed; his hands in his back pockets.

Torrey looked down at her cast, thinking of the changes brought by the breaking of her leg...*perhaps all a part of the Creator's plan. If Helen hadn't stayed, she and Lucas would not have met; Jake would not have had the champion he needed...and now this.* She watched her husband pace.

Suddenly, he stopped. "By God! I've figured it ever' way but upside down an' I just can't see why this wouldn't work," Will boomed.

He turned to look at Torrey, excitement snapping in his black eyes. "Can you see a reason it won't work, Torrey?" She shook her head, trying not to smile.

Then he turned and looked at Dewey. "What about you, old man? You got any reservations, now's the time to spill 'em."

Dewey took a drink of coffee before answering. "Seems like a win-win to me," Dewey said simply from his chair nearest the fire. Queenie was nursing month-old puppies at his feet. One of them, as yet unpicked, was to be Lucas's Christmas present.

Will turned to look at Helen and Lucas who were on the couch, Helen with her boots off, her toes warming under her tense-faced fiancé's thigh. "Willie says the barn was built like a brick shit house, so that sure ain't a problem."

He glared at Lucas. "You sure this whole deal will work?"

411

"My friends in L.A. sure think it will." He looked at Helen then turned back to Will. "And so do we."

Will looked down at Jake's drawings lying on the massive coffee table. "Seems like you thought of ever' thing. Them stalls are just right." Then he said, almost to himself. "Maybe Jake ain't the world's greatest horseman, but he sure as hell can draw!"

Torrey knew then that Will had made up his mind. She suspected the others knew it, too.

Still, it was a big idea; a life-changing idea and anything to do with actually making changes to the ranch made him even more cautious. *Even building the airstrip took him nine years to decide, and they are asking him to decide on this right now.*

She looked over at Helen, who seemed to be fairly relaxed. Clearly, she thought Will would go for it. "I'm missing At and Jake, Helen. He, at least, should be here for this," she said.

Helen heard her, jerked her toes from under Lucas's thigh and sat up straight. "Yikes, I forgot to tell you. Dee Dee called to say they had just dropped Jake off at George's. Evidently, Jake's appointment at ArtCenter is tomorrow afternoon. Sorry about that."

"There's a lot happening all at once," Torrey said, waving her hand.

"Well, at least we got the branding crew out of here before we sprang this whole thing on you," Helen said, grinning.

"We knew you were up to something, we just couldn't figure out what. Certainly, we didn't have a clue you two crazy people would want to live in our barn," Torrey said, with laughter in her voice.

Helen smiled and nodded, looking at Lucas who was looking at Will staring out the window. There was a little frown of worry still between Lucas's eyebrows. *He doesn't know Will like we do,* she thought, *so he's worried our dream might not come true.* She pulled her toes and turned to snuggle up against him and he glanced down at her. "No worries," she mouthed.

She had known the minute Lucas had articulated his dream to her shortly after he had come, that it was not just possible, but probable. At the time, they were standing in the barn, his head swiveling, taking in the space. As he explained his vision, his eyes were intense and the excitement in his voice was unmistakable. "A ballroom? You're seeing a ballroom?"

He'd laughed. "Well, a very big dance studio, anyway...with an apartment for us," he gestured towards the hay mow, "up there."

She'd laughed, catching his enthusiasm. "Oh, my! Tell me the rest," she'd said, slipping her arm around his waist and standing hip to hip with him.

"I will, only I'm counting on you to play the devil's advocate. Here's my thinking so far. It would be a package deal for serious students who want to learn advanced dance and have a ranch experience at the same time."

"Younger kids or older kids."

"Older. High School graduates who want an emersion experience. It would be promoted as a preparatory school for dance. I'd require a video, recommendations, and a completed application form similar to the one Jake was required to fill out for ArtCenter. I'd accept only serious, qualified students."

"Go on," she said, nodding in agreement.

"We'd work out a deal with Will and Torrey to black out other guests during the month of June. That's when the camp would be scheduled...right after the guests have been here helping take the cows up to summer range."

"So far, so good," she'd said. "Though, I'd say you'd better give them and the horses a week or so to recover. Besides, many schools don't get out until sometime in June."

"Good detail," Lucas said. "Now, here's the tricky part. Do you think Will would let me build a simple hay barn and take over this one?"

413

"Take it over and remodel it, you mean?" Helen looked around. The barn was mostly filled with grain, supplement, unused equipment and other accumulations of generations of ranching.

"I think you'd have to put a couple of stalls into the new plans, like he has now. If a mare is due to foal and the weather is bad, or if a horse is sick, it's a space he needs."

He'd turned to her then and folded her into his arms. "God, Helen, I love you. If I'm dreaming too big, I know you'll tell me. It's really something for me to have a partner I can trust. My psychologist says it could be one of my big issues."

She knew what he was saying. "No more deferred dreams," she said simply, as she kissed him.

And so, during the cattle drive and during the branding, they'd talked and dreamed, then brought Jake into their scheme to make it real with his drawings. They had enough money. Jude had caved to Beanie's demands. There had been the one splashy issue of "The Star," that Jude swore she couldn't get stopped, showing the stolen photograph with the torrid headline, "Star Loses Husband to Cowgirl," but that quickly faded.

"Would we live here?"

"That depends on the Rawlings. I think it could work. You don't mind having a home above a barn, do you?"

She had laughed. "It's done all the time on the East Coast and I've rather envied the people that got to live in those quarters."

"And, Helen, there isn't a reason in the world we can't go back to L.A. when we need to…by plane."

"You mean charter an airplane?"

"Maybe at first. But, I've always wanted to learn to fly, and I know just the man to teach me."

Now, they were waiting on Will…who was standing in the "cowboy stance," staring at the

414

drawings, his mind seemingly miles away. He finally looked at Helen. "You sure about the horse-breeding operation deal?"

"I'm not only sure, but excited about it. I have to have something to do while Lucas is teaching. Working with At and Torrey to turn your babies into proper ranch horses is like a dream come true for me, too."

Will stood looking at her, shaking his head. "Thank God I hadn't gotten around to gelding that last colt crop, 'cause one of them is goin' to have to fill ol' Packer's shoes unless I miss my guess. I know you, Helen. You don't do things half-way."

She laughed and looked meaningfully at Lucas. "I sure don't. So make up your damned mind, Will. You're killing us here."

Will walked over and looked at Torrey, sitting in the recliner. She smiled up at him and said. "The spirit horses came to Helen, predicting change. I think this qualifies."

Will nodded and sighed. "And you know how I hate change...but this is the right idea and I believe it's just the right time. He turned to Lucas and held out his hand. "Have your attorney start drawin' up papers."

Helen squealed, and Lucas stood to grab Will's hand, a grin splitting his face. "First thing tomorrow," he promised.

Will lifted his hat and smoothed his hair. "Well, well," he said, as he looked around the room and grinned. "I do believe this calls for a round of Dad's horse piss to seal the deal."